RENEGADES
HARROWMASTER

RENEGADES
HARROWMASTER

MIKE BROOKS

BLACK LIBRARY

A BLACK LIBRARY PUBLICATION

First published in 2022.
This edition published in Great Britain in 2023 by
Black Library, Games Workshop Ltd., Willow Road,
Nottingham, NG7 2WS, UK.

Represented by: Games Workshop Limited – Irish branch,
Unit 3, Lower Liffey Street, Dublin 1,
D01 K199, Ireland.

10 9 8 7 6 5 4 3 2 1

Produced by Games Workshop in Nottingham.
Cover illustration by Jodie Muir.

See Black Library on the internet at

blacklibrary.com

Find out more about Games Workshop
and the worlds of Warhammer at

games-workshop.com

Printed and bound in the UK.

---

*For Will, for hearing one of my 'Hey, wouldn't it be great
if–?' ideas and letting me run with it.*

For more than a hundred centuries the Emperor has sat immobile on the Golden Throne of Earth. He is the Master of Mankind. By the might of His inexhaustible armies a million worlds stand against the dark.

Yet, He is a rotting carcass, the Carrion Lord of the Imperium held in life by marvels from the Dark Age of Technology and the thousand souls sacrificed each day so that His may continue to burn.

To be a man in such times is to be one amongst untold billions. It is to live in the cruellest and most bloody regime imaginable. It is to suffer an eternity of carnage and slaughter. It is to have cries of anguish and sorrow drowned by the thirsting laughter of dark gods.

This is a dark and terrible era where you will find little comfort or hope. Forget the power of technology and science. Forget the promise of progress and advancement. Forget any notion of common humanity or compassion.

There is no peace amongst the stars, for in the grim darkness of the far future, there is only war.

DRAMATIS PERSONAE

SPACE MARINES

THE ALPHA LEGION
THE SERPENT'S TEETH

Drazus Jate – Lord and Harrowmaster

Solomon Akurra, 'the Ghost' – Lord

Qope Halver – Headhunter Prime

Vorlan Xhan – Headhunter

Zreko Chura – Headhunter

Unej Manoz – Headhunter

Dommik Renn – Headhunter

Krozier Va'kai – Captain of the *Whisper*

Derqan Tel – Legionnaire, Eighth Fang

Sakran Morv – Legionnaire, Eighth Fang

Forval Junai – Legionnaire, Eighth Fang

Pentaq Wray – Legionnaire, Eighth Fang

Trayvar Thrice-Burned – Squad leader, Eighth Fang

Kerrig Thrax – Squad leader, Ninth Fang

Titrik Inshu – Squad leader, Third Fang

Urzu Kaibor – Legionnaire, Third Fang

Attas – Harrower, Lernean Terminators

OTHERS

Roek Ghulclaw – Lord of the Guns of Freedom

Jarvul Glaine – Lord of the Shrouded Hand

Vyrun Evale – Lord of the Penitent Sons

Qorru Vayzia – Legionnaire, the Penitent Sons

'Alpharius' – various members of the Faceless

Keros Asid – Lord of the Sons of Venom

Raelin Amran – Lord of the First Strike

Dinal Bloodsinger – Apothecary of the First Strike
Alboc – Legionnaire of the First Strike
Xettus Qeele, 'the Metalphage' – Lord of the Rustbloods

SILVER TEMPLARS

Lampros Hekaton – Grand Oathkeeper
Renus Malfax – Second lieutenant, Fifth Company
Palamas – Captain, Fifth Company
Bedaris Hyrus – Sergeant
Kilus Jesar – Battle-brother
Vastus – Battle-brother
Rhan – Techmarine, Fifth Company

CRIMSON CONSULS

Tythus Yorr – Battle-brother, lifeward to Inquisitor Kayzen Hart

NEW MECHANICUM

Kazadin Yallamagasa, 'Biologis Diabolicus' – Heretek magos biologis
Diabolicus Secundus – Abominable intelligence

HUMANS

THE ALPHA LEGION

Tulava Dyne – Sorceress of the Serpent's Teeth
General Andol – Commander of the Guns of Freedom
Tolly Krace – Alpha Legion factor
Vasila Manatu – Dishonour Guard

THE HOLY INQUISITION

Kayzen Hart – Inquisitor of the Ordo Malleus
(radical recongregationist)

Deema Varrin – Seneschal to Kayzen Hart

Nessa Karnis – Inquisitor of the Ordo Malleus
(puritan monodominant)

Evelyn – Assistant to Nessa Karnis

OTHERS

Jonn Brezik – Pendata trooper

Suran Teeler – Pendata trooper

Kanzad – Pendata trooper

Stevaz Tai – Pendata trooper

Cade – Pendata sergeant

Aemus Speltan – Beharis Delta space port security officer

Morton – Beharis Delta space port security officer

Pashvir – Beharis Delta space port shift supervisor

Raola – Beharis Delta space port logistics officer

PART ONE

CATCHING DEATH'S EYE

Jonn Brezik clutched his lasgun, muttered prayers under his breath, and hunkered further into the ditch in which he and seven others were crouching as the world shook around them. The weapon in his slightly trembling hands was an M35 M-Galaxy Short: solid, reliable and well maintained, with a fully charged clip, and a scrimshaw he had carved himself hanging off the barrel. He had another four ammo clips on his belt, along with the long, single-edged combat knife that had been his father's. He was not wearing the old man's flak vest – not a lot of point, given the state it had ended up in – and as enemy fire streaked overhead again, Jonn began to do the mental arithmetic of whether, right now, he would prefer to be in possession of a gun or functional body armour. The gun could kill the people shooting at him, that was for sure, but he would have to be accurate for that to work, and there didn't seem to be any shortage of the bastards. On the other hand, even the best armour would give out eventually, if he lacked any way of dissuading the other side from shooting at him–

11

'Brezik, you with us?'

Jonn jerked and blinked, then focused on the woman who had spoken. Suran Teeler, sixty years old at least, with a face that looked like a particularly hard rock had been hit repeatedly with another rock. She was staring at him with eyes like dark flint, and he forced himself to nod.

'Yeah. Yeah, I'm here.'

'You sure? Because you seem a bit distracted right now,' Teeler said. 'Which, given we're in the middle of a bastard *warzone*, is something of a feat.'

'I'll be fine, sarge,' Jonn replied. He closed his eyes for a moment, and sighed. 'It's just the dreams again. Feels like I haven't slept properly for a month.'

'You've been having them too?' Kanzad asked. He was a big man with a beard like a bush. 'The sky ripping open?'

Jonn looked over at him. He and Kanzad did not really get on – there was no enmity as such, no blood feud; they just rubbed each other the wrong way – but there was no mockery on the hairy face turned in his direction.

'Yeah,' he said slowly. 'The sky ripping open. Well, not just our sky. All the skies. What does that mean, if we're both having the same dream?'

'It means absolute jack-dung until we get out of here alive,' Teeler snapped. 'You want to compare dream notes after we're done, that's fine. Right now, I want your attention on the matter in hand! And Brezik?'

'Yes, sarge?' Jonn replied, clutching his lasgun a little tighter.

'Stop calling me "sarge".'

'Sorry, s– Sorry. Force of habit.'

A throaty drone grew in the air behind them, and Jonn looked up to see lights in the night sky, closing the distance at a tremendous speed. The drone grew into a whine, and then into a roar as the aircraft shot overhead: two Lightnings flanking an Avenger, all three heading further into the combat zone.

'That's the signal!' Teeler yelled, scrambling to her feet with a swiftness that belied her years. 'Go, go, go!'

Jonn leaped up and followed her, clambering out of the ditch and charging across the chewed-up ground beyond. He desperately tried to keep up some sort of speed without twisting an ankle in the great ruts and gouts torn into the earth by bombardments, and the repeated traversing of wheeled and tracked vehicles. He could see other groups just like his on either side, screaming their battle cries as they advanced on the enemy that were being savaged by aerial gunfire from their fighters. Jonn raised his voice to join in, adrenaline and fear squeezing his words until they came out as little more than a feral scream:

'FOR THE EMPEROR!'

Streams of fire began spewing skywards as the enemy finally got their anti-aircraft batteries online. Jonn heard the *thump-thump-thump* of Hydra quad autocannons, and one of the fighters – a Lightning, he thought, although it was hard to tell at this distance, and in the dark – came apart in a flower of flame, and scattered itself over the defenders below.

'Keep moving!' Teeler yelled as one or two in their group slowed slightly. 'We've got one shot at this!'

Jonn pressed on, despite the temptation to hang back and let others take the brunt of the enemy gunfire. Presenting the defenders with targets one at a time would only ensure they all died: this massed rush, so there were simply too many of them to kill in time, was the only way to close the distance and get into the enemy lines. Once there, the odds became far more even.

They passed through a line of metal posts, some no more than girders driven upright into the mud, and the fortifications ahead began to sparkle with ruby-red bolts of super-focused light. They had entered the kill-zone, the functional range of a lasgun, and the defenders now knew that their shots would not be wasted.

Kanzad jerked, then jerked again, then fell on his face. Jonn did not stop for him. He would not have stopped for anyone. Stopping meant dying. He charged onwards, his face contorted into a rictus of fear and hatred, daring the galaxy to come and take him.

The galaxy obliged.

The first las-bolt struck him in the right shoulder and burned straight through. It was a sharp pain, but a clean pain, and he staggered but kept moving. It was his trigger arm, and his lasgun was supported by a strap. So long as his left arm could aim the barrel and his right could pull the trigger, he was still in this fight.

The next shot hit him in the gut, puncturing the muscle wall of his stomach and doubling him over. He managed to retain his feet, just, but his momentum was gone. He began to curl up around the pain, and the stench of his own flash-cooked flesh. Eyes screwed up, face towards the ground, Jonn Brezik did not even see the last shot. It struck the top of his head, and killed him instantly.

'Die, heretic!' Stevaz Tai yelled, as his third las-bolt finally put the man down. He whooped, partly in excitement and partly in relief, but anxiety was still scrabbling at the back of his throat. Throne, there were just so *many* of them! Even as he shifted his aim and fired again, he thought he saw something off to the left, closing in fast on the Pendata Fourth's defensive line. He blinked and squinted in that direction, but some of the great floodlights had been taken out by that accursed aerial attack, and the shapes refused to resolve for him.

'Eyes front, trooper, and keep firing!' Sergeant Cade ordered, suiting actions to words with his laspistol. It was more for show than anything else, Stevaz assumed, since the heretics were probably still out of pistol range, but it would only be a matter of seconds until that was no longer the case. And those seconds could be important.

'Something to the left, sarge!' he shouted, although he snapped off another shot as he spoke. 'I didn't get a good look, but whatever it was, it was moving fast!'

'Was it in our sector?' Cade demanded.

'No, sarge!'

'Then it's Fifth Squad's responsibility, or Seventh's – not ours! We've got enemies enough in front of us,' Cade snapped, and Stevaz could not argue with that. He jerked backwards as an enemy las-bolt struck the dirt in front of him, and wiped his eyes to clear them of the mud that had spattered across his face.

'Full-auto!' Cade bellowed. 'Let 'em have it!'

Stevaz obediently flicked the selector on his lasgun and joined its voice to the whining chorus that sprang up along the trench. It would drain their power packs rapidly, but the sheer volume of fire should put paid to this latest assault before they needed to reload–

Something exploded off to his left, and it was all he could do not to whip around, lasrifle still blazing. It was immediately followed by screaming: high, desperate screams born not just of pain, but of utter terror.

'Sarge?!'

'Eyes front, trooper, or you'll be the one screaming!' Cade yelled, but there was a note of uncertainty in the sergeant's voice as he fired at the onrushing cultists. 'One problem at a time, or–'

Something large and dark flew into their midst from their left, and landed heavily on the trench floor. It clipped the back of Kanner's leg and she tripped backwards, and her cycle of full-auto shots tracked along Dannick's head and blew his skull to smithereens, then took Jusker in the shoulder. They both fell, and Cade roared in anger and frustration, and not a little fear, as his squad's output reduced drastically. Someone moved to help Jusker. Someone else fell backwards as a lucky shot from the onrushing enemy found the gap between helmet and trench top. Stevaz could not help himself: he turned and looked down at what had caused all this commotion.

It was a headless body, bearing the insignia of Fifth Squad.

Fear paralysed him. What had broken into their lines? What had decapitated this trooper, and hurled their body so easily into Fourth Squad's ranks? It couldn't have been the explosion he heard: what explosion would take someone's head off so neatly, but hurl their body this far?

Cade was shouting at him.

'Tai, get your arse back on the–'

The sergeant never got the chance to finish his sentence, because something came screaming over the top of the trench, and landed on him. The buzzing whine of a chainsword filled the air, along with a mist of blood, and then Sergeant Cade was bisected. His murderer turned towards Stevaz as the rest of the heretics' assault piled into the trench, rapidly overwhelming Fourth Squad.

Stevaz saw a snarl of fury on the face of a woman probably old enough to be his grandmother, and the light of bloodlust in her eyes. He raised his lasrifle, but her howling weapon batted it aside, and the rotating teeth tore it from his grip. He turned and ran, fumbling at his belt for the laspistol and combat knife that rested there, hoping he could at least outpace her until he had his secondary weapons drawn.

Too late, he realised he was running towards where Fifth Squad had been stationed.

He rounded a corner of the trench before he could stop himself, and collided with something enormous and very, very hard. He fell backwards into the mud, and looked up to see what he had run into.

Two glowing red eyes stared balefully down at him, and Stevaz nearly lost control of his bladder until he recognised them for what they were. The eye-lenses of a Space Marine helmet! The promised help had arrived! The lords of war were here on Pendata!

Then, despite the darkness, he took in the colour of the armour plate. It was not silver, but blue-green, and the pauldron did not display a black blade flanked by lightning strikes on a yellow background, but a three-headed serpent. His heart shrivelled inside his chest, because he suddenly realised what he must have seen, moving so fast towards Fifth Squad's lines.

'You're not Silver Templars,' he managed shakily.

The helmet tilted slightly, as though curious.

'No.'

A weapon with a muzzle as large as Stevaz's head was raised, and the bolt-shell it discharged detonated so forcefully that his entire upper body disintegrated.

Derqan Tel turned away from the dead Pendata trooper, and followed the rest of his team into the culvert that ran back from the front lines. No more defenders were coming from that direction: the Legion's human allies had breached the trenchlines now, and could be relied upon to make a mess of this first line of resistance.

'What is a Silver Templar?' he asked the legionnaire in front of him.

'No idea,' Sakran Morv replied. 'Why?' Morv was big even for an Astartes, and carried the squad's ancient autocannon.

'That mortal seemed to think I should be one,' Tel said. He searched his memory, but drew a blank. 'I cannot think of a loyalist Chapter called the Silver Templars. You?'

'Perhaps he meant Black Templars,' Morv suggested. 'Although I think Va'kai would have recognised their insignia.'

Something wasn't sitting right in Tel's gut. Three loyalist strike cruisers had emerged from the warp since the Legion had made planetfall, and were now engaged in void combat overhead with the *Whisper*, the flagship of the Serpent's Teeth. Morv was correct: Krozier Va'kai, the *Whisper*'s captain, would know a Black Templars ship if he was shooting at it.

He activated his vox. 'Trayvar, have you heard of Silver Templars?'

'*Is this really the time, Tel?*' came the voice of Trayvar Thrice-Burned in reply. He was at the head of the advance, farther down the trench. He had also been the first into the defensive lines when Eighth Fang made their assault rush across the ground left dark by the destroyed floodlights; it was that sort of full-throated aggressiveness that had won him the renown he enjoyed, and also seen him doused in burning promethium no less than three times in one particularly brutal assault against a position held by the Salamanders Chapter.

'The mortal I just killed appeared to be expecting them,' Tel informed him. 'It could be a new Chapter. Or, as Morv pointed out,' he continued, 'a misremembering of the Black Templars.'

'*Silver Templars, Black Templars,*' the Thrice-Burned muttered. '*You'd think they would have some imagination, wouldn't you?*'

'The Imperium, endlessly repeating minor variations of the same tired routines?' Morv laughed. 'Surely not.'

'*I'll vox it in,*' Trayvar said. '*The Harrowmaster might know something.*'

'Acknowledged,' Tel replied. Harrowmaster Drazus Jate led

the Serpent's Teeth, and it was his tactical genius that had led to Pendata's fall. Once they broke this last loyalist bastion then the resistance would be shattered, and the raw materials the Serpent's Teeth so desperately needed – promethium, metal, plasteel, perhaps even ceramite – would be theirs for the taking. There would be no sharing of the spoils with other Legions, either: the Teeth were not part of the Warmaster's 13th Black Crusade, and there was no one here but them to claim the winnings. Abaddon would surely fail, as he always did, for all that he was closing on Terra and had ripped the very fabric of reality asunder across the galaxy. If there was one thing the Black Legion could be relied upon to do, it was to fail, and Drazus Jate knew better than to get caught up in *that*.

Trayvar's bolter opened up with a roar, and Tel heard screams as the defenders realised that not only had their lines been breached, but also heavily armoured transhuman killers were now amongst them. The desperate stabs of las-fire cast shadows, but in the narrow confines of the trench Pendata's mortal troops could only bring a couple of weapons to bear at once: nowhere near enough to stop Trayvar. Tel broke into a run as Eighth Fang accelerated ahead of him, stealth abandoned in favour of shock.

'Over the top, and east!' Trayvar barked over the vox, and Tel sprang upwards without thinking about it. The trench through which they were running was still deep enough here that a mortal would think twice before jumping down into it, let alone trying to climb out, but Tel's superhuman muscles were boosted by the servos and mechanical sinews of his power armour, and he cleared the lip with little effort.

A scene of chaos met his eyes.

What had at one point presumably been a highly ordered Imperial camp was now in turmoil. Blazing fires showed where the aerial assault had hit vehicles or fuel dumps, and the burning wreckage of a Lightning had landed on a prefabricated building which, to Tel's eyes, bore the hallmarks of a command centre. Imperial troops – a mix of Astra Militarum forces and the Pendata Bluecoats, the local militia – swarmed like colonial insects attempting to defend their mound, but unlike those minuscule creatures, they had little unity of purpose.

'Let's make some noise,' Trayvar declared, and Eighth Fang opened up.

Their remit was simply to cause as much damage as possible: a simple purpose, and perhaps a crude one, but necessary nonetheless. Eighth Fang would draw the defenders' attention, since eight Traitor Astartes unleashing a fusillade of gunfire could hardly achieve anything else, and during the commotion, the warband's Headhunter teams and the Harrowmaster himself would execute their priority targets.

'Do you think we are being a bit obvious?' Tel asked, gunning down a squad of troopers before they had time to lift their lasguns.

'What are they going to do, ignore us?' Morv snorted. His autocannon coughed heavily as it stitched a line of holes down the side of a Chimera, and the armoured transport exploded. A las-bolt splashed across his pauldron, but he took no notice. 'If they suspect we are not the real threat, and do not engage us fully, we become the real threat. Tank crew,' he added, 'seventy degrees right.'

Tel turned. Sure enough, a ragged group of six Pendatii were running towards a Leman Russ, trying to stay low and avoid notice. The war machine was capable of giving Eighth Fang problems, since its armour was thick enough to potentially turn aside even Morv's autocannon.

'No, I think not,' Tel murmured, sighting along his bolter.

The darkness was no barrier to his visor's thermal sensors, and his weapon barked as he picked the crew off, one after another.

'Move on my mark,' Trayvar ordered. 'We do not want to get pinned down, even by this rabble. Three, two, one... *Mark.*'

The Thrice-Burned went from a standstill to a sprint in under a second, and Eighth Fang followed him. The Imperial resistance, which had just begun to coalesce around them like dark blood clotting over a wound, found that the nature of the threat it faced had abruptly changed. Regular mortals could not adjust their mindsets in time to mount any meaningful resistance, and a ragged firing line of lasgunners splintered as Eighth Fang plunged into them.

Tel did not even draw his power knife. There was no need. He simply stomped and kicked, punched and bludgeoned. Broken bodies flew away from him into their fellows, or went down into crumpled, bleeding heaps. One desperate trooper managed to land a lunge with a bayonet, but the gleaming tip simply scraped harmlessly across Tel's chestplate, and Tel elbowed him in the face hard enough to break both his jaw and his neck.

It was all going exactly as anticipated, until his vox crackled into life with a broadcast on the warband's general frequency.

'*All ground units, be aware that the loyalist strike cruisers have made it past us and are launching gunships,*' Captain Va'kai announced. There was a background thunder as the captured Lunar-class cruiser's guns spoke again. '*Well, two of them are,*' Va'kai added, in a satisfied tone. '*The third one is coming down in pieces.*'

'That's still going to be a lot of company for us,' Morv observed. His autocannon spoke once, detonating an ammo dump that briefly lit the sky as though the sun had thought better of being below the horizon. The shockwave of the explosion was powerful enough for Tel to feel it.

'*Eighth and Ninth Fangs, seize control of the Hydras,*' Harrow-master Jate's voice declared over the vox. '*Since we have such appropriately named tools to hand, let us see how our erstwhile brothers like the taste of our teeth.*'

Tel made sure he was speaking only on his Fang's private vox-channel. 'Brothers, does this seem sound? Even two strike cruisers can hold a lot of gunships – more than we can easily shoot down in the window we will have.'

'You would have us disobey a direct order from the Harrow-master?' Trayvar demanded. 'We have no easy way off this planet without Jate's approval. Besides, if we abandon our brothers now then we make it less likely that they will be able to repel this assault, and we will be easy meat for the loyalists once they have finished with Jate!'

Tel grimaced inside his helm, but the logic of the Thrice-Burned's words was hard to argue against. 'Very well, brother – let us make the best of this.'

It was only a couple of minutes later that they located the Hydra batteries, but those were minutes that clawed at Derqan Tel's mind with poisoned talons. It took time for gunships to punch through atmospheres – he had ridden inside one often enough, wishing for a swift flight so he could face his enemies with weapon in hand rather than waiting to be blown apart in mid-air – but not so long as he would have preferred, in these circumstances. To make matters worse, the defenders had either second-guessed them for once, or had simply decided upon the anti-aircraft guns as a rallying point, because what looked like a veritable company of Astra Militarum was clustered around the looming, quad-barrelled weapons.

'That is a lot of lasguns,' Forval Junai said with feeling, as the air virtually turned red with panicked snap-firing when he poked his helmet out from cover.

'Blind grenades and flanking,' Trayvar ordered. 'Go.'

Each of them hurled one of the sensor-obscuring grenades, which belched out black smoke that would not only render mortal eyes useless, but also confound gunsights and photo-goggles. It did nothing to stop gunfire, however, and the assembled troopers opened up with a volley of las-bolts so concentrated that even power armour would have struggled to stand up to it, yet with such wide coverage that their inability to pick out individual targets would have little effect.

Which was why as soon as they hurled their grenades, Eighth Fang moved laterally, flanking the defenders around prefabricated buildings. It was no better an angle for approach than the original had been in terms of cover or the number of loyalists awaiting them, but with the majority of attention – and critically, gunfire – directed ninety degrees to the side, it had immediately become the safest option.

'Break them,' Trayvar ordered, and sprinted forward with his traditional boldness. Eighth Fang followed, firing their bolters from the hip, yet picking out their targets with a precision and rapidity that a human sharpshooter could not have achieved while standing still. Tel only paused his firing to hurl a frag grenade in the direction of the troops closest to the blind grenade cloud, and was rewarded with another blossom of flame, and more screams.

Pentaq Wray fell, his armour pierced either by a lucky shot, or perhaps simple weight of fire. The rest of them ran on, but even the reaction times of the loyalist troops had caught up to their reappearance now, and although some were breaking and fleeing, it would not be enough. A new volley of las-fire punched into Tel's side and he staggered, his armour flashing up warning signs.

It would have gone badly for them, had Ninth Fang not hit

the other side of the makeshift emplacement at virtually the same time.

Suddenly the defenders were struck on two fronts, and while either attack might have been repelled on its own, albeit with grievous losses, the two together were more than the loyalists could handle. It took a mere handful of seconds for desperate, grim-faced resistance to morph into panic and rout. The Guardsmen broke apart like water splashed out of a puddle by the impact of a boot, and bolter shells chewed into their backs as they fled.

'Morv, with me to hold the loyalists off,' Trayvar instructed. 'The rest of you, get on the guns, and look to the skies!'

'*I hope this works, Thrice-Burned.*' That was Kerrig Thrax, leader of Ninth Fang, speaking over the vox.

'You and me both, Thrax,' Trayvar replied grimly. Tel magclamped his bolter to his thigh and took up station behind the nearest of the anti-aircraft weapons, kicking the mangled body of its previous operator out of the way. The machine-spirit appeared subservient: it did not flicker or power down as he took control and experimentally traversed the barrels back and forth.

'Ready,' he announced.

'Good,' Trayvar said, craning his helmet back as far as he was able. 'Because we've got incoming contacts.'

Tel looked up and saw them too. They might have been mistaken for stars, at least at first, but the motes of light were actually Space Marine gunships thundering through the atmosphere behind a pressure wave of superheated air. He cranked back the barrels to their highest elevation and tapped the targeting auspex.

'Very well, Silver Templars, or whoever in the warp you are,' he muttered. 'Let us see how your equipment fares.'

The auspex's crosshair turned green, and he squeezed the triggers.

A barrage of fire screamed skywards, and even the audio dampeners in Tel's helmet could not prevent him from being buffeted by the concussive thunder of the guns. He checked the auspex, but the target continued to descend unharmed. He had missed.

System inaccuracies? A treacherous machine-spirit recognising its Imperial kin, and deliberately misleading him? Tel aimed again and fired, and this time he kept firing, strafing back and forth across the night sky. It was an alien sensation to a warrior so used to precision operation, but attrition sometimes had its merits. Besides, he had no need to conserve ammunition for a protracted firefight: once those gunships hit the ground, the Hydras would be too cumbersome to be turned on foot troops. It was now or never.

Spent shell casings rattled away on either side of him as the guns thundered their fury into the sky. Tel saw the gunship wink out of existence on his auspex, and he experienced a brief rush of fierce delight that he quickly fought down as he turned to his next target. He had never wanted a weapon other than his bolter, but the sheer power of this array certainly had its own appeal. He had just killed a dozen Imperial Space Marines in a matter of seconds – how many other warriors could make such a boast?

It seemed he was not alone in his appreciation of the ordnance. 'Can we take these with us?' Junai yelled, with a bellowing laugh. Tel saw another point of light wink out as Junai's guns found their target, but the remainder were getting larger by the moment.

'Shoot them down, damn you!' Trayvar roared. 'Shoot them down, or we're ruined!'

Tel's guns found another, blowing it apart in mid-air. Not even a Space Marine could survive a fall from that height, so he did not waste time shooting at the debris. He hit his next target, but only clipped it, and it swung wildly out of his line of fire. The angles were decreasing now, and their window of opportunity was about to slam shut. Tel did not try to chase down the ship he clipped, trusting that a bad landing would put paid to its cargo, and found another. He let rip once more, but the vehicle's sheer velocity meant his shots passed harmlessly above it. He tried to track downwards in pursuit, but it was too late.

THUMP.

THUMP.

THUMP.

In the blink of an eye, they went from burning points of light in the sky to superheated silver craft landing in the mud. Even their retro rockets had barely slowed them, but the hull-mounted hurricane bolters opened up to shred their surroundings. Tel ducked behind his Hydra and attempted once more to depress the barrel: he might get a chance for just one shot before–

The doors slammed down and silver-armoured Space Marines poured out, twelve from each ship. Even knowing what was coming, having been on the other side of it so many times in the past, Eighth and Ninth Fangs still could not mount an effective resistance. Three of their number were killed by the hurricane bolter barrage, either too slow to take cover or risking death for the chance at a shot as soon as the doors opened. Now they were surrounded, and outnumbered.

The Imperials split apart as soon as they exited, to avoid giving the Hydras a target, and their boltguns began speaking. Tel cursed as explosive rounds battered the weapon behind which he sheltered, but he was an experienced warrior. His bolter might not have the power of a quad-autocannon, but he knew just where to land a shot to trouble even Astartes battleplate.

He leaned out of cover just enough and fired. The shell took its target in the knee, exactly as intended.

Tel's transhuman senses immediately noticed two things. Firstly, the armour worn by these Space Marines was not like any he had seen before.

Secondly, the one he had shot, in a place that had incapacitated scores of Imperial warriors in the past, was still standing. And seemed taller than Tel would have expected.

'What in–'

When Derqan Tel's helmet was struck by a bolt-shell, he did *not* remain standing.

Sergeant Bedaris Hyrus felt a small wash of satisfaction as the Traitor Marine went down. The relic boltgun he carried lacked some of the range of his brothers' bolt rifles, but its lineage stretched back through millennia of service in the Ultramarines. Hyrus had been presented with it by Marneus Calgar himself in the aftermath of the Liberation of Novaris, and he was glad that he could once more present it with heretics to kill. However, he lacked any further immediate options; his Intercessor battle-brothers had already eradicated the rest with a combination of overlapping firing solutions and pinpoint accuracy.

'That traitor was mine, brother-sergeant,' Kilus Jesar said testily from beside him. 'He shot me in the knee!'

'Then you should have reacted more quickly,' Hyrus replied. 'Had I delayed, he might have fired again. Is your armour damaged?'

'It is weakened, but will not degrade my effectiveness,' Jesar said, testing the joint.

'Whom are we facing?' Vastus asked. Hyrus investigated the

closest corpse, and a thrill that was part excitement, part trep-idation ran through him as he took in the blue-green armour, the patterning reminiscent of reptile scales, and the sundry other details known to be linked to this most mysterious of human-ity's enemies.

'Alpha Legion,' Hyrus reported grimly. Their adversaries were no mere renegades, but one of the original Traitor Legions them-selves, and a Legion that had plagued the sons of his primarch for millennia. Now Hyrus and his Primaris brothers were here, as the battlefront of Roboute Guilliman's Indomitus Crusade rolled out across the galaxy, and were perfectly placed to wreak vengeance.

'Move out in combat squads!' he barked. 'There are more trai-tors here, but we'll flush them out. Let the Astra Militarum and the Bluecoats repel the cultists unless they are being overrun – our priority is the Alpha Legion. And stay alert, they're Astartes-killers.'

'They might know how to kill Firstborn, brother-sergeant,' Vastus said, as they split into five-man fire-teams, 'but they have not yet faced our like. Brother Jesar's knee will testify to that!'

Some of his squad brothers laughed, but Hyrus did not.

'Never assume the enemy will not learn quickly, Brother Vastus! The Alpha Legion are not to be taken lightly. We may have already lost our advantage of surprise.' He unsheathed his power sword, and led the way as they moved out at speed.

'Do you suppose the traitors we just killed were part of the Heresy?' Jesar asked as they ran. 'That they actually took part in it?'

'It is hard to countenance,' Hyrus replied, choosing to ignore Jesar's use of 'we' when he had in fact contributed nothing more than being shot in the knee. 'Yet we know the Despoiler still lives, if his existence can be called that. It is possible we just struck a blow of vengeance reaching back ten thousand years. And now we have a chance to strike another,' he added. 'Prepare to engage.'

Ahead of them were two Alpha Legionnaires, hunkering down in cover behind the blazing wreck of a Chimera and delivering punishing fire into the loose mob of loyalist defenders trying to engage them. It would have been suicide for mortal soldiers to try to flush even one Traitor Astartes out of such a holdfast, let alone two.

For Primaris, though, it was a far more feasible prospect.

'Blades!' Hyrus ordered, and the rest of the squad drew their combat knives: silver, to match their armour.

'I want one of them,' Jesar growled.

'If you can reach them in time, brother,' Vastus chuckled.

They raised their weapons and fired as one, a barrage of shells that threw up sparks and tore chunks from what remained of the Chimera's armoured hide. The two Alpha Legionnaires ducked with preternatural speed, but the volley had only been intended to get their heads down as Hyrus' squad closed the distance on them. Genhanced muscles and reinforced sinews combined with the finest powered armour ever created by humanity to propel them forwards at speeds of which mortals could barely dream. Hyrus caught a glimpse in his peripheral vision of one of the Astra Militarum troopers – a lieutenant, his mind flashed up, recognising the rank insignia – waving and shouting, but the noise of the man's voice was lost in the thunder of the ongoing combat. Hyrus would speak to him afterwards and find out what it was he had wanted, if indeed it was anything more than a redundant plea for aid, or perhaps him simply hailing his saviours.

However, despite the enhancements they all shared, Primaris Astartes were no more identical than their Firstborn brethren. In spite of Hyrus' best efforts, he and Jesar were being left behind by their fractionally swifter battle-brothers. Vastus was still firing with his left hand as he ran, while his right spun the combat blade with which he was so skilled.

The ground erupted in fiery death, and three of Hyrus' squad were instantly melted into slag from the waist down. Hyrus, half a second behind, threw himself desperately up and over the explosion: his armour's systems screamed at him, and red warning icons flashed up in his vision, but although he was scorched, he was in one piece. So too was Jesar, who landed beside him a moment later.

Contact-activated melta bombs, dug into the ground. Had this pair of legionnaires known the Silver Templars were coming, and set this ambush in an incredibly short space of time, or had they merely blundered into a trap intended for the Astra Militarum?

Hyrus blink-muted the agonised, vox-borne screams of his battle-brothers. A moment's consideration told him that two Alpha Legionnaires would have no need of such a ruse to deal with the Astra Militarum. This had been a trap.

Very well. Two Silver Templars had escaped the trap's treacherous jaws, and two Primaris Astartes were more than a match for two Firstborn, traitors or no. He and Jesar bellowed their Chapter's war cry, and moved to attack.

'Focus and fury!'

The Alpha Legion came to meet them.

They both wore the blue-green colours of their treacherous kind, but whereas the legionnaires killed at the landing site had been more or less uniform in appearance, the wargear of these warriors bore marks of individuality. One, who sported an odd-looking bionic left arm, was protected by a Mark VI suit complete with the pointed 'Corvus' helm, covered with shimmering, darkly iridescent scales. The other's armour looked to be based on the ancient Mark IV design, and showed signs of artisan crafting, with a scale pattern etched into the plate itself, and a coiling, three-headed serpent where the aquila would have normally sat.

Hyrus' bolter shot flew true to strike the hydra symbol, but the flare of a power field negated the impact, and the legionnaire came on undeterred. The spiked circlet of an iron halo glinted behind the traitor's head, and Hyrus' anger flared at the notion of such a valued relic being tainted by the likes of the heretic in front of him. No matter; he would avenge its former owner. He swayed aside from a blast of ravening heat emanating from an arcane-looking energy weapon, and unleashed a cut with his power sword.

He aimed for the Alpha Legionnaire's head, seeking to cleave the ceramite helm in two, but found his blow blocked by a considerably shorter blade which also crackled with the contained energy of a power field. The legionnaire backed off a step, mag-clamping his energy weapon to his thigh, and drew an identical blade in his other hand, then advanced with his twin power knives held in alternate grips. Hyrus stowed his bolter in the same fashion, and attacked double-handed.

He was taller, faster, stronger, and more durable than his opponent: he knew this to be true. He also had the advantage of reach, both with the length of his blade and through the simple fact that his arms were longer, albeit only slightly.

He was also, he realised in under three seconds, losing.

The Alpha Legionnaire was simply never where he should have been. No matter how forcefully Hyrus cut, no matter how swiftly he thrust, the edge of his blade always fell an inch short. In contrast, the Alpha Legionnaire's twin knives found their mark again and again: never doing critical damage, never striking an incapacitating blow, but jabbing into joints, cutting at power cabling, and weakening protective plates.

'Damned warpcraft!' Hyrus bellowed, pulling one cut and switching seamlessly into a different one, which was guided expertly away from his opponent's chest by a power knife. 'What manner of abomination are you?'

'I could ask you the same question,' his adversary hissed through his vox-grille, feinting a backstep, then stepping in to lash out with the tip of his blade at Hyrus' gorget when he pursued. Hyrus swatted the blow desperately aside, but could do nothing about the other knifepoint that caught him in the left elbow as his foe pirouetted past him. He turned to keep his enemy in view, raising the sword again.

The sound of shearing ceramite was immediately eclipsed by Jesar screaming, as some foul weapon penetrated the defences of Hyrus' battle-brother. He gritted his teeth and stepped forward, blade held overhead like the statue of some vengeful heathen god. He was leaving himself open to a fatal counterstroke, but if he could slay his enemy at the same moment, he would count his death as a good one. Better to die in single combat than give the other traitor the chance to bring him down from behind–

Multiple bolt-shell detonations struck him. Mark X Tacticus armour was durable beyond all versions that had preceded it – save for the venerable Tactical Dreadnought armour – but even it could not stand up to repeated bolter fire at point-blank range. The shells ripped through his power pack, tore apart his backplate, and pierced his body. The pain was excruciating, but he was a Primaris Astartes, and he was built to withstand it. It was not that which brought him to his knees, but the abrupt cessation of his armour's functions, and the leaden weight that settled into his arms and legs as his nervous system was irreparably damaged.

The Alpha Legionnaire in front of him stepped back and looked past Hyrus, towards the coward who had struck him from behind.

'He was mine, Solomon,' the knife-armed traitor hissed.

'You were toying with him,' the other heretic replied, from behind Hyrus' left shoulder, 'and we lack time. Kill him now, or I will.'

Hyrus had dropped his sword, but he managed to creep his hand towards his holstered bolt pistol. All he needed was one shot...

The Alpha Legionnaire stepped forward and plunged one power knife into each side of Bedaris Hyrus' head.

'"We lack time"?' Harrowmaster Drazus Jate repeated, withdrawing his knives from the loyalist's helm and letting the body slump bonelessly forward into the mud. 'Did you have somewhere you needed to be, Akurra?'

'Off this planet would be a good start,' Solomon Akurra replied, as his left arm flowed back into its customary shape. The minor daemon bound inside it had briefly forged the limb into a blade with the strength and sharpness to decapitate his opponent, but it always returned to its normal form after its owner no longer required such a tool.

Jate growled in his throat. 'Off the planet? We are so close to success!'

'And it is about to be snatched from us!' Solomon snapped, kicking the Space Marine at his feet. 'What are these, Jate? Our Legion has fought the whelps of the Golden Throne for ten thousand years, yet do you recall seeing anything like *this* in the records?'

'You know as well as I do that the records are far from complete,' Jate replied, scanning the vox for information. He had to admit that it did not paint a promising picture, but the spoils of war were nearly within their grasp.

'This is something new,' Akurra insisted. He raised his bolter, and almost absent-mindedly shot a hotshot-armed loyalist who had sufficiently overcome the fear of seeing five Space Marines slaughtered by two traitors to begin drawing a bead on them from sixty yards away. 'We cannot press on with the attack in these circumstances! Eighth and Ninth Fangs are already dead. We risk being overwhelmed and destroyed by a foe we do not understand.'

Jate plucked his volkite charger from its mag-clamped position on his thigh. He did not intend it as a threat – having his weapon ready was only prudent – but he nonetheless injected a little more force into his voice.

'Do you forget who is the Harrowmaster of the Serpent's Teeth, Akurra?'

'You are,' Akurra replied instantly. 'But do *you* forget that you hold that position not through any appointment by higher authority, or by might of arms or right of conquest, but through the voice of your peers? What was given can be taken away, Drazus. I implore you, let us withdraw. There will be other theatres from which we can take what we need, when we have a better grasp of the opposition we face. Otherwise, even if we survive, I doubt you will remain Harrowmaster.'

'Nor will I if I order the retreat now,' Jate snarled. Akurra was a noted commander in his own right, and a valuable asset, but the Harrowmaster thought he could see the thrust of his supposed ally's hidden blade. 'To give up a prize like this will surely see me accused of timidity, and deposed. No, *Solomon*, we will do as the Legion has always done – we will adapt to the situation, and turn it to our advantage.' He activated his vox. 'Captain Va'kai, what is your situation?'

'*Tenable, Harrowmaster,*' came Va'kai's response immediately. Krozier Va'kai was no mortal starship captain, but a legionnaire whose true genius only revealed itself in the fires of void combat. He was as reliable with a bolter and a power knife as any other, but it was when combat was measured in thousands of miles, and when decisions taken now would influence impacts in ten minutes' time, that he was in his element. *'The strike cruisers galvanised the loyalist ships into making a fight of it, but they only evened the odds, not turned them against us. They're either virtually new or refitted to as near as damn it. Their weapons hit hard and their reactions are as fast as you would expect, but they have no subtlety to them – we have taken one down already. What's more, I think each one wants us for themselves, instead of them working together. It's like they've never seen an actual fight before.'*

'That sounds familiar,' Jate grunted, looking down at the silver-armoured corpses. 'Keep doing what you do best, Va'kai.' He cut the vox-link. 'We press on. Va'kai can hold them in orbit, we will take what we came here for and withdraw as plan–'

His iron halo – the spoils of a knife fight with a Genesis Chapter captain – sparked into action, deflecting a ballistic hit. Jate spun, firing his volkite charger at the point from which his instincts told him the attack had originated. His eyes caught up with the shot a moment later, as the silver-armoured figure he hit was still being punched backwards off its feet.

'More of them!' he snarled, backing towards the cover of the Chimera. Akurra's bolter, the use of which he stubbornly clung to despite his general preference for more exotic wargear – including that warp-cursed bionic arm, which Jate did not trust in the slightest – barked out its defiance as well, but there were still four Silver Templars left, flanked by a gaggle of human defenders, and this time the Alpha Legion had no cunning melta bomb line to thin out the numbers.

'Where is your witch?' Jate demanded. 'We need to get through them!'

'We need to withdraw!' Akurra said desperately. 'By the primarchs, Jate, you are going to get us killed!'

'*We are going through them!*' Jate roared. He risked a look to his left, searching for Akurra's pet sorceress, who had been cowering behind the Chimera the last time he saw her. 'Dyne! Where are–'

Harrowmaster Drazus Jate's iron halo had served him well over the years, but it did not stop everything, and he never saw the shot that struck his helmet and blew his head apart.

HARROWMASTER

Solomon Akurra emptied his boltgun's entire magazine one-handed at the Imperials, causing even the Silver Templars to dive for cover, as he grabbed Drazus Jate's corpse and hauled it farther back behind the Chimera. There would be no recovery on the Apothecary's table for the Harrowmaster – his skull had been pulped by the bolt-shell that had killed him, and he was essentially headless – but his progenoid glands would still be intact, and both they and his artificer armour were too valuable to be allowed to leave the Legion.

'Tul!' Solomon barked, as shots *spanged* off his cover. The loyalists had recovered quickly. 'Hells damn you, where are you?' He had left the witch right here…

Shadows next to him shifted, and resolved into the shape of Tulava Dyne. She was middle-aged by the standards of huma-nity, and the lines on her face were not just from the weight of the powers she wielded. Her skin was maggot-pale – a contrast with Solomon's, which was a deep umber – and the right side of her head was shaved, with the hair on the other hanging in tight braids dyed in greens and blues. She had long ago abandoned the uniform of the Imperial primaris psyker she had once been, in favour of a nondescript navy jumpsuit, although she had added a carapace breastplate taken from the corpse of a Tempestor Prime. Tul had not survived this long in the galaxy by trusting entirely to her innate abilities for protection.

'Don't tell me you still want me to get through them for you?' she said, risking a glance over the top of the Chimera's hull. The flames of the burning vehicle glinted off the bare side of her half-shaved scalp.

'I never did,' Solomon told her, 'and Jate is no longer in a position to argue.' He was reaching for a new magazine when his eyes lit on the body of the Silver Templar the Harrowmaster had killed. A particularly ornate boltgun was clamped to the Imperial's thigh: obviously a weapon of some renown, and with the look of a piece that had been lovingly cared for, repaired, and restored to achieve its current appearance, as opposed to the nearly unscratched and decidedly unfamiliar armour to which it was attached.

'So what are your intentions?' Tulava asked. 'Other than having us pinned down and, if I might offer my opinion as someone who lacks your tactical genius, hilariously outgunned?'

'We are leaving this planet,' Solomon said. He ignored her sarcasm: humans reacted badly to their lives being endangered. Besides, Tul had earned the right to speak her mind to him, many times over. 'The Legion will pull back, and the mortals will cover our withdrawal, but we need a distraction to manage it in good order.'

'A distraction,' Tul repeated flatly. 'And did you want it clean, or dirty?' Some of her old instincts still held sway, sorceress though she might now be. 'Clean' was their code for her innate psykana abilities, which had once made her so valuable to the

Imperium, while 'dirty' meant delving into the realms of gods and daemons in practices the Imperium abhorred.

'Right now, I'll settle for "quick",' Solomon said.

Tulava grimaced. 'Dirty it is.' She sat down cross-legged, and held her force staff across her knees. Solomon reached out and grabbed the Templar's relic weapon, tugging it free from its mooring. The tiny, ancient, and stubborn machine-spirit within objected to his touch: it knew its owner, and it knew that he was not him. Well, it was not the only thing with a spirit.

Very cautiously, Solomon relaxed some of the warding on his bionic arm. Instantly, the daemon bound within it stretched out and overwhelmed the weapon's resistance, breaking its will. Solomon hastily reined the entity back in again, before it could either seek to escape, or to betray him. He had no trouble in maintaining the warding under normal circumstances – Tul had done the heavy lifting for him on that one – but the middle of a firefight was no time to lose control.

The new weapon was bound to him, now. He rose up, aimed, and fired in one fluid motion. The kick was no greater than his old bolter, but the shot struck a Silver Templar in the chest, and when they went down, they did not rise again. Which was just as well, since the rest of the Imperials were getting a lot closer.

'Any time now would be good!' he hissed, taking cover again, then blinked as a sudden chill washed over him. His armour protected him from extremes of both heat and cold, which meant…

Tul was on one knee, with her right hand plunged into the dirt and her left firmly grasping her force staff. Her hair and clothes were whipped by a gale that was not registered by the sensors of Solomon's armour, nor by the motes of ash and dust drifting calmly down around them both, and a fell light flickered in the depths of her mouth as she shouted silent words into the intangible storm. Frost was creeping out from her, hardening the mud beneath them and painting silver tendrils up the side of the Chimera, where it warred with the heat of the flames above, but this was no mere physical cold. This was the bitter bite of warpcraft.

Screams erupted from the other side of the Chimera: the Astra Militarum had seen something significantly worse than Traitor Marines, by the sounds of it. Even the Astartes were taken aback, judging by the harsh curses spat through vox-grilles, and the booms of bolter fire that no longer struck sparks from the wreck behind which Solomon was sheltering.

'This is Akurra,' he said quickly into his vox, broadcasting to all Legion units. 'Lord Jate is dead. I repeat, Lord Jate is dead. I am assuming temporary command as Harrowmaster. The enemy Astartes are something new – an unknown quantity, and dangerous. Commence full withdrawal to orbit. Captain Va'kai,' he added, 'be ready to give us cover.'

The replies came in, crisp and clear: no arguments, not even from Va'kai. The Serpent's Teeth had had their fangs blunted today, and they were not going to throw themselves into a fight against an enemy about whom they knew very little. That was not how the Alpha Legion had survived for ten thousand years.

Deep in his hearts, Solomon Akurra dearly wanted to move beyond merely *surviving*, but that day had not yet come. Right now, he needed to use whatever manner of distraction it was that Tulava had created for him, and–

Drazus Jate twitched, and then the Harrowmaster's hands reached up, clawing for Solomon's throat.

Solomon spat a curse, one of the few things he remembered from his home world, and dropped his newly acquired weapon to grab at Jate's wrists. He was still wearing his helm, but he knew better than to trust to ceramite against one possessed by the Neverborn. He had seen their flesh melt through armour, or their diabolically enhanced sinews tear it apart, so he wrested the dead warrior's fingers away from him, and did his best not to look at the swirling shadows with flashes of fangs that flickered in and out of view where Jate's head had once been.

'Tul!' he shouted. 'Tulava!'

The witch jerked as if waking from sleep, and the psi-storm around her ended as abruptly as it had begun. Jate's reanimation did not, however – at least until Tul laid her hand on his pauldron and spoke hurried words that saw the dead Harrowmaster's form relax and sent him slumping backwards into the mud, once again a lifeless corpse.

'What did you do?' Solomon demanded, taking up the captured boltgun again and readying it. No enemies appeared around or over the Chimera, though, and from the sounds of it they all had other, more pressing concerns.

'You wanted a distraction,' Tul panted, 'and you wanted one quickly. The Despoiler's ripped the fabric of the galaxy apart – the Neverborn answer the call readily now, even here. They won't abide for long, but there are enough freshly dead bodies for them to play with to keep the Imperials occupied.'

Solomon grimaced. Daemons were not natural allies for the Alpha Legion. Other Traitor Legions or later-born renegades might fight alongside them, might even offer themselves up as vessels, but the sons of Alpharius Omegon rarely flew so close to the dark energies of the warp. The Neverborn were tools, to be used only when they could be properly controlled, such as the minor warp-thing bound into Solomon's left arm, which helped guide his shots, and his blows in combat. It ran against Solomon's instincts to summon so many Neverborn and leave them to their own devices in such a manner, but he was low on options.

'Is this happening across the whole battlefield?' he demanded. Tulava shook her head.

'Not right away, I'm not that strong. I gave the power a beach-head here, and it will reach out and grow.'

'Then we should be going,' Solomon said. He hoisted Jate's limp body onto his shoulder, and stood up cautiously. The weight of his former comrade would slow him, but he would need to keep his pace to one that Tulava could match. Besides, another body sheathed in ceramite over his pauldron would provide excellent ablative armour.

What met his eyes as he stood was not the sight of Imperial troops battling against reanimated corpses. It was much, much worse.

Something monstrous, malformed and hideous squatted on the ground: a quivering heap of flesh that must have been ten feet tall, at least that across, and perhaps twice so in length. Even as Solomon watched, he saw a glistening tendril reach out of the warp spawn and latch around the body of another fallen Guardsman, which was wrenched into the rest of the mass and absorbed with a soft squelching sound. The monstrosity quivered and expanded accordingly, paying no attention to the las-bolts that seared its hide, or the bolter shells that blew gobbets of newly dead flesh out of it.

Shapes moved beneath the surface, and then what looked like arms emerged, lying horizontally within the skin and each hand clasping the upper bicep of the other limb, as though two bodies had been pushed forward side-on from within the thing against its outside. When they moved suddenly, bonelessly apart, the space between them was no longer the spawn's hide, but a fanged mouth that roared its hatred of the material universe. More tendrils shot out and snared victims, this time living ones, who fell helplessly to their knees as the purplish lengths tightened around their necks.

No, Solomon realised, they weren't tendrils. They were, or had once been, intestines.

'Was this supposed to happen?' he asked, as a Silver Templar was hoisted into the air by his wrists, struggling futilely.

'You said you needed a distraction, this is no time to get picky about details!' Tul snapped.

'So this was *not* what you intended.'

'Off-the-cuff daemonancy is not an exact science! Now can we please start running?'

She had a point. Solomon turned his back on the manifestation of the sorceress' work and began to run – or jog slowly in his case, since Tul needed to keep up with him – away from the warp beast she had summoned. Behind him, choking and screams spoke of the destruction it was wreaking on his enemies.

It was not alone. As Tulava had predicted, the maleficarum was spreading, and bodies that had been lying lifelessly were now stirring with unnatural vigour. Isolated corpses simply rose, as the daemon that had taken temporary residence in the deceased flesh began to manipulate it to its will, but a grotesque slurping sound drew Solomon's eye to a pile of bodies that had been thrown together either by an explosion, or in a hasty and undignified attempt to clear a path through them. These were starting to bleed together into an unholy whole, and he altered his path to give it a wide berth. Panic was setting in throughout the Imperial camp now, as the Alpha Legion and their human allies became a less obvious threat than the reanimated dead.

Mostly, at any rate. A volley of lasgun fire from his right struck Solomon's side, but his armour held. He subvocalised a command and the scales of his custom battleplate shifted from matt to reflective. The next volley splashed off him harmlessly as he half turned and raised the captured boltgun. He let his arm guide his shots: a trio of shells claimed a total of four victims, one punching clean through the man in front to detonate in the chest of the trooper behind him, and the rest cowered back and fled. However, no sooner had the dead hit the ground than they began to stir again.

'This is far from ideal,' Solomon told Tulava, as something exploded in the distance. A bit more distraction, courtesy of one of his Fangs, or an unexpected battlefield occurrence? He was too far away to tell. He flipped the scales of his armour back again: the reflector plates were enormously effective against energy weapons, but a ballistic impact would damage the finish and render them useless.

'The entire situation is far from ideal,' Tul said testily. 'I was working with very limited time, and only the barest notion of wards to prevent the entire thing getting out of control. If we had planned this from the start, I would have been considerably more prepared!'

Solomon shook his head. Tulava Dyne was a powerful ally – and she truly was an ally, unlike the Neverborn – and a valued advisor, but he always had to remember that she was not a legionnaire. She lacked the mental fluidity: the ability to adapt immediately and instinctively to developments and setbacks, to recognise the most likely path to survival or the realisation of goals, and even to alter what one's goals were based on the current situation. No one could completely achieve that ideal, of course – even the twin primarch – but it was something to which all legionnaires aspired.

Many martial arts throughout humanity's history had stressed the importance of perfect balance, the ability to immediately move in any direction to attack or defend as required, but mental balance was just as important as physical, if not more so. The greatest warrior was the one who stood at the intersection of will and reality; the one who would pursue their vision to the limits of what was possible, and no further, and would change their vision when necessary.

For example, Solomon had intended to reach one of the Imperial shuttles that standard defensive doctrine declared would be waiting for the senior commanders in case of the need to retreat. As a line of reanimated corpses appeared between command bunkers to bar his way, their movements growing more and more certain as the daemons inhabiting the bodies gained full control over their fleshy vessels, he re-evaluated that goal.

He trusted that the Neverborn would fall first upon the followers of the Emperor, but there were none nearby; and in any case, the Serpent's Teeth and their human followers were not dedicated to any of the Chaos gods. To these beasts, most of the combatants here were functionally similar. He had to be ready to fight, and against an enemy whose abilities were uncertain.

'Can you ease our passage?' he asked Tulava, pressing a stud on his gauntlet. 'Still them, as you did with Jate?'

'I'd have to be touching them,' Tul said, readying her force staff. 'We're going to have to do this the hard way.' Her staff was a formidable weapon even against mortal enemies, when empowered with her will. Against the Neverborn, even those housed in mortal flesh, it would be a tool of agonising banishment.

However, she would still have to strike them; and the Neverborn, well aware of their fleeting presence in this realm, were not inclined to patience. They would throw themselves at her in their desire to taste her blood, and care not if three of their number were struck down so long as the fourth succeeded. Tulava was human, with human reflexes, and only the shape of the creatures now advancing on them were human: the rest was something very different.

Solomon dumped Jate's body off his shoulder in a clatter of ceramite, snatched a frag grenade from his belt, and hurled it at the onrushing revenants. It detonated and threw at least half a dozen of them sideways, but each one staggered back up to its feet despite its shredded flesh. Degrading a body made it harder for the daemon to control, and shortened the creature's time in the material universe, but wounds that would incapacitate or kill a human were only inconveniences.

It had slowed some of them. He began to fire with the boltgun, obliterating the heads of those at the forefront of the rush. Even the loss of a head might not stop a Neverborn – Jate's corpse had demonstrated that – but it made it more difficult for them, and Solomon lacked the shredding firepower of an assault cannon that would easily and quickly render the bodies utterly useless. Given the choice of destroying a couple and then having to deal with the unharmed remainder at close quarters, or impeding many of them before they reached him, he would take the latter option.

Heads burst, and headlong rushes turned into stumbles. Solomon switched his aim to knees, blowing out lower limbs and sending revenants crashing to the mud. They would still come on, but any damage he did now increased their chances of survival.

'Ready?' Tulava asked from behind him.

'Ready,' Solomon replied, and threw himself flat. They had done this many times before, albeit usually against enemies for whom death was a more definite state of affairs.

Tul screamed as she swung her force staff. This was not daemonancy, or sorcery, or any other form of bargaining with the Ruinous Powers; this was Tulava's own psychic abilities. She unleashed a psychic shockwave that ripped through the air above Solomon's head, and slammed into the onrushing scrum of animated corpses.

Some fell, and made no further moves except for twitches. Others staggered, but came on as though drunk. It was Solomon's opening. He sprang to his feet, clamped the boltgun to his thigh, and drew his power knife. Then he commanded the daemon that resided in his left arm to alter the form of its metal housing.

If the warp creature bound within his limb felt any reluctance at harming its own kin, it gave no sign of it, for Solomon's arm lengthened into multiple razor-edged tendrils from the elbow downwards. These were no mere flails, tools only of momentum, but were each under Solomon's independent control. Part of the challenge of mastering his arm's abilities had been learning how to wield such weapons, when the sensory feedback from it was so different to usual. As was the way of the Alpha Legion, he had adapted.

Solomon whirled into the attack. His arm's unnaturally sharp edges sliced through the bodies of former Astra Militarum and Bluecoat troopers, decapitating, lopping off limbs, and carving great rents in torsos. His enemies did not stop, but nor did Solomon: he spun and cut, evading the clumsy strength of his daemonic foes and taking off hands, severing spines, whittling their numbers and their effectiveness down with a welter of precision blows. Here and now, he was their own personal harrowing.

According to his helmet's chrono, it was thirteen point four seconds later that he came to rest with the last of the possessed bodies at his feet, the corpses now too damaged for the minor entities within to exert any further meaningful control over them. His subjective experience had suggested a rather longer combat, but that was the way of his advanced bioengineering: not even a Space Marine could entirely reconcile what occurred when in the grip of their highly accelerated metabolism with the external passage of time.

Solomon scanned for new threats and listened to the vox bleed while his arm re-formed, and attempted to piece together what had happened while he had been otherwise occupied with fighting for his life. Snippets suggested that despite the unexpected nature of Tulava's distraction, the withdrawal was proceeding approximately as planned. Second and Fourth Fangs reported successful extraction from the combat area, others were on the verge of completely disengaging, and even some of the human support had been able to leave the defenders to fighting their newly risen dead.

'Solomon!'

Tul's shout drew his attention a moment before the sound of movement would have done. He whirled and brought the bolt-gun up, but hesitated as the mass of flesh lumbered into view around a barracks. He was not sure if it was the same monstrosity that had formed next to them originally, or another that had taken shape somewhere else, but it was certainly significantly larger. The boltgun would not touch it, and using his arm would be akin to trying to kill a Helbrute with a spoon. Even Jate's volkite charger probably would not trouble the thing.

The vox crackled, and disgorged words laced with a sneer.

'Cover your ears, witch.'

Tulava did so, although her expression suggested that she was not best pleased by the manner in which the advice had been framed. The blocky shadow of *Shadowstrike* swung in overhead, much more quietly than might have been expected given its size, and opened fire.

Two wing-mounted lascannons punched their tank-killing beams into the flesh-thing's bulk, drawing forth bellows of pain that only increased as the twin-linked heavy bolter roared out its support. Against this sort of firepower, not even the unholy amalgamation of dead bodies could survive: it came apart in a matter of seconds, damaged beyond its ability to reconfigure itself. With the threat gone, *Shadowstrike* descended and lowered its access ramp. The gunship was smaller than its Thunderhawk cousins, more intended for aerial warfare than transport, but it had enough infantry-carrying capacity to make do when required. Tulava jumped on as soon as it was low enough for her to do so; Solomon picked up Drazus Jate's body before following her.

'We're on,' he voxed to the pilot. 'Go.'

'*Acknowledged.*'

The ramp began to retract, and Solomon pressed the stud on his gauntlet for a second time to deactivate the homer that had called the craft to him. *Shadowstrike* was an Alphawing, a variant of the Raven Guard's Darkwing-pattern Storm Eagle. Many pieces of – and schematics for – that Legion's technology had found their way into the Alpha Legion's hands during the Horus Heresy, including the Alpha-Corvus armour that Solomon wore: or at least, the original version of it. The suit had had many previous owners, and enough repairs had been done over the millennia since that it was doubtful any of the original components remained.

Shadowstrike's troop bay held eight other Alpha Legionnaires, armoured in black. Headhunters. Qope Halver, the Headhunter Prime, was a vulpine-featured warrior with russet-brown skin and hair so black it seemed to hold a faint blue tinge. He saluted Solomon with a fist to his breastplate, although the gesture had no warmth behind it. Solomon returned it nonetheless.

'The Harrowmaster is lost?' Halver asked, looking down at Jate's corpse. 'A bloody price for no gain.'

'The price would have been higher had we stayed,' Solomon said. 'Did you face the silver Astartes?'

'We did,' Halver replied. 'We lost two before we could disengage.' He shook his head. 'What were they?'

'I don't know,' Solomon admitted. 'And that is a situation

that I intend to change before we next meet the Imperium in open battle.'

Halver scowled. 'Another setback. The Imperium might be encouraged by how easy it was to rout us here.'

'Look on the bright side,' Tulava said, from where she had already strapped herself in. The Alphawing was accelerating towards orbit and the waiting sanctuary of the *Whisper*, but the ride would inevitably be rougher for her than for the rest of them.

'And what is that?' Solomon demanded, turning to her. He had no regrets about the order he'd given, but that did not change the fact the Serpent's Teeth were withdrawing without the resources they came to claim.

'You're the mysterious, unknowable Alpha Legion,' Tul said, and the mockery in her voice was not directed at him, or his Legion. 'The odds are good that whatever you did here, the Imperium will be jumping at shadows assuming that it went exactly as you planned, and that they're somehow missing the bigger picture.'

Solomon grimaced. 'If only that were true.'

'I fought for them for twenty years,' Tul pointed out. 'Trust me. It'll be true enough.'

DANCE OF THE LONG GUNS

'Captain!' Solomon called, as the bridge door slid aside to allow him and Tulava entry. 'What is our status?'

'Teaching these whelps a lesson in manners, is our status,' Krozier Va'kai replied with a grim smile. Va'kai was unusually tall, even for an Alpha Legionnaire, yet he seemed coiled like a spring even when sitting in his command throne. The Alpha Legion made much of the hydra insignia that was its symbol, with many warriors bearing scale designs on their warplate, but there was nothing reptilian about Krozier Va'kai. He put Solomon more in mind of an avian predator, permanently ready to swoop on victim or carrion, as the mood or opportunity took him. 'Come to port fifteen degrees, launch prow torpedoes.'

'They will evade,' Solomon said despite himself, taking in the tactical hololith and focusing on the strike cruiser that Va'kai was targeting. The enemy ship's momentum would bring them into position to be struck by the barrage, but the distance was great enough that they would see the torpedoes coming.

'Of course they'll evade,' Va'kai said with a snort. 'But that will open them up for a lance shot from the *Sinister*, and bearing in mind the damage they've already taken, it should split them right down the middle. At the least, they will be out of the fight.'

'Torpedoes away, lord captain!' the gunnery officer reported. She was Alpha Legion through and through: all the bridge crew were. Indeed, the vast majority of the *Whisper*'s crew, and that of the *Sinister* and the *Dextral*, its two escort ships, were dedicated Legion serfs. Others amongst those the Imperium designated as the 'Traitor Legions' might press slaves into service, but there was always a risk that even such feeble creatures might rebel at a critical moment. The Alpha Legion – or at least the Serpent's Teeth – preferred a more enduring sort of loyalty.

'Roll starboard ninety degrees,' Va'kai commanded, apparently content that matters would resolve themselves as he predicted. 'I suspect the two merchantmen above us have more guns than they would appear to, given where they have positioned them-selves. Give them a taste of the port batteries.'

The *Whisper* shuddered as its ancient drives and thrusters com-plied with the instructions relayed to them by the bridge crew, and the pinpricks of stars visible outside began to tilt. It shud-dered again as its batteries fired, the concussive recoil of guns the size of super-heavy tanks moderated into nothing more than a slight vibration through the enormous superstructure. Some-where off to port, Solomon had no doubt, two Imperial vessels were in the process of becoming expanding flowers of metal.

'How is the withdrawal proceeding?' Solomon asked.

'We have' – Va'kai glanced at a read-out – 'eighty-seven per cent of expected landing craft back on board. Just the stragglers left now.'

'Give them as much cover as you can,' Solomon said. Va'kai glanced sidelong at him.

'I did not eliminate those two gunships for our safety, Solomon. Nothing they might have been hiding could have scratched the *Whisper*, but our transports would be a different matter.'

Solomon nodded. 'My apologies. I should know better than to offer you advice in matters pertaining to the void.'

'Offer as much advice as you see fit,' Va'kai replied. 'I am not arrogant enough to believe that I am infallible. Just do not be offended if I have already thought of it.'

'Noted,' Solomon said. That was something else that set the Alpha Legion apart from others: the fluidity of command and rank. Ego was rigid, and rigid tools were liable to break under pressure. The Alpha Legion used each member, be they Astartes or unaltered human or even, on occasion, xenos factor, in the manner to which they were best suited. Expertise was prized, and differing opinions sought, so that the best solutions to any problem might present themselves.

At least, that was what Solomon thought of as the Alpha Legion's way. It was fair to say that, scattered and diverse as the Legion was, it was by no means a universal approach.

All the same, it was something that had kept the Serpent's Teeth, and its previous incarnations, alive and functioning for a hundred centuries. The corrupted sons of the other Traitor Legions might mewl about the 'Long War' against the Imperium, but what did they know of it, lurking inside the time-distorting realms of the warp? Much of the Alpha Legion had never taken refuge in the Eye of Terror, or the Maelstrom, or any other place where realspace gave way to the immaterium. They had lived and fought and died in the time between the other Legions licking their wounds from one raid and planning the next. Solomon was two hundred and forty-two years old, by his best reckoning, and any warp-distortion to that figure was no more than any Imperial Space Marine might encounter as he travelled from conflict to conflict.

'What manner of foes are these, that put us to flight so easily?' Va'kai asked. 'They have little experience at void combat, I can tell you that.'

'I do not know,' Solomon replied, 'and that alarms me. We know the Imperium, we know their ways. Guilliman laid down their laughable Codex Astartes, and by and large they hold to it.' A rigid tool, again, and one prone to breaking when exposed to the correct pressure. He shook his head. 'But what we saw down there was like nothing I have heard of. It's as though they've created a new breed of Space Marine, Krozier, with new armour, new weapons...'

'What you're suggesting would be a greater innovation in one go than the Imperium's managed in ten thousand years,' Va'kai retorted. 'I am not saying it is impossible, but it sounds unlikely.'

'Take a look at this,' Solomon said. He unclamped a bolt weapon one of Fifth Fang had managed to capture, and passed it to the captain of the *Whisper*. Va'kai took it, and examined it for only a second or so before passing it back.

'Consider me convinced, Solomon. That is no model I've seen before, although I do not walk planetside as often as many of you.'

'Lord captain!' The shout came up from the bridge's central well. 'The strike cruiser fired upon by the *Sinister* is heeling towards us!'

'Do they have any weapons systems active?' Va'kai demanded. 'Any target locks?'

'Negative, my lord. Scans suggest they have lost power to all weaponry, and they're moving slowly.'

'What are you playing at?' Va'kai murmured, his eyes narrowing as he stared at the tactical hololith, its bright icons casting faint reflections on his smooth, copper-skinned features, as though he had adorned himself with glowing glyphs. 'You are practically begging me to shoot you, but an overloaded reactor blast would not catch us from this range...'

New flecks of light appeared on the hololith, emanating from the stricken strike cruiser's bow. Solomon frowned at them, the faintest flicker of concern tugging at him. 'Are those torpedoes?'

'Strike cruisers do not typically come armed with torpedoes,' Va'kai replied. He glanced at the captured bolt rifle again. 'Although I will concede that today is a day of surprises. No, I believe that what is approaching is–'

'Boarding pods!' the auspex operator shouted, as if on cue.

Va'kai laughed. 'Oh, this is almost embarrassing! Beyond desperate, at this range. The turrets will take care of them.'

'Don't kill them all,' Tulava said suddenly. Solomon turned to look at her, and Va'kai did as well.

'I beg your pardon, lady sorceress?' Va'kai asked. His tone was polite, but there was a steel beneath it. Krozier Va'kai would accept advice on his bridge, but he might bristle slightly at being instructed by a human, even one with Tulava Dyne's power.

'Leave one pod intact,' Tul elaborated. 'We need to study this enemy, and we'll need evidence to convince other warbands of what we've faced here today. Perhaps the Biologis Diabolicus can be of assistance, as well.'

'You are asking me to let my ship be boarded?' Va'kai demanded.

'By one pod only,' Tul insisted. 'They'll be overwhelmed within–'

'That is not the point, it's the principle–'

'Captain,' Solomon broke in, putting a slight emphasis on Va'kai's title. He was addressing the master of the ship, not a warrior with whom he had, if not friendship, at least a camaraderie. 'I understand your position, but I ask that you accede to the lady sorceress' request. We need to study this new enemy, and they are presenting themselves to us freely.'

He held Va'kai's eyes for a moment, and then the *Whisper*'s captain nodded.

'Very well, Solomon, but I want you to lead the defence yourself. If these new warriors are as formidable as you say, I do not want to give them any chance to disable us somehow.'

Solomon placed his fist on his breastplate. 'You have my word.'

'Assuming all goes to plan, we will have the last of our craft back by the time the boarders have breached,' Va'kai said. 'We will break from combat and jump to the warp, in case our exuberant friends have more help on the way, but to what destination? With Jate dead, I'll take your guidance, Solomon.'

Solomon did not have to think. He had been hoping for this from the moment he entered the bridge, but had no guarantee Va'kai would look to him over any of the other senior Legion members.

'Make for the *Unseen*,' he instructed. 'And send word to the Faceless, the Sons of Venom, the Redacted – anyone else we can make contact with. They need to know what's coming for them, if they have not already encountered it.'

'It will be done,' Va'kai replied. He raised his eyebrows. 'Speaking of "coming for them"…' He glanced meaningfully towards the bridge door.

'Of course.' Solomon turned and made for it, keying his vox to alert other legionnaires and bring them to his position. The quicker, lighter rhythms of Tul's hurrying steps followed him.

'Would you like my assistance?' she asked.

'That depends,' Solomon replied, his lips twisting in a slight smile. 'Am I going to have to fight it again?'

BIOLOGIS DIABOLICUS

So much of the Legion's history was lost.

In that sense, Solomon had to admit that they were not so different to the Imperium. Some of the gaps in their knowledge were accidental, as records disappeared due to technological failure, or enemy action. More frustrating, at least to him, was the fact that so much of what they had once known had been deliberately occluded. Even as the Inquisition worked to keep the vast majority of humanity ignorant of the truth, both about the wider galaxy and their own civilisation's history, so had the Alpha Legion, over millennia, become more and more withdrawn into its own cells and warbands, guarding their true intentions even from those who shared their heritage.

It had not always been that way, or so the tales suggested. In the era of the primarchs, before the Horus Heresy had begun, Alpharius Omegon had known the full extent of the Alpha Legion's operations, and had coordinated it across the galaxy. When Horus had turned on his father, however, everything changed. Brother betrayed brother, and secrets that had once been kept only from outsiders were now walled away from those with whom they had once been shared. Some rumours even suggested that the twin primarchs themselves had ended up at odds with one another, as some long-hidden difference caused their shared soul to turn against itself.

But then again, they were only rumours. Much of what the Alpha Legion had left were only rumours. Some of the Legion said Alpharius had been killed in the Battle of Pluto, others that he had been killed on Eskrador. Some said one or other event had been Omegon instead. Some deliberately obtuse fools even denied that either incident had seen the end of a primarch's life, and that either or both of the twins were still alive somewhere in the galaxy, watching and waiting, or subtly guiding events in the pursuit of some unknown plan.

The whereabouts of artefacts said to be associated with the primarch were unknown. No one Solomon had ever spoken to knew what had happened to the *Alpha* or the *Beta*, the Legion's twin flagships. It beggared belief that two such notorious Gloriana-class battleships could have been lost without trace, but neither were there any reliable records of a sighting since the days that followed the Heresy. After Eskrador, the Legion had splintered: not in the manner of a shattering glass, but of a fragmentation round entering a body. Each piece dug into the flesh of the Imperium, and stopping and removing one would do nothing to affect the progress of the others, but the splinters were, by that same token, no longer part of a unified whole. Some notable commander had presumably taken the *Alpha*, and another perhaps the *Beta*, and they had passed out of everyone's histories.

The *Unseen*, on the other hand, was a known quantity, at least to the Alpha Legion of the area of space designated by the Imperium as the Ultima Segmentum. It was not a ship so much as it was a conglomerate: a combination trophy heap and junkyard, built around the core of a Universe-class mass conveyor, with innumerable other smaller ships now attached to it. It looked like a small space hulk, but the *Unseen* had been constructed by the Alpha Legion, not thrown together by the capricious whims of the warp, despite the pieces of ork, t'au, and other, stranger xenos vessels that nestled in its superstructure alongside those made by humans.

It had long ago, by dint of some unrecorded agreement between powerful warlords, been designated as neutral ground, and not for the use of any one individual. So it was that one of the greatest strongholds of the Alpha Legion – in the records that Solomon knew of – lay within an asteroid cluster on a decades-long orbit around their parent star. It was here that the warbands gathered, on the infrequent occasions when they came together, and it was here that certain of the Alpha Legion's retainers, resources, and associates remained.

Solomon had expected to need to go in search of the Biologis Diabolicus. He had certainly not anticipated being greeted by the former priest of Mars as soon as the airlock that led from the access passage into the body of the station itself hissed open.

'Commander,' Magos Kazadin Yallamagasa buzzed, with what Solomon interpreted as excitement. The magos was an imposing figure, approximately nine feet tall, and with a number of arms within his voluminous robes that Solomon was not certain he'd ever had an accurate count of. The original robes had long disintegrated, of course, for Yallamagasa had broken from the teachings of the Omnissiah some three thousand years before, and he now wore deep green, with silver stitching that picked out patterns of coiling serpents. He was flanked by two of his Dishonour Guard: massive, genetically enhanced warriors, much of whose armour had once belonged to Ultramarines. Without the black carapace enabling full integration, their movements were slower, more deliberate and sluggish. The one on the magos' left had her head shaved apart from a topknot, and sported a line of gemstones adhered to subdermal piercings across her brow. The other, whom Solomon knew to be Vasila Manatu, had golden eyes split by slit-like black pupils, which allowed her to see better in low light.

'You again,' Halver growled at them. 'Still aping something you will never be, I see.'

'Who did you kill to get your armour?' Manatu shot back, with a mocking quirk of her eyebrow. She tapped her chestplate. 'I took this from the corpse of its former owner.'

'Yes, yes, they are not Space Marines,' the Biologis Diabolicus said, with an irritated wave of one of his hands. 'There are many different forms of genhancement in the galaxy, Lord Halver, and the result is far more important than the method. Speaking of which, Commander Akurra,' he continued, 'I believe you have some specimens for me to examine?'

Solomon smiled wryly. He should have anticipated that Yallamagasa would be eager to examine the corpses. 'We do, but surely you would prefer to conduct this in your sanctum?'

'Of course,' Yallamagasa replied crisply. 'However, I could not risk allowing another to intercept the cadavers before I could do so.'

'Magos, I assure you that I would hand them over to no other,' Solomon said. It was the truth: idiosyncratic though Yallamagasa undoubtedly was, he was undeniably a genius, and his genelabs in the bowels of the *Unseen* were one of the main reasons why the Ultima Segmentum warbands were able to maintain their numbers at such viable levels. Other renegades might struggle with failing technological knowledge and ancient, irreparable equipment as they sought to induct aspirants through the harrowing procedures that all Space Marines had to endure, no matter where their loyalties lay. The Biologis Diabolicus, however, had been able to meld his knowledge of gene-smithing and flesh-crafting – knowledge that had seen him exiled from the Adeptus Mechanicus – with the existing wisdom of the Alpha Legion's Apothecaries. So it was that Solomon had been raised into the Legion's ranks, and without the corrupting effect of warp anomalies such as those within which other renegades concealed themselves, his biology and anatomy were scarcely any different to one of his distant Imperial kin.

'Bring them, then,' the magos said eagerly, his upper half rotating in a swirl of robes while his lower limbs, so far as Solomon could make out, made no such motion. This did not stop Yallamagasa striding immediately away, his two Dis-honour Guard in tow.

'You heard him,' Solomon instructed, and Legion serfs hur-ried forwards, pushing gurneys on which lay the bodies of the Silver Templars killed during their desperate, doomed boarding attempt. There were three in total: the rest had fought with such ferocity that the only way to bring them down had been to essen-tially hack them apart. The three bodies Solomon had brought over for the magos to examine, while not exactly whole, did at least have one undamaged head, torso, and so on between them.

'Are you coming?' Solomon asked Halver, who shook his head.

'I'll take a look around to see who's been by recently, and what news they had.'

'If they chose to share it,' Tulava put in.

'Our ways have kept us safe and active for longer than you can comprehend,' Halver said dismissively. 'So mind your tongue, witch.'

'Mind yours, prime,' Solomon retorted, and felt the slight rush of chemical responses in his blood as Halver's sharp features turned towards him with narrowed eyes. The Alpha Legion was not a brotherhood in which slights were regularly met with drawn blades, but neither did they hold to the absolute authority of rank so common within Imperial Chapters. Their command structure was fluid, with those best suited to a role taking it with the approval of their peers, but sometimes peers could not agree.

And when all was said and done, while many of the Alpha Legion were by no means as far under the sway of the Ruinous Powers as most of their so-called traitor brethren, neither were they immune to the lures of the Blood God.

'Careful, Ghost,' Halver said, his voice roughening a little. 'You are not Harrowmaster here, and you have not yet been appointed commander of the Serpent's Teeth.'

'And if I am, I shall expect my brothers to speak to the lady sorceress with respect,' Solomon said levelly. 'That is as true now as it will be then, so consider it when the time comes to make your voice heard.'

Halver's eyes flickered to Tulava once more, then back to Solomon. 'I have already seen the costs of your leadership, Akurra. I have no wish to go the same way as Kyrin Gadraen.'

Solomon's nostrils flared. 'Kyrin understood the risks, and accepted the mission of his own free will. I gave no order. Do you think I wanted to lose him? We hailed from the same world, we told the same tales, and sang the same songs. He was all I had left of my old life.'

Halver looked for a moment as though he would speak again, but then he simply nodded: not an acknowledgement of an error, but of what Solomon had said.

'We will compare notes once we are back on the *Whisper*, brother.'

'Indeed,' Solomon replied. Halver turned and made for the bridge, and Solomon set off after the Biologis Diabolicus.

'Does your closeness to me jeopardise your chances of becoming commander?' Tulava asked, hurrying to keep pace with him. Solomon could have slowed his strides to match hers, but then he would have risked losing the party ahead of him completely, and he had no intention of giving Yallamagasa a chance to start the autopsy in his absence.

'Perhaps,' he acknowledged. 'But you have earned my loyalty, just as I have earned yours. I will not abandon that to appease others who do not realise the benefits such bonds can bring. I will either become overall commander, or I will not.'

'For a Legion so notorious for its scheming, you can be remarkably fatalistic at times,' Tulava said, with a snort of laughter.

Solomon considered how to respond to that. Tulava had been with him for two decades, but still she – like virtually every other human factor of the Legion – did not truly understand their mindset. Perhaps that was not surprising; perhaps it was something that only an Astartes brain could properly comprehend, and one that had received the particular gifts of the Alpha Legion's gene-seed at that.

'We always seek to influence outcomes to our advantage,' he said, after a few seconds. 'However, some outcomes cannot be meaningfully changed without changing ourselves. Sometimes that is necessary, even desirable… and sometimes, doing so would render any victory won by such methods essentially meaningless. I try to value my allies according to their worth, not according to their origin. If I were to depart from that mindset in order to win power then I believe the forces under my control would no longer be as effective, and so it might be better had I never achieved that level of command at all.'

'You could always lie about it,' Tulava pointed out, and Solomon laughed.

'The Alpha Legion was born in lies, and to this day we breathe them as easily as we do oxygen, but that also means that we can sniff them out with great readiness. It would take a matter of great importance for me to risk attempting to deceive so many of my brothers all at once, when their attention would be fixed on my words and the intentions behind them.'

THE NEW BREED

Magos Yallamagasa's sanctum had once been a ship's primary medical bay and apothecarion, and it still contained ancient machinery which likely dated back to the Great Crusade. However, there were many other, newer devices installed, few of which had ever been seen, let alone approved, by either the Adeptus Mechanicus or any Apothecary of the Space Marines. Solomon's armour registered a drop in temperature of several degrees as soon as he entered the chamber, the result of cold-bleed from the cryo-store units scattered around, in which resided the various organs and implants the Biologis Diabolicus would use to usher the next generation of Alpha Legionnaires into the galaxy. Most of these creations were the work of the Diabolicus Secundus, Yallamagasa's abominable intelligence engine. The magos liked to keep his circuits focused on matters of biology, and so had delegated his knowledge of machines – which was lesser, although still substantial – to his spider-legged automaton, which spoke in a static-edged version of Yallamagasa's own voice.

More than once, Solomon Akurra had pondered the wisdom of leaving his Legion's future so largely in the hands of someone who was technically an outsider. However, Yallamagasa had been working aboard the *Unseen* for longer than most of the Legion could remember, barring those who had spent significant periods within the warp, and no one could fault his work. His payment was the protection afforded by the galaxy's finest web of guerrilla warriors, and therefore the freedom to pursue his other works without fear of interruption from the Adeptus Mechanicus, the Inquisition, or any of his renegade rivals; that, and access to certain organic materials or test subjects with which warbands would return to barter for his services. Yallamagasa would not risk anything so rash as holding the Legion's gene-seed stores hostage, but he could easily refuse to undertake work for any given commander should he feel that he was not being fairly recompensed.

But on some occasions the work itself was its own payment. Such was the case now, as the Biologis Diabolicus had laid out the corpses on ancient restraint couches that more usually bore those undergoing the surgeries needed to make a warrior truly transhuman.

'This promises to be a fascinating endeavour,' Yallamagasa said, as the door slid shut behind Solomon and Tulava. Solomon removed his helm and set it down, letting his locks swing free. The air was laced with astringent medical smells, of disinfecting sprays and anti-contaminants. The body of an Astartes could shake off most infections, but aspirants were nowhere near as hardy, so the places in which they were created needed to be clean. Even Imperial Chapters sometimes struggled for supplies of gene-seed, and while the structures of the Imperium were lumbering and prone to waste and error, they still easily eclipsed the resources the Alpha Legion could bring to bear. As such, profligacy could not be tolerated, so the survival of aspirants once they had been granted their first implants was of the utmost importance.

'I am glad you did not remove the armour,' the magos said, firing up a plasma cutter and las-scalpel. 'It is not just an existing form that has been upsized, and it should be examined in its own right.'

Solomon, who had spent over two centuries becoming immensely familiar with the different ways in which Space Marines were armoured, both to kill his enemies and to repair and replace the components of his own warplate, decided not to comment. Yallamagasa did not always consider the knowledge base of his audience before speaking, which was an idiosyncrasy that had to be tolerated.

However, as the magos began his autopsy, Solomon's familiarity with the subject decreased. He knew Space Marine anatomy, both from his own wounds and those he had patched up on his brothers, and from those he had inflicted. It was quickly becoming clear that these new Space Marines were similar in most respects, but very different in others.

'Fascinating,' Yallamagasa said, as his tools flensed an arm and laid bare metallic coils built into the sinews. 'This is a new level of bioengineering, beyond that which I have seen before. At least from the Imperium,' he added, for the Diabolicus Biologis was not one to admit that his own work was second to that of any other.

'What about Fabius Bile?' Tulava asked. Solomon opened his mouth to try to head off the impending eruption, but the damage was done.

'Bile?' Yallamagasa said, outraged. 'That charlatan? How many millennia has he been tinkering with Astartes biology, and to what end? He kills as many as he enhances, and the so-called "benefits" of his work are temporary and unstable! The study and improvement of living flesh is not his passion – he merely pursues it to inflate his own ego!'

Solomon, who was not in the mood for another of the magos' incandescent and envious rages about the former Apothecary of the Emperor's Children, shot Tulava an unimpressed look. She responded with a smirk; there was something about her human sense of humour that relished enraging Yallamagasa. On another day Solomon would have tolerated it; might even have been vaguely amused himself. Right now, though, the shadow of this new threat was still hanging over them all, and he had no patience for levity.

'–allowed him access to their gene-seed, and where are they now, I ask you? He is–'

'Magos,' Solomon said firmly, interrupting the torrent of recycled complaints. 'The ability of Fabius Bile to have produced these warriors is irrelevant, since there is absolutely no possibility that he is responsible for them. Someone has, however – and on a large scale, at that. These were not small numbers of elite troops. There were at least a hundred of them, almost certainly more, and these ones threw their own lives away in the hope of closing with us.'

'The level of resources required to bring such a thing about is hard to calculate,' the magos said thoughtfully, his rage subsiding as he applied his brain – or whatever mechanical parts now replaced it – to the issue at hand. 'Just as considerable would be the effort needed to make the Imperium adopt a new procedure. This would never have been officially sanctioned. The research must have been conducted in secret, I cannot estimate over how many years, and then for it to not instantly be declared heretical...'

'Space Marines are not the Imperium,' Solomon said. His

eyes drifted over the butchered torso of another of the strange warriors, where a solidified ribcage designed to act as a natural armour against the galaxy had been severed by Yallamagasa's whirling mono-molecular blades and pulled apart by his mecha-tendrils, leaving an odour of superheated bone in the air, and the flesh within open for inspection. There was an organ connecting the Space Marine's two hearts, and Solomon was sure that no such thing resided within his own chest. 'Which is not to say that they are not stubborn in their own ways.'

'If anything, it makes it more remarkable,' Yallamagasa said, returning to his dissection. 'What Space Marine Apothecary could have devised such advances, and incorporated them so seamlessly into the pre-existing transhumanism? They treat wounds and collect the gene-seed of the fallen, they are not innovators. But if not an Apothecary, who would have the ability to influence a Chapter to incorporate them?'

Solomon rubbed his chin, and the wheels of his mind began to spin in new directions. 'Perhaps no existing Chapter *was* influenced to incorporate these changes.'

Yallamagasa's body did not move, but his head rotated one hundred and eighty degrees to look at Solomon. 'A new founding, then?'

'Perhaps,' Solomon said, thinking it through as he went. 'The tension between the High Lords of Terra and the Adeptus Astartes is well known to us. If the High Lords have somehow come into possession of a means to enhance Space Marine biology, they would use it. Perhaps they seek to create a force with greater allegiance to them. I suspect many of the existing Chapters would react poorly to something that could see them replaced, and the High Lords might count on such resentment to make the new warriors less likely to bond with their existing kin. And even if that is not the case,' he added, as a new thought occurred, 'it might be possible to encourage it, and widen a few cracks in the Imperium's shell.' He fell silent as he began considering options. It would take a much more complete picture of the situation to make it even potentially viable, but the possibility of an operation conducted under loyalist colours, 'accidentally' conflicting with that of these newcomers and resulting in a perceived betrayal...

His vox chimed. *'Akurra.'*

'Halver,' he replied. 'We agreed to compare notes back on the *Whisper.'*

'You will want to see this for yourself. Get to the communication deck as fast as you can.'

Solomon blinked in surprise as the vox disconnected again. There had been tightly wound urgency in Halver's voice. The Headhunter Prime was worried, and had ended the call rather than engage in any further conversation.

Solomon might not like Halver, but his battle-brother was not one to exaggerate or overstate matters. If he wanted Solomon to see something as soon as possible, then it was important.

'Magos, please continue, and let me know your conclusions,' he said, striding towards the door. Tulava was already hopping down from the operating table on which she had seated herself, having recognised the change in his demeanour. 'Something requires my urgent attention.'

The Biologis Diabolicus did not respond, but merely went back to his autopsy with various clicks, whirrs and buzzes of intrigue and surprise. Tulava caught hold of Solomon's arm as they left the sanctum.

'Where are we going?' the sorceress asked, running to keep up.

'The communications deck,' Solomon told her, without slowing. 'Halver told me to get there as fast as I could.'

Tulava nodded. 'Say no more.' She muttered something, and

suddenly Solomon's feet were wrapped in darkness instead of thudding into the solid decking of the *Unseen*. It flowed up his body like a wave of night before he could open his mouth to object, and congealed around his head. His stomach lurched for a moment, a particularly disconcerting sensation for a warrior who never normally experienced such things, and then the darkness cleared from his vision to reveal the *Unseen*'s communication deck. Slightly less welcome was the sour visage of Halver, turning towards him. However, the Headhunter said nothing about Tulava's sorcery, which spoke volumes as to how important he felt it was for Solomon to have reached him as soon as possible.

'What is it?' Solomon asked him, making a mental note to speak with Tulava Dyne later about using her powers to warp-walk him without warning.

'See for yourself,' Halver replied, bringing up a transmission on the vid-screen. 'It is date-stamped as having arrived here three days ago, but given the disruptions caused by the Despoiler's rift, the warp alone knows when it was sent. No one else has seen it. Even the Diabolicus probably does not know about it.'

It was from one of the Serpent's Teeth's agents, a mid-ranking Imperial official on the world of Vorlese. All the correct cyphers, codes, and clearances were in place, but when Solomon had finished reading it he went back and checked them again. Then he read the message again, and then he went back and checked its authenticity for a third time.

'I told you that you would want to see it for yourself,' Halver said. The Headhunter Prime had the slight, grim smile of someone who had received bad news, but had at least got to then deliver that news to someone whom he did not particularly like.

'Guilliman,' Solomon said flatly, prompting a gasp from Tulava. 'Resurrected. After ten thousand years, he is... back?'

'That has to be a mistake,' Tul said. 'That can't be true. It can't be!'

'What's the matter, witch?' Halver sneered. 'Are you worried you have thrown your lot in with the wrong side?'

'Enough!' Solomon snapped, before Tul could reply. He was in no mood to hear them argue, and should frayed tempers cause matters to escalate then it was highly likely that one would lose their life. Halver might disparage Tulava, but Solomon knew well enough that the sorceress' gifts could end his battle-brother, just as surely as Halver's bolter could blow Tulava apart were he able to fire before she could bring her powers to bear.

'The message has every sign of authenticity,' Halver said to Solomon, choosing to ignore Tulava. 'Either our factor has become acutely delusional, our security protocols have been compromised to a level we have never before seen, or he speaks the truth.'

'Under normal circumstances I would believe the first, or even the second,' Solomon said slowly. 'Given the nature of what the magos is currently dissecting in his sanctum, I am inclined to believe the third.'

'Truly?' Halver said softly. 'You believe the primarch of the Ultramarines has returned?'

'Something seismic must have happened to the Imperium for them to make the advances we have seen and fought against,' Solomon said. 'The return of a primarch would explain that. Who else would have the authority to command such upheaval of the Space Marines themselves? It fits the facts we have, Halver, unbelievable though it might seem.' His temper flared suddenly, and he slammed his fist into the wall. 'All the hells take Abaddon! What else has his meddling made us miss? What other information from our factors has never reached us?'

'That's of secondary importance right now,' Tulava said. 'We need to know what to do, surely?'

'The witch is correct,' Halver said immediately, prompting a look of surprise from Tulava. 'We are without a Harrowmaster, and this piece of information only suggests that there is even more we do not know about what we now face. We need to consolidate.'

Solomon nodded, his mind whirling again. 'Agreed.' He had never planned for the return of a loyalist primarch, because who could have foreseen that? However, the Serpent's Teeth had any number of options prepared, to cover most eventualities to the best of their abilities and resources. The true mettle of a commander lay not in what options he had available, but in the decisions he made. The question was the same as always: how could this situation best be turned to benefit the Legion? If benefitting the Legion was not possible, how could it best benefit the warband? If benefitting the warband was not possible, how could it benefit the individual? The Alpha Legion had a reputation for always getting what they wanted, but that was easier when you could change the outcome you were pursuing based on how likely the current situation meant you were to achieve it.

He made his choice. All choices were a gamble, but this was, perhaps, more of one than most.

'We must send out word to all of our contacts,' he declared. 'It is not enough to simply warn our brothers of what we've faced. We need a coordinated response. The warbands of the Ultima Segmentum must be summoned as soon as possible, for a Council of Truth.'

Halver nodded his agreement, but Tulava looked uncertain. '*All* of our contacts, lord?'

'All of them,' Solomon said. 'Reach out, Tulava. If we are to roll the dice then I will roll them all, and see how they fall.'

NEW FACES, OLD FACES

They came.

Solomon had not been certain that they would. The Alpha Legion was, by its nature, independently minded. They had no primarch, no First Captain, no Chapter Master. Nor did they have a home world: the *Unseen* was the closest thing to a base of operations, at least in the Ultima Segmentum. The very fluidity of command structure that made them so adaptable also meant that a call such as the one he had put out held no more authority than that which the recipients chose to give it.

The Legion was splintered into warbands, and warbands into cells, and so on. How could there be any single authority in such a situation? Two Alpha Legion operatives might pass each other on a street wearing identifying marks without blinking, for those marks would have been set by groups that had no knowledge of each other. Solomon was certain that Legion factors had fought each other before, each group pretending to be Imperial loyalists, and assuming their counterparts were the real thing.

It was infuriating.

'Whom do we have?' he asked Qope Halver, as they stood side by side in the council chamber he had chosen for the assembly. The Serpent's Teeth had yet to formally appoint a new commander, and Solomon had simply proceeded as though he had been awarded the role. Captain Va'kai had raised no objection, which likely carried a lot of weight. More surprisingly, the Headhunter Prime, and others, had been silent on the issue as well. Solomon suspected that they were waiting to see how he performed before deciding whether to challenge him.

That suited him. He had confidence that he could lead them well, and at least he was getting the opportunity to do so. If he could not, he would be replaced by another suitable candidate, and the Legion would be the stronger for it.

'A good response,' Halver replied, 'and a varied one. Although that might lead to its own problems.'

Solomon grunted non-committally. Another element of the Alpha Legion's fluidity was the fact that they were, by far, the most diverse of the renegade Legions in terms of their methods and ideologies. Many warbands were utterly dedicated to the Ruinous Powers, and wore the marks of Chaos proudly and openly, but others were not so far gone. The Serpent's Teeth stood in fierce opposition to the Imperium, but Solomon paid the Chaos gods no more heed than he did the Emperor. Power, that was the only question that mattered to him and his brothers: what power could something give, in exchange for what cost? Gods so rarely seemed to provide enough of the former without the latter being far too high.

Of course, it was rumoured that some of the Alpha Legion had never truly turned their colours at all: that they were still performing their acts of infiltration, subterfuge, and sabotage for the Imperium, without even the Imperium being aware of it. That would be a thankless task indeed. Solomon had a certain grudging respect for warriors who could risk everything in aid of those who would execute them without mercy, but he had no time for their idealism. Those who could not see that the Imperium was beyond help were delusional fools.

'Who are the notables?' he asked. He had an idea himself, from what he had seen, but another perspective was always welcome.

'The Shrouded Hand are here,' Halver reported. 'Mainly veterans, and experienced in xenos combat.'

Solomon nodded. He had seen a small group of warriors in ancient but well-cared-for battleplate, with an easy confidence to their movements. Their apparent leader went bareheaded aboard the *Unseen*, and at first sight had skin the colour of blood. Only a closer look revealed that his flesh was in fact translucent, and the colour was lent to it by the blood and muscle beneath. Solomon had seen many deformed and disfigured servants of the Ruinous Powers in his years in the Legion, but this more subtle mutation was somehow one of the most disquieting he had encountered.

'Who else?'

'The First Strike,' Halver said, nodding towards another band of legionnaires.

Solomon sucked his teeth as he studied them. 'They have more than a few skulls in their iconography. And about their persons in general,' he added, as one warrior shifted position and revealed the spiked trophy rack of the one behind him.

'And a fair number of chainblades, brought to a peaceful council,' Halver observed.

'Assault specialists?'

'How did you guess?' Halver said with a snort.

'Just do not seat them next to the Faceless,' Solomon advised, studying the council chamber as intently as though it were a warzone. The trouble was that it could become exactly that, if they were not careful. Even the Imperium's lapdogs came to blows with each other from time to time, over matters of honour, or pride, or one Chapter considering that another had killed the wrong people, or in the wrong manner, or had enjoyed it too much. For renegades such as the Alpha Legion, the constraints of a shared cause were so loose they were practically non-existent.

'You invited the Faceless?' Halver groaned.

'We invited everyone,' Solomon pointed out. 'The Faceless are a part of the Legion, and they operate in this segmentum.'

'I cannot stand those fools,' Halver said, although he had the sense to say so quietly, and barely moving his lips. The chamber was awash with noise, but that did not mean that someone was not listening. All Space Marines had sharp senses, and that was to say nothing of the dubious gifts the Chaos gods might have bestowed upon their followers, or any of the myriad surveillance devices employed by a Legion specialising in espionage.

'You are not the only one,' Solomon said. His dislike for the Faceless was not as strong as Halver's, but there was little harm in seeding more common ground between the two of them. And besides, his statement was not untrue: even within a Legion where warbands were distrustful rivals as often as they were cautious allies, the Faceless were unpopular. 'I see the Sons of Venom are here as well,' he added, before Halver could voice his displeasure further.

'I do not know much about them.'

'Biowarfare specialists,' Solomon told him. 'They believe that their method of war is the ultimate realisation of the Legion's principles.'

'Doesn't everyone?' Halver snorted. 'The giant over there is Roek Ghulclaw. He has few battle-brothers with him, but he does command sizeable militia forces called the Guns of Freedom through General Andol, beside him. They helped take down a world called Makenna VII somewhere in Segmentum Obscurus. Most of the original Guns of Freedom died there, of course, but they have been recruiting since.'

Solomon studied the pair of them. Ghulclaw's armour was liberally decorated with the eight-pointed star of Chaos, and encrusted with protuberances that could have been horn, or bone, or possibly something else entirely. Andol was a thin man, and so tall that he was only a head or so shorter than the huge legionnaire beside him. His uniform, evidently once Imperial, now bore similar markings to that of his lord. Solomon caught a glimpse of the man's hard, dark eyes, set in a tawny-skinned face with sunken cheeks and a lantern jaw, and saw the light of fanaticism within. Andol was no weak-willed or intimidated puppet, obeying Ghulclaw out of fear. If Solomon was any judge, his soul had long ago been willingly signed over to the forces of the warp.

'I heard of a new cell calling themselves the Unsung,' he said. 'Anything from them?'

'"New" is a debatable term,' Halver replied. 'They claim to have been stuck in a warp storm since the Heresy, and only recently got out again thanks to some sorcerer.'

Solomon pursed his lips. 'Do we believe them?'

Halver shrugged with a clank of ceramite. 'You know as well as I that anything's possible. It is something of a moot point though, since the message they sent back told us to eat the business end of our own bolters, in not so many words.'

Solomon nodded slowly. He was not distraught by that news: a warband claiming to have known the primarchs themselves might turn more than a few heads, and make things unpredictable. 'What about the Redacted?'

'That bunch of impersonators? Possibly dead, certainly disappeared,' Halver replied. 'Rumour has it that they were at the heart of that mess which saw the end of the Angelbane, and the rest of the Sons of the Hydra.'

Solomon grunted. Quetzel Carthach, the Angelbane, had been one of the more prominent Legion figures in the Ultima Segmentum. His war against the sons of Guilliman had struck important blows against the Imperium, while also providing useful distractions for those warbands who preferred to operate a little more circumspectly.

'Carthach's absence may pose an issue,' he said quietly.

'Are you sure?' Halver asked. 'I cannot imagine the Angelbane doing anything other than wanting to take the war straight to Guilliman, and given what we have heard about the size of the crusade that is rolling out–'

'True, but he would inevitably be reined in to an extent,' Solomon pointed out. 'Even Carthach would not go for the primarch on his own, so he would have to compromise to gain the support of others. But without him, who will be pushing for an aggressive response?'

Halver snorted. 'My wager would be on the First Strike.'

'True enough,' Solomon conceded, 'but how much voice do they have? They muster, what, thirty legionnaires in total?'

'Plus one battered strike cruiser,' Halver said.

'Not a large force. Not sufficient to sway the council,' Solomon said. He shook his head. 'I am worried, Qope.'

He felt the slight change in posture of the warrior beside him, and his sensitive olfactory organs detected the faint chemical shift that indicated surprise. Halver was slightly wrong-footed by Solomon's admission.

'Worried by what?' Halver asked, his voice not betraying the uncertainty he was now feeling.

'Our mindset. Our mentality,' Solomon said. He took in the room with a gesture of his bionic left hand. 'Fighting from the shadows is fine – it is tactically sound to use pawns and proxies to do our work, and to strike at our enemy without revealing ourselves. But when our enemy comes bringing fire and light to burn us out, along with all the other things he hates and fears, how will we react? Will we gather ourselves and strike at him, and give him reason to fear what his light may reveal? Or will we crawl away into smaller and smaller shreds of shadow, diminishing as we go, and let him proceed unchallenged?'

Halver looked at Solomon, then grimaced and looked away again. 'Open warfare has never been the Legion's way.'

'"Never" is a strong word,' Solomon said, 'and not one that I believe, in this context.'

'Lord Akurra?'

That voice did not belong to Qope Halver. Solomon turned to see a trio of legionnaires behind them, having paused just before they got so close that their unannounced presence might have constituted a threat. Two of them, including the one in front, were very similar facially, with the bald heads and olive skin tones so common within the Legion as a whole. The other had skin a couple of shades darker, and although the sides of his skull were shaved, he wore a single braid of hair down the centre of his scalp. Most notably, to Solomon's eyes, the heads of all three were marked with multiple small scabs, as if each had recently gone head first through a pane of glass.

'The Penitent Sons?' he asked, although he was already reasonably sure of the answer. He stepped forward and offered his left forearm. The leader obliged, clasping Solomon's wrist with his hand in a warrior's grip, and allowing Solomon to do the same in return.

The bound daemon in Solomon's arm licked out, lightly tasting the soul of the Astartes facing him. It was a new experience, Solomon felt through the bond: he had not met this warrior before. It was always a good idea to check when dealing with fellow members of the Alpha Legion.

'Vyrun Evale,' the other legionnaire said. 'New commander of the Penitent Sons.'

'Thank you for coming,' Solomon said. 'I was sorry to hear about the death of Lord Arkay.'

'This so-called Indomitus Crusade has taken a toll upon us all,' Evale said sombrely. Solomon felt a momentary twinge of regret in the other warrior's soul, just before he released Evale's arm, but there were other emotions mixed in there as well. Joy, ambition, guilt, and… fear? Yes, fear, being savoured like a mortal gastronome might enjoy a delicately spiced new dish. It was not a sensation Solomon knew well, but his daemon was familiar with it, both its own and others'. Yet Vyrun Evale's face was impassive, giving no indication of the kaleidoscope of feelings whirling beneath the surface.

'Please be seated,' Solomon said, stepping back and gesturing to the benches arrayed in a semicircle around the front of the room. Space Marines had no need to sit, of course, but the Alpha Legion had always valued the input of all its factors, be they human, transhuman, or even xenos, and not all were as hardy as the sons of Alpharius Omegon.

'What's that about?' Halver asked quietly, as the Penitent Sons passed out of earshot again, so far as could be reckoned.

Solomon's lip twitched. 'Loyalists, or so they proclaim. They wear barbs inside their helms as penance for the crimes our Legion has committed against the Emperor's vision.'

Halver screwed his face up, clearly trying to come to terms with that explanation. 'Then what in the name of all the dead stars are they doing *here?*'

'Looking for another excuse to punish themselves, is my guess,' Solomon said. 'They have no hesitation in attacking the Imperium, or in supporting others to do so. They just pretend to be remorseful about it afterwards.' He thought again of the guilt his daemon had sensed. 'Perhaps they genuinely are, in a way, but it seems they desire that feeling as much as they abhor it.'

'If you lead us down a path like that,' Halver said flatly, 'I will kill you myself.'

'If I led us down a path like that,' Solomon said, turning his head to look at him, 'I would probably enjoy it.'

Halver growled, deep in his throat. 'Is everyone here now?'

Solomon tapped the finger of his gauntlet on his lips. 'Not quite. But we should get underway regardless. We will deal with late arrivals as and when they turn up.'

Halver sighed. 'I wish Kyrin was here. His counsel would be invaluable.'

'Do not presume to think that you are the only one who valued his presence,' Solomon said acidly.

'"First for the Legion, second for the warband, third for the individual",' Halver recited. 'Those are our priorities, are they not?'

'Are you insinuating that I place my own wishes above the good of the Legion?' Solomon demanded.

'I merely find it coincidental that the risks you propose for "the good of the Legion" so rarely involve your own skin,' Halver said, his tone a study in neutrality. 'Your successes are hard to argue with, Solomon. Just remember that when those successes dry up, there are those of us who will have been counting the costs.'

He turned and walked away to where Krozier Va'kai and Tulava Dyne were already waiting. The captain of the *Whisper* greeted the Headhunter Prime with a nod; Dyne simply shifted a little farther away, and refused to look at him. Solomon remained where he was for a moment more, and softly sang a few bars of the tune that was all he had left of Kyrin Gadraen.

Qope Halver was not the only one who counted costs. Now Solomon just had to hope that after the council was concluded, the books would still be balanced in his favour.

RADICAL

Inquisitor Kayzen Hart breathed deeply, letting the blessed incense that laced the air of his respirator fill his lungs, and silently recited the twenty-fourth verse of Hauptmann's *Ode to Terra*. His mind jumped back to when he had actually seen the musical epic performed in the legendary St Lucia's Hall, on the North Jovian polar plate; two hundred and thirteen years ago, but still as clean and sharp in his memory as the combat knife sheathed at his belt. He could recall the texture of the rich but old velvet that covered the seats, the faint scent of the layers of polish applied to the wood, and above all, the crystal-clear tones of the soprano, Nulia Wehrmark. Her performance that night had truly embodied Hauptmann's work, and had reduced many audience members, including him, to tears. At times, Hart had almost felt that the Emperor was indeed speaking through her.

He killed her, thirty-seven minutes after the performance. She had been a singular talent, it was true, but she had also been an operative of one of humanity's most insidious foes. The successful culmination of that investigation, and the foiling of the so-called Undersong Massacre, was what ended his apprenticeship to Inquisitor Druman and gained him the Inquisitorial seal currently nestling in his jacket pocket. It was the ultimate authority in the galaxy, second only to that of the will of the Emperor Himself.

Now it was time to see if it would be respected.

The shuttle doors began to lower. Hart waited until they had touched the hangar deck before he descended from the transport, his left hand resting upon the carved ivory head of the sword-cane in which nestled the long, thin shape of Helorassa, his antique power sabre. It had been an heirloom handed down through the family of the governor of the Bruzas System, and presented to Hart as a gift in thanks for his leadership in the cleansing of Southstar Hive. Hart was perceptive enough to realise that the gesture had been motivated by more than just gratitude – Governor Reen had desperately wanted to prove her loyalty to the Golden Throne – but the weapon was an excellent one, and he had seen no reason to refuse.

'Inquisitor,' a deep voice boomed, at the precise moment Hart's right foot made contact with the deck of the hangar bay. 'Welcome aboard the strike cruiser *Dawnblade*.'

Six silver giants waited: Primaris Marines, Roboute Guilliman and Belisarius Cawl's new breed of transhumans, released upon the galaxy to drive back the darkness that had engulfed the Imperium in the aftermath of the Cicatrix Maledictum's opening. These were descended from the Avenging Son himself, and Hart was not entirely certain what sort of reception he was going to receive. The vox-officer to whom he had spoken had been respectful, but that was a mortal man, not one of the masters of this ship.

'I am Renus Malfax of the Silver Templars, second lieutenant of the Fifth Company,' said the Space Marine who had previously spoken. 'We are honoured to welcome another of the Emperor's servants aboard.'

Hart ducked his head in acknowledgement. It seemed that the Silver Templars were prepared to recognise his authority, at least in part. This was good: the Adeptus Astartes could be prickly, and loath to accept that anyone else spoke with the voice of the God-Emperor, from whom they claimed descent. An experienced inquisitor such as he knew that the wisest course of action was to make requests of Space Marines, not demands.

'My seneschal, Deema Varrin,' he said, gesturing to the stocky woman at his left shoulder, then turned his attention to his right. 'And Tythus Yorr of the Crimson Consuls, who does me the honour of serving as my lifeward.'

Malfax inclined his head to them both in turn, the model of a polite warrior, but his brow furrowed as he looked at Yorr. 'Your pardon, brother. My history may be in error, but I was under the impression that your Chapter had been destroyed.'

'To all intents and purposes, it was,' Yorr rasped. His voice box had been damaged when a heretic sniper's shot took out half of his neck in Southstar Hive, but he had fought on and saved Hart's life in the desperate melee that ensued when the traitors closed with them. 'The accursed Angelbane saw to that. However, I was serving with the Deathwatch, and so escaped the fate of my kin... If "escape" is the correct term.'

Malfax's expression altered slightly. Space Marines were hard to read for most mortals, but Hart had encountered several in his time, and Tythus had been with him for over a decade. If he was any judge, Renus Malfax had just been confronted for the first time with the concept of being the lone survivor of his own Chapter, and had been roundly discomforted by the notion.

'You have our greatest sympathies,' Malfax said, inclining his head somewhat more deeply to Yorr.

'Under such circumstances, I understand that a lone warrior would normally be reassigned to another Chapter – probably one with a similar ancestry and tactical outlook,' Hart said. 'But this would leave him beholden to whims of fate in terms of his future operations. He might fight on for centuries more without ever bringing to battle those who took his brothers from him. Tythus travels with me because doing so allows him the greatest chance of striking back at his enemy.'

Malfax nodded. 'The foes of humanity are many, but I have heard of the Angelbane, Quetzel Carthach. He is a warlord of the Alpha Legion – the traitors whom we put to flight on Pendata, if our guess as to their identity was correct.'

'Indeed,' Hart said. 'Hence my presence here. I have dedicated centuries of my life to opposing their schemes, and I have vital intelligence to inform your Chapter's next move.'

This was the moment. It was entirely possible that Malfax would politely refuse him, citing the greater authority of Roboute Guilliman, and the Silver Templar's planned role in the Indomitus Crusade. Hart had already prepared his soul for the taste of disappointment, and even given some considera- tion to his options should he be unsuccessful here, but none of those met his requirements so well. For some things, only Space Marines would suffice, but this was not a situation that justified the requisition of the Grey Knights.

For a slightly surreal moment, Kayzen Hart found himself wishing that his adversaries were more inclined to use daemons. At least then his way forward would be clearer.

'We will be glad to accept your counsel,' Malfax said, and some of the tension in Hart's chest began to ease. 'You have arrived at an opportune moment, as we are currently discuss- ing our next moves.'

Hart raised his eyebrows in surprise. 'I am honoured that a

lieutenant would come to greet me, if you are in the middle of a council of war.'

Malfax smiled, but Hart got the impression the expression was more for his benefit than the result of any natural response in the warrior making it. 'It seemed the right thing to do, given I extended the same courtesy to the other inquisitor.'

Hart could be just as impassive as any member of the Adeptus Astartes if he put his mind to it, but it took considerable effort not to let his shock show. 'The other inquisitor?'

'Of course,' Malfax said, and now his smile took on a slightly puzzled air. 'You were not aware of her presence?'

'I was not,' Hart replied. Malfax looked a little uncertain, the reaction of a trained warrior encountering an interpersonal issue of unknown provenance, so Hart decided to smooth things over. 'You understand that we operate independently – it is entirely plausible for another inquisitor's work to have brought them here.'

Malfax nodded, although he did not look completely convinced. It was understandable, Hart supposed: the Silver Templars had been founded for the Indomitus Crusade, and so every action of Renus Malfax's comparatively short existence as a Space Marine so far would have been in the service of a thorough, detailed plan. That was probably even more true for successors of the Ultramarines, a Chapter noted for their adherence to tactical doctrine. While the Silver Templars might prize individual skill, and seek single combat with prominent enemies, they were unlikely to ignore orders and do as they pleased as one might expect of, for example, the Space Wolves. The notion of individual thinking, of making decisions outside of a command structure, would be entirely foreign to them.

'If you will follow me, then,' Malfax said. 'We can reconvene the council and proceed.'

* * *

Hart had been aboard more ships of the Imperium than he could count. He had travelled incognito on charter vessels, hitched rides with mining crews, and been the guest of honour on the palatial cruisers of rogue traders. He had explored the forgotten corners of solar systems with junker captains, ridden to war alongside the Astra Militarum, and commanded one of the Inquisition's infamous Black Ships. He had even been granted permission to briefly travel in the Ark Mechanicus *Caestus Metalican*, although his hosts had stopped just short of stating outright that to step outside the quarters he had been assigned for the duration of his journey would be considered a betrayal of their trust that would be met with violence, and the warp take the consequences (Hart hadn't pressed the issue: the Adeptus Mechanicus, much like the Adeptus Astartes, were not worth an inquisitor aggravating over a matter of pride, or indeed anything much short of proven heresy).

However, despite his vast experience in the many different ways humanity sailed amongst the stars, Kayzen Hart still felt that there was something distinctive about Space Marine vessels. The universal scents of lubricative unguents and stale, recycled air permeated them as thoroughly as in any other ship, but the little details were different; and as an inquisitor, he instinctively focused on the details. 'Functional' was an adjective anyone might hope would apply to a starship in which they were riding, given that the alternative was 'inoperable', but Space Marine ships always felt *purely* functional. Hart had met voiders who regarded their ships as something halfway between home and lover, an integral part of themselves from which they hated to be separated for any length of time. He had seen devotional prayers etched into walls for no apparent reason other than a human deciding that the pla-steel panel needed it, aquila pendants hanging from door frames and touched for luck by anyone who passed through, and Navy ratings almost coming to blows over which unlikely hat an obli-vious servitor would be decorated with.

Space Marine vessels had none of that. They were giant machines used to travel from the last battle to the next one, and that was, so far as Hart could tell, the limit of their pur-pose in the eyes of their masters. Even such individualisation as did occur seemed, to him, to be an expression of the Chap-ter's mindset upon the setting that happened to be around them, rather than intrinsically linked to the ship itself. Space Marines would not mourn the destruction of a ship past the loss of resources, mobility, and ability to strike against their enemies that it represented; and their serfs, indoctrinated into their masters' way of thinking, were no different.

You could just about forget for a while, Hart thought, that Space Marines were no longer entirely human, and then you saw something like the inside of a strike cruiser and remem-bered how very different their viewpoint was to that of most other members of the Imperium.

So it was that when they came to the chamber that appeared to be serving as the Silver Templars' centre of operations, there was no frippery or decoration. The door through which Malfax led him held nothing more than a designative number, and the walls of the room beyond were as stark and bare as the hangar bay they had left behind, several levels below. The holo-projector and tactical displays in the centre looked nearly new: the benefits, Hart supposed, of being a newly formed and freshly equipped Chapter.

There were a dozen Silver Templars in the room, who turned towards him as he entered. He was not yet fully used to the ranks used by Primaris Marines, but there appeared to be at least two captains present, an Apothecary, three other lieutenants, and the one holding a staff was almost certainly a Librarian...

And then he laid eyes on the other baseline humans in the room.

Several were Chapter-serfs, of course: hard-eyed people in simple robes who had sworn life-oaths. Two women, however, stood out. One held an air of obvious menace that belied her slight build, drawn cheeks, and the smart lines of her jacket; had he encountered her in a dark street or a dive bar on a hive world, Kayzen would have kept one hand on his valuables and both eyes open for a knife. The other was altogether rounder and softer to the eye, with the faint wrinkles of laughter lines visible on her face, but it was she who caused his hackles to rise.

+Kayzen Hart,+ the voice of Nessa Karnis said, entering his brain unbidden while the woman who owned it regarded him from behind an expression of deceptive calm. Her mental touch gave his name the psychic stench of animal dung as she dropped the words into his mind like someone flushing waste out of an airlock. +What in the name of the Emperor are you doing here, you radical filth?+

ALLEGIANCES

'Lady Karnis,' Hart said politely, clasping both hands on the head of his swordstick and bowing his head to her in greeting. 'I trust that you are well.'

It was a statement, not a question that invited a reply; Kayzen Hart did not care one way or the other whether Nessa Karnis was well, although had he discovered that his old rival had contracted a debilitating or possibly fatal sickness then he would hardly have been upset. He did not, however, draw his weapon and attempt to end her life. Nor did she, which was an improvement on how they had last parted ways.

'You are familiar with each other?' Lieutenant Malfax enquired, looking between the two of them. Hart smiled slightly.

'We have had dealings before. After all, we hunt the same quarry.'

'Indeed,' Karnis said frostily. 'Although our methods differ.'

Malfax was still glancing from one of them to the other, clearly trying to interpret the niceties of baseline mortal communication with a brain no longer well suited to the task. It struck Hart again exactly how blunted these transhuman warriors were by the changes that made them into humanity's greatest fighting force. Or at least some of them, he corrected himself; some had either never truly forgotten what it was like to be mortal, or had taken the time to learn once more. Renus Malfax, though, was not one of those. He was almost like a giant, exceptionally deadly child wondering why his parents were arguing.

'Our methods cannot be that different, since it appears we have both approached the Adeptus Astartes for assistance,' Hart said, with a slight smile. He would gain nothing by antagonising Karnis here, and it was not as if the woman was not intelligent, simply close-minded. She was a monodominant puritan, whereas Hart was a recongregationist, and viewed as radical by those who could not see the necessity of his beliefs.

Karnis' eyes narrowed, and for a moment Hart thought she was actually going to attack him, either physically or psychically. Instead, she pursed her lips in a gesture of only mild distaste.

'I hope you have something worthwhile to contribute to our discussions, Kayzen.'

Hart smiled. Two inquisitors coming to blows in a room of Space Marines would do nothing except make it less likely that either of them would receive the assistance they desired. It seemed Karnis had come to the same conclusion he had: it was best to work together to launch the projectile of the Silver Templars at the Alpha Legion. Each of them would then undoubtedly seek to direct that projectile according to their own desires, but at least it would hit a target of some sort.

A new Space Marine stepped forward from behind his battle-brothers. This one was hooded, and armoured in black, and his breastplate was decorated with a rib-like moulding. Hart stiffened for a moment, and not just from the natural wariness any human would feel at being approached by such a giant warrior, for the iconography was not dissimilar to some of that used by worshippers of the Lord of Disease. However, this was no heretic glorifying death, he realised after a moment – it was inconceivable that such a being could be here – but an Astartes Chaplain whose stylised armour reminded his enemies of their own mortality.

'I am Lampros Hekaton,' he intoned, in a voice like a solemn bell, 'Grand Oathkeeper of the Silver Templars. I am in command here.'

'Lord,' Hart replied, with a deeper bow than the one he had offered Nessa Karnis. This was the most senior Chaplain of the Silver Templars, and already a great hero of the Chapter. His statement might have riled a less discreet inquisitor, but Hart chose to take it as relating only to the Silver Templars and their attendant fleet, rather than claiming authority over the Inquisitorial representatives as well. 'I have heard of your heroism during the Liberation of Novaris.'

'And I yours, during the cleansing of Bruzas,' Hekaton replied. 'Lady Karnis was about to address us with her learning of the Alpha Legion, as we lack such specialised knowledge. I would welcome your counsel in addition.'

'I would not like to impose,' Hart said, with a polite smile at Karnis, 'and I am sure that we can still learn things from each other, despite both having made individual study of this enemy. If Lady Karnis would like to go first, I will supplement her knowledge with my own afterwards.'

Nessa Karnis glared at him, apparently trying to find an insult in his words, but it seemed she came up short. She cleared her throat, and Hart was treated to the sight of the Space Marines in the room all turning their attention to her, like giant pupils in a scholam run by a tiny tutor.

'The Inquisition has access to many secrets, which we guard for the good of all,' Karnis began soberly, scanning the room as though she were indeed the tutor Hart had imagined her as, and was looking for any student not paying full attention. 'You may be aware of some of what I will say. There is other information I am confident you will not have heard. I will detail what I think is relevant to this discussion, so I ask your forbearance if I touch on things of which you already have knowledge.'

The assembled Space Marines nodded, or made small noises of assent. Hart had to admire the way in which Karnis handled her audience; educating Space Marines on their traitor brethren was not something to be undertaken lightly, but she had to make sure that they were informed. Or at least, as informed as it was prudent for them to be.

'The Alpha Legion were the last of the First Founding to be brought to full operational strength,' Karnis stated. 'Much information has been lost since then, of course, but the records we have suggest that even at the time of the Great Crusade it was not apparent exactly when they became active. They have always been shrouded in secrecy and mystery, and it is quite clear that this was deliberate on their part. The fact that many still choose to go by the name "Alpharius" is an indication of this, although it remains a matter for conjecture whether this is intended merely as a tribute to their damned primarch, a title that has essentially become an indication of rank, an attempt to make the Imperium believe that he is still active, or a combination thereof.'

Or because they think themselves so very clever, Hart added to himself. He did not speak out loud, in case the Silver Templars got the wrong idea about how familiar he was with these heretics. Or perhaps, he conceded to himself, the right idea.

'Their status as the newest Legion appears to have always been a sore point for the Alpha Legion and their primarch,' Karnis continued. 'Alpharius drove his warriors to prove themselves the equal of those that had come before them, by adopting ever more inventive and involved methods of waging war – indeed, Lord Guilliman apparently suggested at the time that their tactics, although ultimately effective, were inefficient and brutal.'

And how I know that rankles with you, monodominant as you are, Hart thought. *You saw the same records I did, when we studied together under old Druman. The Tesstra Compliance was everything you would want: an object lesson of how nothing outside the Imperium can be tolerated. Guilliman was still methodically working his way towards compliance in the outer system when the Alpha Legion tore the heart out of the resistance in a matter of hours.*

'That ideology appears to have persisted to this day,' Karnis declared. 'More than any other heretic faction of which we are aware, the Alpha Legion sows discord and dissent amongst Imperial citizens, and works to turn our own people, systems, and bureaucracies against us. Alpha Legionnaires taking the field in force, as you encountered on Pendata, is comparatively rare – usually only seen when the Legion is either desperate, or particularly confident.'

'So they are cowards?' Renus Malfax said, with just the hint of a question in his tone.

'Worse,' Karnis said, shaking her head. 'They are *calculating.* Unlike the other Traitor Legions, who mainly sought refuge in the Eye of Terror after the Emperor triumphed over Horus, the Alpha Legion have maintained a large presence in realspace. They have plagued us ever since, striking unseen, a constant thorn in our side.'

'I have studied some of the bodies of those heretics slain by our warriors on Pendata,' the Silver Templars Apothecary said. 'I am not familiar with this Legion's gene-seed, or its effects, but there appeared to be a cross-section of newer recruits and seasoned veterans, as one might expect in any force that had been in existence for some time. They did not appear to be either greatly aged, nor greatly malformed.'

'And from our experience fighting the Flawless Host on Novaris, I can assure you that we are familiar with the twisted bodies of those who worship Chaos,' Hekaton added. Hart nodded silently. Those traitors had once been the loyalist Shining Blades Chapter, before their pride saw them fall to Slaanesh. The Silver Templars might have little understanding of the nature of the different Ruinous Powers, but at least they were not completely unversed in the ways of the Great Enemy.

'We believe that many of the Alpha Legion are insurgents in the truest sense of the word,' Karnis said. 'They live within the Imperium, feeding off us like parasites. They use networks of spies and agents to infiltrate our societies – hypno-conditioned, coerced, or outright fanatics – and plunder us for resources, or indeed acquire those resources through their perceived authority as members of the Adeptus Astartes. I have personally investi-gated no fewer than five occurrences where tithes of weapons, ships, or personnel were handed over to what the authorities believed were Imperial Space Marines, but whom I concluded were Alpha Legionnaires who had disguised their armour and equipment. Their continued existence in realspace might mean that the legionnaires you face lack some of the horrifying muta-tions we have come to expect from those traitors who took shelter in warp anomalies, and suggests that most of those who took part in the Heresy have long since perished of old age, but it also means they are more likely to be able to pass as loyalists when it suits their purposes.'

Renus Malfax hissed through his teeth. 'They are cowards indeed!'

A Chapter of duellists, Hart thought grimly, as others muttered their agreement, *who take offence if the enemy does not meet them on their terms. If we can bring the Alpha Legion to battle then the Templars will serve us well, but they are not made for hunting a wily quarry.*

Karnis shot Hart a quick glance which made him wonder if she had been listening in on his thoughts, and gave him the idea that she was in agreement with him in any case, whether she knew it or not. 'Cowards or otherwise,' she said instead, 'they cannot be underestimated. They set schemes within schemes, and too many victories won against them have turned out to be pyrrhic in nature. There is almost always a secondary target not seen until too late. My mentor likened it to fighting smoke – you might succeed in driving it out of somewhere, but it has already flowed in somewhere else while your back is turned, and your efforts may cause you to draw it down into your own lungs.'

'He also said something else,' Hart broke in. 'Something which I find important to remember.'

The heads of the Silver Templars turned towards him, although had looks been able to kill then the one Nessa Karnis shot him would have rendered their attention redundant.

'Lord Hart?' Malfax prompted. Hart could practically hear the eagerness in the lieutenant's voice. Tactically cognisant though all Space Marines were, the Silver Templars did not want to be told that their enemy was everywhere and nowhere, impossible to predict, or to land a telling blow against. They wanted something they could find, and see, and fight.

Hart would give it to them.

'Lord Inquisitor Druman devoted his life to fighting the wiles of the Alpha Legion,' Hart said. 'He did liken them to smoke, it's true, but he also likened them to a shadow on the wall cast by a flickering flame. It moves, it shifts, and if you look hard enough then you can convince yourself that you have seen the shapes of monsters and enemies within. However, it may only bear a passing resemblance to what is actually casting that shadow, and that is what your focus should be on.

'The greatest threat to those who know of the Alpha Legion is to assume that they will always be one step ahead of you,' he continued, and he noted the subtle, but eager changes of expression on the faces of the Space Marines as they took in his words. 'Yes, they might appear to claim a victory out of a defeat, but a secondary objective is only secondary. We should not take a failure to defeat them utterly as an utter defeat for ourselves. Every blow we strike that damages them more than it damages us is a victory. We have the full might of the Imperium behind us, they only have that which they can scavenge.'

'They are still a threat, even with that,' Karnis snapped. 'Lord Hekaton, the Alpha Legion will not be caught off guard by you a second time. I am happy to offer my experience to help safeguard your arm of the Indomitus Crusade against their inevitable attempts to infiltrate it–'

'I know where they will be,' Hart interrupted.

All eyes focused on him again. Even the serfs. Even the dangerous-looking woman who had to be Nessa Karnis' apprentice, or interrogator, or whatever term she was using.

'Lord Hart, let me be clear,' Grand Oathkeeper Hekaton said slowly. 'You have information about… a base of operations? A stronghold?'

'A conclave, if you will,' Hart said, taking grim delight in the look on Karnis' face, although not letting it show on his own. 'They were not prepared for you, or your weapons, or your manner of war, or the Indomitus Crusade in general. They are shaken. The Alpha Legion are not the only ones who can use infiltration and espionage, and over the years I have managed to place my own agents within their network. I have intercepted communications calling their disparate elements together – I suspect to plan how they are going to react to this new threat. A great portion of their strength in the Ultima Segmentum will be gathered in one place, and a task force of sufficient size might be able to strike them a blow from which they will struggle to recover.'

'Foolhardy!' Karnis snapped. She was practically vibrating with fury.

'Bold!' Hart retorted.

One by one, the assembled officers of the Silver Templars turned to look at Lampros Hekaton. The huge warrior stood in silent contemplation for a moment, then nodded once.

'Please bring forth this information, Lord Hart. If it is tactically sound, this may be an opportunity that we cannot pass up.'

Now Hart allowed himself a smile, and he heard the slight exhalation from beside him as Tythus Yorr let out the breath he had been holding. Finally, the galaxy's last Crimson Consul was going to get the chance to see a military operation underway against those who had robbed him of his brothers.

Kayzen Hart stepped up to the cogitator powering one of the hololith displays, brought out the data-spool on which he was pinning his hopes, and began to prepare his mind for war.

COUNCIL OF TRUTH

'I am Raelin Amran, and I speak for the First Strike,' the warrior said, rising to his feet. Solomon assessed him with a glance, as he knew the rest of the chamber was also doing. Amran was almost slight, as Space Marines went, with cheekbones that looked nearly as sharp as the selection of blades hanging from his belt, and at first glance he seemed to be standing straight and tall and calm, like all the others who had spoken so far. However, Solomon's enhanced senses allowed him to see the faint twitches of eyes and fingers, and his knowledge provided him with an explanation. Raelin Amran had bloodlust nagging at the edge of his thoughts: a bloodlust that he was suppressing, but which was there nonetheless.

'We do not and will not shrink from combat,' Amran continued. Solomon saw his pupils dilate slightly as the words fired neurones in his brain, bringing back memories of past battles. 'We have faced the cravens of the Imperium head-on, and will do so again.'

'Is that why there are so few of you?' someone shouted. Raelin Amran whirled with his lips twisted in a snarl, and one hand reaching for his long-handled chainblade. There were still shreds of decaying flesh stuck between the chainsword's monomolecular-edged teeth, Solomon noted: the sure sign of a warrior for whom the maintenance of weapons was becoming of less importance than the usage of them.

'Peace!' Solomon shouted. 'We have all lost brothers to this new Imperial offensive, and mockery will not swell our numbers!' Amran's hand remained clamped around his weapon's grip, but he neither drew it, nor activated the motor. 'Lord Amran, please continue to speak,' Solomon urged, and the other legionnaire reluctantly subsided.

'I have little else to say,' Amran said gruffly, 'and we have little patience for the games played by the rest of you. We will bring this Indomitus Crusade to battle. If we can do so in a way that complements a wider offensive, so much the better. If not, we will fight alone.' He took his seat again, but his eyes were still searching for whoever had shouted.

'At least his is a voice calling for action,' Krozier Va'kai muttered from Solomon's left. 'There have been precious few of those.'

'Not strictly true,' Solomon replied quietly, but he knew what the captain of the *Whisper* meant. The commanders who had spoken so far might have suggested courses of action, but those actions were of subversion, infiltration, and deception. All were worthwhile parts of a whole, but no one of consequence had yet called for what surely had to be the culmination of such efforts: battle.

'Do they all wish for their lackeys to do the fighting for them?' Halver growled. 'Are they not warriors of the Legion?' He tailed off with a grunt of disgust as a group of legionnaires rose to their feet and removed their helms as one. They revealed heads that were all bald, all olive-skinned, and if not identical, then near enough that a person might lose their mind trying to map the minuscule differences of brow, of forehead, of cheek, and of chin. These were the Faceless.

'I am Alpharius,' said the foremost, and the entire chamber erupted.

'You are *not!*' bellowed Jarvul Glaine, the translucent-skinned leader of the Shrouded Hand, his voice rising above the general chorus of derision that greeted this statement.

'We are nameless!' the leader of the Faceless shouted angrily into the storm. 'We bear the sacred features of our primarchs–'

'You bear the closest likeness that can be achieved after ten millennia with no contemporary images to work from, and you bear those courtesy of my tools!' the Biologis Diabolicus shouted from his position on the sidelines. He amplified his voice to make himself heard, and his statement was greeted by laughter from several quarters, including from Qope Halver. Insults were exchanged at volume, and began to morph into threats.

Solomon sighed, and rose to his feet.

'*Brothers!*'

The Alpha Legion of the Ultima Segmentum were not yet so absorbed in their infighting that they would ignore the one who had called them all together. Voices died down while they waited to see what he would say.

'Taking the primarch's name is a tradition when the role is what is important, not the identity of the speaker,' he reminded them all. 'Our brother speaks for the Faceless in this council, his true identity need not concern us beyond that. He has every right to assume the name Alpharius, so long as he does not seek to command us with it.'

'You are more diplomatic than I,' Halver muttered, as Solomon took his seat again.

'And that is why he speaks for *us* here, and you do not,' Va'kai said quietly, without looking past Solomon at the Head-hunter Prime. Solomon schooled his face to stillness, rather than showing the amused smile that twitched at his lips. Halver grunted, but made no argument, rather than risk going against Solomon and Va'kai both.

'I am Alpharius,' the leader of the Faceless restated, and this time was met with a few grumbles and sighs, but no outright hostility. 'We have suffered from this Indomitus Crusade, as have you all. If our enemy is truly Guilliman reborn, then he has succeeded in mobilising the Imperium to an extent not seen in centuries, if not thousands of years. The Despoiler may have torn the galaxy apart, but he has only awoken a more dangerous foe. We now face a new breed of Space Marine who outmatch us physically, and whose weaponry is unfamiliar to us. We must return to the central principles of our Legion.'

'Oh, this should be good,' Va'kai murmured. 'What are our central principles according to him, I wonder?'

'If the enemy seeks to bring you to battle, you should refuse him,' the pseudo-Alpharius declared. 'The Legion must disappear. The galaxy is wide and cold and empty, and the Imperium has many enemies eager to throw themselves onto these new guns of theirs. Let Guilliman think he has broken our spirit and scattered us – even a primarch cannot pay great mind to a single threat, now absent, when so many more are crowing for his attention. Whatever changes he has made to the bureaucracy that governs his empire, he cannot remove or reshape that monolith completely, and the Faceless are the experts of the long game. We have already begun the work of reseeding our own operatives within the Administratum, and expanding on the influence we had already gained. Wheels are turning, my brothers–'

'Turning to what end?' demanded Raelin Amran of the First Strike, from across the chamber. 'Is there a purpose? Or do you just amuse yourself with endless games, congratulating yourselves on your cleverness at escaping detection, while ignoring the fact that your schemes are beneath the notice of anyone who matters?'

'He's got a point,' Tulava observed, to no one in particular.

'And this is why we made sure they were not seated next to each other,' Solomon said with a sigh, as voices rose around them again. He glanced at Krozier Va'kai. 'There is no unity of purpose here, and no one who appears willing to take responsibility. Too many wish to crawl away and hide instead of fighting. Another confrontation with the Indomitus Crusade will see them scatter. It is down to us to convince them.'

Va'kai's eyes were hard. 'You understand what you are asking of me? The *Whisper* was my ship before I ever joined the Teeth. It will not carry the day alone, and will likely be lost.'

'I understand,' Solomon said soberly. He could read the intent behind Va'kai's words as clearly as if the veteran captain had spelled them out: if he went through with this gamble and it did not pan out, he would lose Krozier Va'kai's support. In fact, he would be lucky if Va'kai did not attempt to kill him. The way of the Alpha Legion – or at least, the way into which Solomon Akurra had been inducted – was to seize the advantages of any situation, even if that ran contrary to the initial intent. However, sometimes that involved taking risks.

The Legion was indecisive and rudderless. Solomon would not have chosen to step up now, not while his authority within his own warband was so uncertain, but the greater cause could not wait for him to gain security. A crisis must be forced, and decisions made, and if no one else would be the catalyst, then he would. If he was the commander who gained in the long run, so much the better. If he was not, then the Legion would still surely be stronger, more unified, than it was now.

'Do it,' he told Va'kai quietly. 'I will take the consequences.'

'You will,' the captain replied grimly, but he pressed a stud on his gauntlet that would send a tightbeam signal to the *Whisper*. The signal was encrypted but also, on this occasion, meaningless; merely a jumble of code, which would yield nothing to even the most fervent listener who somehow managed to intercept it. It was not the content of the signal, but the presence of the signal itself, which carried the meaning today.

Beyond the collective hull of the *Unseen*, out where the ships of the Alpha Legion lurked and formed a massive flower of mismatched metal, the splinter that was the *Whisper*, along with the *Sinister* and the *Dextral*, began to subtly shift position.

Other ships would notice. The various warbands were too watchful of each other – too paranoid, was another interpretation – to assume that a ship which began to manoeuvre had no hostile intent. However, that same distrust meant it was unlikely that any of the *Whisper*'s neighbours would jump too quickly into opening fire when surrounded by strangers, lest they unintentionally insert themselves into a trap never intended for them. Transmissions would be sent back through the void, converging on the commanders present on the *Unseen*, updating them and asking for guidance. Solomon just had to hold everyone's attention for a while, so they were focused on him rather than on the blinking vox-rune on their helmet's display, or the chiming in their comm-bead.

He got to his feet once more, and spread his arms.

'Brothers!'

He did not wait to see if they decided to listen to him this time; there was a momentary dip in noise, and he leaped into it.

'I have heard the statements from those who have chosen to speak, and I have noted those who remained silent,' he began. 'What I have not heard, from any corner of this chamber, is leadership.'

That was less well received than his previous words. The Alpha Legion of the Ultima Segmentum turned towards him, like a multi-headed predator newly aware of an intruder in its lair.

'I have heard declarations of intent to wage war on the Indomitus Crusade, but with no proposals for how they can be part of a greater whole,' Solomon said. 'More commonly, I have heard the same old narrative – that we hide, manipulate, bide our time and wait, and I would ask everyone here' – he swept the chamber with his eyes, careful not to let his glance come to rest on any individual for more than a moment, lest they decide he was singling them out – 'is ten thousand years of waiting not sufficient for you?'

That stung. Solomon felt its sting himself, and he had delivered the words. The Alpha Legion might scoff at the other so-called Traitor Legions, who hid in warp anomalies and for whom time passed differently; they might laugh about how those warriors might be ten thousand years old by the reckoning of the galaxy outside, but had spent only a fraction of the time the Alpha Legion had fighting against the Imperium. However, with that came a harder, sharper fact that was more painful to grasp.

They had spent all this time fighting, but they had not won.

'What would you have us do, then?' called out Vyrun Evale, of the Penitent Sons. 'Face the full might of the Indomitus Crusade in open battle?'

Solomon smiled and shook his head. 'Brothers, why is your insistence on either throwing ourselves onto our enemies' guns, as the Faceless put it, or meddling with records behind the scenes and tricking baseline humans into rising up against their masters? We should be using all the tools at our disposal. What is the Legion's greatest weapon?'

The other commanders knew a rhetorical question when they heard one, or at the very least had no wish to be an example of the ancient adage that it was better to keep quiet and be thought a fool than to speak out and remove all doubt. They waited, perhaps to see whether Solomon was about to reveal himself as a fool, at which point they could safely ignore him.

Solomon took a deep breath.

'Our greatest weapon is the truth.'

He was not shouted down, although neither did voices clamour in agreement. He had their attention, though, which was his main purpose at this point.

'I am two hundred and forty-two years old,' Solomon said. 'My people thought I had been selected to be one of the Emperor's Space Marines. At first, so did I. The lineage of the Serpent's Teeth does not run through a warp storm. None of my warband were, or claim to have been, alive at the time of the Great Crusade, or the Heresy. Our records of that time are fragmented, but there is one thing that we hold to.

'The Alpha Legion knew the truth. We knew all the truths – the dirty, twisted, uncomfortable truths that others refused to recognise. We saw the need for subterfuge, for sabotage, for assassination, for insurgency and counter-insurgency. We could redden our hands on the field of war, no matter how we seem to have forgotten that in the years since, but we were subtler, too, and our methods ran deeper. Other Legions could ensure that an enemy lost a war before it had begun – we eliminated the enemy before they even knew they *were* an enemy!'

Heads nodded. The paths of the Legion might have splintered and separated, to turn it into the myriad shapes and ideologies Solomon saw in front of him, but each one of them still felt connected to that past; they took pride in it.

It was time to jerk them out of that pride.

'But now?' he continued. 'We have become lost in lies. We have become so enamoured by lies that we can no longer see the truth, and when you cannot see the truth then how can you lie with any effect? We have fought the Imperium with shadows and deceit for ten thousand years, and to what end? Nothing. It is still there, still clinging on in defiance of time, and attrition, and entropy, and even common sense. When we lose – and how we have lost, over the years – we smile and tell each other that this is fine, that we are playing the long game, that all of this is part of the Legion's plan. A plan that no one now remembers. A plan which, if it even once existed, is now ten thousand years out of date. We pride ourselves on flexibility, but our vision has become so narrowed that we are trapped by our own ego and self-image.

'We cannot defeat the Imperium with lies, *because they can lie better than we can.*'

That sparked outrage. Solomon might have laughed, had he not been concerned about keeping the attention that he had so carefully captured, but there was something grimly amusing about seeing transhuman warriors who could slay a score of mortals within the space of a couple of breaths angry at having their capacity for untruths maligned. It was a symptom of the greater problem.

'The Imperium is built on lies!' he told them. 'It breathes lies every day! To fight the Imperium with lies is like trying to drown a flood. They abhor change, but now they bring forth new warriors in new armour, and bearing new weapons. They rip up their own laws on how Chapters should be structured. Roboute Guilliman, the son of the Emperor and the brother of our primarchs, accepts the worship of those who think his father is a god. The very identity of the Imperium, for one hundred centuries, has been built on a dichotomy – that its enemies are weak and worthless, and so its primacy through strength is righteous, but that its enemies are also powerful, and subversive, and could bring ruin upon them at any moment, and so anything less than complete obedience is punishable by death for the good of all. How can our lies touch such utter hypocrisy, when our enemies are steeped in it from birth?

'I am *not* Alpharius.' He stared around the chamber, letting them hear the words, and understand the weight of them. 'We, of all the Legions, should be able to reach beyond our progenitor. Whatever plan the primarchs had for us, if ever they did, must be adapted for this new era. It is time for us to forge our own destiny, and become a Legion again in more than just name.'

'And how do you propose we do that?' demanded the warrior of the Faceless who had called himself Alpharius; or perhaps it was a different one, Solomon was not quite certain. 'Would you set yourself up as our Harrowmaster, commander of us all?'

'Would you have me?' Solomon countered. 'We have always assigned ranks and responsibilities based on suitability for the task at hand. I have, on occasion, pulled out a warrior's heart and shown it to them, still beating, as they died. I intend to do the same to the Imperium. I wish to reach into its chest, rip out its rotten core, and watch its systems go into failure from the shock. Perhaps, when everything is done, there may be something worth saving. There might still be some future for humanity, the race that originally birthed us all, but the Imperium, that foetid carcass that spreads its entrails across the stars and bleats glory to its own name, will be *dead*.

'And if humanity cannot survive without the Imperium,' he said, 'then it does not deserve to survive at all.'

There was silence for a moment. The giant, Roek Ghulclaw, rose to his feet.

'That was a good speech, Lord Akurra. But I would hear more

specifics of your plan before I commit the Guns of Freedom to your cause. What are your planned targets? What are your intended methodologies of war?'

Solomon allowed himself a small smile. Being asked to prove himself was a big step up from being ignored.

'I envisage a combined arms approach,' he began, addressing Ghulclaw directly. 'The Legion's tactics of destabilisation and infiltration can be key, but they must work to a goal. If our warbands work together and pool our resources, we can form a fighting force to equal–'

He was interrupted by the *Unseen*'s alarms sounding, echoed by dozens of individual alerts over vox-channels. This was not crews surreptitiously informing their commanders of a ship moving suspiciously: this was something altogether more serious.

'Warp wake!' someone shouted.

'Ships translating!' reported someone else.

Krozier Va'kai looked up at Solomon with eyes as hard and as flat as hull metal as he received his own transmission. 'It is the Silver Templars – fleet-strength, at least.

'And the *Whisper* is right in their path.'

THE HYDRA AT BAY

Inquisitor Kayzen Hart was not a military man. He knew just enough about battles and strategy to know that he was no expert, and that these were things that should most definitely be left to experts. His talents lay in unravelling threads, piecing together loosely related facts into something approaching a cohesive whole, and making connections that others missed. He had spent literal centuries studying intensely and travelling widely, learning more about and combatting the schemes of the Alpha Legion, who were themselves just one of humanity's countless enemies. For Hart to assume that the intellect which had allowed him a degree of success in his field meant he would also be able to easily understand the logistics of battle, and the ebb and flow of combat, was laughable – as laughable as the notion of a Space Marine thinking he could uncover a cell of heretics in a city the size of a continent. That was why the Emperor had inquisitors, and why He had Space Marines: to perform their different roles in His service.

All the same, when the Silver Templars task force translated from the warp back into realspace, and the protective shutters lifted from the viewports of the bridge of the *Purity's Edge*, Kayzen Hart's spirits soared for two reasons. Firstly, the Alpha Legion were where his intelligence had said they would be, and the Silver Templars' Navigators had succeeded in bringing the fleet out of the warp at exactly the right point. And secondly, he could tell that the traitors were both outnumbered and outgunned.

Grand Oathkeeper Hekaton had commandeered a sizeable force, albeit a minute speck when set against the leviathan that was the Indomitus Crusade as a whole. Still, a force comprising one Space Marine battle-barge, Hekaton's flagship the *Purity's Edge*; three strike cruisers, the *Dawnblade*, the *Riposte*, and the *Silver Fury*; and eight Gladius-class frigates would be a potent threat to any enemy. When the Imperial Navy element was added to that – two Armageddon-class battle cruisers, the *Hammer of Glory* and the *Thunder of Fury*; a total of sixteen light cruisers, made up of nine Endeavour-class, five Endurance-class, and two Defiant-class vessels; and over two dozen escort ships in the form of various frigates and destroyers – it became a task force that few foes short of a tyranid hive fleet or a full-scale ork Waaagh! would have much hope of matching in void combat.

'What are we facing?' Hekaton demanded. Sensor read-outs began to flash up, and Hart did his best to interpret them, but this was not his area of expertise.

'Six capital ships, twice that many light cruisers, and various support craft and escorts,' the Grand Oathkeeper announced a moment later, as though talking to himself, 'clustered around what appears to be a small space hulk.' Hart had a fair idea that Hekaton was actually verbalising what he was seeing for the benefit of the inquisitors present, just in a manner that was not obviously condescending, and suppressed a smile. Who said that Space Marines were entirely without interpersonal skills?

'That is not a standard defensive formation,' observed Captain Palamas, commander of the Fifth Company.

'Indeed,' Hekaton agreed. 'Their ships appear to be guarding against each other as much as they do any potential threats from without. It is as you said, inquisitor,' he continued, inclining his helm towards Hart. 'The traitors are so deceitful that they cannot even trust themselves. This plays to our advantage.'

'A word of caution, Grand Oathkeeper,' Hart said politely. 'I would never counsel you not to press an advantage in battle, but appearances can always be deceiving with the Alpha Legion.'

'We can only defeat what the enemy puts in front of us,' Hekaton said, which was not precisely what Hart might have hoped to hear, but he nodded as though he were in full agreement. The Silver Templars were the experts here, after all.

'It appears that your information was accurate,' Inquisitor Karnis said from beside him. Hart turned, and noted the twist to her mouth, as if the words themselves were bitter on her tongue.

'If you set fire to every bridge you encounter which is flawed, you are soon left with no ways across the river,' he said, trying not to sound too smug. 'I do not doubt that your methods have reduced the number of heretics the Imperium is faced with, Nessa, but the big fish will always be out of your reach if you leave no one to lead you to them.'

'Your attempts at mixing metaphors are as unwise as your radical leanings,' Karnis said crisply. 'I am yet to be convinced that *we* are not the ones taking the bait in this scenario. However, since we are here, I will assist where I may. Evelyn, my data-slate.'

The hollow-cheeked woman who shadowed her produced the requested device, and Karnis called up a document which appeared to be half list and half diagram, with various names and phrases circled and connected by lines. Hart glanced at it, and saw several words he recognised.

'You have a list of vessels connected to the Alpha Legion?'

'Of course,' Karnis said absent-mindedly, glancing between her data-slate and the tactical display, which was now starting to flash up ship identifiers. 'It is hard to know where truth ends and deception starts with this filth, but still–'

'The *Whisper*,' Hart broke in, pointing at the icon that represented the vessel closest to them. 'Connected to the warband known as the Serpent's Teeth.'

'A vessel we fought over Pendata,' Hekaton confirmed, his voice grim. 'It claimed the *Heartblade*, twin ship of the *Dawnblade*, before the traitors withdrew. However, it appears that revenge is ours today. Open fire!'

Even Hart could see that the *Whisper* was vulnerable. It was a captured Lunar-class cruiser, and as with all ships constructed by the Imperium, its strongest armour was at the front. They had come across it with its back turned, so to speak: the *Purity's Edge* was at the spearhead, flanked by the *Hammer of Glory* and the *Thunder of Fury*, bearing down on the exposed engines at the rear, out of the traitors' fire arcs. The faster escorts ranged ahead on the flanks, above, and below, looking to confuse and damage enemy ships before the cruisers closed into weapons range. The *Whisper*, on the other hand, was left unmolested, for reasons that soon became obvious.

Hart thought he felt a slight shudder in the *Purity's Edge* as the dorsal bombardment cannon loaded a magma bomb into its monstrous firing chamber. He certainly did not imagine the vibration through the deck as it fired on the hapless Lunar-class, which was still attempting to come around and bring its broadsides to bear, so it could at least spit its defiance into the face of death.

The bombardment cannon of a Space Marine battle-barge was a weapon primarily used for delivering punishing barrages from orbit. It would destroy ground defences and break open fortification lines ready for the insertion of warriors of the Adeptus Astartes, arriving via drop pod or gunship, who would sweep away any opposition whose will had not already been shattered.

Of course, a munition that could break open the most stoutly built land-bound fortifications from fifty miles above could also wreak havoc on a capital ship a third of that distance away.

Hart watched the white glow of the magma bomb's tail as it screamed silently through the void towards the *Whisper*. He imagined the desperate shouts and cries aboard it as it strove fruitlessly to evade, and hoped fiercely that the crew were not so far gone down the dark paths of heresy that they no longer had any fear of death. He wanted their final moments to be filled with fear and misery, and the bone-deep knowledge that their end had been brought about by servants of the Emperor's light.

It took perhaps half a minute for the magma bomb to reach its target: still not long enough for a ship the size of a Lunar-class cruiser to do anything other than twist a little on its axis, caught from a standing start as it was. The futile flare of manoeuvring thrusters lit up for a few seconds, and then the mighty munition struck home.

The flash of light was blinding, as destructive energy of cataclysmic proportions was released. The *Whisper* had been struck amidships, and it came apart as though a giant had seized it and broken it in two with her hands. The fore and aft segments, now twisted and broken, were thrown apart by the force of the explosion, and what had been the *Whisper*'s prow struck one of its two escort ships, dooming that as well. Innumerable shards of metal, which were themselves the size of Titans but looked little larger than dust, began to spread outwards in a bloom of death, opening against the fixed points of light that were the stars beyond it.

Beside Kayzen Hart, Tythus Yorr exhaled, a deep breath which sounded almost sensual in terms of the amount of raw emotion laced within it.

'The first blow lands,' Hekaton said, and the slight mechanical twinge lent to his voice by his helmet did nothing to disguise the pleasure in it. He activated the vox with an armoured finger. 'All ships, pick your targets and engage. If any enemy tries to break from the pack, pick them out. If they cluster together, use overlapping fire lanes. You have permission to board,' he added, not without a certain amount of relish.

Hart looked at Karnis, and found her looking back at him. They held each other's gaze for a moment, and Hart had a sudden memory from nearly three hundred years before, when they had both realised that old Lord Druman was on the verge of making a very rare mistake.

'Are you seeking to recapture traitor ships, Lord Hekaton?' Karnis asked carefully.

'We are seeking to eradicate this filth, Lady Karnis,' Lampros Hekaton replied. 'There is no surer kill than the one made face to face, especially against foes as deceptive as these. If we board ships and find traitor legionnaires awaiting us, we may conclude that the other ships are similarly crewed. If we do not, we must consider that the ships are decoys, and the traitors are sacrificing some void capability to convince us that we have killed a large portion of their fighting strength.'

Hart grimaced. There was a certain logic to what the Grand Oathkeeper said, although to his mind it smacked of justification for what the Silver Templars longed to do in any case: find their enemies, and fight them one on one. He had hoped that simple ship-to-ship combat would slake that urge, but it appeared that these particular sons of Guilliman would not be satisfied unless they proved their physical superiority.

'I see,' Karnis said, nodding. 'In that case, may I advise that this cruiser' – she highlighted one on the tactical hololith, below the *Purity's Edge* and some way to port – 'is not boarded? It is registering as the *Blind Agony*, which my records suggest is associated with the warband known as the Sons of Venom. They specialise in biowarfare, and may have weapons and traps that would trouble even Primaris Marines when deployed at close quarters.'

Hekaton grunted an assent. 'Your counsel is well taken, Lady Karnis. That vessel will be marked for destruction by different means.' He began issuing orders, and Hart saw the *Riposte* and a trio of frigates peeling off towards the ship Karnis had identified, which looked like a Murder-class cruiser. From Hart's limited knowledge of voidcraft, that would be a vicious and close-matched fight, but Hekaton clearly had confidence in his captains.

'And now,' Captain Palamas said, with unmistakeable eagerness, 'we see what our enemies can truly do.'

Hart watched the icons on the hololith as they shifted position. The Alpha Legion had been caught unawares, that much was true, but now they were starting to re-form. The ships closest to the Imperial fleet were dropping back, while those behind were pushing up to support them. Hart saw new icons appear, blinking as they streaked forward: torpedoes, launched by the traitors in an attempt to disrupt the attackers' formation. Turrets sparked into life in response as soon as the projectiles came into range, blazing thousands of cannon rounds and turbo-las charges into space, seeking to blow the building-sized projectiles apart before they struck and detonated.

'A desultory offering,' Palamas said, as icon after icon winked out.

'One which was never intended to succeed,' Tythus Yorr rasped. He pointed at the blue light indicating the *Thunder of Fury*. 'That ship is at the centre of a weak spot in turret fire arcs, and the traitors will have noticed it.'

Grand Oathkeeper Hekaton leaned forward slightly, and if his helmet lenses could have narrowed then Hart was sure they would have. 'Hmm. You might be–'

A new flurry of blinking torpedo icons appeared, in far greater numbers than before. What had looked to be a mess of enemy ships, all jockeying for position and getting in each other's way, were aligned for a few moments; and in those moments each one spat a full volley of torpedoes, from multiple directions, but all aimed at the same place.

This was not a general disruption pattern, seeking to inconvenience the attackers and buy time. This was an execution.

The *Thunder of Fury* noticed that death was coming for it, of course, but it was as helpless as the *Whisper* had been in the face of the *Purity's Edge*'s bombardment cannon. The Alpha Legion had conceded ground, allowing other ships to further close with them unmolested, in order to punch a gaping hole in the attackers' line. Orders and calls for aid leapt back and forth across the vox, to no avail: escorts and light cruisers could not get into position fast enough to lend sufficient defensive firepower. The *Thunder of Fury* tried to go head-on, to present the smallest possible target profile and its strongest armour to the incoming attack, but the Alpha Legion never committed everything to one strike location. The *Thunder*'s turrets blazed, but fully half of the torpedoes struck home, all along the ship's superstructure.

Hart tasted bile in his mouth as explosions lit up the starboard viewports. An Armageddon-class battle cruiser was a beast of a ship, and a stalwart of the Imperial battle line. The *Thunder of*

Fury might not be completely destroyed, but it was not going to be able to take further part in the battle, and would have to be given a wide berth even by its own allies, lest it explode and take some of them with it. Its loss was a blow to the Imperium, and a significant blow to this task force, which now found itself with only two-thirds of the centralised firepower with which it had entered the engagement.

'The hydra has teeth,' Hekaton said grimly. 'But they made the mistake of allowing us to reach into their throats!'

The faster escort ships began to fire, as the range became close enough for their lances and weapons batteries to target the traitors. The Alpha Legion's gambit had slain a monster, but now they found themselves harried by multiple smaller antagonists, as frigates and light cruisers set about them. Hart bit his lip as contacts began to flare and die, on both sides. The Alpha Legion had worked in harmony to kill the *Thunder*, but they were not a unified fleet. Did this sort of individual combat play to their strengths, or at least eliminate some of their more obvious weaknesses?

The bombardment cannon of the *Purity's Edge* spoke again, and in its wake Hart saw the drive trails of multiple wings of Thunderhawks and boarding torpedoes leaving the battle-barge, and heading towards a light cruiser of a design so archaic he couldn't place it. The Silver Templars were out for blood.

Only time would tell how much of it would prove to be their own.

TRAPS WITHIN TRAPS

Space Marines did not panic. Panic came from fear, and fear was something that warriors of the Astartes had only a theoretical understanding of. Imperial or renegade, loyalist or traitor, it barely mattered; fear was something to be inflicted upon others, with varying levels of enjoyment. It was not an emotion that clouded the minds of Space Marines, except to provide an extra edge to self-preservation when there was no greater cause that required a warrior's sacrifice. All of which explained why there was no panic aboard the *Unseen* when the Silver Templars translated from the warp and began to hammer the assembled ships of the Alpha Legion.

Although, Solomon conceded to himself as voices rose and orders flew hither and thither with increasing urgency, if you didn't *know* that...

'The *Whisper* is destroyed,' Krozier Va'kai reported, in a voice like an adamantium-jawed trap. 'The very first shot those bastards fired. We only have the *Sinistral* left.'

Solomon felt a hollow ache in his gut, and not just from the tactical impact on the Serpent's Teeth, now reduced to one escort frigate which would surely struggle to survive the forthcoming combat. The *Whisper* had been the closest thing he'd had to a home for over two hundred years. Space Marine though he might be, renegade though he might be, he was not completely inured to a sense of loss.

Adaptability. That was the key. The ability to take a setback and turn it into an advantage was what had always marked the Alpha Legion out from their so-called peers, and they would do the same today.

He nodded. 'Then our feasible options are greatly reduced. We have only one course of action reasonably left open to us, especially if we wish to maintain authority here.'

'If *we* wish to maintain authority?' Qope Halver repeated. 'You are the one setting yourself up as Harrowmaster.'

'And that authority, should I achieve and maintain it, would extend to my fellow commanders,' Solomon assured him. He looked at Va'kai. 'Are you ready?'

'If this fails then we are all going to look like fools,' Va'kai growled. 'Probably dead fools, at that.' He shook his head. 'But there is no point wishing for more time – this will have to be the test. Very well, Solomon.'

Solomon turned to Tulava. 'Sorceress, if you would?'

Va'kai set his jaw as Tulava's eyes rolled back in her head. Purple-edged darkness rose up from her feet to engulf them both, and they disappeared a moment later.

'I do not understand how you can put up with that,' Halver said, with distaste.

'It works,' Solomon said simply. 'We must make use of all the tools at our disposal, provided we can control them adequately, and I trust Tulava.'

'I do not doubt the witch's commitment to you,' Halver said. 'I have less faith in her ability to rein her powers in. You were not on Vannamir IV. I've seen what can happen when a mortal loses control.'

'She is stronger than you give her credit for,' Solomon told him. 'Don't forget that she was an Imperial first. The Imperium might be fools, but when it comes to their psykers, only the most resilient minds make it to the battlefield.'

'I have not forgotten that she was Imperial,' Halver said. 'It fills me with less confidence than it does you.' He jerked his head at the rest of the room. 'Should you not be doing something about *that?*'

Solomon looked around. The commanders of the various warbands were engaged in furious conversation with their respective vessels, but Solomon was pleased to see that none of them had yet made a run for the hangars. Quite apart from the time it would take to get there, braving the void in a Thunderhawk or a looted shuttle while a battle raged would be reckless; and if the council so far had shown one thing, it was that few of Solomon's counterparts from the other warbands were reckless. Even Raelin Amran of the First Strike was still present, although Solomon could see the micro-signals on his face that indicated how frustrated he was at not being engaged in the combat himself, or even able to see it. It would not be long before he could stand it no longer, and left to seek out his ship. Once that happened, the others would start to waver: was it best to sit tight on the *Unseen*, which would give protection from the guns of the Imperial fleet by dint of its sheer size, or follow Amran's example, and possibly even use the distraction of his inevitable frontal assault to try to cut and run?

Solomon had to give them something to focus on.

'Brothers!' he bellowed, above the noise. 'Follow me to the bridge! We must coordinate our defence!'

Heads snapped up and around as he strode towards a hatchway. One of the Faceless stepped forward, as though to block his path.

'What foolishness is this?' the Faceless demanded. 'The *Unseen* is a hulk, it has no single bridge!'

'The Serpent's Teeth have not been idle,' Solomon told him, and brushed past the Faceless without slowing, with Halver on his heels. The effect on the rest of the chamber was immediate, and predictable. Wary of each other though all the warbands might be, no one wished to let a potential tactical advantage pass them by, and the assembled warriors of the Alpha Legion fell in behind Solomon out of necessity. Which was of course the plan: get them used to following now, and it would be easier in the future.

Assuming they had a future left after this battle.

They were in the central part of the *Unseen*: the former Universe-class mass conveyor, one of the largest ship classes the Imperium had ever created. Such a beast of a craft had the internal infrastructure to move large quantities of either goods or personnel around quickly, and the massive turbolift Solomon led them to could have accommodated an entire Astra Militarum company. It certainly had space for the various command groups of the different Alpha Legion warbands, despite them being far bulkier than mortal warriors. Solomon did not vox Va'kai to see whether things were going according to plan: they either were, or they were not, and there was nothing he could do about it either way yet.

When the huge, curved door of the turbolift rolled back, Solomon led them the short distance to the bridge. The craft's original designation had long since been lost, so now it was simply the nerve centre of the hulk, and fairly close to being the physical centre as well, despite its asymmetric form. It had once been a dead room, nothing more than a collection of old consoles and equipment that had stared out onto the star-speckled void for millennia. The Serpent's Teeth had been making changes, however.

Now, ancient lumens glowed once again. The faint tang of ozone and burned dust in the air marked the life throes of machinery coaxed back into operating order, but this was no mere resurrection of the ancient past. New power couplings had been fitted, new cables run across floors and into walls, and fresh servitors sat at the control stations. Tactical hololiths were blinking into existence, giving a three-dimensional picture of the battle raging outside.

'The sensor arrays still work?' Vyrun Evale asked in surprise. 'We were not aware of this.'

'We have amalgamated the systems from across the entire structure, so far as we have been able.'

The Alpha Legion turned, and Solomon turned with them. He knew what he was going to see, but even so, he had to admit that it was an impressive sight.

Krozier Va'kai sat on the captain's command throne: a monstrous hunk of metal, festooned with gadgets and devices, with Tulava Dyne unobtrusively positioned behind him, and to one side. From there, he could call up and study any number of read-outs, from the mundane to the critical. It was a picture only spoiled for Solomon by the knowledge that they had no real idea if it worked.

'What have the Serpent's Teeth done to the *Unseen*?' demanded Jarvul Glaine of the Shrouded Hand, his tone laced with suspicion.

'We have adapted it to better fit the needs of the Legion,'

Solomon said. He gestured at the hololiths. 'For which we might all be thankful.'

'The *Unseen* is neutral ground!' one of the Faceless spat.

'Of course it is!' Solomon retorted. 'The Serpent's Teeth make no claim to it, other than that brought on by necessity! We are under attack, brothers! Do you wish to apprise yourselves of the situation, or not?' He turned his own attention to the tactical hololiths, since he had little enough idea himself of how the battle progressed.

It turned out that the answer was 'badly'.

It was hardly surprising. The Silver Templars might be reckless and headstrong, but they had arrived in the sort of force that allowed them to indulge their impulses. With the Imperial fleet elements in support, they combined powerful short-ranged weaponry and boarding capability with the cover of massed long-range firepower.

'We are trapped here,' said a voice beside him, and Solomon breathed in the sour stink of Keros Asid, lord of the Sons of Venom. Asid was a mighty-looking warrior, tall and broad, but his skin was nearly grey, and bore an unhealthy, waxy shine. 'Had they come upon us as a fleet, we could have scattered and lost them, or drawn the faster ships away to isolate them,' Asid continued. 'As it is, our ships face the choice of being pinned in place and destroyed or boarded, or leaving all of their commanders to their doom. If our vessels were to escape, even the *Unseen* would not be sanctuary from the Templars' wrath.'

'One way or another, we will die here,' Vyrun Evale said. 'We should send word to our ships to save themselves – they must escape, and continue the fight without us.'

'Is this how the Alpha Legion operates in the Ultima Segmentum?' demanded the sepulchral tones of Roek Ghulclaw. The giant Space Marine stepped up behind Evale, towering over him by a head. 'It gets trapped and executed?'

Another light winked out on the hololith. Unless Solomon missed his guess, the *Blind Agony* had just been destroyed by three Imperial ships working together, although the impassive expression of Keros Asid might as well have been watching three ants kill another from a rival colony.

'No,' he said, in answer to Ghulclaw. 'It is not. At least, not if I can help it.' He turned and pushed his way through the other commanders, who were clustering around the hololiths and using them to coordinate their ships' effort. 'Captain! Are we ready?'

'As ready as we will ever be, Harrowmaster,' Krozier Va'kai replied. Solomon's gut tightened as the veteran fixed him with a steady glare. Va'kai had lost the *Whisper*, and if this did not work, then Solomon would lose much more. That was the way of the galaxy, however: you rarely had time to make sure that everything was exactly as you would like it before you had to rely on it. Solomon had decided to roll the dice, and it was time to see how they would land.

Va'kai flicked a switch. 'Engines: activate.'

For a long moment, nothing happened. Then a shudder ran through the deck.

It was barely perceptible. Mortals would not have noticed it, unless they were hard-connected to the ship's systems. Space Marines, on the other hand, had senses more acutely tuned to minute alterations in their surroundings, lest they miss the first signs of an attack. Voices stopped in mid-sentence as the assembled Alpha Legion commanders realised that something had changed.

'What's happening?' Raelin Amran shouted, rounding on Solomon. 'How is this possible?'

'Diligent work for two decades,' Solomon answered him, lifting his chin. 'You all saw a hulk, nothing more than a base of operations or a hideout – somewhere to lick your wounds and replenish your ranks. The Serpent's Teeth saw an opportunity.'

It had taken much more than that, of course. Adepts of the New Mechanicum had been given the pick of the warband's loot for five whole years, including a Goliath-class forge tender that Solomon had led a raid specifically to capture, in exchange for their assistance. Reactors had been salvaged and repurposed, power grids forced into some form of unity through means that were as sorcerous to Solomon as anything Tulava did, and drives refitted and repositioned under the guidance of the Diabolicus Secundus. The fresh servitors were not just for show: each one was plugged into a chimeric mess of mainframes and controls.

The *Unseen* was not a Gloriana-class battleship; was not one of the beautiful vessels of ancient times that slid between the stars like a mega-predator through the ocean depths. It was far bigger, and far cruder, and far, far uglier.

But, Solomon realised with a fierce excitement, it was working.

There had been no opportunity to test it. He might say that the Serpent's Teeth made no claim to the *Unseen*, but that was a lie. Drazus Jate had ordered the hulk refitted in secret for a reason, lest another commander tried to benefit from the fruits of their labours. Testing it now, in front of everyone, was a great risk – not only because it might fail, but because all the most ambitious members of the segmentum's Alpha Legion were aboard.

'Is it armed?' Raelin Amran asked, his expression lighting up as the possibilities for destruction occurred to him.

'It is,' Krozier Va'kai declared. 'A somewhat eclectic mix, but we are making do with what we have available.' His fingers skated over the control pads around him. Solomon had visions of the techno-sorcery of the Mechanicum sleeting the instructions out through the *Unseen*'s bulk, interacting with a score of different power grids and receiving feedback in a dozen versions of machine code. Thrusters fired, and the *Unseen* began to tilt as it shifted ponderously towards a new heading.

'It appears we have been noticed,' Roek Ghulclaw observed. The hololith icons indicating the closest Imperial ships were falling back, rather than pressing their advantage against their beleaguered Alpha Legion counterparts.

'Then let us make sure we have their full attention,' Va'kai said. He glanced at his read-outs and grimaced for a moment, then snorted humourlessly. 'Well, we may as well find out if this works. Starboard Battery One, target and fire.'

An icon became ringed in red, as the *Unseen*'s weapons locked on. Solomon edged towards the bridge's viewport and looked out. He found himself wanting to see the results with his own eyes, rather than through the impersonal hololith displays.

There was no shudder, no matter how faint: the recoil of the weapon was insufficient to make the smallest vibration in a vessel the size of the *Unseen*. However, a projectile streaked away, and a few seconds later a tiny speck in the distance erupted into flame as its oxygen-laced atmosphere gave life to the explosions that ripped it apart.

'What was that?' Jarvul Glaine asked.

'T'au railgun,' Krozier Va'kai replied, and now he was smiling the smile of a carnodon that had scented blood. He flexed his gauntleted fingers, and looked up and out at the voidscape beyond the viewports. Solomon smiled in turn, as the other commanders turned their attention to the hololiths, or to the battle raging outside. Excited. Eager. Impressed.

Biddable.

'My lords,' Va'kai said, selecting targeting solutions with

inhuman speed. 'Let us teach these stripling bastards how the Alpha Legion makes war.'

The drives roared, the *Unseen* ploughed forwards, and its arsenal of mismatched guns spoke as one to hurl death out into the stars.

THE BITER BIT

It was everything that Kayzen Hart had dreamed of.

He had spent centuries hunting the Alpha Legion – tracking their movements, rooting out their operatives, and disrupting their schemes. He had seen actual legionnaires only three times, twice fleetingly. He had nearly lost his life to them in the one longer engagement in which he had been embroiled, some fifty years before, and had only been saved thanks to intervention from a squad of Crimson Fists. Lord Druman had been correct: it *was* like fighting smoke, and poisonous smoke at that. Hart had never managed to bring his enemy to bay and force them to engage, yet here they were.

'Strong resistance to boarding parties on the vessels identified as the *Null Void* and the *Freedom's Cry*,' a vox-operator was reporting.

'Then these are no decoys,' Hekaton breathed. 'The traitors are here in truth, and in force.'

It seemed a strange realisation to come to, well after a battle had started and several capital ships had already died, but such was the nature of the Alpha Legion. You could not be certain where they were until you actually saw them, and even then you still probably only had a partial picture. Hart could feel the atmosphere on the bridge grow more eager, as the crew of the *Purity's Edge* gained confidence that their efforts were indeed bringing the fury of the Emperor's wrath to heretics and traitors. Hekaton's commands grew bolder, and even the Navy elements of the fleet began to throw themselves into the battle with a passion bordering on recklessness. Hart saw ships flare and die in the cold void, but the Silver Templars' joy in battle was almost infectious; or maybe it was simply his own emotions, finally released. All he knew was that what he might once have thought of as grievous losses were outweighed by the damage being inflicted on this most deceptive of enemies. A war of attrition might be brutal and wasteful, but if that was what it took to destroy the Alpha Legion of the Ultima Segmentum, then it was a price that he – and therefore the Imperium – would happily pay.

'They are not using the space hulk to their advantage,' Tythus Yorr rasped. 'They could have withdrawn, and used it as cover while they escaped into the warp.'

'Indeed, brother,' Captain Palamas said. 'Inquisitor Hart told us that he had word of a conclave of sorts occurring here – it seems likely that this is taking place aboard the hulk, and the ship crews have too much loyalty to their commanders to leave them.'

Yorr smiled nastily. 'May their misplaced loyalty prove to be their undoing!'

'We must pressure the hulk in order to keep them pinned,' Hekaton said. 'If they feel they must engage us to prevent us from boarding it, we can corral them against it and use our superior firepower to–'

He broke off as an icon flared and died on the hololith: an Imperial icon, and one that, so far as Hart's inexpert eye could tell, had not to that point been taking heavy fire.

'What just happened?' Karnis asked, her voice laden with suspicion. Hekaton tapped his console.

'That shot came from the space hulk,' he reported, in tones like lead.

'Throne of Terra, that thing's functional?' Karnis hissed.

'It's manoeuvring, and coming about,' Captain Palamas reported. 'Grand Oathkeeper, I–'

This time, there was no possibility of confusion. The blaze of light was visible to Kayzen Hart's unaugmented mortal vision, as he looked out at the battlescape. The space hulk, previously dead and inert, had come alive, and had joined the fight.

For the size of it, it was not heavily armed. Its weapons were isolated pinpricks of light against its massive, dark flank; however, it was so large that even isolated weapon points still totalled an immense amount of firepower. Escorts and light cruisers came apart before it as it moved inexorably forwards, propelled by whatever unholy conglomeration of engines the traitors had managed to rig up. The remnants of the Alpha Legion fleet began to flow into place around it, incorporating it as the brutal anchor of their new formation.

'Disengage!' Hekaton roared. 'All ships, disengage and fall back!'

Hart bit his lip in anger and frustration. In theory, he was one of the most powerful men in the galaxy, wielding the authority of the Emperor Himself, and yet there was nothing he could do here. They had gone from punishing the Alpha Legion, using their superior numbers and firepower to overwhelm the traitors, to being overextended and exposed. Had this been yet another accursed trap, sacrificing elements of their fleet to lure the Templars in before the space hulk revealed its true power?

'No!' Tythus Yorr snarled, and it took Hart a moment to realise that his lifeward was actually arguing with Lampros Hekaton. 'We must press the attack! By remaining at close range we limit the ability of the hulk to target our ships, lest it hit its own! If we withdraw, we allow them clear firing solutions!'

The *Hammer of Glory* had pressed in to exchange broadsides with a Lunar-class cruiser. The traitor ship had received much the worse of it, but now the *Hammer* was vulnerable. Much like its sister ship, the *Thunder of Fury*, it attempted to present its heavily armoured prow to its adversaries, but once more, such measures were insufficient. The space hulk's guns raked along the *Hammer* from bow to stern and back again, stripping away void shields and then punching deep into its superstructure. Hart watched in silence as tens of thousands of Imperial lives were claimed by the airless void of space.

'We withdraw,' Hekaton said, the eye-lenses of his skull helm fixed on Tythus Yorr. 'The losses we have inflicted upon the enemy today are meaningful, and still stand proudly against those we have incurred. However, the nature of the engagement has changed dramatically. To persist further is folly, and would hand the Alpha Legion a significant victory.'

Hart felt the familiar thrum of the warp engines powering up, and the protective shutters began to lower over the bridge's viewports once more. The *Purity's Edge* was preparing to enter the immaterium, and from the looks of it, the rest of the Imperial fleet was planning to do the same.

'You will abandon your battle-brothers who have boarded their vessels?' Tythus Yorr demanded, pointing towards what remained of the combat. Hart could imagine his pain: given he was the lone surviving member of his Chapter, the notion of leaving brother warriors to die was one that would not sit well.

'I will not be questioned further aboard my own ship!' Hekaton snapped. 'Do not forget your place as our guest here, *brother*. The boarding parties knew the risk of death, regardless of how our fleet fared. They will meet their fates with dignity and honour, and now we will withdraw in the same manner, before this becomes a rout.' He turned away from Yorr and raised his voice. 'Prepare for translation!'

'Lord Hekaton!' a crew member shouted. 'We have reports of hostiles aboard!'

'What?' the Grand Oathkeeper thundered. 'Has there been a teleport flare?'

'No, my lord, but systems are showing malfunctions at several external airlocks–'

'Have we passed near where the *Whisper* was destroyed?' Hart cut in. Hekaton's helmet snapped round to look at him, which was an unnerving visage to be presented with so suddenly, even for an inquisitor.

'Yes,' Hekaton replied, after a moment. 'Within a mile or so.'

Hart nodded. 'Assault troops, then – survivors in the wreckage who have equipped themselves with jump packs, or some equivalent. I imagine they would be too small for your sensors to detect, unlike Thunderhawks or boarding torpedoes.'

'If you cut off the Alpha Legion's arm, they will seek to blind you with their own blood,' Nessa Karnis said bitterly.

Hekaton growled, deep in his throat. Through the vox-grille of his death's-head mask, it was an alarming sound indeed. 'Dispatch assault squads to those locations,' he ordered. 'Captain! All other battle-brothers aboard are to be assigned to guard locations of strategic importance, with particular emphasis on the enginarium, the life-support systems, the bridge, and the

Navigators' quarters. Once those are secure, I want this ship scoured until we have found every intruder.'

'Of course, Grand Oathkeeper,' Captain Palamas said, saluting. He turned to Tythus Yorr. 'Brother. If it would ease your soul, you may hunt with us.'

Yorr took a deep breath. 'It would, brother-captain. But I am oath-sworn to act as lifeward for Inquisitor Hart. Even vengeance must give way to duty, or we are no better than the filth we fight.'

For a moment, Hart considered it. However, he was known to the Alpha Legion, and their schemes ran deep. It was not out of the realm of possibility that they would seek to lure his lifeward away from him, then manage to create some other emergency that would see him ejected from the bridge and the additional protection he enjoyed here, simply in order to kill him. It was not arrogance that made him think this way, nor was it paranoia. Kayzen Hart had seen innumerable lives ended by the Alpha Legion and their operatives, and often those which had required considerable effort and complex planning seemed the least significant, or the most tangentially connected to the Legion's apparent goals. He could not afford to assume that he was too unimportant to be eliminated.

'By assisting me, we are doing more damage to these traitors in the long run than you could with blade and bolter alone,' he said. 'Never forget that.'

Tythus nodded slowly. Captain Palamas turned and left the bridge, already giving orders to organise the defence of the *Purity's Edge* against the insurgents, and klaxons began to sound. The battle-barge was not going to give the Alpha Legion any chance to maroon it here in realspace, not with the might of the space hulk bearing down on them.

Kayzen Hart tried to think of the day's events as Lampros

Hekaton had put them, of a punishing blow delivered to an enemy that had eluded him for so long, but he tasted bile nonetheless. They had come so close, *so* close to a true victory, only to have it snatched away from them.

He was still lost in his own thoughts when reality tore open, and the Silver Templars' task force fled.

Solomon watched the sliver of the enemy's flagship shimmer away into unreality, followed moments later by the battered remnants of the rest of the fleet, and sighed.

'Mourning the one that got away?' Qope Halver asked, from next to him.

'Some of our brothers from the *Whisper* managed to get aboard,' Solomon told him. 'I had hoped they might be able to disable its warp drives. Had we then been able to board it, we might have presented Krozier with a suitable replacement for his loss.'

Halver smiled wryly and looked over his shoulder. 'I would say the old scoundrel has traded up well enough.'

Krozier Va'kai sat back in the command throne of the *Unseen*, and disabled those targeting systems which were still active. Lit up by command runes and hololith screens, he looked like a god of war: not an ancient deity clutching a primitive hand weapon, but one sitting on firepower equivalent to a fleet of starships, and with the ability to use that to its full potential. It was difficult to picture him anywhere else.

'Masterfully done, Captain Va'kai,' Keros Asid said, making a bow with his fist to his chest. The other commanders made mutterings of agreement, and Solomon smiled. The Alpha Legion believed in roles going to those with the greatest suitability for them, and after Va'kai's demonstration of his abilities, it would be hard for anyone here to argue that someone else should have command of the vessel that the *Unseen* had become.

And if Va'kai had command of the *Unseen*, then the Serpent's Teeth had command of the *Unseen*.

'Lord Akurra,' Roek Ghulclaw intoned, turning towards him. 'I have primarily operated in Segmentum Obscurus, and I have no ties to anyone here. The foresight of the Serpent's Teeth in preparing and improving this hulk has impressed me, as did your words earlier. The Guns of Freedom will accept you as Harrowmaster, until you give me reason to change my mind.'

Solomon inclined his head in acknowledgement. Ghulclaw's Guns of Freedom were a sizeable militia force, exactly the sort of raw materiel the Alpha Legion liked to use to wear down enemies before a more surgical Astartes strike.

'The First Strike concurs,' declared Raelin Amran. 'You are prepared to fight, and we will fight alongside you.'

Solomon did not try to hide his smile. Any Legion commander would be gratified to have others place their trust in him; and as with all things, once momentum had started, progress became easier and easier.

One by one, the other lords of the Alpha Legion inclined their heads to him, and voiced their acceptance. This was not final: it would only take one mistake for them to withdraw their support, and perhaps leave him as isolated as the *Whisper* had been when it was destroyed.

On the other hand, it was no coincidence that the majority of the Serpent's Teeth were currently concealed in the depths of the *Unseen*, allegedly in case of problems from the other warbands, with only a skeleton crew of legionnaires left aboard the *Whisper*. It was also no coincidence that those unlucky legionnaires happened to be ones, or at least led by ones, Solomon had considered the least likely to support him as Harrowmaster.

The arrival of the Silver Templars had not been guaranteed,

but Tulava had set the lure when she had contacted all of their assets, and Solomon had been ready for the bait to be taken. Persuading Va'kai that his ship was a worthy sacrifice had taken some doing, but the veteran had accepted that their losses had to be real, in order to avoid suspicion from the other lords, and seal their claim to the *Unseen*.

Now, Solomon had command, and Va'kai had one of the most powerful vessels in the Ultima Segmentum at his fingertips. More importantly, the Alpha Legion itself was united.

'My lords, we still have work to do here,' Solomon declared. 'There are boarding parties aboard some of our vessels, and the Silver Templars will not cease fighting just because their fellows have abandoned them. Let this be our first joint action – we must reinforce each other, and assist in retaking each others' vessels from the Imperium scum! Once we have done that, I will outline to you my vision for our next move.'

'Are you still intending to go through with this?' Tulava asked, moving to his side as the other commanders began to coordinate their forces, and vessels moved to each other's aid.

'I am.'

'I hope you know what you are doing,' Qope Halver said quietly. 'The subsector is a fine target, and would solve our supply issues for months to come, but it is going to be a big ask. Especially since we have no idea how well this lot are going to work together.'

Solomon took a deep breath. 'It is the way of the Legion, brother.

'We will adapt. Or we will die.'

AFTERMATH

When the battle group returned after nearly three weeks sidereal time, the Alpha Legion were gone, leaving nothing but the wreckage of those ships too damaged to be worth salvaging. Kayzen Hart stared at the bare stars with disappointment, but without much surprise. The likelihood of the traitors remaining in place long enough for a larger force to arm and return had been slim indeed, but Grand Oathkeeper Hekaton had no intention of allowing the Alpha Legion to scour the site of the battle for materiel at their leisure.

'Shall I order salvage crews deployed, lord?' one of the bridge crew asked.

'No,' Hekaton replied coldly. 'The traitors may have trapped the wreckage in the hope of delaying and disrupting us further. We have our orders from the primarch, so we shall waste no further time here.'

Hart stepped forward. 'Lord Hekaton. The space hulk is no longer present.'

'This had not escaped my notice, inquisitor,' Hekaton replied. There was an undercurrent of tension in the Grand Oathkeeper's voice. Hart suspected that his flagship being boarded by Alpha Legionnaires had angered Hekaton more than he was letting on, despite the fact that the intruders had achieved little of note before they were killed. However, Kayzen Hart was an inquisitor of the Ordo Malleus, and while he knew better than to antagonise members of the Adeptus Astartes, nor would he be browbeaten by them.

'It is clearly warp-capable,' he pointed out. 'While we normally expect space hulks to move relatively randomly, it would be naive of us to expect the same from a vessel that was clearly under Alpha Legion control. If it can move and fire as they wish in realspace, and it is warp-capable, we must assume that they can direct its movements in the immaterium.'

'Your logic is sound,' Hekaton acknowledged. 'But I fail to see the relevance. Although it pains me to say so, inquisitor, the Alpha Legion are gone. I will not set this battle group to chasing shadows, when such a delay might be our enemies' primary goal. We shall continue as planned.'

'I am not asking you to chase shadows, Lord Hekaton!' Hart protested.

'No, you would have us walk into another trap,' Nessa Karnis said acidly. Hart rounded on her, his temper rising.

'My information was accurate! The Alpha Legion were here, in force!' He drew himself up and looked down his nose at her, well aware that making an issue of his superior height was petty, but unable to restrain himself. 'Had we come in battle group strength to begin with, even that accursed space hulk would not have availed them!'

Karnis smirked and looked past Hart's shoulder, just as he became aware of a giant presence looming behind him.

'Is that a criticism, inquisitor?' Hekaton rumbled. Hart turned back to him.

'As an inquisitor, I deal in facts, Lord Hekaton,' he replied levelly. 'I was not able to inform you of the Alpha Legion's exact strength, and so I did not try. You used your best judgement based on incomplete information, and the other requirements placed on your battle group. There will always be unknown factors that can make a mockery of our best efforts. However, I will not allow my colleague to accuse me of providing false information. The intelligence from my sources was accurate so far as it went, and I made no claims of which I was not certain.'

Hekaton neither moved nor spoke for a moment. Then he nodded, very slightly.

'The battle tactics of the Alpha Legion fleet suggested that even its other ships did not know the space hulk was an active combatant until it joined the fray. The traitors could have dealt us even more damage had they coordinated with it more effectively from the start, and I do not attribute that failure to a lack of tactical awareness. I suspect that the majority of them were unaware of its capabilities, so it is unsurprising if your intelligence was lacking on that count.'

'And it is further evidence that the Alpha Legion are not unified,' Hart pressed. 'They are individual warbands, not a combined force. They can be hit until they splinter, or turn on each other in desperation.'

'Perhaps,' Hekaton acknowledged. 'However, that is not the role of this battle group. Should the Alpha Legion set themselves in our path again, they will be dealt with summarily, but I will not allow us to be sidetracked.'

Hart fought down his frustration. 'Grand Oathkeeper, I believe I know where they will strike next.'

Hekaton's skull helm regarded him for a couple of seconds. 'Go on.'

'If I may.' Hart moved to the tactical hololith and tapped the keys to bring up a map of the galaxy, then highlighted a system. 'Here.'

Hekaton joined him, as did Tythus Yorr and, with an expression of considerable dubiousness on her face, Nessa Karnis.

'The Charadon Sector?' Hekaton said.

'Specifically the Psyphos Subsector,' Hart elaborated, expanding the map to show an area of space comprising five different solar systems, two of which were centred around binary stars. 'They are key supply systems, providing huge amounts of food, medical supplies, and munitions to the Indomitus Crusade, and recently liberated. It also sits on the Angel's Way, one of the primary stable warp routes to Ultramar. The Alpha Legion specialise in disruption – if this subsector was lost, or even embroiled in a drawn-out conflict, the knock-on effects on the crusade could be significant.'

'Inquisitor Karnis?' Hekaton said. 'Your thoughts?'

'I am not aware of any reason why the Alpha Legion would target Psyphos over any other suitable location,' Karnis said. 'Still,' she added, with audible reluctance, 'I must concur that it would appear to fit their criteria. Inquisitor Hart's analysis of its importance is broadly accurate, and so it cannot be ruled out. If my fellow inquisitor would share the nature of his so-called "sources", perhaps we could be more certain?'

Hart snorted. 'You would track them down and kill them, Nessa, and I have not spent a lifetime developing a web of contacts in order for you to execute them. Justice will come to them, but only when I deem their usefulness to be at an end.'

'I am uninterested in your infighting,' Hekaton said bluntly. 'My judgement stands, the battle group will proceed as directed.

However, Lieutenant Malfax and the Second Demi-Company of the Fifth Company will take the *Dawnblade* and oversee additional defences at Psyphos. Either or both of you may accompany them – or you may continue with the main battle group, and take your leave when convenient.'

Hekaton's face was still hidden, but there was something in his voice that suggested to Hart that any such departure would be at the convenience of the Grand Oathkeeper, not himself. He inclined his head.

'I will travel with Lieutenant Malfax and his warriors. Should the authorities of Psyphos show any reluctance to comply with the directives of the Silver Templars, they will surely not resist the will of the Emperor's Inquisition.'

He let that hang in the air for a moment. It would not do Hekaton any harm to remember that although Hart might tread carefully around the Adeptus Astartes, the rest of the galaxy lived in fear of him, and the power of his office. He knew well enough that supreme defenders of humanity though they were, the Space Marines were not universally loved, particularly not by those in positions of power. Lord Guilliman's return had changed things to an extent, but that was still not licence for Space Marines to treat the Inquisition as an afterthought.

'I will come too,' Nessa Karnis said, breaking the brief silence. She glanced sideways at Hart. 'I am eager to see how accurate my colleague's intelligence is.'

Tythus Yorr had been almost vibrating throughout the time they were on the bridge, but he had sufficient restraint to wait until he and Hart were back in their quarters before he exploded.

'We were supposed to break the Alpha Legion!' he snarled. The Crimson Consul's rage was not directed at Hart – at least, not precisely – but it was an alarming thing to witness nonetheless.

Yorr was not just an oversized human thug in bulky armour; he was a bioengineered killer, the product of ten thousand years of genetic manipulation and psycho-conditioning. Oath of fealty or otherwise, Hart never let the safety Yorr's presence conferred blind him to how dangerous the warrior was.

'We will,' Hart assured his lifeward. 'I have dedicated my life to this end, do you doubt me now?'

'We handed them a victory,' Yorr seethed. 'A victory which, if your information is correct, has allowed the one known as Akurra to achieve pre-eminence within their ranks. He has started to unify our foes!'

'You are a son of Guilliman,' Hart said, 'and so your instincts naturally run to seeing an end goal, and devising the best plan to get there. That is not how the Alpha Legion thinks. To truly fight them, we must think like them. A setback is only a setback if you compare it to your previous aims, and if you allow those to blind you to the new best course of action.'

'There are those who would suggest that thinking like the Alpha Legion is heretical,' Yorr said, regarding Hart from beneath his prominent brows.

'Do not let Nessa Karnis' words trip from your tongue,' Hart replied. 'The privilege and curse of the Holy Ordos is the requirement to understand our enemies without tainting ourselves.' He sat down at the utilitarian desk with which the Silver Templars had furnished his quarters. 'I would have liked nothing better than for our forces to crush the Alpha Legion in void combat, and I regret our losses. However, to see it as a defeat is blinkered. We have a new opportunity now, one we would not have had before.'

'What is that?' Yorr demanded dubiously.

'My sources do indeed suggest that Solomon Akurra has risen to prominence,' Hart said. He tapped the nail on the third finger of his left hand in a particular pattern, and it flipped up to reveal a tiny storage compartment built into the artificial finger. From here he extracted a data-spool, unrolled it, then took up a pen and began to write.

The data-spool was his most prized possession: more so than Helorassa, his power sabre; perhaps even more so than his Inquisitorial rosette itself. It was a genuine Alpha Legion cypher, taken from the body of a cell leader in the catacombs under Starmark City on Berna Majoris. It would not grant him access to all of the Legion's secrets, of course – the traitors were too well subdivided, and distrustful even of each other, to allow that – but it had given him a foothold within one element.

The cypher was, he had to admit, ingenious. The precise code used depended on the different elements of the date: check number, the year fraction, the year, and the millennium. Someone with the cypher would be able to apply the correct decoding procedures according to when the message was dated, and the best bit of all was that the message's date did not need to relate to when it was actually composed – it was simply a way of telling the recipient how to read it.

'With prominence comes power,' Hart said, carefully composing the text. 'With power comes the expectation of action. The Alpha Legion are not so different from you in some ways, my friend.'

'Be careful of your words, Kayzen,' Yorr said warningly.

'I mean only that they are warriors,' Hart reassured his lifeward. 'Depraved, deceitful, and traitorous, of course, but they are still Space Marines, of a sort. Their purpose is, and will always be, warfare. A leader who does not lead them to war in some respect will not remain leader, and a leader who commands a sizeable force will be expected to wage war on a grand scale. Akurra's rise to power may serve to unite disparate elements of the Legion, it is true, but this means that rather than chasing the work of isolated cells, we have a chance to strike a telling blow against multiple enemies simultaneously.'

He smiled as he wrote. Nessa Karnis might imagine that his sources were rumour-mongers or whisper-merchants; she surely did not suspect that Hart was corresponding directly with Alpha Legion factors. Of course, he had to provide accurate intelligence of his own every now and then, in order to maintain his cover, but he made sure it was never anything that would work against the overall interests of the Imperium.

'Provided, of course,' he added, 'that they can be lured out of the shadows en masse by an appropriate prize.'

Tythus Yorr grunted. 'When you told Lord Hekaton that you believed the Alpha Legion would attack Psyphos, was that because your sources suggest that they will, or because you intend to bring it about?'

'If it allows us to crush the majority of the Alpha Legion active in the Ultima Segmentum,' Hart said, finishing his encoded missive, 'does it really matter?'

Yorr was silent for a moment. Then he shook his head.

'No.'

'Precisely,' Hart said. 'They will attack *somewhere*, that much is inevitable. It is good strategy to dictate where that is, and it is a necessity that it be somewhere of sufficient importance for them to risk their forces.'

He replaced the data-spool, folded the note up, and secreted it in his pocket. Messages sleeted back and forth constantly from a fleet this size all the time, when they were in Imperial systems. Even aboard a Space Marine vessel, his Inquisitorial authority would allow him use of a transmitter terminal with no questions asked, and once it was away, he could be sure of it reaching its intended destination.

Hart doubted that many others understood the true scope of the Alpha Legion's presence within the Imperium's systems. It had kept him awake for more nights than he cared to remember, envisaging it as a massive underground network, like the tendrils of a fungus. Oh, Nessa Karnis was not the only one who dreamed of uprooting the whole thing, but she had never had the patience for this sort of work. Kayzen Hart knew that even if he burned all his contacts, even if he exerted all his influence, even if he pulled in a thousand or more Alpha Legion operatives, he would find little of substance. Most knew nothing of who they truly worked for: they were simply bribed to pass on a message to here, or to there, or to redirect something somewhere else. Those with influence would be several steps removed, and by the time he had gathered enough information to work out how to reach them, they would have been tipped off by the disappearance of their underlings, and would have made themselves scarce.

No, you couldn't fight this sort of infiltration. You had to use it, had to direct it for your own purposes. Misinformation, or accurate information with a hidden purpose behind it, that was the key. He had to draw his foe out, with the poison of his intentions masked by the honey of a sweeter truth.

Then he had to strike. And when he did, he must not miss.

PART TWO

DELTA PRIMUS

Security work could, in the professional opinion of Aemus Speltan, go and do one.

He'd been working security at the space port for seventeen years. He'd been working security during the Noctis Aeterna, when the sky bled light, and half the town had lost their minds and gone on a rampage. He'd been working security when the first ships of Lord Guilliman's Indomitus Crusade had arrived, bringing what they claimed was salvation, but which turned out to be little more than demands for a doubled tithe, and a recruitment drive for the Astra Militarum that had seen Aemus' oldest son snatched away and stuffed into a uniform. He'd lost uncountable nights to grainy eyes and a persistent headache that fitful sleep during the daylight hours was unable to shift. He still had his marriage, but it was on its last legs. The thing was, if he and Imara split, they would both be reassigned to even smaller dwellings, and who knew where that would be, or what sort of condition it would be in? Their compartment was hardly spacious, but they'd managed to make it reasonably comfortable over the last twenty years, as such things went. It was easier to tolerate each other's presence and work opposing shift patterns, than be uprooted and risk being dumped into a multi-dorm compound somewhere with the other old divorcees.

Of course, part of the reason his compartment was comfortable was because of Tolly Krace. Imara didn't like it when Aemus started doing favours for Krace, but she had no problem using the comfortable chair those extra few thrones had bought, or the rations he'd been able to pick up at the market even when the Imperium's tithes were biting the hardest. Tolly Krace was a small-time hoodlum, but he wasn't actually *dangerous*. He wasn't one of those monsters who went around hurting people. He just made sure that some goods moved from place to place without inconveniencing those people who thought it was their responsibility to know about such things.

Sometimes Tolly wanted a certain gate left open, to allow people who definitely weren't there to not get in and definitely not remove anything before it had been inspected and tallied. Aemus would nip out of the control room for a comfort break and see to it while someone else was on patrol. You didn't do such things on your own patrol: that was just asking for trouble if the problem was found before you could rectify matters again, once everyone who shouldn't have been there definitely wasn't there any longer.

As for the pict-sentries – well, they were always on the blink, weren't they? Granted, that was mainly because Tolly had set Aemus up with a cunning little device which ensured that happened. Aemus didn't understand how it worked – that was enginseer stuff – but it slotted neatly into a power outflow and didn't look at all out of place alongside the rest of the control room's equipment, half of which was never used anyway.

Aemus didn't even have to turn it on and off himself: he could program it to work at a certain time. That way, the mysterious vid-outages didn't only happen when he was on shift. Oh yes, Tolly Krace knew what he was doing, and he knew how to make sure his helpers didn't get rumbled, either. That was the sort of thing that made Aemus willing to go along with it. In many ways, he got the feeling that Krace cared more about his well-being than his own superiors did.

He didn't see who came in, of course. You didn't linger, or try to snatch a look. Although nothing had been explicitly said, Aemus was savvy enough to know that such things would not go down well, and while Tolly Krace wasn't one of those monsters who went around hurting people, there was no point in pushing your luck just out of idle curiosity. He blinded the pict-sentries and opened the gate, and put everything back as it should be once the allocated time was past – so no one in authority started to get suspicious that the reason there was nothing out of place in the shipping manifests was because the extra items had already disappeared – and then he went down the market at the end of the month and someone slipped his second wages into his pocket when no one was looking, including him.

No one got hurt, a few people got things they wanted without inconveniencing anyone, and Aemus got a bit richer. Well, slightly less poor, anyway. Where was the harm?

This request was an early one, to be completed one hour after the start of his fourteen-hour shift. Aemus resorted to 'sneaking' out for a lho-stick, although it cost him a stick to each of the others in the control room for them to let him, and an extra one to the supervisor. He sorted the gate as per, then hurried back, careful to save the last of his stick for the moments before he walked back through the door, so the smell of the smoke was still fresh on him.

'Imagers down again?' he tutted as he came back in and saw the blank screens.

'Yeah, went off just after you left,' Morton grumbled, thumping one of them. It responded by flickering back into life again, and was quickly followed by the others.

'Hah!' barked Pashvir, the shift supervisor. 'Why didn't you try that before?'

'I did!' Morton protested, but was cut off by a collection of swear words from Raola, who coordinated the landing schedules.

'Something up?' Aemus asked, sauntering over to her. He had no understanding of the complicated details of Raola's work, but it was important to act naturally.

'We've got a *lot* of shipping traffic coming in,' Raola said, juggling the printouts the cogitators were vomiting at her. 'I'd say a sixty per cent increase on usual. A whole bunch of bulk carriers just hit upper orbit, and they all want allocating.'

'Are you complaining about doing your job again, Raola?' Pashvir demanded.

'Yes, chief,' Raola said bluntly. 'And I know you can fire me for it, but *you* know you can't find anyone else who can find slots for these bastards half as efficiently as I can.'

Pashvir threw up his hands theatrically. 'The woman knows her value, though it pains me to admit it.'

'You pulled me up last week for complaining,' Morton said, in a tone that stopped just short of being a complaint in and of itself.

'Tell you what,' Pashvir said, smiling, and Aemus recognised that smile as one that could disappear at any moment. 'If you can bring the imagers back online every time they go down, I might see my way to overlooking the odd grumble or two. Otherwise' – and now his smile was gone, with no hint that it had ever existed – 'you can keep your mouth shut when you do your job.'

'Yes, chief,' Morton replied sulkily, and went back to studying the imagers. Aemus settled down into his seat, ready to do nothing much for the next hour or so.

One of the imagers went off again.

'Morton?' Pashvir said. Morton shrugged, leaned forward and thumped it, but nothing happened.

'That's weird,' Aemus said, taking a step towards the display.

'What's weird?' Morton asked. 'They go down all the time. They were down just now! Piece of Throne-damned junk...'

Aemus realised he'd made a mistake, and tried to cover himself. 'Well, yeah, but the whole system tends to go down at once, doesn't it? I know it's been that way when I've seen it.'

Morton shrugged. 'Do I look like a tech-priest to you? If it's just one rather than all of them, I'll take it.'

Another one winked out.

Pashvir hissed through his teeth. 'I swear, this thing is mocking us. It's going to make us watch it fail on us, one by one–'

Another imager flickered and died, and something chilly took hold of Aemus' spine. The others were used to the technology only working intermittently, but he knew why that was. This was nothing to do with him; nothing to do with Tolly Krace's clever little gadget, wired inconspicuously in next to the vid-imagers. This was a genuine failure, and there was something alarming about the pattern.

'It's coming here,' he said, the words reaching his tongue at the same time as the concept formed in his brain.

Pashvir snorted. 'Come again?'

'It's coming here,' Aemus repeated, certain he was correct, and increasingly alarmed at what that meant. 'The blind spots. They're on a path through the complex, from the loading bays up to the control room.' He reached out, seventeen years of experience telling him which of the almost-identical displays was the next on the route. 'This one will go next.'

It did.

None of the features of Pashvir's face changed. His eyes, his mouth, his nose, all studiously remained exactly as they were. However, the rest of his expression somehow settled around them, morphing from irritation into alarm. He reached for his vox.

'Patrol, report.'

Only the hiss of static answered him.

'They would have got to here by now,' Aemus said, pointing to the second screen that had gone dead. Another screen went blank, this one within two hundred yards of the control room.

'Morton, Aemus,' Pashvir said. 'On the door.'

Aemus looked at Morton, and found the younger man looking back at him. Still, there was nothing for it, although part of Aemus wanted to bolt out of that door and run the other way, away from whatever might be making its way towards them.

Another imager went black, and they both made a grab for the guns racked on the wall.

They were sturdy shotguns, Deliverance pattern, straight from the forges of the noble Raven Guard's home world, loaded with solid slugs for stopping power, and scattershot for what Torwin – the shift supervisor when Aemus had started work at the space port – had phrased as 'a more even-handed approach'. Aemus racked a solid shell with hands that barely shook, and took up position to the left of the door, while Morton went to the right. The door itself was high-grade plasteel, six inches thick, secured by three bolts as thick as Aemus' arm at all times that someone wasn't actually passing through it. It wasn't a mechanical one, with controls that could be overridden: the only way in was if the shift currently inside the control room decided to let you in.

The imager that covered the corridor directly outside the door went out. Aemus swallowed.

'Want me to see who's there, chief?' Morton quavered, nodding towards the vision slit. It was a slide-aside job, like you might get in an old-style gaol.

'Let's not put your head in the way of whoever's out there, eh, Morton?' Pashvir said. He had drawn the autopistol he always kept on his belt, and was holding it low in two hands, like he knew how to use it. Aemus had never known what Pashvir did before he became a shift supervisor, but he got the abrupt impression that it might have involved guns.

'Yes, chief,' Morton replied, the relief obvious in his voice. 'Thank you, chi–'

The door crashed in.

Six inches of high-grade plasteel flattened Aemus. One moment he was standing, and the next he was on his back, sliding across the floor with the door on top of him. He heard voices start to yell, and then...

Thwip.

Thwip.

Thwip.

...and three soft thumps. It was over within a second. It was over before he'd had time to register that one of his hands was still clutching his shotgun, although admittedly it was in no position to shoot anything other than his own foot.

Not that Aemus had any intention of shooting anything. His head was almost completely covered by the door, and heavy and uncomfortable though it was, and bruised though *he* was, he could just about breathe, and maybe if he lay very, very still, whatever had just broken in would not notice him, or at least not consider him enough of a threat to do anything about–

Footsteps, soft but heavy, crossed the floor towards him. So much for that plan. He tensed, but it was pointless. He couldn't free himself, and anyone could just walk around and shoot him in the head without him being able to get away, or bring his weapon to bear.

The door was pulled off him in one swift movement, as if it weighed virtually nothing. Aemus wailed and raised his shotgun with his eyes shut, not wanting to see what was inevitably going to kill him before he could pull the trigger, but the weapon was slapped out of his hand so hard he felt the bones in his wrist crack with a white-hot grinding sensation.

'Ah, Aemus. There you are.'

Death hadn't arrived. Aemus cautiously opened his eyes, trying not to whimper at the pain in his wrist, and saw, to his shock, a familiar figure standing over him.

'Tolly?' he managed. Then he saw what was standing off to one side, and this time he did not manage to restrain his whimper. A black-armoured giant, his battleplate worked with a scale motif, with a boltgun the size of Aemus' torso clamped to his thigh, but a much more delicate weapon in his mighty gauntlet. It looked like a needle pistol, although upsized for its bearer, and suddenly Aemus understood what the soft noises he had heard were. Of course, his mind said desperately, trying to cover over its own fear with logic, a needle weapon wouldn't risk destroying the control room's machinery...

'When's the next shift due on, Aemus?' Tolly Krace asked, sitting down onto his haunches. He'd never been a nice-looking man, had Tolly Krace; Aemus had always got the impression that every smile was planned, and every friendly remark weighed for effect before it left his lips. Now, though, he looked positively predatory.

'The lords are waiting, Aemus,' Krace snapped, when Aemus' terror prevented him from answering.

'Th-thirteen hours,' Aemus managed. 'More or less.'

Tolly Krace rose back to his feet, and bowed his head to the black-armoured giant. 'Lord Alpharius.'

Aemus saw the needle pistol come up.

Thwip.

Qope Halver turned away from the security guard. He was already insensible, and the cocktail of potent toxins would end his life beyond hope of revival within the next thirty seconds. 'Well done, Krace.'

The mortal known as Tolly Krace bowed again. 'My lord.'

'Return to your dwelling, and resume your life as normal until we contact you again,' Halver instructed him. The factor had proved himself reliable and useful, and his little crime empire and its pre-existing bribery network had provided the perfect cover for Halver's team of Headhunters to make planetfall in a shipping container. Now they simply had to ease the way for the rest of the force.

'Hydra Dominatus,' Tolly Krace replied, his eyes shining, then turned and disappeared out through the control room door.

'Shall I begin?' asked Vorlan Xhan, in a voice two octaves too high for his build. Halver couldn't keep a smile from his face.

'You sound ridiculous, Vorlan.'

'I sound like a mortal,' Xhan replied. He flattened out the printouts he had taken from the body of the woman, activated the cogitator, and set to work. Codes started to rattle out into the blackness above, accompanied by vox signals carrying Vorlan's altered voice, issuing instructions. Some ships were ordered to hold position, but the new arrivals – the bulk carriers containing the Alpha Legion's strike force – were prioritised and allocated landing pads. Slowly, Beharis Delta's shipping system began to welcome its conquerors down with landing beacons.

Halver smiled again, for a different reason. Crashing planet-wards in a Thunderhawk or a drop pod was one thing, but a leisurely drop in a bulk carrier, without the issues of incoming fire, was far more efficient. Akurra had planned it well. The Faceless had done their part by offering up Tolly Krace, one of their many contacts in the subsector. The Serpent's Teeth, specifically Halver's Headhunters, had opened the way.

Now it was time for the Alpha Legion as a whole to remind the galaxy why they had once been so rightly feared.

THE MAILED FIST

The numbers on Solomon's helmet chrono ticked down, and reached zero. He activated his vox, and spoke a single word.

'Attack.'

The engine of the vehicle in which he stood roared into life, like a predator claiming ownership of a kill. Ahead of them, the loading doors of the bulk carrier would be halfway to the ground. Everything had been coordinated precisely. To activate their engines too early would have warned those outside that something was amiss; too late, and they risked surrendering the initiative. Solomon strongly doubted that there was anything within this space port, or indeed any of the others, which could stand against what was coming. Nonetheless, that was no excuse for sloppiness.

The Mastodon heavy assault transport thundered forwards, its treads reaching the lip of the ramp at the precise moment the ramp's far end touched the deck. It was an ancient vehicle, possibly dating back even to the Horus Heresy or before. Or perhaps it had been captured more recently, taken from a loyalist Chapter; there was no way to be sure. The Shrouded Hand had offered its use as Solomon's command vehicle for the assault, and he had accepted. Its immense size and heavy armament made it the perfect spearhead for a shock assault.

Nor was the Mastodon alone. Behind it came three Land Raiders – one of the ancient Mark II units, and two in the more modern Crusader pattern – and two Rhinos, and behind them were four Predator battle tanks, two Whirlwinds equipped with Scorpius launchers, and a Deimos Vindicator Laser Destroyer. The other Alpha Legion transport which had touched down in the same space port was disgorging its own cargo: a pair of Fellblade tanks, with half a dozen bike-mounted Astartes of the First Strike and two Hellhounds from the Guns of Freedom to ride as escort and keep enemy infantry away from the cumbersome super-heavies. It was a fearsome armoured convoy, and it was just one of seven such strikes taking place in the major cities across the planet.

The Alpha Legion did not engage the menials or servitors who scurried out of their way as their vehicles roared towards the space port's main gate. Solomon's plan hinged on a lightning attack that would hit before the Imperials properly understood what was going on, and the longer the Alpha Legion waited before they opened fire, the more confusion they would sow. The vehicles being used for this assault were, so far as possible, free from any insignia relating to the Ruinous Powers, or the sort of macabre trophies collected by warbands like the First Strike. To those who knew little of the Alpha Legion – and they were the vast majority, amongst the population of the Imperium at large – the convoy would look like Imperial vehicles, including those belonging to one of the multitude of mighty Space Marine Chapters, heading for the governor's palace. There could be legitimate reasons for that, and it would be a foolhardy local military commander who would order their underlings to open fire on Astartes vehicles.

They were out of the space port now, and onto the main transport artery connecting it to Delta Primus, the capital. Other vehicles, be they smaller domestic groundcars, hulking cargo haulers, or anything in between, swerved aside to clear the way for the military convoy that ground its way along the rockcrete.

'We should pass the city boundary within four minutes,' reported Titrik Inshu, the leader of Third Fang. 'From there, estimated time to the palace is ten minutes.'

'It would be a lot faster if we weren't bringing the Fellblades,' remarked Urzu Kaibor, also of Third Fang.

'We may be glad of them soon enough,' Solomon said. 'Our intelligence suggests that the governor takes his security very seriously, and has not inconsiderable resources at his disposal.' He turned to Qorru Vayzia of the Penitent Sons, who was monitoring the vox. 'Anything on the security channels?'

'Nothing important, Lord Akurra,' Vayzia replied, holding the earpiece to one side of his scabbed and scarred face. 'We're being challenged by the local gunrats, but nothing we would respond to if we were who we're pretending to be.' He tilted his head. 'Ah, here we are. It sounds like they've woken up a colonel. Beharis Seventy-Third, Astra Militarum garrison.'

Solomon nodded. 'Let's hear it.'

Vayzia flicked a switch on the Mastodon's vox-console, and a voice was patched through to Solomon's helm: male, mortal, slightly nasal, with overtones of accustomed command blending uneasily with the fear any sensible Astra Militarum commander would feel when an armoured cavalcade of Astartes were bearing down on his capital city.

'*–is Colonel Iobar of the Beharis Seventy-Third. State your identity and purpose or we will open fire. I repeat, this is Colonel–*'

Solomon nodded. 'Give me a general broadcast frequency.'

Vayzia flicked another switch. 'You have it.'

Solomon activated his vox. 'This is Brother-Captain Trokus of the Iron Snakes Chapter of the Adeptus Astartes, broadcasting on wideband communication to the defenders of Delta Primus, including Colonel Iobar of the Beharis Seventy-Third. Are you aware that Governor Morvane has been declared Excommunicate Traitoris by the High Lords of Terra?'

'I... What?'

'If you and your forces stand down at this time and apprehend the governor, no further action will be taken against you, colonel,' Solomon continued, as inexorably as the advance of the Mastodon in which he rode. 'Failure to comply with this edict will result in the destruction of you, your regiment, and your city.'

'They've already scrambled flyers,' Inshu reported. 'We've got one Marauder and two Vultures approaching, probably more on the way.'

Solomon switched frequencies. 'Ready the Skyreaper battery, and fire as soon as they come within range.' The Mastodon was equipped with a formidable anti-aircraft capability, and they would use it. Space Marines expected immediate compliance to their decrees, and many Chapters viewed any challenge to their authority as an act of aggression, to be punished. Destroying a potential threat was well within the remit of the Alpha Legion's deception. He switched back to the general broadcast. 'I am waiting, colonel!'

Tulava Dyne was smiling. 'Iron Snakes?'

'They are real,' Solomon told her, muting his vox once more. 'As is Brother-Captain Trokus, I believe. But I would be sorely surprised if anyone here has ever seen an Iron Snake, and snakes are similar enough to hydras for our iconography to go unremarked for now.'

'*Now hear this, Captain Trokus,*' the voice of Colonel Iobar declared, shaky but defiant. '*I will need to see evidence of this declaration before I am willing to take any such action against our governor! I can assure you that should I be satisfied of the authority of your claim, you will have my full support–*'

'I grow tired of this man's bleating,' Solomon said into the vox, in a bored voice. 'Defenders of Delta Primus, I will say this once more: your governor has been declared Excommunicate Traitoris by the High Lords of Terra. We are here to ensure this sanction is carried out. Should you not wish to suffer the same fate, you will turn all your efforts to aiding us. You are either loyal citizens of the Imperium, or you are traitors in your turn – there is no standing by in the face of treachery!' He cut the vox-link.

'Very good,' Inshu said, with mocking applause. 'You hit just the right note of pompous threat. If at least a third of the garrison don't soil their fatigues and turn on their companions, then I'm an ork.'

'The Marauder's pulling away,' Qorru Vayzia reported from the vox-station. 'The pilot is saying she is no traitor to the Imperium. The Vultures are still coming in. No, one is still coming in – the other's going after the Marauder.'

The faintest of whines reached Solomon's ears, amplified by the audio receptors in his helm. Above the Mastodon's armoured assault bay, and protected by the vehicle's void shields, the Skyreaper battery was opening up.

'And one is going down,' Vayzia said, a moment later.

Solomon signalled him. 'Patch me in. I want full access to their command frequencies.'

Vayzia obliged, and Solomon began to scan through the transmissions of Delta Primus' defenders. Orders were being broadcast and, by the sounds of it, largely ignored. The units stationed nearest to him were the most reluctant to engage with the approaching Space Marines, whereas ones from elsewhere in the city were beginning to mobilise in order to, as they saw it, defend the governor. The 73rd's major had already declared his colonel a traitor, and was attempting to assume command. Orders to get more flyers airborne were being resisted by most squadron commanders, although it sounded like certain individual pilots were attempting to defy that countermand.

All in all, the vox painted a picture of utter chaos.

The two Fellblades spoke as one. The Imperial Knight which had been pounding the Mastodon's void shields with battle cannon shells came apart like a child's toy, and fell into flaming wreckage at the foot of the grand stone steps which led up to the main doors of the Summer Palace.

'You were correct, lord,' Urzu Kaibor said, as the Mastodon growled to a halt. 'I am glad to have them with us now. I do not know how this governor won the loyalty of a Freeblade.'

Solomon checked the relic bolter he had taken from the fallen Silver Templar on Pendata. Its faint machine-spirit was utterly broken to his will now, and it would serve him as well as any other weapon.

He activated his vox. 'Disembark.'

The Mastodon's assault doors ground open, and Solomon led his warriors out. Himself, Tulava Dyne, five Lernean Terminators of the Serpent's Teeth, as well as Third Fang, ten veteran legionnaires of the Shrouded Hand, and another ten from the Penitent Sons. The Crusaders each disgorged five First Strike assault troops, who immediately took off on jets of flame from their jump packs, aiming for the mansion's higher windows. The Mark II Land Raider carried another five Terminators, also from the Shrouded Hand, while the squads in the Rhinos had formed a perimeter around the palace. One of those consisted of ten bolter-armed Astartes from the Sons of Venom, and the other eight warriors were from a small warband known as the Soulfangs, wielding a variety of heavy weapons between them. Solomon had seen their twisted armour, and how the guns almost seemed a part of them, and knew that the warp had found them. No one could look on them and see an Imperial Space Marine, but the time of that deception was past. Most of the Imperial forces were at war with themselves, now.

The Alpha Legion had committed to this attack as a unified force, the different warbands supporting and complementing each other, and it had worked exactly as Solomon had hoped.

The Penitent Sons and the Shrouded Hand led the way up the steps, ignoring the fire from inside. The governor had surrounded himself with a sizeable force of his loyalists, but most were only armed with lasguns. The faster-moving Space Marines breached the main door and ground-floor windows in a matter of seconds, adding to the confusion within, where the First Strike were already fighting their way down from above. Solomon and Tulava kept pace with the solid wall of ten Alpha Legionnaires in Tactical Dreadnought armour, and so had little to fear from the gunfire that still flashed out at them. It was overkill – a single squad could have taken the palace with ease, and against such mortal opponents, Solomon might have managed it on his own – but it was all part of the plan for a decisive strike.

Massed bolter fire annihilated the defenders. There was no resistance to speak of: they fell back, or they fell in pieces. The Alpha Legion advanced at a steady pace, and the humans could do nothing to even slow them. Solomon fired his bolter only once after they passed through the first wing of the main building and into the private gardens beyond. He let his daemon arm guide his hand, and the bolt-shell found its mark in the skull of a sniper who had been lining up a shot, presumably on Tulava.

The sorceress looked up as his weapon discharged, and then to where a silhouetted body was falling from its vantage point. 'Thank you.'

The central building was where the governor would be holed up. Protective metal shutters had descended over all the windows and doors. They were no match for melta bombs: the Alpha Legion entered the building from all sides, and proceeded to draw the net ever tighter.

They met in the middle, but of the governor, there was no sign.

Solomon looked from the face of one squad leader to another. 'Is there any possibility we could have missed him?'

'Not unless he was dressed like the rest, and shooting a lasgun at us,' Titrik Inshu said. 'Nothing got out of this building once we went in, I would stake my soul on it.'

Solomon knew that Inshu would not make such a statement lightly. The Alpha Legion might not be as deeply embroiled in warpcraft as many of their fellow renegades, but every one of them knew how real the soul was. Quite what awaited Solomon's soul after his death, he was not sure: he had never walked in the supposed light of the Emperor, but nor had he courted the favour of the Ruinous Powers. He supposed he was destined for torment one way or the other. All the more reason to put off dying for as long as possible.

He activated his vox again, raising the squads outside. 'This is Akurra. Has there been any movement fleeing the palace?'

The reports came back in the negative, and Solomon bit down on a curse. The governor was not vital – no part of a good plan was vital – but finding him would greatly benefit them. He had important command codes that would open armouries, activate the planet's most powerful weapons systems, and allow the Legion to take control of the orbital defence stations.

Tulava sighed. 'Find me someone who's still alive.'

Qorru Vayzia turned his helm to look at her. 'What?'

'I need one of them who's not dead yet,' Tulava said, gesturing at a couple of the broken, blood-spattered bodies of defenders who had fallen in their last-ditch defence of, apparently, nothing. 'Still breathing? You and your Astartes senses will find one quicker than I can.'

Vayzia's voice took on a note of anger. 'Listen to me, witch–'

'Do it,' Solomon said.

The Penitent Sons found her one in under a minute: a guard who was unconscious from loss of blood, and would surely be dead within a minute or two, but whose life still barely fluttered in her chest. Tulava dipped the first two fingers of her right hand into the wound that was killing the other woman, then began to chant.

Solomon felt the temperature drop, and tasted burned sugar on his tongue again. Tulava lifted her bloodied fingers up, then drew them down over her opened eyes, still reciting a chant in the same tongue-twisting language.

Her eyes burned with blue fire, and she looked around, then smiled.

'Move.'

The warriors of Inshu's squad did not need to be told: they stepped aside. Tulava reached out with her bloodied hand, changed the cadence of her chant, and twisted her fingers through the air.

A section of the room's wall crumpled and fell aside, revealing itself to be a concealed door. Beyond it lay a passage, lit only by dim, dust-covered lumens. A set of fresh footprints in the dust of the floor indicated where someone had passed through it recently.

Solomon noticed Qorru Vayzia exchanging glances with another member of his squad. Clearly, a witch who could pull walls down with her mind was one they might think twice about antagonising.

'You can't fit down there, can you?' Tulava asked Solomon conversationally. Solomon shook his head.

'Not even without my armour.'

'I guess this part's up to me, then,' Tulava sighed. She rolled her shoulders, producing a clicking noise from the left one.

'He may well take his own life rather than cooperate,' Qorru Vayzia warned. Tulava smiled at him as she stepped into the passageway.

'Don't worry. I don't need all of him.'

THE ENEMY OF MY ENEMY

The hospitality of the Silver Templars had been somewhat lacking: mainly in actual hospitality. That was unsurprising, Hart supposed, since the only baseline humans that the Space Marines were used to accommodating were their Chapter-serfs, who endured a spartan standard of living. The governor's palace on Qampar, capital planet of the Psyphos Subsector, was far more comfortably appointed. Hart had graciously accepted the use of a small suite of rooms: nothing too opulent, but at least the bed was softer than the floor, and the food tasted of something.

In fact, it tasted very good indeed. He was just sitting down to supper, having taken a small sample of each dish with his poison-sniffer – since the appearance of an inquisitor could sometimes provoke strong reactions, both from those who actively wished to see them dead and those who simply wanted someone else to catch the consequences for it – when there was a rapping at his chamber door.

'Come,' he said, tapping the rings on his right hand to activate the digi-lasers set within. He did not deactivate them when the door opened to admit Nessa Karnis.

'Inquisitor Karnis,' Hart said, picking up his goblet. 'To what do I owe this interruption?'

Karnis strode across the carpet towards him, letting the door swing shut behind her with the gentlest of clicks. 'How did you know the Alpha Legion were going to attack the Psyphos Subsector?'

Hart paused with his goblet halfway to his mouth. 'The phrasing of your question suggests that this is no longer theoretical. Are we under attack?'

'The Beharis System has fallen,' Karnis said bluntly, stopping at the other end of the small table from which he had been about to dine.

'Fallen?' Hart repeated. 'Already? I had not been informed of a conflict.'

'It barely deserved the name,' Karnis said, with a derisive sniff. She eyed his rings. 'Are you going to incinerate me if I have the temerity to sit?'

Hart waved a hand. 'Feel free, so long as you keep your mind inside your own skull and use your tongue to talk, like a civilised person.'

Karnis gave him a flat stare, but pulled out one of the luxuriously upholstered chairs and sank into it with a puff of breath that was somewhere between a sigh and a grunt. She was old, Hart realised suddenly: centuries old, just like him. Juvenat treatments, high-end bionics, and the sort of ferocious willpower that all inquisitors carried at their core could drag a human body forward for far longer than nature had originally intended, but even those measures had their limits. Hart could still move like he had done in his distant youth, when he needed to, but there was always a price to pay afterwards, and an ache in his bones that never left him.

'So far as we can ascertain, Beharis Delta fell in a matter of hours,' Karnis said wearily. She reached out to pick up a candied vehrum fruit, and popped it into her mouth. 'It seems that the traitors infiltrated the control tower at the main space port and prioritised the landing of certain bulk haulers from orbit, which turned out to contain Alpha Legion mechanised elements. They struck at the heart of the principal cities and wiped out the chain of command. Planetary officials, senior military officers, everyone.'

Hart took a mouthful of wine. 'I thought our doughty Silver Templar allies had been busy impressing on everyone the importance of being ready for an attack?' Lieutenant Malfax had taken his watchdog assignment with the sort of stolid acceptance that would have constituted a furniture-smashing tantrum in anyone with less devotion to duty than a member of the Adeptus Astartes, and he and the fifty or so Space Marines under his command had spent the last three months trying to make improvements to the defences of the various systems in the subsector.

'The Alpha Legion announced themselves as Iron Snakes, and claimed the governor and other senior officials were heretics,' Karnis told him. She poured herself a goblet of wine without asking, but Hart didn't stop her. 'With the military briefed for an attack by traitors, it seems a fair percentage of them decided that the traitors must already be in charge. By the time they realised their mistake, the damage had been done. Assuming it was a mistake, and they weren't heretics already,' she added grimly.

'If only we hadn't been concerned about the impact on morale of giving the officer corps details of the faction we believed was likely to attack,' Hart said mildly. 'Perhaps then the Alpha

Legion's subterfuge would have been more easily penetrated, leading to less confusion.'

Karnis glared at him. They had argued bitterly over that detail, with Hart pressing for greater transparency and Karnis insisting that only the highest echelons should even hear the Alpha Legion's name. Hart had eventually backed down, when he became concerned that they could no longer pass their wrangling off as professional disagreement in front of the subsector governor and the Silver Templars lieutenant. The Inquisition's authority hinged on any individual inquisitor being seen to enact the will of the Emperor. If two inquisitors were known to be in direct opposition, how could they both be embodying His will? Better to preserve the appearance and reputation of his ordo to ensure future cooperation from others, rather than argue so ferociously over details that both he and Karnis risked losing any influence whatsoever.

'There's another inhabited planet in that system, is there not?' he continued, when Karnis did not rise to the bait. 'Beharis Beta?'

'There are mining teams present on almost all of the rocky planets and moons,' Karnis corrected him primly. 'But yes, Beharis Beta is the other main population centre, and the seat of the system governor. They dispatched their fleet in force as soon as the first distress signals arrived. They were unaware at that point of the nature of the threat, and that no identified Alpha Legion vessels were actually in orbit around Beharis Delta, since the traitors made landfall in captured Imperial vessels.'

'I can see where this is going,' Hart said gloomily. He picked up a roasted tennek leg and bit into it with slightly more force than was truly required. 'The Alpha Legion warfleet came in from the edge of the system once the Beharis fleet had been dispatched?'

'From behind the star, actually,' Karnis replied. 'They must have calculated their angle of approach to avoid or target the sensor relays that would have picked them up. The Beharis fleet got to Delta and found no way of attacking the Alpha Legion without bombarding the planet essentially at random, and were then engaged and largely destroyed by the orbital defence platforms and planet-based batteries, which the traitors had seized. The Alpha Legion's fleet, including that accursed space hulk, overwhelmed and corrupted Beharis Beta's orbital defences, which was when Beta thought to actually call for help from their neighbouring systems rather than trying to deal with the problem themselves – I was with Governor Alzyn when the first transmission came through. However, the Beharis ruling class are genetically bred for command, and the last transmission we received, a mere hour or so later, spoke of a virus bomb attack from orbit releasing a pathogen that was almost immediately fatal to them, but left their underlings untouched.'

Hart sighed. An inquisitor grew somewhat inured to mass loss of Imperial life – in some situations, they were the cause of it – but the incompetence of others exacted its own toll on his mental well-being. 'What a mess. I presume the governor intends to send a task force?'

'The speed and manner of the system's fall has made everyone cautious,' Karnis said. 'Lieutenant Malfax has been in touch from the *Dawnblade*, and urged against committing too much too quickly, given what happened when Beharis Beta tried the same thing with their fleet. Alzyn concurs.'

'Giving the Alpha Legion time to consolidate their position, should they choose to do so.' Hart finished his tennek leg and took another sip of wine. 'Inaction allows them as much time as they need, overzealousness has the potential to play into their hands. As ever, the trap they set for us is as much made from our own minds as it is their capabilities.'

'Malfax is now angry that we paid so much heed to the increased cult activity within the Lilliath System,' Karnis said, and took a gulp of her own wine. 'He thinks we should have recognised it as a decoy.'

Hart raised his eyebrows. 'The lieutenant said that?'

'Well, not in so many words,' Karnis admitted. 'But you know how Astartes are. You learn to read them after a while.'

Hart snorted a laugh. 'Very true. Did you explain to him that had we ignored it, and focused our attention elsewhere, it is likely that it would have turned into a catalysing force for an Alpha Legion attack after all?'

'I did not,' Karnis admitted. She gave him a crooked smile. 'You know how Astartes are.'

'I do.' *And I know how you are, too,* Hart thought. *An attempt to bring back our camaraderie of old, before we trod such different paths? This is something I trust less than outright hostility.*

Nonetheless, something within him ached for that camaraderie. Their time together under Druman had been hard, and at times desperate. Both of them had been broken and rebuilt, as they saw the true horrors that the galaxy had to offer, and steeled themselves to face them. However, there had been a kinship born of shared experience in that. Hart had once entertained notions that he and Karnis might remain close throughout their careers – trusted allies, each knowing that they could turn to the other for support in times of need, despite the knowledge that their work would inexorably lead them down different routes.

But when he realised that the Imperium was flawed and needed rebalancing in order to bring it back into line with how the Emperor must have intended it to be, and that Nessa Karnis still clung to the idea that everything was unfolding according to the Emperor's plan... Well, there was nothing he could do. That was the sort of schism that would prise apart any friendship.

'So,' Karnis said, after a few pregnant moments. 'You did not answer my initial question, Kayzen. How *did* you know that the Alpha Legion would attack the Psyphos Subsector?'

I hope you are usually more subtle than this with your manipulations, Hart thought, hiding a smile behind the napkin with which he wiped his mouth, *else the Imperium's foes will lead you a merry dance.*

Still, perhaps subtlety was not required. Throne help him, but Hart missed having someone in whom he could confide. Deema Varrin was a thoroughly able seneschal, but while she was ferociously capable in the realm of numbers and logistics, and able to ease his work by effortlessly absorbing and relaying the local laws and customs of anywhere they might travel, she lacked much in the way of imagination. She understood her job, but when Hart had tried to speak with her about his own work, she had mainly just stared blankly: so far as Varrin was concerned, if the inquisitor wanted her to listen, then she would listen, but she was neither required nor particularly able to formulate an opinion on such things. Tythus Yorr was better in that regard, but suffered from the problem common to many Space Marines of seeing most things in relation to physical combat. Besides, at the end of the day, he was not fully human, and it was humanity that Hart was entrusted with protecting.

He sighed, and pulled out a data-slate. His thumbprint called up what he had been studying before, and he slid it across the table to Karnis. 'There. Downreach.'

'Downreach? The second moon?' Karnis frowned, and began to scroll down the screen. She stopped after a second or two, and looked back up at him. 'Kayzen, what is this?'

'The moon, yes – or more precisely, the shadow directory Ordo Malleus storage facility upon it,' Hart said. 'I only discovered its existence a few years ago, mainly by chance. I half suspect the inquisitor or inquisitors who commissioned it passed on without entrusting the details of it to anyone else. It appears that entire protocols exist for its maintenance and security, including the hiring of personnel, without anyone concerned knowing the true nature of what they're guarding, or even to whom they ultimately answer.'

'And what are they guarding?' Karnis asked. 'Don't tell me to look at the list, Kayzen – summarise.'

'With regard to the Alpha Legion, and why I think their ultimate goal will be to assault Downreach, take a look at artefact three-nine-seven-kappa,' Hart told her. 'No, look for yourself. I don't want to influence your impression of the listing one way or another.'

Karnis looked at him for a long moment, but then returned her attention to the data-slate and typed in the entry. Hart knew when she found it, because her face adopted the studious blankness that it gained whenever she was reading something intently. He remembered it from their long sessions together, devouring texts on the nature of the enemy they were fighting, in wherever Druman had dragged them to this time: Emperor-forsaken hellhole; palatial, upper-class manse; or any number of places in between.

It was a simple enough entry: four lines of text, descriptive without being evocative. It was dry and factual, and would mean nothing to anyone without the right knowledge. To such a person, however, it would mean a great deal indeed. In its own way, the entry itself was the very essence of the Alpha Legion.

Nessa Karnis read it, and then read it again. Then she swallowed.

'Is this what I think it is?'

'I have not been to the facility to inspect it,' Hart admitted. 'However, your reaction suggests to me that my own was not just wishful thinking.'

'Wishful thinking?' Karnis pushed the data-slate back towards him. 'I can't imagine why you would want to see this resurface.'

Hart waved a hand. 'A figure of speech. I cannot imagine how long this has been *somewhere*, archived and mouldering. Was it misidentified once? Did it get misfiled? Was its true nature deliberately obfuscated when it was first interred, with the intention that with no accurate record, it could never be found again?' He shrugged. 'We will most likely never know. But I believe that for all the excellent tactical reasons the Alpha Legion could have for attacking this subsector, this' – he tapped the data-slate – 'is their true reason. Or at least, a reason as true as any other, and the reason why they decided to come here instead of, as you pointed out aboard the *Purity's Edge*, any number of different locations which would equally serve those other purposes.'

Nessa Karnis sat back and studied him. Hart found the experience surprisingly uncomfortable. It was the novelty of it, he realised: most people actively sought to avoid an inquisitor's gaze, lest they be punished for a crime imagined or, indeed, very real. It had been centuries since he had been used to someone who knew his true identity having the nerve to simply look at him, without explanation, apology, or excuse.

'So what should we do about it?' she asked, after a few more seconds had passed.

Hart did not comment on her use of 'we'. If she had finally decided that he might know what he was talking about, so much the better. 'I predicted the attack on the subsector. This has been borne out. Although I regret that I was correct, hopefully we can now trade off the accuracy of that prediction to ensure that the moon is appropriately defended. The traitors will strike there at some point, I am certain of it.'

Karnis tapped her index fingers together thoughtfully. 'Should we not remove the artefact concerned?'

Hart shook his head. 'Think about it, Nessa. If this is what has lured them here, then there is every risk that our removal of it would be noticed. At the moment, we have one solid prediction for what our enemy will do, even if we don't know when or how – if we change the layout of the board, we may find the game changed on us in turn. There is no safe play here, but I feel we must see this through. The Psyphos System has sufficient resources to repel even an Alpha Legion force of magnitude, so long as we don't end up fighting shadows. We are strong, and they must come to us.'

Karnis pursed her lips, but finally nodded. 'Very well, Kayzen. You are much changed from when we were interrogators together, and hardly for the better, I would say. But, your instincts are still good. Thank you for extending this trust to me. We must work together to ensure the Alpha Legion take no more territory, and are sorely punished for what they have already done.'

Hart smiled, and nodded. 'I agree. They are a slippery foe, but we will break them in the end.'

Karnis finished her wine with a single gulp, then set the goblet back down and nodded to him. 'In which case, I believe our combined presence will be useful to assist in shaping the forthcoming strategy of Governor Alzyn and Lieutenant Malfax.'

Hart rose with her, and they made their way to the door of his chamber together.

THE RUSTBLOODS

Success begets success. That was an adage as true in the theatre of war as it was in so many other contexts.

The fall of the Beharis System was fast, brutal, and comprehensive. The Alpha Legion under Solomon's command had not actually killed that many people, in the grand scheme of things; it was the identity of the deceased that mattered. High-ranking officials, military commanders, and senior members of the Ecclesiarchy had all been wiped away by swift surgical strikes – and even, to Solomon's surprised pleasure, an incredibly precise virus, courtesy of the Sons of Venom. The remaining population had in no way all converted to worshipping the Ruinous Powers, but they were rudderless and leaderless, and the coordination of their resistance had been effectively broken.

'*Everything is proceeding ahead of schedule, Lord Akurra,*' the human known as Tolly Krace reported from one knee, appearing on the bridge of the *Unseen* via a communication hololith. Krace was a factor of the Faceless, but it turned out that his history of crime and smuggling had left him with a good working knowledge of where important resources were located, and he had proved to be highly capable in matters of logistics, as well as almost entertainingly ruthless. Solomon had had to break him from his habit of addressing all legionnaires as 'Lord Alpharius', but other than that, the man was a useful find.

Solomon inspected his data-slate, taking the details in at a glance, then passed it to Roek Ghulclaw and dismissed Krace by the simple measure of flicking a switch. The commander of the Guns of Freedom studied the read-out, then nodded. 'Good. This will go a long way to resupplying my forces.'

'But not ours. Promethium will fuel our vehicles, and we can eat mortal rations as well as we can our own, but we need bolter rounds and ceramite plating, not las power packs and flak vests,' said today's Alpharius. Solomon was still struggling to tell them apart, but it was more force of habit than anything else. Whichever member of the Faceless represented them at any given time, they apparently had the authority to do so, and that was all that mattered.

'Which dictates our choice of next target,' Solomon said. He was not actually intending to give anyone else a say in the matter, but so long as it fulfilled the needs of his warband, he was unlikely to hear much in the way of dissent. He called up the display on the tactical hololith and a slightly fuzzy, translucent image of a planet winked into life. 'Anthras. The heart of the Anthras System, which is itself situated at the mouth of the Angel's Way, a stable warp route into the heart of Ultramar.'

'And which is a forge world of the Adeptus Mechanicus,' said Alpharius.

'Anthras supplies at least six Imperial Space Marine Chapters,' Solomon pointed out. 'Its forges and stores contain enough materiel to sustain us for a year or more of incessant warfare, especially now we have the captured ships from the Beharis System to act as carriers.'

'It is protected by the Legio Regis, amongst other measures,' Alpharius said, highlighting the crowned cogwheel icons dotted about the planet's surface. 'You would have us go up against a Titan legion? We do not have the capability.'

'Not in a straight fight,' Solomon agreed. 'Although the main strength of the Legio marches with the Indomitus Crusade, and those engines left behind are primarily under repair. Still, we are not Iron Warriors or Death Guard. We do not need to throw ourselves into a head-on conflict if it is not to our benefit to do so.' He activated his vox. 'Tul, would you send our new guests in?'

'*Gladly,*' Tulava Dyne replied in his ear, her voice laced with distaste. One of the doors onto the bridge hissed open, and in walked an atrocity.

It was huge: or rather, it was not huge, being somewhere between a bike and a Rhino in size, but it was huge in the context of a ship's bridge. It had seven legs – four down one side, and three on the other – and moved with an uneven, jerky gait that nonetheless promised deadly speed when required. Its mechatendrils writhed and coiled as it stalked forward, for this was a creature made of metal and animated by diabolical energy, and the muzzles of the powerful guns protruding from its back kept twitching from one place to another, constantly covering all angles.

Atop it sat something that was arguably even worse.

The Helstalker was a daemon engine, and it was fearsome indeed, but more fearsome still was the mind that commanded it. The Alpha Legionnaire in question looked down at Solomon from his mount's back, and inclined his helmet ever so slightly.

Four pallid human wretches pushed forward to stand in

front of their master. Their eyes had been replaced by optical sensors and their mouths with vox-grilles, their legs with tracked units and their arms with clawed cybernetics, all of which melded with their remaining flesh in ways that the eye could not quite comprehend. Solomon could see wires and corrugated tubing beneath their flesh where veins would normally run.

'All hail Xettus Qeele the Metalphage, Lord Discordant, and lord of the Rustbloods,' the human thralls barked, growled, and squealed through their vox-grilles, the edges of the synthetic words bleeding with static and unpleasant harmonies. The effect put Solomon in mind of someone running a dirty, greasy finger down his spinal column.

The Rustbloods were a powerful force. The Metalphage was a heretek hunted by the Adeptus Mechanicus, and was steeped in the mysteries of the New Mechanicum. The Space Marines under his command were more closely aligned to that mirror of the Imperium's Machine Cult than they were to the Alpha Legion, but it was in the Alpha Legion that they had their origin, and it was the Alpha Legion's colours they wore. Xettus had ignored the original call to council aboard the *Unseen*, but word of Solomon's conquest of the Beharis System had spread quickly, and the Rustbloods had smelled the metaphorical blood in the water.

Success begets success.

Solomon eyed the Helstalker, then looked up to meet Xettus' helmet lenses. 'I take it that you wished to make an impression.'

'I could have left my mount unfettered in the bowels of this craft,' Xettus declared. The natural tone of his voice was surprisingly rich, but it was also laced with the snarl and hiss of scrap code. 'All may not have been as I left it once I returned, however.'

'Hear me, warpsmith,' called Krozier Va'kai from the captain's throne. 'The *Unseen* may have been attended by the New Mechanicum, but it is not given over to your corruption, and I am increasingly attuned to its systems. If I get a whiff of your code in its cogitators, I will destroy you. Is that clear?'

Xettus' crested helm turned towards Va'kai briefly, then back to Solomon. 'You brought me here to threaten me?'

'My captain's words are no threat,' Solomon said, 'simply a promise. You are a predator of machines, but we are content with our systems the way they are. The forge world of Anthras, on the other hand, is a target for which your talents are eminently well suited.'

Xettus' helm expelled a squall of static which might have been a disdainful sniff. 'Your initial message said as much. Ceramite. Mass-reactive munitions. You scrabble at the lock of a treasure chest, but you intend to take only the dross.'

'I do not preclude more esoteric methods of waging war,' Solomon informed him, 'but our basic requirements must be fulfilled. Neither you nor we can take Anthras with only the resources currently at our disposal: we cannot neutralise the defence systems and the great war engines, you lack the numbers and power to counteract its more mundane armies. If we act in accordance with each other, the forge world will fall. So long as we get what we want, you may indulge yourself to your hearts' content in whatever hidden mysteries the tech-priests of Anthras are sitting on.'

'Assuming you still have hearts,' put in Jarvul Glaine of the Shrouded Hand.

Xettus did not react to Glaine's jab, although the Helstalker's mechatendrils lashed a little more fiercely for a second or two. The daemon engine's head barely qualified for the term, and the glassy red orbs that seemed to serve it as eyes had no iris or pupil to give any indication of which direction it was looking, but Solomon was getting the distinct impression that it was focused on his bionic arm. This was partly because the daemon bound within his limb was reacting in a way he had never experienced before.

It almost felt... afraid.

'The Titans,' Xettus said eventually.

'What about them?' Solomon asked.

'They are mine,' the Metalphage declared. 'Regardless of whether our arrangement continues, whether we conquer more worlds or go our separate ways forever, the Titans are mine.'

'Done,' Solomon said. 'You may destroy them or take control of them as you will.'

'And I will have command of the attack,' Xettus said, eagerly.

'No.'

The four-strong chorus of altered humans hissed in displeased static as their master was contradicted, but Solomon stared Xettus down without flinching.

'I am Harrowmaster here,' he said. 'I was selected for this role by my peers, and I vindicated that choice with the triumph over Beharis. I will not relinquish that authority to a newcomer.'

'Beharis is a backwater system of miners and grain farmers,' Xettus growled. 'It is not a forge world, and it does not have a forge world's defences!'

'All the more reason not to give overall command of the assault on a forge world to a warrior whom we know only by reputation,' Solomon said firmly. 'You refused our initial invitation, so you are an auxiliary to this operation, albeit one who stands to be well rewarded from his involvement. Should everything proceed to our mutual benefit, then there may be a place for the Rustbloods with us, if you wish to ally your cause to ours. For now, I will take your counsel, but the command remains with me.'

Xettus said nothing for long enough that Solomon was half sure he was going to refuse. However, if the Metalphage was waiting for a break in the ranks before him, he was to be disappointed: none of the other commanders spoke up to voice dissatisfaction with Solomon's pronouncement. Eventually, Xettus inclined his head once.

'So be it. I shall begin constructing an electrogheist to bring down the defence systems.' He turned, manoeuvring his Helstalker adroitly given its size, and made for the bridge door with his altered retinue trailing behind him. Solomon caught a glimpse of Tulava's unimpressed expression as the lord of the Rustbloods stalked through the doorway, before it closed behind him again.

'You entrust such a dangerous individual to your witch?' asked Keros Asid.

'Tulava is formidable,' Solomon assured the rest of them, 'and carries nothing with a machine-spirit. The Metalphage might even succeed in turning our weapons or armour against us, but although she is physically weaker, Tulava is in some ways less vulnerable to him than we would be.'

'He has less than thirty Space Marines with him,' Alpharius declared. 'He has a high opinion of himself, for someone whose command is so limited.'

'I command merely six Astartes,' Roek Ghulclaw said, a tone of menace wrapping around his voice. 'Do you wish to measure yourself against the Guns of Freedom?'

'Peace,' Solomon said wearily. 'The Rustbloods' power does not lie in the number of our battle-brothers who march with them, but in their mastery of machinery. Their war machines and daemon engines are valuable on their own, let alone the New Mechanicum's ability to make a mockery of our enemies' systems.'

'You should not have let him lay claim to the Titans,' Raelin Amran declared. 'That was poorly done.'

'We stand no chance of securing them without him,' Solomon replied. 'If he can turn some of them, and bring them to our side for future engagements, so much the better. If he tries to hold Anthras for himself, or ventures off on his own with his captured god-machines, he becomes a useful distraction to further divide the Imperium's attention, especially since they will have no way of knowing that he is not a part of our greater plan.'

Amran subsided, but Solomon did not ignore his words. He kept an eye on the lord of the First Strike while he outlined his plan of attack on Anthras. So too did he keep an eye on Roek Ghulclaw, and Jarvul Glaine, and Alpharius, and Keros Asid, and the other commanders of factions both large and small.

The Alpha Legion made the most of any opportunity that presented itself, and Solomon had no intention of being someone else's opportunity.

WHITE-OUT

'Are we sure we need to be here?' Tulava Dyne yelled over the blizzard and the noise of weapons fire. The icy, snow-laden gale whisked her words away as soon as they were spoken, carrying them up into the dark sky of Anthras' northern polar region.

'Xettus was insistent that this was the best location from which to corrupt the forge world's governing machine-spirit,' Solomon replied. He needed to put little effort into his voice, since it was boosted by the vox-amplifier within the beaked helm of his Mark VI armour.

'Then allow me to rephrase my question!' Tulava shouted, as a new volley of galvanic rifle shot fizzed by overhead, cutting a brief swathe through the billowing snow. 'Are we sure that *I* need to be here?'

'Surely a powerful sorceress like you is not afraid of a little snow?' Solomon chided. He reached around the ferrocrete block behind which they were sheltering and let the daemon in his arm guide his shots. His bolter barked three times, and he knew without looking that each one had found its mark and dropped one of the skitarii firing on their position.

'That's easy for you to say, in all your get-up!' Tulava snapped. She was swaddled in cold-weather gear, with goggles over her eyes and thermal cloth wrapped over her nose and mouth, but even with her expression entirely hidden, she still managed to radiate an aura of utter misery. 'I don't know how much use a sorceress is going to be when she can't feel her fingers!'

'Can't you call on one of the gods to take your suffering from you?' suggested Attas, the Harrower of Solomon's Lernean Terminator bodyguard.

'That's not a bargain I'm prepared to make yet,' Tulava said, with a shudder that Solomon suspected had nothing to do with the temperature. 'I'm not here because I'm sworn to the Ruinous Powers, I'm here because the Imperium has to pay for what it did to my family!'

'The Changer cares not what you think your motivations are,' Attas declared. He straightened up to let rip with a blast of combi-bolter fire and took three galvanic rifle shots in return, which did nothing to damage his armour, then lowered himself back into cover with a whine of servos. 'All purposes serve him.'

'This is not the time for a theological debate,' Solomon said. The Serpent's Teeth had never been amongst the particularly devout, but it was inevitable that individuals would find their way into the worship of Chaos from time to time. For some that took the form of Chaos Undivided, whereas others might find a particular patron. It appeared Attas had devoted himself to the Changer of Ways. There were certainly worse options, to Solomon's mind – the Harrower was unlikely to start killing his comrades to satisfy the urges of the Blood God, or develop a contagion that might kill others who lacked the blessing of Nurgle – but it was still worth keeping an eye on. Solomon had seen warriors overwhelmed by the power of Tzeentch dissolve within seconds into a monstrous flesh-thing with myriad fanged maws, and grasping tentacles which dripped acid that could eat right through ceramite.

'I agree,' Tulava said, with feeling. 'How about we concentrate on getting out of this warp-forsaken weather before my hands drop off?'

Solomon stole a glance at the enemy's position. 'They are too well dug-in for us to assault them, and they are not taking the bait.'

The plan had been reasonably simple: advance on the skitarii position, pretend to withdraw under heavy fire, and draw a counter-charge onto the explosives with which the Alpha Legion had mined the ground before they even committed to the dummy attack. It was a tactic with a high chance of success, since the Adeptus Mechanicus approached the concept of heretics setting foot on their sacred worlds with just as much fanaticism as that displayed by the most ardent worshipper of the Chaos gods. The tech-priest in command was unlikely to be content with sitting safely in cover and taking potshots, when there was an apparently disorganised enemy within reach.

The problem was, while the sub zero temperatures were no real concern to Solomon and his power-armoured warriors, they did have an impact on the nature of the engagement. The massed ranks of the Guns of Freedom lacked both the fully enclosed power armour of the Astartes, and the skitarii's various cybernetic enhancements; they would suffer just as much as Tulava, if not more so, and had insufficient cold-weather gear to function here. The Alpha Legion's human troops were being put to use fighting in the planet's more temperate zones, so choking the defenders of this node with weight of numbers was out. The blizzard's vicious gusts and crosswinds meant that air support was impractical, and the First Strike's jump pack tactics were similarly negated. Their assault squads were grounded and, from what Solomon could tell, increasingly chafing at the lack of combat. The Adeptus Mechanicus were no fools, either: the control node was covered by a teleport jammer, so even a shock assault by the Lerneans was out of the question.

'Perhaps they are relying on waiting us out,' Attas suggested. 'They may think we will risk everything to achieve a swift end to this engagement.'

Solomon considered this, and disregarded it. 'No, if they are waiting for something then it will be something specific. The priesthood of Mars are only patient under certain circumstances, and this would not be one of them.'

'Which implies we should make a move before whatever it is occurs,' Attas pointed out.

'I definitely agree with that,' Tulava put in.

Solomon considered. He had nearly a company's worth of Alpha Legionnaires here, by Imperial reckonings, which was a potent force indeed: three of what might have been termed as tactical squads, two from the Serpent's Teeth and one from the Penitent Sons; a full twenty of the First Strike's assault troops; his Serpent's Teeth Lernean bodyguard; the eight Havocs from the Soulfangs; and the twenty-four Astartes warriors of the Rust-bloods, along with Lord Xettus Qeele himself, and a detachment of their own skitarii. It was a well-armed and well-armoured force, and he had no doubt that they could punch through the killing ground currently covered by the weapons of the node's defenders. The question was how many lives it would cost them, because even Space Marines were not invulnerable to sufficient weight of fire. Besides, Solomon would hardly continue to impress his fellow commanders if a force he led had been cut to ribbons conducting a frontal assault. However, his options were limited: sometimes subterfuge failed, and the Alpha Legion had to fall back on their most basic nature.

His helm's audio receptors picked up the *swish-swish-swish* of multiple mechanical legs moving through snow moments before the faintest hint of static interference crept in around the edges of his vision. The dark shape of Xettus loomed up out of the flurrying whiteness, his chainglaive balanced across his shoulders.

'What is the delay, Lord Akurra?' Xettus asked, his voice crackling through the vox. Solomon's organic ears had not reacted to the Metalphage's voice, but the link seemed to vibrate as it delivered his words.

'An unexpected reluctance to engage on the part of the Mechanicus,' Solomon replied. 'You know this foe the best, Lord Xettus – is there some way in which you can provoke them?'

'Fewer than a thousand of the enemy stand between us and our goal,' Xettus declared. 'Do you fear death, Harrowmaster?'

'There is a difference between not fearing something, and not rushing to embrace it,' Solomon said sharply. What was it about those who had given themselves over to the influence of the Ruinous Powers that made them so eager to spend their lives in the pursuit of whichever cause they were a part of today? 'We are outnumbered ten to one, and our enemy has a significant heavy weapons presence. We might reach the control node that is your target, but the impact on our force would mean that such a venture would hardly be defined as a success.'

'Reaching the control node is the only criteria by which success can be measured,' Xettus said. 'Access to the forge world's machine-spirit is everything, Harrowmaster.'

Solomon silently cursed the very notion of an Alpha Legionnaire who had lost any grasp of subtlety. Still, he had been eager to work Xettus and his following into the Alpha Legion's plans, and so it behoved him to deal with the consequences of that decision. The Rustbloods' skitarii were just as able to deal with the weather and terrain as their Mechanicus counterparts, at least, and would not slow down an advance. If he sent them ahead to soak up the initial enemy fire–

'Lord Akurra, there is a big contact on the auspex, moving in from the north-west.'

That was Titrik Inshu over the vox. Solomon instinctively looked in the direction indicated, but his armour's senses were useless beyond a couple of hundred feet thanks to the howling blizzard, let alone the ridges and dips of the frozen landscape and its snowdrifts.

'How big a contact, and what manner? A flanking force?' he asked.

'Difficult to tell, lord, this accursed weather seems to be affecting the equipment, but I think–'

The blizzard roared, but it was no longer just the voice of the wind.

'Titan!' Solomon shouted, as part of the dark polar horizon took a lurching step. This was what the Mechanicus had been waiting for, and he had sat still long enough for it to get into position and trap them.

The massive shape lit up with searchlights that speared out through the night and the storm, piercing the twin veils of darkness and snow. They picked out the Alpha Legion where they were sheltering from the ongoing fire pouring from the Adeptus Mechanicus position, now caught between the hammer and the anvil. The god-machine was still perhaps half a mile away, but that was no distance at all for the mighty weapons it carried. In contrast, the Alpha Legion had nothing that could scratch it, even were they within range: the terrain was too rough for the super-heavies such as the Fellblades to have accompanied them, and they had no such walkers of their own.

'Cover!' Solomon yelled, as the carapace-mounted batteries of the Titan opened up, and kicked up massive sprays of dirt, rock, snow, and steam just short of their position. There was precious little cover to be found, that was the problem: there were some ridges between them and the Titan, certainly, but even if the massive war machine's weaponry couldn't punch straight through, it might just bury them in debris. Besides which, by seeking the sparse shelter available from the Titan, they were only revealing themselves to the skitarii and Kataphrons firing on them from their other flank. One member of Third Fang, hurrying for the questionable cover of a rocky overhang, was engulfed in the white-hot blast of a plasma culverin, and died instantly.

'A Warlord,' Xettus said lasciviously, as though the warp-damned thing wasn't about to obliterate them all. It wasn't even one of the smaller kinds, although that would have made little practical difference: no, Solomon was about to get vaporised by the mightiest terrestrial war machine in the Imperium's arsenal, short of the colossal Imperator Titans.

Unless, of course, he got Tulava to warpwalk them out of there. She couldn't move the whole force, of course – he'd not known her to be able to teleport more than one Space Marine, beside herself – but if she and he could get clear, they might yet survive. Even the Mechanicus would struggle to find a pair of renegades, one of them mortal, in the aftermath of this sort of engagement. He could find a way to link up with the other forces still contesting other key regions of the planet, and–

And he would have failed. He would lose his command; he might lose his life, depending on the reactions of the factions whose warriors he would have left to die. The alliance he had brokered would splinter, the Legion would slide back into insularity and infighting, and the Imperium would escape yet again.

Solomon Akurra believed with all that was left of his soul

that he was the best commander the Alpha Legion currently had, and he would either prove that to be true, or he would die.

'All units, prepare to advance on the command node!' Solomon shouted over the vox. Galvanic rifle shots ricocheted around him; he fired back with his bolter, but even his daemonic arm's uncanny accuracy was not going to be enough to guarantee any of them safe passage across the killing ground.

'*Have you lost your mind?*' snarled one of the Soulfangs, the words mushed and distorted by whatever mutating forces had done to his mouth. '*We will surely die!*'

'We cannot fight the Titan!' Solomon snapped. 'We *can* fight the Mechanicus foot troops!' He turned off his vox, and grabbed Tulava's shoulder. 'We need a distraction! Something to grab their attention, even for a few moments, just to give us an edge!'

Tulava raised one gloved hand to shield her goggled eyes from the storm, and peered towards the Mechanicus lines. 'Do you want it clean or dirty?'

'After last time?' Solomon asked. 'I would prefer clean!'

Tulava rolled her shoulders. 'Trick question, I've got nothing clean that can help us here! Hold on to something – this isn't going to be pleasant!'

She spun her force staff through the air, chanting in a brutal tongue Solomon had never heard her utter before, then let out a feral scream and slammed the sharp butt of it down, right through her clothes and into the meat of her thigh. She yanked it out again and spun it once more, still chanting, as flecks of red spun off into the storm and were instantly frozen into ice.

Solomon blinked in confusion. Was that...?

Blood.

The taste of it was suddenly in his mouth, rich and coppery and slightly salty. He had tasted blood before, of course: he had fought without a helm at times during his two hundred years of warfare, and there was no escaping it when bodies were falling around you with wounds inflicted by high-velocity ballistic weapons, or explosive rounds, or chainblades. His Astartes physiology could detect the differences between the blood of baseline humans, Space Marines, xenos species, and more besides. Having tasted someone's blood he could, to a certain degree of accuracy, track them if they were wounded. These were all simple facts, just another part of his experiences.

He had never known blood to taste *good* before.

Solomon tried to speak, but words would not form on his tongue. His tongue itself felt swollen within his mouth, and continually grazed by his teeth as he tried to manoeuvre it around and form the guttural grunts that were all he could give voice to. It would be so easy to do more than just graze it: to bite down, and let the sweet blood flow as his vision clouded with red…

And then, as abruptly as the sensations had flooded through him, they were gone. He could taste nothing more than the faint remnants of his last ration pack, and the slightly stale air of his helmet's recycling systems, his tongue was back to its normal size, and the power of speech was returned to him.

'What,' he began, 'in the name of the primarchs, was th–'

New screams split the air, but these were not from Tulava.

The assault squad of the First Strike, some twenty Space Marines, were screaming. They were falling to the ground and clawing at themselves, or standing rooted to the spot, backs arched and trembling. A galvanic rifle shot ricocheted off the pauldron of one of those so afflicted, to no reaction.

'Tulava,' Solomon said, reaching for his sorceress. 'What is happening?'

Then their armour began to split, and he understood.

Their champion was first. He dropped his weapons as his ceramite breastplate sundered in two, pushed apart from within.

Literally pushed: two black-taloned hands, the skin as red as the fresh blood in which they were coated, wrenched it aside, to allow egress for a narrow, horned head, with eyes that blazed fire. Wiry shoulders followed it, and then the rest of the beast pulled its way clear, like a monstrous insect emerging from a blue-green cocoon. One clawed foot on a backward-jointed leg, steaming in the frigid air, touched down in the snow and stained it crimson, followed by another. A hand reached back into the champion's body, and wrenched out a long, jagged blade of black metal, at an angle from which there would have been no room for it had things been unfolding in accordance with standard physics, rather than the unnatural dimensions of the warp.

The daemon of Khorne raised its head to the snow-whipped heavens, and howled.

Its brethren followed, each one clawing its way out of the vessel that had allowed it entry to this plane of reality, until twenty of the daemons stood steaming in the snow. Long tongues flickered in and out of their pointed muzzles as they cast around for blood, and their eyes began to fall on those who had been the battle-brothers of their host bodies.

Tulava, leaning on her force staff for support, yelled something in the same language she had used to cast the summoning incantation. The daemons tensed as though whipped, then whirled around and began to lope towards the Adeptus Mechanicus lines, their long legs eating up the ground.

'That's… the best I can do,' Tulava panted, staggering sideways. Solomon caught her without effort. 'Can't run. Can't really see, for that matter…'

'It will be enough,' Solomon said. He activated his vox again. 'Detonate the charges! Now, before they get there!'

It took a lot to shock a Space Marine, particularly one who

had lived his life in opposition to the Imperium and been surrounded by the varied natures of those with similar allegiances, but seeing daemons claw their way out of the warriors beside them had pushed those under Solomon's command close to that point. However, someone recovered himself in time to press the detonator, and a thick cloud of steam rose up as hidden melta charges intended to vaporise onrushing skitarii simply did the same thing to the snow under which they had been concealed. The Adeptus Mechanicus fire faltered and became less focused. It was not much of a barrier, and it would only conceal the Alpha Legion part of the way towards the enemy, but it was as much as Solomon could conjure.

'Forward!' he bellowed. 'Hydra Dominatus!'

'*Hydra Dominatus!*' roared the vox back at him, and with the world about them beginning to explode as the Warlord found its range, the Alpha Legion plunged into the teeth of the lesser of two evils.

TAKING CONTROL

There was little to be gained from hanging back where the Titan's guns were more likely to strike. Solomon hoisted the weakly protesting Tulava up over his right shoulder, and charged ahead into the snow and steam with the rest of his troops.

The steam cover did not last long – the howling winds saw to that – but it lasted long enough to achieve at least a part of what Solomon had intended for it. The fire of the Mechanicus, their visual and heat targeting systems both thrown off by the thick white cloud, was less effective and accurate for a few critical seconds. Once the Khornate daemons emerged into view, the defenders of the node had a new problem to wrap their logic circuits around.

Solomon did not trust the New Mechanicum, but at least they would adapt to new knowledge and situations, and actively worked towards innovation. The Adeptus Mechanicus were as hidebound as any priest of the Ecclesiarchy, and could be even more inclined to ignore evidence if it conflicted with their pre-existing worldview. That could sometimes make them annoyingly difficult to distract or fool, but it also made them vulnerable.

The Adeptus Mechanicus knew precious little about daemons: Solomon knew that had to be true, because if they did, Mars would be overrun with them by now thanks to someone's ill-advised experiments. They might understand that traitor war machines had been corrupted somehow, and might even have an idea that the same thing could happen to humans (although most tech-priests were likely to dismiss that as a generalised weakness of the flesh), but actual daemons which had taken form in realspace were something at which the Mechanicus at large would stare in paralysed surprise while they tried to fit them into some sort of known category. A soldier of the Astra Militarum would know instinctively that a daemon was the enemy, and would scream and open fire; a skitarius would waste time trying to identify this being, which did not match parameters for either ally or foe. It would only take a second or so for new subroutines to come online and create the classification of 'Hostile: Other', or similar, but even a second or so could make a crucial difference.

Solomon heard much of the gunfire pause for a couple of moments as the howling Neverborn bounded out of the artificial fog, then start up again as their behaviour clued the defenders into their purpose, even if their identity was a mystery. When the last of the steam was blown away, he got his first view of Khornate daemons in action.

They did not move as normal creatures did. Their strides held no grace or fluidity, for all their long-limbed build, yet they ate up the ground hungrily nonetheless. Their actions were subtly *wrong* somehow, even through the rangefinders of Solomon's helmet, but he knew that it would be the same if he were observing them with his naked eyes. They left bloody footprints behind them, but the creatures seemed almost superimposed upon the landscape of white snow and grey rock, as if they were not truly there. Every now and then one of them would blur or shudder faintly, something entirely unrelated to their progress, and then snap back into a focus so sharp it almost hurt the eye.

The Adeptus Mechanicus fire was focused on the Neverborn now, as the adept in charge realised that unlikely though it might seem, the danger they posed was more immediate than that of the renegade Astartes beyond, but even that firepower did not conform to normal expectations. Solomon saw what must have been the combined output of an entire unit of Kataphron Destroyers engulf one of the daemons in a coruscating ball of plasma and energy that would have been sufficient to incinerate a Dreadnought, but the horned creature loped out the other side without a scorch mark to show for it. In contrast, one of the frontrunners dropped, its pointed skull split by a single galvanic rifle shot. Khorne truly did not care from whence the blood flowed.

Solomon didn't care either, at least not in terms of the daemons. The creatures that had clawed their way out of the First Strike would have a limited amount of time in realspace, no matter how badly Abaddon had wounded the galaxy with the Cicatrix Maledictum. So long as they either soaked up fire that would have otherwise targeted the remaining legionnaires of the Alpha Legion, or made an impact on the Adeptus Mechanicus defensive line – preferably both – he would be happy. Or at least, as happy as he could be when charging into a gunline with a Titan behind him.

'What's Xettus doing?' Tulava shouted, insofar as she could manage that whilst being jolted around by Solomon's frantic pace over the uneven ground. Solomon snatched a glance over his left shoulder and his targeter locked on to the dark shape of the Rustbloods' leader atop his daemon engine mount, still standing where he had been before this charge had begun, even as pulverised rock flew up all around him. However, his skitarii and Astartes were thundering through the snow, so Solomon was not inclined to worry too much about it. Let the Lord Discordant get himself torn to shreds by the Warlord's macro gatling blaster or vaporised by its volcano cannon, assuming he did not have some cunning New Mechanicum trick to hide himself from its targeting auspexes. Given the amount of firepower with which the Warlord was indiscriminately raking the Alpha Legion's former position, the god-machine's ability or otherwise to target him was unlikely to make much difference.

Solomon looked back towards the Adeptus Mechanicus lines, his daemon arm flashing up without thought to intercept a shot that would have otherwise struck his helmet, and he witnessed the Neverborn's charge strike home.

Perhaps two of the beasts' number had fallen to the fusillade of firepower through which they had charged. The daemons' pace accelerated to unnatural speeds now they were within range of their tormentors, and they vaulted into the air almost as though propelled by the jump packs their mortal hosts had been unable to employ. The wind seemed to get no purchase on them, and they flew as straight as any missile to clear the defensive emplacements and land in the midst of the skitarii.

'Tul,' Solomon said. 'Your work has my compliments.'

There were certain warrior-forms employed by the Adeptus Mechanicus which specialised in close combat, but if they were present here, they did not meet the charge of the Neverborn. The daemons howled in murderous joy as their hellblades buried themselves in the bodies of the skitarii, and the blades themselves seemed to sing a dark song as they tasted blood, strange and altered and chemical-laden though it might be. In mere seconds, an entire section of defensive fire winked out as those warriors garrisoning the line were either killed, or became preoccupied with trying to kill the unnatural horrors which had just landed amongst them.

The impact spread out like shockwaves, or ripples caused by a rock thrown into a pool, and Solomon could almost see the defensive machine reorganise itself. With the closest threat now engaged, some of the defenders who had been firing upon the Neverborn's charge now calmly redirected their guns towards the Alpha Legion's second wave, while those directly on either side of the breach in their lines prepared to fire at the daemons should they murder their way through the troops with whom they were currently in combat.

'Left flank!' Solomon yelled over the vox. 'Hit their left flank!'

The Neverborn had struck the Adeptus Mechanicus lines in the middle, with all the directness one might expect of the followers of Khorne. The rest of the Alpha Legion's charge veered to one side, into the teeth of one of the remaining flanks, but away from the guns of the other side, now the centre had been taken out of commission. It was a brutal advance, and Solomon saw half a dozen legionnaires and at least forty of the Rustbloods' skitarii fall, but their own fire was taking its toll as well. There were no better marksmen in the galaxy than the warriors of the Astartes, and even a defensive redoubt such as the one behind which the Anthrasians were sheltering was no guarantee of safety. Nor were they wholly reliant on inhuman accuracy alone: the Havocs of the Soulfangs paused in their advance to steady their weapons and unleash a concentrated hail of fire that obliterated a section of the wall and most of those behind it, punching another gaping hole in the defensive line.

Solomon grinned behind his helmet's faceplate. A crucial

tipping point had passed; the defenders were retreating from this fresh breach, trying to find new and more defensive firing positions, and were on the back foot. He emptied his bolter's magazine, each shot snapping back the head of a skitarius, then mag-clamped it to his thigh and commanded his arm's fingers to extend into their flail form.

'You'd better put me down before you do that!' Tulava raged.

'Can't you heal your wound so you can actually walk?' Solomon demanded, deflecting another incoming shot. 'I've seen you do it before.'

'No!' The motion sensors in his armour actually detected Tulava's shudder at the thought. 'Do you want us all to die? You don't just *heal* a blood offering to Khorne, you overgrown fool!'

Solomon's eyes narrowed. 'I would have the head of any other mortal who spoke to me like that.'

'And any other of your warriors who threatened my life would find his bones breaking within his flesh,' Tulava laughed. 'I gave you your distraction, Solomon – just put me down somewhere safe before you go off and kill things.'

The Alpha Legion let loose with one last volley of supra-accurate bolter fire, shredding the bodies of the nearest skitarii, and charged with power knives drawn. They might not have been dedicated assault troops, but they were superior to the defenders in every way: larger, stronger, better armoured, and more skilful. Solomon dumped Tulava to the ground next to a sizeable pile of still-smoking rubble, and joined his efforts to those of his warriors.

Solomon was a Space Marine; he might not have been bred for combat, but he had been moulded for it since his youth. The methods used to induct neophytes by the Alpha Legion of the 41st millennium likely differed from those of their own history, and almost certainly differed from those practices used by the Chapters in service to the Imperium, but the end result was essentially the same: a knowledge that violence was the only true purpose of their existence. No matter what lineage a Space Marine hailed from, that was always true. However, whether it was the residual influence of the Blood God left over from the ritual which had summoned the Neverborn still wreaking havoc further down the defence line, or the relief of having made it through what could well have been a suicidal charge with a decent portion of his force intact, this combat held a joy above and beyond the usual thrill for Solomon.

He spun and lashed out, and his flail-fingers wrapped around the neck of a skitarius trying to bring its weapon to bear on him. He squeezed, and the razor edges sliced through flesh and metal to decapitate the Mechanicus warrior with a gout of blood. Another flew at him from the side while he was dropping the first, and he punched it in the chest with his other hand. His ceramite-encased fist smashed through the metal of its ribcage and buried itself inside; his fingers closed around some sort of internal organ, and he heaved the spasming skitarius off its feet and into two of its fellows. What turned out to be a heart was ripped out in his fist as the hapless cyborg's body flattened its comrades, and he threw the bloody chunk of metal-laced flesh at yet another, smearing its optical sensors with blood as the heart struck it in the face. The skitarius' wild shot flew wide, and Solomon re-formed his daemon arm into a single long blade, then split its hooded skull with a thrust.

The psychic shout that crashed into his mind was not formed into words: it was just a stark, raw warning. Tulava's talents did not lie in the direction of telepathy, which was why the Imperium had not sent her to the City of Sight, but she could reach into another's brain in a very limited way. The first time she had done so with Solomon, the shock of it had startled him so much he had nearly been killed by the very xenos she had been trying to alert him to. These days, he was better able to control his reactions, and Tulava had learned to slightly refine her sendings.

The images were warped and blurred, little more than hulking shapes with glowing arms, but they were enough. Solomon activated his armour's reflective capabilities, just as the trio of Kataphron Destroyers from farther down the defensive line opened fire.

'Cover!' he yelled again, but there was precious little to be had.

Plasma culverins spat death, and bolts of ravening energy ripped through attacker and defender alike, searing them where they stood. Solomon saw skitarii fall with gaping holes burned right through them, and Space Marines collapse as everything from the waist up was melted into slag. He was hit: intense heat washed over him and bled through the ceramite of his armour, causing red lines to spike on his helmet's read-outs, but the highly reflective scales of his protection did what they were designed to do and shed the worst of the blast. Then he was up and running, weaving through the dead, the dying, and the miraculously untouched.

'Alpha Legion! With me!' he cried. He drew his bolt pistol and fired three rounds at the nearest Destroyer while moving at a dead run. The first one sparked off a section of armour plating, the second shattered the battle-servitor's targeting matrix, and the third blew out the back of the construct's skull. Limited though the guidance provided by the half-dead cranial matter was, the servitor still required it to function, and it immediately drooped.

The other two discharged their primary weapons at him, but Solomon's speed was more than a match for their simplistic targeting programs, and the plasma blasts ripped up the ground behind him. Cognis flamers ignited and Solomon was engulfed in burning promethium, but he burst through it unscathed and launched himself at the nearest servitor.

Kataphron Destroyers were mobile heavy weapons platforms, and were not equipped with melee weapons. The servitor clumsily swiped at him with the still-steaming barrel of its plasma culverin, but Solomon vaulted over it and put two bolt pistol shots into the top of its skull before he had even landed on its tracks. However, the third one was already pivoting around to target its fellow, and the enemy currently balanced atop it. Servitors were not sacred to the Adeptus Mechanicus, not like their precious machines: a servitor would not hesitate to fire on one of its own kind if that was the best way to eliminate an enemy of the Machine Cult. Solomon did not trust the protection of his reflective scales at such close range, and dived aside as the active Destroyer opened fire. Plasma engulfed the servitor he had just killed, melting its armour plating and charring its remaining flesh; then the plasma canister went up, and the polar night briefly turned to day as blistering energy roiled out.

The shockwave slammed into Solomon just as he was rolling back up to his feet, and sent him sprawling. His helmet's lenses automatically shifted down to dull the flash, leaving him virtually unsighted for a moment, but he could hear the remaining Destroyer spinning around to target him again. He raised his bolt pistol and fired the remainder of his clip at the noise: the *spanging* sounds of bolts ricocheting off armour plating told him that his efforts were unsuccessful. His trigger clicked dry just as his lenses cleared to show the battle-servitor's main weapon lining up on him.

A wave of psychic force hit the Destroyer from behind, rocking it on its tracks. Sparks flew as cables were torn loose, and its aim was knocked wayward for a moment, but Tulava Dyne's intervention had not taken the Destroyer down, merely given Solomon a moment's grace.

He did not waste it.

He dropped his bolt pistol and drew his power knife, activated the matter-distorting field with a flick of his thumb, and threw the blade overhand. It flashed through the air and buried itself to the hilt in the battle-servitor's forehead, punching deep into what remained of its brain. It flailed for a few moments, its tracks whirring and its weapons waving uncertainly, before it too lapsed into the stillness of the death its lobotomised core had been denied for so long.

Solomon could hear the howls of the Neverborn on the wind as they continued to kill, farther up the battle line. The explosion of the Kataphron had drawn the attention of some nearby skitarii away from the daemons and towards him, and he hastily reloaded his boltgun as a galvanic rifle shot caromed off his pauldron. He put a shell through each of their skulls, then retreated to retrieve his knife.

'Thank you,' he voxed to Tulava, as he wrenched the blade from the grey flesh of the Destroyer's forehead.

'It seemed unfair for you to have to deal with all three of them by yourself,' the sorceress replied dryly. Solomon tensed as skitarii came filing between the battle-servitors' corpses, moving in their mechanical lockstep, but he relaxed as he realised that these were Rustbloods. They advanced down the defensive line, their guns firing munitions that seemed to suck in what light there was, in marked contrast to the glowing projectiles of the Adeptus Mechanicus. Behind them came Solomon's legionnaires, content for the moment to save their bolt-shells and let the skitarii carry the fight to their Imperial counterparts. With this end of the defences broken, and the Neverborn wreaking havoc in the

centre, the node was as good as secured. All the same, Solomon knew better than to congratulate himself too soon. The priest-hood of Mars were full of unpleasant surprises, and he would not put it past the tech-priest in command of these defences, if they were still operational, to enact some form of self-destruct protocol on the command node rather than let heretics get access to it…

Almost against his will, Solomon's gaze was dragged towards the massive shape of the Warlord Titan.

The god-machine's weapons had chased them across the ground, but had fallen silent when the Alpha Legion reached the Adeptus Mechanicus battle lines. Solomon ignored it after that: he had been too busy killing the enemies immediately around him, and could do nothing about it in any case. Now, however, the massive shape of the Warlord appeared to be rising out of its stationary stance, and Solomon had a vision of the princeps receiving a transmission from whichever tech-priest was in command of the defence, calling its gargantuan fire-power down as a last-ditch sacrificial ploy. He saw the distant points of brightness as energy weapons began to power up.

'We may have a problem,' Tulava panted, struggling up level with the Kataphron Destroyer on which Solomon was still standing.

'Yes,' Solomon agreed. 'We may.' There was nothing to be done: he just had to hope that the rest of the Legion would still manage to take Anthras somehow, and continue driving a knife into the Imperium's rotten heart.

The Warlord roared, its war-horns ringing out through the blizzard.

Then it screamed.

It was a mechanical scream, one of distorted electronics and distressed metal, and at first Solomon could not understand why the enormous machine was making such a noise. Then the dim light reflected on something else metallic, something that appeared to be reaching up from the ground.

'What's going on over there?' Tulava asked, rubbing at her goggles. Solomon kicked up the magnification on his helmet's lenses.

'What in the name of the primarchs…?'

The ground beneath the Warlord had come alive with serpents.

It was hard to judge the scale against the massive shape of the Titan, but Solomon would have guessed that each one was large enough to swallow him whole. His mind wrestled with what he was seeing for a moment, until he realised that his first impression had not been erroneous: they were indeed metal, there were at least four of them, and they were slithering up the Warlord's legs in showers of sparks.

'Is there a reason we're not dead yet?' Tulava asked, her flippant words belied by the tension in her voice. Solomon scanned the ground around the Warlord, and finally found what he was looking for: the dark, multi-limbed shape of Lord Xettus of the Rustbloods, and his many-legged steed.

'It seems Xettus had some daemon engines he did not tell us about,' Solomon said. The serpents had reached the Warlord's waist, and judging by the way the god-machine was trembling, its machine-spirit was under a concerted assault from the warpsmith's creations. Xettus had been very reticent on how exactly he was going to corrupt the Adeptus Mechanicus' planetwide systems; were these machines always intended as a part of that process? Had they come down in one of the Rustbloods' transport ships without Solomon's knowledge, and then burrowed through the snow in his force's wake? Had they teleported? Had they somehow dropped down directly from orbit? Solomon's knowledge of the capabilities of such infernal constructs was limited, but it was lucky for them all that Xettus had them in the right place at the right time.

Unless…

'You treacherous little swine,' Solomon bit out. He turned to Tulava. 'The wretch used us as bait! He must have known the defenders intended to flank us with a Titan, and we lured it out so he could take it down.'

'Is he managing it?' Tulava asked.

Solomon looked back. The Warlord was trying to shake its assailants loose, but it was not designed for such measures, and could move neither swiftly nor sharply enough to succeed. One serpent's mouth opened into five-part jaws, like the petals of some obscene flower, and clamped on to the Warlord's chest where the reactor that powered it was housed. Another slithered down the macro gatling blaster, while a third coiled around the volcano cannon. The fourth and final daemon engine opened its mouth, reared back, and struck at the Warlord's head.

The Titan screamed again, and staggered. Energy crackled and flowed from the war machine to its parasites, and then in reverse. Solomon saw Xettus' Helstalker scuttle closer, and the warpsmith raise his arms as if in impeachment. The machine-spirit of a Warlord Titan was a mighty thing indeed: Solomon's knowledge of such things was limited, but he was aware of that much. It would take a true master of the New Mechanicum's knowledge to break its will and harness it to his own.

It appeared that Xettus Qeele of the Rustbloods was such a master.

Little by little, the Titan stopped shaking, and the daemonic serpents attached to it stopped thrashing. Solomon could almost feel the power resonating from the unholy union, as the Warlord's machine-spirit was dragged down into a dark place and ripped asunder by forces against which it had no defence. Its crew were in all likelihood already dead, their cerebral link to the war machine having fried their brains; either that or they were themselves being corrupted by the power of Chaos, or possibly digested alive as the Warlord's control room took on a new and horrifying form. Anything was possible with the New Mechanicum.

Solomon breathed out. 'Well, at least that problem is solved.'

'I'm not entirely sure about that,' Tulava said. 'This is what I was going to tell you before – the Rustbloods are hanging back.'

Solomon opened his mouth to disagree, then realised that he had seen skitarii marching past, but the legionnaires themselves? He had been too busy killing the Kataphrons to keep track of how many had been lost in the fighting. He leaned out to peer around the corpse of the Destroyer on which he was standing, and saw a dark mass of Space Marines unmoving at the far end of what had once been the Adeptus Mechanicus defensive line, past even the breach blown in the redoubt by the Havocs' heavy weapons.

He just had time to realise the true nature of Xettus' betrayal before the Warlord opened fire.

Its weapon batteries obliterated what was left of the breach point and began to march down the line towards Solomon, faster than even a Space Marine could run. Mega gatling blaster, volcano cannon, and carapace-mounted laser blasters threw up snow, flame, pulverised rock and smashed ferrocrete in a tidal wave of destruction that marched towards him.

'Oh *crap*,' Tulava had time to say, and then everything went black.

FOR THE GOOD OF ALL

Kayzen Hart closed the door behind him and threw his interrogation tools down in disgust. 'They are mocking us!'

Deema Varrin cocked her head inquisitively. 'They are?'

'These accursed tattoos,' Hart muttered. 'Nothing more than a smokescreen.'

Tattoos were not uncommon on Qampar: devotional ones to Saint Stevanus Imannis, who had claimed the system in the name of the Imperium, were the most prevalent. However, many of the population carried designs on their skin of one form or another, be they holy or purely decorative in nature. The first time Hart had seen a three-headed serpent on the neck of a labourer, he had nearly drawn Helorassa and slain the menial on the spot, for the symbol was believed to be borne on occasion by the Alpha Legion's mortal agents. Then he had found out that several of Qampar's most prominent socialites had taken to sporting the same design, and that the general population had followed their example.

Hart had moved swiftly, and arrested the entire households of everyone so implicated. Then he interrogated them all, ruthlessly, barely pausing for sleep. Now, some three weeks after his personal crusade had begun, he was no closer to finding a genuine Alpha Legion operative.

'The man knows nothing of our enemy,' Hart spat, stripping off his long protective gloves, which were now spattered with the blood of the Margrave Rebb. 'He is a venal oaf, reasonably inter-bred, and greatly invested in the well-being of his spouses and children. Were I interested in the minor corruptions of business here, or the sexual and political scandals of his peers, I would have information enough to last me a lifetime. But actual leads on the Alpha Legion's activities? Nothing.' He sighed, unstoppered a decanter of the margrave's best wine, and took a swig. He had commandeered the manse's kitchen for his work, since it was already possessed of bare surfaces that would not stain, and could be easily cleaned. It also had the benefit of being next to the well-stocked pantries.

'You think the Alpha Legion are not active on Qampar?' Tythus Yorr asked. Hart shook his head.

'No, I know they are here. These wretched tattoos have to have their origin *somewhere* – there is no cultural explanation for something so close to the Legion's iconography, especially not emerging so recently. Rebb claimed to have got the idea for his from the Duchess Reida, who in turn implicated Baron Connill, and so forth. I suspect the genuine operatives exerted some form of influence to bring the icon into the minds of the nobility in order to camouflage their own kind.' He took a smaller sip of the wine. 'Perhaps there are subtle differences within the hydra tattoos – certain marks, placements, or configurations that allow cell members to still identify their own amongst the white noise. I may need to make a more in-depth study of this.'

Varrin cleared her throat. 'You might recall, inquisitor, that Governor Alzyn was unimpressed by your decision to apprehend all these noble households. If you were to attempt to incarcerate a sizeable portion of the working population–'

'That will not be necessary,' Hart cut her off, waving the hand that was not holding the decanter. 'I would simply need to remove the area of tattooed skin from every individual for future study, and record from whom it was taken. Once I had identified patterns or recurring features, we would be in a much better position to apprehend the heretics. Of course,' he added, warming to the subject, 'anyone who sought to avoid having their tattoo removed would instantly mark themselves out as a heretic, and likewise anyone who disappeared after the removal had taken place. That in itself could turn up a sizeable crop of useful–'

'*Where is he?*'

The voice carried in from the grand entry hall. Hart looked up, because it was a voice he recognised. It was a tone he recognised as well, although not one he had heard in the past few weeks. However, it sounded like his cordial relationship with his fellow inquisitor was going to prove just as short-lived as he had expected.

'I'm in here, Nessa.'

A clatter of footsteps down a narrow passageway announced the arrival of Inquisitor Nessa Karnis and Evelyn, her aide. Both women looked positively murderous, although in Evelyn's case that appeared to be her natural state anyway. Karnis had a rather greater emotional range, but both the arrogant stand-offishness of their reunion and the guarded camaraderie of recent weeks were gone as if they had never existed. In their place was the white-hot fury of a fanatic – a side of her Hart had not seen since their days purging cults together.

He armed his digital lasers again. Formidable psyker though Karnis was, Hart had spent his entire career working on his mental fortitude. Karnis liked to rely on a psychic thrust that would incapacitate her opponent and allow her to strike unopposed: lazy, but often effective. However, Hart was fairly certain that he could resist her mental attack, and shoot her down before she completed her physical one. Her aide was an unknown quantity, but would surely be significantly outmatched by the towering presence of Tythus Yorr.

'You traitor!' Karnis seethed, as her eyes fell upon Hart.

He raised his eyebrows. 'I was not aware you held such strong feelings about the nobility of Qampar.'

'I care nothing for the nobility of this planet!' Karnis snapped. 'Under any other circumstances, I might applaud you for actually getting your hands dirty instead of tolerating heretics as you are wont to do, but this does not excuse your flagrant manipulations!'

'Manipulations?' Hart asked. 'What in the name of Terra are you talking about, Nessa?'

'The artefact,' Nessa bit out. 'The artefact of which you told me. The one you *happened* to discover in the vault on Downreach.' She pulled out a data-slate. 'I did my own investigations, *Kayzen*. Are you going to deny that it was moved here three years ago on *your* orders? That you did not in fact use your knowledge of it to predict the Alpha Legion's movements, but actually placed it there in order to use it as bait, to deliberately draw an attack onto an Imperial system?'

Hart sighed. 'Nessa, where is your commitment? Druman trained you better than this, I know that. What is the price of half a system, if we eliminate the Alpha Legion's ability to function in this segmentum as a result?' He shook his head. 'Yes, I lied to you – I freely admit that, and I would expect no different from you. I had hoped that as and when you learned the truth you might appreciate the subtlety with which I am letting this scheme play out, but it appears not. As ever, your puritanical nature blinds you to the wider picture, and makes you focus only on the more minor threat in front of you.'

'You dare throw your radical rantings in my face?' Karnis demanded. 'You are as bad as Kryptmann!'

Hart's fists clenched involuntarily. 'Do not be ridiculous! Kryptmann was a short-sighted fool! Furthermore' – he paused, and got a grip on himself – 'this is pointless. Regardless of your outrage about my actions, your authority does not exceed my own. I had every right to order a change in storage location for that artefact, and I warned the relevant forces of the likelihood of the Alpha Legion's interest in this system – the other details are irrelevant.'

'Brother Yorr,' Karnis said, turning her gaze on the Crimson Consul. 'The Adeptus Astartes are renowned for their lack of deceit. Can you truly condone Inquisitor Hart's actions?'

'We lack patience with petty politics,' Yorr rumbled. 'That does not mean we lack an understanding of the necessity of deception, on occasion. Inquisitor Hart's actions have but one purpose: to bring destruction to the heretics who slew my Chapter. Of this, I can only approve.'

Hart raised his eyebrows expectantly. 'Well, Nessa? What now?'

Karnis curled her lip. 'That is up to you, Kayzen. If you are sensible, you will leave the subsector immediately for the good of all, and leave me to clean up the mess you have made here. I will be sure to mention your cooperation, late though it may be, when I contact the conclave.'

'And have you take the credit for the Imperium's eventual triumph?' Hart said with a snort. 'Out of the question. Not only is this my life's work, but you simply cannot be trusted to prosecute this in the correct manner. For success to be guaranteed, I must remain. Perhaps if you have such a great objection to my methods, *you* should leave. And do not try to intimidate me with the conclave,' he added, with a sneer. 'You know as well as I that many would consider my stratagem entirely justified!'

Karnis drew herself up. 'Do not make me do this, Kayzen.'

'Do what?' Hart flapped one hand irritably, although he kept the other's digital lasers primed and ready.

'I had hoped to keep the ordo's reputation intact,' Karnis bit out, 'but I see that is no longer possible. Since you will not bend to reason, I must employ force. You seem to forget that your lifeward is not the only Space Marine in the system. I do not think that the Silver Templars will be happy about you leading them by the nose, and withholding important tactical information from them.'

Hart's nostrils flared. 'You would involve the Adeptus Astartes in a matter of internal ordo politics? That is a dangerous step.'

'It is one I am prepared to take,' Karnis retorted. 'My conduct has been exemplary, after all. This is your last chance. Leave now, and hope that whatever ordo investigation takes place into your behaviour does not conclude that you must be branded a heretic who has conspired with the enemy. Otherwise, Lieutenant Malfax may render it a moot point.'

Hart took a deep breath. 'Nessa, are you threatening my life?'

Too late, Karnis realised the trap she had stepped into. Tythus Yorr was sworn to protect Hart's life, unless his execution was ordered by someone whom Yorr considered to have unquestionable authority over him, which, given the Crimson Consul no longer had a Chapter Master, probably consisted of Roboute Guilliman, and very few others. If Karnis was threatening an action that would endanger Kayzen Hart's safety – indeed, if she was threatening it precisely *because* she believed it would endanger his safety – then Yorr was duty-bound to eliminate that threat.

The Space Marine shifted position slightly, to better draw attention to his power-armoured bulk, and began to speak in a tone which, although polite, brooked no argument. 'Inquisitor Karnis, I recommend–'

He stopped, nothing more than a faint hiss of expelled air emerging from his lips. Hart looked at him, shocked; Yorr's eyes were wide and wild, and a vein throbbed in his forehead, but he was apparently unable to either move or speak.

'What are you waiting for?' Karnis gasped, her words mangled by the strain of holding Yorr in place with her psychic abilities. 'Kill him!'

Fire leaped into life around Evelyn's hands, and she threw it at Hart's face with a scream.

The aide was a pyrokine! Hart turned and ran, one hand up in a desperate attempt to protect his eyes, and the other firing his digi-lasers blindly behind him. Even beneath the panic any human would feel when engulfed in fire, Hart's ferocious mental conditioning allowed him to focus. Distance, that was the key: pyrokines were devastating psykers when close, but few were able to control their powers to any great effect at range, and almost all needed to see their target. Running was not just an instinctive reaction, it was the one that made the most tactical sense.

He crashed through the door and burst out into the manse's internal courtyard, pursued by the charred stink of his own hair, his face and hands already cracking and blistering agonisingly. He did not dare stop, but veered immediately to his right, while he reached into his coat to find the grip of his heavy Ripper autopistol. He tugged it out of its shoulder rig, swearing in pain as the textured grip bit into the newly damaged skin of his palm. At least his clothing was flame-retardant as standard:

a wise precaution for an inquisitor. It was just a shame that he could not extend the same chemical protection to the rest of his body...

'Treachery!' he bellowed at three Qampari Dragoons standing in the main gateway, who looked up and raised their lasguns uncertainly as he barrelled towards them. 'I am Inquisitor Kayzen Hart, and I–'

He saw the signs of betrayal at the same moment he realised that none of these three had been in the group who had secured the Rebb manse under his command. His first shot took the left-most guard in the neck, dropping him in a shower of blood; his second shot punched clean through the flak jacket of the woman in the middle and into her torso, splintering bone and shredding flesh – the powerful toxins laced into the ammunition were almost certainly redundant, given the nature of the wound. The third one got his own shot away before Hart could squeeze his trigger again, and a beam of super-focused light speared through Hart's body just beneath his left collarbone. He returned fire a moment later, and the guard's face disappeared to leave nothing but a bloody mess beneath his helmet.

Hart came to a panting halt in the midst of their bodies and turned to aim his pistol back the way he had come, ready to empty the rest of the magazine into the pyrokine. A blast of flame erupted out of the door through which he had fled, but instead of Evelyn, it instead disgorged Tythus Yorr. The Crimson Consul fired his bolter back through the doorway, then turned and thundered towards Hart, his armour trailing wisps of smoke. The skin of his face was burned as well: he clearly had not had time to don his helmet, although he did so now.

'Deema is dead,' Yorr reported as he drew alongside Hart. 'The inquisitor is protected by some manner of force field, while the psyker shrouds herself in flame, making it impossible to place a shot.' He looked down at the bodies of the guards. 'Has she turned the local military against you as well?'

'Some of them, at least,' Hart replied, his mind racing. He could not risk Karnis going to Governor Alzyn or the Silver Templars with the truth; they were unlikely to share Hart's strategic vision. However, despite the damage it would do to the ordo's reputation, not to mention the decrees she would be violating by making outsiders party to their secrets, there was every possibility that she would do just that. Karnis was truly unhinged, prepared to endanger everything over her hatred of him.

'Inquisitor, we should depart,' Yorr said tensely. 'I cannot protect you efficiently against multiple assailants from different angles, and you require medical attention.'

'Yes,' Hart said, coming to a decision. 'Yes, we should. We will acquire a transport and make for the space port with all speed.'

'The space port?' Yorr asked, as they broke into a run – or at least, Hart broke into a run, whereas Yorr was moving at what was for him no more than a gentle trot. 'You intend to leave after all?'

'The planet? Yes,' Hart replied through gritted teeth. The breeze on his face and hands caused by the running provided some blessed relief from his burns, and although the lasgun wound was a red-hot core of pain through his upper chest, at least the destructive energy had cauterised it. 'Nessa called my bluff. I am not so foolish as to call hers, for there is no course of action she will not pursue to bring me down. Returning to the governor's palace will risk both of our lives, but my authority should suffice to get us off-world. That is what Nessa wants, after all,' he added bitterly. 'She may be content to let the ordo decide my fate at some point in the future, so long as I am not around to get under her feet and prevent her from taking the credit for my schemes.'

The transports in which they had arrived were still parked on the manse's grounds, just off the main drive: a Chimera, and two hulking, soft-sided trucks in which the Qampari Dragoons had ridden, since it had not seemed necessary to equip them with armoured carriers simply to bring them to a noble's house. Two dragoons were stationed on watch to ensure no enterprising criminals made off with the vehicles, but Yorr's bolter spoke twice, and they fell before they could even look surprised.

Hart was just trying to remember how to drive a Chimera when a Nighthawk gunship swung around over the manse's roof.

'Inquisitor Hart, Brother Yorr,' the pilot's voice declared over the vox-emitters, as it closed in. 'Stand down, or we will open fire by the command of Inqui–'

Tythus Yorr did not stand down; he jumped *up*.

The Crimson Consul leaped onto the top of the Chimera, then vaulted from that into the air with an agility that belied his size and the weight of his power armour. The Nighthawk, which had dropped to little more than the altitude of a two-storey hab in an effort to intimidate them into compliance, was unable to swing away in time, and Yorr landed on its nose. He wrenched open the cockpit with one hand, seized the pilot, broke his flight restraints, and tossed the luckless man out. The pilot hit the ground with a bone-breaking thud, and Yorr manoeuvred himself into the cockpit with surprising alacrity, given the disparity in size between himself and the former occupant, although he did swat the hanging canopy clean off with a swipe of one arm.

'The transport bay is empty,' Yorr said into Hart's ear, via his comm-bead. The Nighthawk began to swivel around and lower to the ground. 'This vehicle will take us to the space port with the greatest speed.'

'I was not aware that you knew how to pilot such a craft,' Hart said, surprised.

'*I know how to operate many vehicles,*' Yorr said, sounding almost absent-minded.

The access ramp was lowering, and had nearly touched the ground. Hart looked back at the manse's gateway, then raised his Ripper pistol and fired indiscriminately at the knot of dragoons that was emerging, clustered around the familiar shapes of Nessa Karnis and her aide. At least one of the dragoons fell, and there was a bright flash as a shot caused Karnis' conversion field to flare into life. Then Hart hurried up the ramp and into the shelter of the transport bay as the dragoons began to fire back, and before Evelyn the pyrokine could unleash her witchfire.

'Go!' Hart yelled, slapping his elbow against the door controls. The ramp began to close again, and Tythus wasted no time in feeding power to the engines. Hart had a glimpse of a fireball streaking towards them before the ramp closed, just before the Nighthawk pulled away at a speed that would leave even the most uncanny of powers behind.

'*There should be a medikit in the locker on the left-hand side of the bay,*' Yorr said over the vox. '*You should treat your wounds, inquisitor.*' He hesitated for a moment, then spoke again as Hart wrenched the locker in question open and found the kit exactly where it was supposed to be. '*I apologise for my failure when Inquisitor Karnis confronted us. I was rendered unable to move or speak for a few seconds, and so I was unable to discharge my duty as your lifeward.*'

'Think nothing of it,' Hart replied, prepping a spray gun of synthskin. 'Nessa is a powerful telepath. You have saved my life on several other occasions, and I am still alive now.'

'*Even so, the notion of an outside force interfering with my brain is one with which I find I am profoundly uncomfortable,*' Yorr said. '*What if she has compromised me in some manner?*'

Hart smiled to himself, although only momentarily, since it

created a flash of agony in his cheeks. 'My friend, it seems there is some baseline human in you still. These are the worries many of us have around psykers of all sorts, particularly telepaths. How can we know that our secrets have not been discovered? How can we know that our thoughts are still our own?' He sprayed the synthskin on the left side of his face, and breathed a deep sigh of relief as it immediately began to cool and heal the burns. It would be an unsightly fix, but it only needed to reduce the damage until he could access more advanced medical care.

'*How do you know the answers to those questions?*' Yorr asked. Hart had never thought he would hear a Space Marine sound plaintive, but there was the faintest edge of it in Yorr's voice. Something about the encounter had shaken him deeply.

'We do not,' Hart admitted. He applied the liquid bandage to the other side of his face, then moved on to his hands.

'*That seems inefficient and unsatisfactory,*' Yorr muttered. Hart laughed, and replaced the synthskin dispenser.

'You have just summed up the experience of being human in a single sentence, my friend. Our humanity is what makes us most fallible, while at the same time is the thing that separates us from and sets us above the myriad mewling species that would steal the galaxy from us. Not that I need to tell a former member of the Deathwatch that, of course,' he added. 'Do you need to stop to treat your own injuries?'

'*I can endure far worse hardships than this,*' Yorr replied stolidly.

'Good,' Hart said. He moved to the cogitator terminal at the front of the bay, and punched up their location. 'Then let us continue to the space port with all speed. Human, fallible, and betrayed though I might be, we still have work to do if we are to bring ruin to the Alpha Legion.'

LIES AND GREAT EXAGGERATIONS

The Rustbloods might have laid claim to the polar node of Anthras in the aftermath of the bloody engagement which had claimed the life of Solomon Akurra, but they were more New Mechanicum than they were Alpha Legion, and Qope Halver did not trust them one bit.

Shadowstrike had taken them within thirty miles, and was now sitting buried under a snowdrift with two Headhunters left behind to watch it. The other five were with him, advancing on the thermal port which the plans suggested lay just beyond the next ridge.

'Contact,' Vorlan Xhan reported, looking up from his auspex. His voice was back to normal now. 'Two, from the north.'

'Go dark,' Halver ordered, and his team obeyed, melting into the snow and rock of the ridge beside them. The Headhunters of the Serpent's Teeth paid little attention to the normal livery of their Legion, wearing black most of the time in acknowledgement of their role, and adapting the chameleonic nature of their armour's scales to best suit their surroundings. The cameleoline cloaks they also wore served to break up the distinct outline of power armour as much as anything else, for those skilled in stealth knew that shape was as important for concealment as colour and movement.

The kill team powered down their armour, letting the frigid wind steal away its remaining warmth. Halver knew it would not be long before he began to feel the bite of the polar chill: power armour might be a fully sealed system, but it could not moderate its internal temperature without that power. However, in a snowfield like this, the heat signatures of their power packs would stick out to anyone – or anything – with any form of heat sensors. Only the visual displays within his helmet remained active, so he could get a tactical view of what was in front of him; it was a tiny flicker of energy, too small to be detected by any enemy unless they were on top of him.

At least, that was the theory. With the New Mechanicum, anything was possible.

The two daemon engines came over the ridge, multi-limbed legs stabbing down through snow and somehow getting purchase on icy rock. They had been forged in the shape of monstrous arachnids, the high arch of their backs at least twice Halver's height, and although their metallic carapaces were a familiar blue-green, they bore many markings of the Ruinous Powers and the New Mechanicum, but none of the Alpha Legion.

Halver held his breath instinctively. If either of these creations could hear his breathing inside his helmet then their senses were keen enough to discover his kill team in any case, but some reactions were so ingrained within the psyche that even Space Marines still adhered to them. He was ready to reactivate his armour's power at a moment's notice if needed, and one hand was already on a melta bomb. His instinct was to go for the daemon engine's head, but who knew if that would have the expected effect on one of these monstrosities? Halver knew little about the Neverborn and their ways, especially not when they were animating a metal war machine.

The two daemon engines stalked closer, chittering as their heads swung from side to side. Their mechanical tendrils lashed as if tasting the air, and their multiple eyes constantly flickered to and fro. Halver had seen creatures such as these when they had sighted an enemy, and these two were not behaving with that sort of focus, but he was not reassured. Their senses were undoubtedly sharp, and although the daemons inhabiting these metal bodies would not perceive the world in the same way as a human did, there was no way of telling what might attract their attention. And certainly, the Serpent's Teeth and the Rust-bloods were theoretically allies, but Halver was not inclined to take chances when only the Rustbloods' battle-brothers had survived the operation to take the node. That was the sort of coincidence that would make anyone suspicious.

He did not know what it was that gave them away. Perhaps it was a minuscule movement of a finger creeping nearer to a trigger, perhaps a flutter of a cameleoline cloak, or maybe the faintest noise of cooling metal or ceramite. Whatever it was, one of the daemon engines ceased its steady patrol, and its head snapped towards them.

The Headhunter team did not move. Every one of them would wait for Halver's lead before they attacked, or fled.

The two infernal creations changed direction and began to stalk closer, with tendrils waving, and the cannons that pro-truded from their swollen abdomens swinging back and forth. Halver knew within a second that they were not going to stop and resume their patrol; they were going to scour the ground in front of them until they had found whatever it was that had attracted their attention. His team could not melt out of the way, so they were down to two options: run openly, or fight openly.

Or, given that they were Alpha Legion, take the third option.

He cautiously shifted the position of the hand that was resting on the melta bomb until his index finger lay against a different detonator on his belt, and pressed it. A mile and a half back the way they had come, a placed charge exploded, sending snow flying and starting a mini-avalanche. The two daemon engines whirled around in a skitter of legs, and set off at a pace the Headhunters would have been unable to match.

Halver waited until they were out of sight, then waited a further twenty seconds. Only then did he fire his armour up again. A new flush of warmth spread through him as his suit's life-support systems came back online, and the servos and artificial muscle fibres lent increased strength to his limbs once more.

No words were needed: he made a single hand signal, and his kill team followed him onwards.

They reached the thermal exhaust port they were aiming for just over ten minutes later. It was situated under a rocky overhang, and was belching out warm air as a near-constant cloud of steam. Xhan scanned it, then shook his head.

'No obvious security measures or alarms.'

Halver grunted. 'Mechanicus or Mechanicum, it makes no difference – there's no way of telling whether something is the result of absent-mindedness, overconfidence, or diabolic cunning.' He waved a hand. 'Open it.'

Zreko Chura stepped forward with an arc-cutter, and set to work on the grille blocking their way. Ninety seconds later, their entry point was clear. A mild adhesive from Chura's belt pouch secured the grille back in place once they had passed it, sufficient to hide the cuts from a cursory inspection, and the kill team pressed onwards with their armour darkening to its usual black, the better to hug the shadows of their new environment. Who knew whether these tunnels had once had an intended purpose other than for airflow? With the Machine Cult, things could be forgotten, rediscovered, and turned to new usages with no attention paid to what had come before, just as easily as they could be held in unchanging reverence.

The security servitors came at them out of a side tunnel. There was no approach noise of clumsy footsteps or tracks: one moment they were dormant, the next they were activating and attacking. Halver dived aside from the swipe of the chain-blade arm of a swollen brute roughly the size of an ogryn, but the thunder hammer on the other side caught him in the chest as he came back up to his feet. Energy discharged with a crack, and the next thing he knew he was on his back, thirty feet down the tunnel.

'Halver!' Xhan shouted, slashing at the attackers with his power knife.

'I'm fine!' Halver replied, although the screaming of his ribs as he began to rise gave the lie to his words, and a grinding noise from his chestplate let him know that the ceramite had fractured.

There were three of the enemy, he saw as he raised his bolt-gun: each significantly larger than a Space Marine, and moving with the sort of speed and coordination that spoke of something far more than basic security protocols. His team opened fire, drawing bolt pistols and power knives where they could for ease of use in such close quarters, but the tunnels were cramped, and the servitors pressed their advantage. Vorlan Xhan was swatted aside by the thunder hammer; another construct pinned Unej Manoz against the wall with a massive drill bit that chewed into his armour and sent ceramite scales flying.

Gobbets of flesh followed a moment later, as the servitor began to bore right through him.

Halver fired three times, striking the drill limb on its joint and severing it. Manoz fell to his knees, the drill bit still embedded in his chest, and Zreko Chura attacked with his power knife. However, although his blade struck home several times, the servitor appeared largely unaffected by the blows; it rounded on him, swinging the pneumatic mace that served as its other arm, and struck Chura clean on the helmet hard enough to shatter it. Chura collapsed, and the servitor raised one metal-shod foot to stamp on his head.

Then froze, transfixed by a spike that burst out of its chest from behind.

A shout split the air – a mortal shout, from mortal lungs – and another of the servitors was slammed into the opposite wall so hard that it began sparking. The third, the thunder hammer-armed one that had struck Halver in the first place, was impaled in the same manner as the first, and joined its companion in immobility. The remaining Headhunters cautiously lowered their weapons, and Qope Halver picked himself up as the mysterious spike withdrew from the servitor, and its wielder moved into his view.

'Headhunter Prime,' Solomon Akurra said in greeting, his daemonic arm re-forming into its normal configuration. His warplate was battered and chipped, and one lens of his helmet was cracked, but he was still in one piece. The relic boltgun clamped to his thigh without a magazine in it spoke to how much effort and ammunition it had taken him to remain that way.

'Harrowmaster,' Halver replied. 'I find that I am unsurprised by the Ghost's survival.' He grunted as Tulava Dyne appeared, leaning heavily on her force staff, which at least explained the fate of the second servitor. 'Her, more so.'

'A pleasure as always, Halver,' Dyne hissed. The witch looked drawn, even by mortal standards.

'These ones die easiest if you hit the central processing unit in their chest,' Akurra said, nudging one of the fallen servitors with his foot. 'We found that out the hard way.'

'What happened, Lord Akurra?' Vorlan Xhan asked. His left pauldron was shattered, and his arm was limp and apparently useless.

'Xettus betrayed us,' Akurra said, without bile or anger. 'To an extent, at least. He orchestrated the destruction of our forces which were not directly loyal to him before he began to corrupt the machine-spirit of the planet's defences. Tulava was able to warpwalk us out of the path of the Titan's weapons at the last moment. We took shelter in the node, and have been observing the Rustbloods' work since.'

'What have you seen?' Halver asked. 'Are they planning to betray the rest of us?'

Akurra shook his head. 'The Mechanicum's ways are a mystery to us both, but I have had no indication of that. Xettus and his minions appear to be doing exactly as they promised, barring the fact they slew their allies beforehand.'

Halver considered this. He had led this mission to determine Xettus' trustworthiness for himself; discovering Solomon Akurra still alive was an unlooked-for occurrence. 'Does Xettus know of your survival?'

Akurra shook his head. 'I have had no indication of that. So far as I am aware, he believes me dead, and probably intends to propose himself as the new Harrowmaster by dint of his command of the captured Warlord Titan.'

'That is unlikely to be well received,' Halver said.

'Indeed,' Akurra agreed. 'Which is why it is crucial that the Serpent's Teeth support his claim.'

Halver's surprise at this statement was only mild: the subtle arts of politicking were as common and finely honed in the Alpha Legion as were the more brutal arts of war. 'You are not intending to contest it?'

'Not yet,' Akurra said. 'I intend to remain dead, so far as anyone knows, until a better opportunity presents itself. Xettus has a strong position in any case – he has indeed been crucial in subduing Anthras' defences, and he now commands a formidable force of daemon engines. I will not strike to reclaim my place from the traitor until I have what I need to ensure my authority is unquestioned. So long as Xettus sticks to the plan of attacking the Psyphos System next, that is still within my grasp.'

Halver snorted. 'He can most likely be prodded in that direction, but even though that was your plan, you cannot expect to take the credit for it if he leads us to success.'

'The success itself will be sufficient,' Akurra replied. 'I have another goal, the achievement of which will reinforce the Serpent's Teeth as the most prominent and powerful faction within the Alpha Legion.' He spread his arms. 'Unless, of course, you intend to ensure that I remain dead permanently, Halver.'

The tunnel went very quiet, and Qope Halver became acutely aware of the boltgun in his hands, and the lack of ammunition in Akurra's corresponding weapon.

'We have not always seen eye to eye,' Akurra continued calmly. 'You could probably gain considerable standing with Lord Xettus if you were to return with my corpse, and present it to him discreetly. Deceit and betrayal is, after all, the lifeblood of our Legion.'

Halver nodded slowly.

'It is.'

The Headhunters who were still on their feet stiffened, just noticeably. In all honesty, Halver did not know who they would follow, if it came to it. However, he was certain that once the matter was resolved, they would all align behind the survivor. The Alpha Legion was as pragmatic as they came; there was no point holding to the cause of a leader who was dead.

And Halver was certain that he could kill Solomon Akurra within seconds.

'So how could I trust Xettus?' he asked. 'Bringing him your corpse would suggest that I knew of his betrayal, which would make me a liability – or he could serve me up to the other warlords and tell them with total honesty that it was I who slew you, not he.'

Akurra nodded in his turn. 'Valid points. Therefore, if you are not going to kill me, I will instead request that you assist Tulava and me to escape from here.'

'Preferably involving something that means I don't have to walk to the equator,' the witch added acidly. 'And also soon, if possible. If we heard the commotion you were making, others might have too, and there are more dangerous things in this complex now than some leftover Mechanicus watchdogs.'

It came down to trust. Qope Halver did not particularly like Solomon Akurra, but so far he had been good to his word in terms of unifying the Alpha Legion, and striking at the Imperium.

'Better the daemon you know,' he said. 'Move out.'

PART THREE

FOOL ME TWICE

Lieutenant Renus Malfax was frustrated.

His attempts to rally the defences of the subsector had largely come to naught. The Beharis System had been taken off guard by the Alpha Legion's barefaced effrontery at launching an assault while claiming the identity of a loyal Chapter. This was just another example of the traitors' depravity, in Renus' opinion; he maintained the faintest iota of respect for heretics who at least made no bones about their allegiances. Then Anthras had fallen, or certainly had been compromised enough for the Alpha Legion to seize a considerable amount of resources, according to the astropath messages Governor Alzyn had received. The tech-priests' confidence in the technological superiority of their defence systems had been misplaced, and their dismissal of Renus' earlier warnings confirmed as nothing more than arrogance. Typical Adeptus Mechanicus behaviour: Renus would not try to instruct them how to bless a cogitator or repair a Repulsor, and they should not try to tell him that they could repel an assault by Traitor Astartes.

The Psyphos System itself was surely the next target. The Alpha Legion had struck at a supply system and at a forge world. Unpredictable and unorthodox although they might be, everything now pointed to a thrust at the heart of government. Renus had ordered astropathic messages sent out, but he had little illusion that help was on its way. The Indomitus Crusade had already liberated these systems and passed on, and the Grand Oathkeeper had directed Renus' demi-company to oversee the defences here, rather than return himself with greater force. Several of the other systems in the Charadon Sector were dealing with their own problems, as various forces both traitorous and xenos sought to destabilise the Imperium's re-established rule. For the first time in his life, Renus saw the Imperium not as a galaxy-spanning monolith, a massive, cliff-sided edifice rising above the crashing waves of those who sought to bring it down, but more as a loosely connected series of islands amidst a raging and ever-rising sea.

It was a sobering realisation, and one with which he was not comfortable. It did nothing to change his resolve to defend the Imperium, but there had been moments as the *Dawnblade* tirelessly patrolled the orbits of the Psyphos System that Renus Malfax had questioned himself. Was his new perception of the Imperium as vulnerable a sign that he had been compromised in some way? Or was it simply a deeper understanding of the perils humanity faced? Doubt was a potential chink in the armour of his faith, but was overconfidence not a similar weakness, merely inverted?

Part of his mind was still musing on this while he studied the shipping patterns over Qampar. He had ordered all schedules to be forwarded to the *Dawnblade*, so he could inspect them and bring a Space Marine's tactical awareness to bear. The Psyphos System, at least, would not be taken without a fight. Security had been tripled at all space ports, and the fleets and orbital stations were on a constant high alert. No matter how subtle the Alpha Legion were, there was no way they would be able to sneak in here while evading notice.

Something tugged at his awareness, and he frowned, casting his eyes back and forth across the three-dimensional swarm of icons, and their various ident tags. He tapped an instruction into the keys of the cogitator and turned a dial, and the display began to move backwards in time an hour... Three hours... Six hours... A day... Three days...

Renus nodded to himself, then highlighted a dozen individual ships and let the display play forward again at an accelerated speed. Vessels orbiting planets, the *Dawnblade* included, made frantic circles while the rest of the traffic went about its business. Some ran from planet to planet within the system, ferrying goods and people back and forth; others burned out to the Mandeville point and disappeared into the warp; still others translated from the immaterium and began to make their way inwards, towards one planet or another. The entire system within the Mandeville point was a massive sphere, far too large to patrol in a manner that would allow the apprehension or inspection of ships as soon as they arrived.

Once they got close to the planets, though...

Renus smiled tightly. The dozen ships he had picked out had all translated into the system from the warp within a day of each other, and had made their way towards Qampar at different speeds, and on different trajectories, from then onwards. However, their arrivals into the outer reaches of the planet's orbital security systems were almost precisely coordinated, with less than half an hour between them. If processed by shipping control, they would set down on the planet's surface virtually at the same time.

And each one was a bulk hauler, the same sort of ship as those with which the Alpha Legion had hoodwinked the Beharis System.

'Give me a channel to the fleet and the Ramilies star forts,' Renus ordered. The vox-operator threw the various switches, and signalled him to go ahead.

'This is Lieutenant Malfax of the Silver Templars, aboard the *Dawnblade*,' Renus declared. 'I am sending you the identities of twelve vessels–'

An alarm blared across the bridge. Renus had spotted the cause within half a second, and tapped a key to bring the information up. Long-distance scans were always unreliable, but he had little doubt of the veracity of what he was seeing.

'*Lieutenant?*' someone prompted over the vox. Renus' brain absent-mindedly identified it as belonging to Commander Priam of the star fort *Tenacity*.

'Systems are picking up a major incursion at the edge of the system,' Renus reported. Alarms would be ringing all through the fleet, now. 'The Alpha Legion are here.'

He took in the information as it sleeted across the terminal. This was a larger fleet than the one the Silver Templars had attacked on the advice of Inquisitor Hart, so it seemed that the heretics' successes had drawn others to their banner. That damnable space hulk was at the centre of the fleet, a blunt-nosed battering ram which could probably smash its way through the combined defensive firepower of the Psyphos System with nothing more than momentum and sheer mass, but that was not what drew Renus' eye. He was becoming more used to looking past the obvious threat with the Alpha Legion, and seeing the secondary blade lurking behind the first thrust.

'Heavy transports,' he said, highlighting them for the attention of his fellow commanders. They were shadowing the hulk, well protected behind its bulk and the encircling ring of dedicated warships; for despite their size, they were poorly armed. It was not their guns that concerned him, however, but what they might carry.

'They can pack an awful lot of cannon fodder in there,' said Captain Al-Shawa of the *Revenger*, a Styges-class cruiser. 'If they're full, we're talking a few hundred thousand ground troops in each, at the least.'

'Or a few Titans,' Renus said.

There was a shocked silence.

'They have just sacked a forge world,' Renus reminded his fellow officers. 'We lost contact with Anthras – we do not know exactly what occurred, or what might have been looted. It would be foolish of us in the extreme not to consider the possibility that the traitors now have god-machines in their arsenal.'

'The ground defences have nothing that can stand against Titans,' Captain Al-Shawa said, her voice shaking.

'The bastards still have to land them, though,' pointed out Commander Priam. 'I'm expediting emergency landing procedures to clear the civilian traffic out of orbit. The last thing we need is some terrified merchant getting in the way of our guns.'

'Belay that,' Renus ordered. He signalled the vox-officer, who transmitted the information he had prepared before the Alpha Legion's arrival had been detected. 'Here are the twelve ships I mentioned earlier. If we let them land, we risk the Alpha Legion establishing a beachhead on the ground before we have even engaged their fleet. Destroy these ships, then proceed with the expedited procedures.'

No one argued. A Space Marine lieutenant might command a mere fifty warriors of his own kind, but Renus had the full weight of the Adeptus Astartes behind him. Even a general of the Astra Militarum would be well advised to listen to what he had to say. For these officers of Psyphos, now with a heretic fleet bearing down on them, his word was as good as law.

Guns flared, and bulk transports died, one after another. Only when the last had come apart in a shower of glittering shards did Commander Priam send out the order to clear the orbit. Those ships waiting to make planetfall were sent into an accelerated landing pattern, launches for anything other than military vessels were cancelled, and those ships with destinations elsewhere were ordered to either return to Qampar, or otherwise take their chances with the Alpha Legion and make themselves scarce before the invaders arrived.

Renus checked the chrono, and measured it against the signal delay from the scans. At the speed the traitors were moving into the system, Qampar had approximately eighteen hours before all hell began to break loose in the sky above it.

All he had to do was make sure that it never made it to the ground.

It was in fact after seventeen and a half hours that the Alpha Legion fleet became visible to the naked eye; at least to the crews of Qampar's defenders, crowded together in orbit above the system's primary world. The central smudge of light that marked the presence of the ugly mass of the space hulk was ringed by its own constellation, as starlight reflected off a myriad of other hulls.

Renus Malfax did not know fear, but he would have been lying had he denied the presence of a certain apprehension. The true strength of the Alpha Legion force could not be known: they might have ships packed full of warriors, or conversely be running a skeleton crew on virtually all of the vessels in order to increase their apparent numbers, and therefore the alarm in their enemies. However, if even a majority of those ships were running anywhere near close to complement, then this was an

Alpha Legion mobilisation of greater size than any of which he had heard in the Imperium's recent history.

'It seems the serpents no longer feel the need to cling to the shadows,' he remarked. 'Let us make them regret this.'

'Some of their outliers have already broken away to harass shipping,' the auspex officer reported.

'And an Administratum facility on the moon Downreach is broadcasting a distress signal,' the vox-officer added.

Malfax waved his hand. 'Those are afterthoughts, at present.'

'Another incoming signal,' the vox-officer said, as another light began blinking. She swallowed. 'This one is from the traitor fleet, my lord.'

Renus looked over at Brother Rhan, the Techmarine. The fall of Anthras had left him cautious. 'Is it hostile?'

'No evidence of scrap code, brother-lieutenant,' Rhan replied, checking his instruments. 'It appears to be a simple audiovisual broadcast.'

'Then we can assume that the deceit lies in their words,' Renus concluded. 'Still, let us see what the traitors have to say for themselves.' He would have valued the counsel of the two inquisitors, but it appeared that their differences, be they personal, professional, or both, had boiled over. There had been a violent altercation at the manse of one of Qampar's nobles, and now neither one could be found. Renus had accepted the news with the same slightly disgusted resignation as he would any other report of baseline human allies putting their own petty concerns above that of their duty to the Imperium. It was always disappointing, but rarely truly surprising, and a valuable reminder that even the Inquisition was no more sound than the humans that made it up. It would always be the lives and the blood of the Space Marines that kept the Imperium safe.

The holo-generator in front of him flickered into life. The light flowed and hardened, and formed itself into something Renus Malfax had not been expecting at all.

The head and shoulders of a Space Marine.

The Alpha Legion were Space Marines, of course, he knew that; or at least, they had the same origin. However, Renus' first contact with his heretic brethren had been the warriors of the Flawless Host, and it would be hard to find more altered and disfigured servants of Chaos. He had not made a study of the bodies, but it seemed that many of them had deliberately altered their own flesh, quite apart from the twisting effects of the warp. That had stuck with him, and had formed his impressions of what renegade Astartes looked like.

The visage with which he was now presented, on the other hand, was as unremarkable as it was possible for a Space Marine to be. The head was bald, and while no one who looked upon it could mistake its features for that of a baseline human, there were no indications of mutilation or mutation. The skull was smooth, the brow prominent but not overlarge, the nose slightly aquiline, the cheekbones high, and the jaw strong without being disproportionately wide. The traitor's countenance was... almost noble. But despite that, Renus felt that he might have some difficulty in bringing the exact nature of the face's features to mind again, even though he – like most of his brethren – possessed very accurate powers of recollection.

What could be seen of the traitor's armour was no more distinctive. He wore a Mark VI suit, and barring the slight dints and nicks which spoke of warplate that had protected its bearer through many battles, it was not ornamented or decorated in any manner other than the coiling hydra on the right pauldron. For all the galaxy, he looked like he could have been a new recruit about to step onto his first battlefield at the height of the Horus Heresy.

It was, Renus had to admit, all somewhat unnerving.

'State your name and purpose,' he said. He deliberately kept his voice flat and uninterested, as if the Chaos-aligned fleet bearing down on the planet he had sworn to protect was of no concern.

A faint smile twitched across the face of his opposite number.

'I am Alpharius.'

'I highly doubt that,' Renus replied. All the same, something inside him twisted slightly at the heretic's words. Inquisitor Karnis had spoken of how readily individuals of the XX Legion assumed the identity of their primogenitor, for reasons best not guessed at, but that did not make it easy to ignore the impact of the name. The Imperium at large might have hidden or forgotten the history of its darkest days, but the Adeptus Astartes still knew the names of their founding fathers, and more specifically the names of their brothers who had turned against them. Some were known to be dead, some were known to be living – if their warp-altered forms could truly be described by that term – and the fates of some were unknown. Alpharius, however, was an enigma. He had supposedly been slain by the Ultramarines on Eskrador, in the aftermath of the Heresy, and yet rumours of his existence persisted.

Perhaps that was the best indication of the truth, Renus reflected. If the Alpha Legion had allowed word of Alpharius' presence to spread, that was a likely sign that he was indeed dead.

'Your belief, or lack thereof, is of no concern to me,' the so-called Alpharius declared. He had a deep, resonant voice, unhurried and used to command. Had Renus not stood in the presence of a true primarch, the Lord Commander and Imperial Regent Roboute Guilliman, he might have found it harder to persuade himself that the Alpha Legionnaire was indeed lying about his

identity. *'My purpose is simple, lieutenant. I will not insult you by suggesting that you surrender.'*

Renus smiled despite himself. 'And I thought you traitors believed your foul gods were capable of anything, including turning the hearts of warriors such as myself.'

'You are a Space Marine, lieutenant,' the heretic declared. *'You have no ties, no loyalty to this world. You care nothing for its fate after you give your life in its defence, because your own death is all you care about.'*

'Believe me, traitor,' Renus replied, 'I care a considerable amount about yours, as well.'

'Your human counterparts, on the other hand?' Alpharius continued, as though Renus had not spoken. *'Drawn from this system, perhaps from this very planet. They should consider surrender. They have families, friends, loved ones – all of whom will suffer if we are forced to prosecute a war to achieve our ends.'*

'You speak as though war is not what you seek,' Renus scoffed.

'But it need not be here,' Alpharius said levelly. *'We seek a tithe – weapons, supplies and recruits. Our requirements would be considerably less of a drain on this world's resources than the punishing demands of the Indomitus Crusade, which bleeds its conquests dry and calls it "protection".'* The traitor smiled. *'The protection of the Alpha Legion can be arranged for a far lower price, so long as we do not have to fight to take what we want.'*

'It is your "protection" which would be a lie,' Renus said. 'Qampar is loyal to the Imperium, and is protected by the might of the Emperor!'

'You are confusing protection with revenge, lieutenant,' Alpharius said. *'I have no doubt that after we shatter the poor excuse for a defensive fleet you have mustered, annihilate the various fortresses and strongpoints on the planetary surface, level every single shrine to the Imperial faith, slaughter the rulers, and take the resources*

we need, the Imperium will find its way here in weeks or months and re-establish its brutal rule on the miserable survivors, many of whom will be executed for not fighting harder. However, we will be long gone.'

Renus clenched his teeth in anger, but he dared not look away or give any sign. The Alpha Legion were the masters of deception, so it followed that they would be able to read it in others.

'Of course, if Qampar were to surrender, we would not need to destroy your defensive emplacements, making it all the easier for you to protect yourselves from the Imperium's inevitable reappearance,' Alpharius continued. *'All we need as a sign of good faith is for the defending fleet to fire upon and destroy the* Dawnblade. *Once this is done, assuming there are no other hostile actions, we can discuss terms.'*

It was a well-baited hook, Renus had to admit. This was the danger in allowing heretics a chance to speak; there was always the possibility that rather than howling rants about the supremacy of their so-called deities, they might find a way to seed doubt in the hearts and minds of those who lacked the steel of a Space Marine. But Renus had counted on the Alpha Legion seeking this sort of advantage, and had prepared for it. Rhan, out of sight of the imager which was broadcasting Renus' own likeness to the traitor vessel, gave the prearranged signal, and Renus was freed from having to continue the conversation.

He cut the feed. 'Brother Rhan, you have a fix on the signal's origin?'

'Yes, brother-lieutenant,' Rhan confirmed. 'It comes from the space hulk, as we suspected, but I have narrowed it down to this section.' He fiddled with some dials, and a rough image of the hulk, a small area of which was highlighted, took shape where the features of the pretender Alpharius had been only moments before.

'My friends,' Renus said, widening his broadcast to bring in the various captains and commanders of the Qampar fleet. 'The traitors have unwittingly bared their throat to us.

'Let us rip it out.'

CHARGE

The Imperial fleet moved into the attack almost as soon as their leader broke off the transmission. Qope Halver watched from the viewports of the *Unseen* as battle was joined, and once more felt the familiar tension in his gut. He was a warrior, an infiltrator, an assassin, and a saboteur – none of which he could do from the deck of a warship. Here, he could merely watch, and potentially die without ever striking another blow at the Imperium.

Of course, his odds of dying were theoretically considerably lower when aboard the *Unseen* than they might have been on any other ship in the fleet, but things were not quite the same as they had been when Solomon Akurra had been in command.

'Get back to your vessel,' Lord Xettus ordered the member of the Faceless who had taken on the mantle of 'Alpharius' for the conversation with the Silver Templar.

'The *Void* is about to engage the enemy,' the Faceless replied. Xettus rounded on him, his mechatendrils waving ominously, and his four-strong living chorus hissing their electronic displeasure.

'I do not recall asking for your opinion of my orders,' Xettus declared.

The Faceless held the gaze of the Lord Discordant's helmet for a moment, then inclined his head slightly. 'As you command, Harrowmaster.' He replaced his own helm, and made his way to the bridge doors, but Halver had no illusions that the instruction had been accepted as calmly as the other legionnaire had made out. In fact, he would be amazed if 'Alpharius' even left the *Unseen* at all. If it had been Halver, he would have relied on the battle occupying Xettus' attention until it was safe to make the crossing between ships in a transport craft, and blamed an engine failure or similar for the delay. In fact, if it had been Halver, he might well have already ensured his craft was suffering from just such an issue, in order to give some veracity to his story.

Xettus had been Harrowmaster for only a short time, raised to the rank by voices including Halver's own, and he was already acting as though his authority was untouchable. Akurra had his flaws, there was no doubt about that, but he was diplomatic enough not to order his supposed allies out into the middle of a void battle with only a Thunderhawk or similar for protection, simply because he no longer saw any need for them on the bridge of his warship.

On the other hand, Akurra was not *here*. Halver was here, left in danger while Solomon pursued his own goals, just as Kyrin Gadraen had been. Kyrin had been gone for eleven years now, as the Imperium managed time, and–

And those were thoughts best left alone for now. Solomon Akurra was still very much alive, despite what Xettus Qeele believed, and was on the small transport which had peeled off from the main fleet as soon as they emerged from the warp. Xettus thought that was a minor diversion, an excuse to pack the remnants of the First Strike off and let them sate their bloodlust on a small moon; the new Harrowmaster had little patience for followers of the Blood God, nascent though their allegiance might still be. As Qope Halver understood it, the mission was actually something far more crucial, but he did not know the full details. No one ever did, with Solomon Akurra. Not until you were counting the bodies, and sometimes not even then.

On the other hand, from what Halver had seen so far, Akurra was vastly preferable to Xettus.

'They are not breaking formation,' Xettus said, looking up from his inspection of the tactical hololith.

'I can see that,' replied Krozier Va'kai, from the captain's throne. That had been a notable battle of wills: the Metalphage clearly wanted nothing more than to get his noospheric fingers into the space hulk's systems, whereas Va'kai had told him that, Harrowmaster or not, an interference with his ship would see Va'kai use its armaments to lay waste to all the transports Xettus had filled with his playthings stolen and warped from Anthras. Xettus had apparently decided to back down in the face of such stiff opposition, backed up by impressive firepower, but Halver could practically smell the ambition on him. Xettus was lurking on the *Unseen*'s bridge like a powerful predator waiting for his opportunity to charge in and dispatch a rival who was crouching, teeth bared, over a succulent carcass.

Halver eyed the hololith, then turned back to the viewports. He could make little sense of it, which frustrated him. He could look at a landscape and instantly see the vantage points, the blind spots, the places from which a sniper could have a commanding field of fire and, conversely, where to take cover from each of them. That was what made him such a good Headhunter Prime: the ability to read terrain, and make it work for his purposes.

He had no such affinity for void combat. There were no physical surfaces, no structures, nothing to work with other than huge distances and the projected movements of ships that were under the control of different minds. How anyone could read anything into it was a mystery, but although trust did not come easily to Qope Halver, he trusted that Krozier Va'kai knew what he was doing.

'What is their strategy?' Xettus demanded. 'You said they would remain between the protection of the star forts!'

'I said that was what *I* would do,' Va'kai corrected him. 'They are coming at us fast, and tight. All warships, no transports – they are concentrating their firepower.'

'It will not matter,' Xettus said. 'We outnumbered and outgunned them even before they split their force like this. We can pick their fleet off, then engage the star forts at our leisure before landing the ground forces.'

Halver eyed the hololith, where icons flashed up to represent detected weapons fire as the onrushing defenders began to engage the slower-moving Alpha Legion fleet. He shook his head. 'There is something more to this. Even I can see that their survivability would have been greater had they remained within the aegis of the star forts. The Silver Templars are Space Marines, and while they are eager for combat, they are not orks to rush in without any consideration for a strategic goal.'

'They are definitely eager for combat,' Va'kai said thoughtfully. 'I saw that over Pendata, when they engaged the *Whisper*. But they are not taking the lead here, do you see?' He did something with the controls of his throne, and one of the Imperial ships buried within the formation began to pulse. 'That is the Silver Templars' strike cruiser.'

'They are not exactly leading the charge,' Xettus mused.

'The rest are protecting it,' Halver said. This was not too different to targeting a convoy in which a mark was riding, it was just that the potential fields of fire ran through three hundred and sixty degrees instead of the more usual one hundred and eighty. 'Look at how the other ships shift to ensure it is always covered. The rest of their fleet is an escort detail.'

Va'kai nodded, and opened a vox-channel. 'This is Captain Va'kai of the *Unseen*. All ships, disengage immediately, break formation, and scatter.'

'What are you doing?' Xettus snarled, rounding on him.

'This is a targeted thrust, disguised as a hammer blow,' Va'kai replied calmly. 'They are coming in at full speed, baiting us to encircle and engage them. They know we can destroy them, and they know we know that, but they are gambling on being able to get that strike cruiser close enough to their target to achieve their objective.' He smiled wolfishly. 'Since we know neither their target nor their objective, let us make them chase it. Not everything in their fleet has the manoeuvrability of a strike cruiser, so if they want to keep the escort in place, they can only change direction at the pace of their most sluggish ship.'

Xettus nodded. 'We can keep them at arm's length and pick them off, and if the strike cruiser makes its move without protection, it will be vulnerable.'

The forward portion of the Alpha Legion fleet was breaking away into a huge sunburst of metallic splinters, through which the Imperium was punching. A light escort went up in a blaze of explosions as the weapons of an Imperial heavy cruiser found it, but the majority of the ships quickly escaped beyond the effective range of lances and gun batteries.

'All forward torpedoes, fire,' Va'kai commanded.

The bridge servitors responded to his order, and a lopsided ripple of metallic projectiles the size of hab-blocks swept out from the various prows that made up the *Unseen*, directly towards the defenders. The armouries of Anthras had been good to the Alpha Legion, and magazines were full again.

'Now pitch down forty degrees, roll and yaw to starboard the same amount, and fire portside batteries when we have targets,' Va'kai commanded. The *Unseen* began to respond slowly, the thrusters straining against the hulk's sheer momentum.

'You cannot hold your course now,' Halver heard Va'kai mutter. 'So which way are you going...?'

The icons depicting the Imperium fleet began to shift on the hololith.

Downwards.

'That answers the question of what their target is,' Halver said. 'It's us.' He instinctively fingered the boltgun clamped to his hip, as though he could smash open a viewport and pick off their enemy with a few well-placed shots, but this was far outside his sphere of influence.

'Or the heavy transports,' Xettus said. He sounded concerned: clearly, the Metalphage was in no mood to lose the prizes he had secured from Anthras.

'Which are still shadowing us, I note,' Va'kai said with displeasure. 'What part of "break formation" do they not understand?'

'They are not to be left unprotected!' Xettus ordered. 'They may yet be the defenders' true targets – the Imperials cannot hope to damage the *Unseen*!'

'In my experience, the slaves of the Golden Throne are capable of hoping a great many things,' Va'kai commented. 'Sometimes, they even manage them. I am calling the rearguard up to target them.' He moistened his lips as he studied the hololith, and cones and lines began to emanate from the various icons shown: projected courses, unless Halver was much mistaken. They extended, solidified, began to cross over...

'They are not aiming to get into broadside position,' Halver said, as realisation dawned. 'They are going to ram us. This is not a thrust disguised as a hammer blow, it is a hammer blow disguised as a thrust!'

COMBAT DROP

The ship transporting Solomon to the moon of Downreach, several hundred thousand miles from the battle for Qampar's orbital supremacy, was a junker scow called the *Old Victorius*. It was the kind of odd-job vessel of which there might be thousands in any populated system: it could haul freight, carry tools for the crew to mine asteroids, or perform salvage jobs on wrecked ships – or possibly, with a few cunningly fitted guns, on ships that might not have been entirely wrecked before the scow reached them. It lacked the speed or inbuilt firepower for dedicated piracy, but might serve a small fleet of such scavengers as a supply vessel. As with many such craft, it had been altered, repaired, and refitted so extensively that its original designation was unclear. The *Old Victorius* was a mongrel beast, unique but unremarkable, just another slight variant on a familiar design. In fact, Solomon concluded, it was very fitting for the Alpha Legion.

Apart from the internal scale.

'I feel like a prisoner,' growled Alboc. He was a massive Space

Marine, half a head taller than any of his remaining brethren in the First Strike. There were only a dozen of them left in total: seven in Alboc's squad, a mere three from a team headed by a warrior named Venuen, the Apothecary known as Dinal Bloodsinger, and Raelin Amran himself.

Solomon checked his chrono. 'This will be over soon.'

'I do not need your platitudes,' Alboc retorted, rising from his crouch against the hold's wall. The ship's corridors and hatchways were designed for baseline humans, and without much consideration given even for them. For Space Marines, attempting to move through the ship was an invitation to become inextricably wedged. Only the cargo holds gave them the room they needed, and Solomon had spent the last day and a half in the same space as a dozen killers with the short tempers characteristic of those who had attracted the gaze of Khorne.

He had weathered it without Tulava, too. Neither of them fully trusted that her tongue would not land her in trouble; and in any case, Tul had no wish to spend extended periods of time in the same space as warriors whose comrades she had possessed with the Neverborn without their consent.

'Peace, brother,' Raelin said, stepping forward and placing one hand on Alboc's breastplate. 'The Harrowmaster is not your enemy.'

It had been simple enough to tell the First Strike the truth of Xettus' treachery: Solomon had simply left out the part where their battle-brothers had already been taken over by daemonic forces. Xettus had fired on them just the same, and their fate would have been just as sealed.

Alboc's jaw worked, and Solomon could see the war going on behind his eyes. Part of the other Space Marine wanted to vent his rage on Solomon, to lose himself in bloodlust and violence, and forget about higher thought processes. However, Alboc was still Alpha Legion, and that was the other side pushing back at his psyche: the abhorrence of the simplistic, and the prevalence of strategy over brutality. Alboc knew that he was starting to lose himself, starting to lose the core of what it meant to belong to his Legion, and the frustration of that knowledge merely stoked his anger all the more.

Had Solomon been a part of the XX since its early days, one of those mythical veterans who had fought alongside the primarchs, perhaps he would have mourned what the Alpha Legion had become. Perhaps he would have felt pity for Alboc, who had fallen off the knife-edge they all walked between doing what they had been bred to do, and losing themselves in it until it was all they could think of.

Solomon did none of those things. He had been inducted into the Legion as it was today: a shattered, ragged, ever-shifting quagmire of warbands and alliances, the full extent of which was unknown even to themselves, let alone their enemies. He had encountered the warp-touched like Alboc for all of his existence as a Space Marine. They were tools to be used for the ends of those who were still fully in command of their own minds, and one did not feel pity for tools. So he remained still and unspeaking, keeping his hands away from weapons, and without letting any emotion show on his face. Showing deference to the Khornate was as dangerous as responding with aggression.

Alboc settled a little. His pupils contracted again, the tic around his left eye subsided, and he returned to the standard manner of a Space Marine: deadly at a moment's notice, to be sure, but not actively seeking bloodshed.

Solomon's chrono pinged. 'It is time, brothers.'

He placed his helmet on his head. This was not just a precaution for what was to come, but to conceal his identity. His armour had not been serviced since the Battle of Anthras, for he trusted none of the new crop of tech-priests that had seeped through the fleet since Xettus had arrived. The Metalphage's entourage of New Mechanicum adepts was welcome in many ways, but Solomon could not risk the news of his survival reaching his rival. So it was that he wore the identity of a nameless legionnaire in battle-scarred plate who was attached to the remnants of the First Strike for a minor terror mission, something to make the Imperium glance in a different direction and wonder if this attack heralded another, as-yet-unseen thrust.

He and the First Strike made their way to the service corridor that ran between this hold and the next one. This at least was large enough for them to traverse with ease, since it had been built to accommodate loading vehicles, and they emerged into another massive space. In the middle of it, somehow not dwarfed despite its comparatively small size, was the next stage of their transport.

A Kharybdis Assault Claw.

It was a truly ancient design, an assault craft that probably dated back to the Horus Heresy itself. Solomon took in its squat shape, heavily heat-shielded, with multiple insectoid legs and a fanged maw at the base armed with melta cutters and cyclic thermal jets. It looked predatory, even before you took into account the tales of how the machine-spirits of some such craft had degraded over time to become highly unpredictable. It was very possibly not safe, even for Space Marines. However, it was their only chance of getting where they wanted to go in one piece: the scow was not intended for atmospheric entry, and its shuttles were slow and poorly armoured.

The tech-adepts around the Kharybdis were moving away from it, having finished fuelling it, and performing whatever arcane – or possibly profane – rituals it required to operate. The First Strike pushed forward, almost jostling each other in their impatience to board. Solomon could sense their eagerness as the prospect of imminent combat grew more and more tangible, and he wondered again how wise it was to enter the Kharybdis: not because of the vessel itself, this time, but the simple presence of a dozen proto-berzerkers eager to shed blood.

He had no choice. If he was to reclaim his place as Harrowmaster, he needed the authority this mission would give him. Otherwise he would resign himself to watching Xettus doom the greatest alliance of the Alpha Legion the Ultima Segmentum had seen in millennia to... adequacy. A threat, a nuisance, a force that would pillage planets and spill blood, but which would ultimately splinter apart again without having torn the gaping wound in the Imperium for which Solomon had forged it. Xettus was no fool – no one achieved a position of command within the Alpha Legion if they were a fool – but he lacked vision.

One of the tech-adepts, little more than a shadow in a robe, drifted towards him. Solomon tensed, wary in case this was one of Xettus' underlings that had identified him at the last moment. However, the voice that emanated from the deep cowl was far more familiar.

'Good luck, Harrowmaster,' murmured the unmistakeable tones of Magos Yallamagasa.

Solomon frowned in surprise. 'Diabolicus Secundus?'

'The circuits of this individual were amusingly easy to override for my own purposes,' the abominable intelligence said, with an electronic chuckle. 'Rest assured, Harrowmaster, that I have no interest in Lord Xettus retaining his current prominence within the Legion. You will have my support in your endeavours.'

Solomon took that in. It made a certain amount of sense that the part of Yallamagasa which was focused on machinery had no wish to see the Metalphage in command of the Legion. In fact, should Xettus Qeele lose his influence, there was no question as to who – or in this case, what – would be most likely to take command of the various daemon engines and captured war machines that were currently the core of Xettus' power.

'You want me to get in that thing?' said a voice at Solomon's elbow, announcing the arrival of Tulava Dyne. She was swathed in a hooded robe and her face was covered with a rebreather mask, to limit the chances of her being identified by anyone who happened to remember what the former Harrowmaster's sorceress looked like.

'The anatomy of a baseline human is insufficient to withstand the physical stresses of a drop pod descent and landing,' Solomon said. 'However, someone with your gifts might be able to compensate.'

'You're not selling me on it.'

'The alternative is Xettus as Harrowmaster.'

Tulava shuddered, and heaved a long-suffering sigh. 'Fine, where's the door?'

The Kharybdis launched with a kick like an enraged grox, and screamed towards the moon of Downreach like a bloodthirsty meteor. There was no subtlety about this, no distractions, no clever masking of intentions. The scow had been all the subterfuge necessary: now the Alpha Legion fell groundwards with blades bared, and dared the defenders to stop them.

A single falling object would initially be treated as an anomaly, of course. It might be a piece of debris coming loose from an orbiting ship and caught in Downreach's gravity well, in which case it would almost certainly burn up in the atmosphere and be no threat to anyone. However, if there was anyone competent on an auspex then they would realise after a while that the object in question was not burning up, and was moving faster than could be accounted for by gravitational pull alone.

'What are the defences like?' Dinal Bloodsinger asked. He

seemed the least swayed by the influence of Khorne, and while most others of the First Strike were gripping their restraints and, Solomon imagined, staring off into the distance with pinned pupils behind their helmets at an imagined enemy, the Apothecary still seemed focused on the here and now.

'The moon's defences should be basic,' Solomon replied. 'It is unlikely to be targeted by most reavers, since it is relatively sparsely populated, and without major riches of any sort. Our objective, on the other hand, is likely to be well protected, although not obviously so. It is disguised as an Administratum facility, but will almost certainly have highly trained troops and defensive ordnance.'

The Apothecary nodded, and Solomon could hear the smile in his voice. 'That sounds like an invigorating challenge, Harrowmaster.'

Solomon became aware of a consistent low muttering emanating from his left, and looked sideways at Tulava Dyne. The sorceress was strapped in as best she could be, but she looked like an infant in the restraints designed to hold a warrior of the Legiones Astartes in place during a drop. She had removed her respirator now there was no risk of being recognised by hostile forces, and her lips were moving non-stop as she appealed to any powers that might be listening to safeguard her.

'Are you well, Tulava?' he asked with false cheer, anticipating a barbed response. Dyne did not look at him, but continued her muttered refrain. Solomon strained his hearing, but could not detect anything that led him to believe that she was actively working an incantation, so he tried again. 'Tul!'

She jumped, and looked at him with wide eyes. Solomon was reminded once more that she was still mortal, a powerful mind housed in a fragile body which had not yet been granted any boons by the Ruinous Powers. It was remarkable to think that such a powerful being could be killed by physical stresses that would cause him no more than mild discomfort.

'Are you well?' he asked again, more seriously. She inhaled deeply, without taking her eyes from him, exhaled again, sniffed sharply once, and nodded.

The Kharybdis jolted violently, and Tulava cried out in alarm.

'The retros should not be activating already,' Dinal observed.

'Indeed,' Solomon agreed. 'We are taking fire.' The drop pod rang again, as another shot struck them. 'I suspect the defences of the Inquisition site have targeted us.'

'And what are we planning on doing about that?' Tulava demanded. 'You might survive if this thing is cracked open like an egg, but I'm not so confident!'

'There is nothing we can do,' Solomon told her calmly. 'This vessel has weathered countless attack runs – we must simply trust that it will survive one more.'

'I swear to all the gods, Space Marines are the most aggravating beings in the galaxy, no matter what cause you follow!' Tulava raged. Another shot clipped them, and the Kharybdis tilted violently. 'Gah! The warp take this, Solomon! Do you *want* to get shot out of the air, and leave Xettus to rule unchallenged?'

'Of course not,' Solomon replied. Had he ever felt the fear he could see in Tulava's eyes, even as a child? He found it hard to believe: he certainly could not recall it. 'But there are no alternatives. This is our only possible approach.'

Tulava's eyes narrowed. 'How far above the ground will we be when the retros fire?'

'Fifteen hundred feet,' Dinal Bloodsinger responded.

'And when will that occur?'

'In seven seconds.'

Tulava's mouth widened into a humourless grin. 'Then this is not *my* only possible approach.'

'Five seconds.'

Solomon realised her intention immediately. 'Tulava, no! You would be placing yourself into even greater danger if you warp-walk to the ground alone!'

'Two seconds.'

Tulava's grin widened, beneath desperate eyes.

'I know.'

She released her restraints, fell to the deck of the Kharybdis, then reached out and placed one hand on Solomon's greave. He had time to open his mouth, but not the time to protest, before the familiar purple-edged blackness swept up to engulf him.

DEATH OF THE DAWNBLADE

'Give me the helm!' Va'kai snapped to his servitors. A moment later he tapped commands into his throne, and the *Unseen* began to change course again, the mismatched propulsion systems straining to obey his wishes.

'What are you doing?' Xettus demanded, rounding on him. 'The transports–'

'The warp take your transports!' Va'kai snarled. 'We are a hulk, stitched together from wrecks and salvages! We have the size to weather most ordnance fire for long enough to destroy who-ever is attacking us, but we do not have the structural integrity to withstand multiple full-speed collisions with vessels of this size! And I,' he added tightly, 'have no intention of dying today.'

Halver watched as the *Unseen*'s projected course began to disentangle from those of the Imperial fleet. The Imperi-um's ships tried to alter their courses as well, but as they got closer and closer, the window for successful readjustment grew smaller and smaller. The *Unseen*, guided by Krozier Va'kai's expert hand, slipped away from the possible trajectory of one after another, until only one remained.

The *Dawnblade*, pulling into a steeper and steeper dive, finally emerged from its escort.

'All guns, target that vessel,' Va'kai ordered. Every weapon for which they had ammunition kicked its payload repeatedly out into the void, seeking to break the shining strike cruiser apart before it could complete its suicide run. Impact after impact was shrugged off by multicoloured void shields at a rate they surely could not maintain, but the *Dawnblade* was now so close that Halver could see the flashes of its protection as it shed the power of the shots into the immaterium.

'They are aiming for us,' he said, unable to keep the tension from his voice. 'For this section specifically.'

'They are aiming to die, and I intend to oblige them!' Va'kai snapped. 'Increase rate of fire!'

'Increased rate of fire will lead to weapons overheating,' a servitor intoned emotionlessly.

'Acknowledged!'

The servitors, their rote warnings dispensed, obeyed. The rain of death pouring out from the space hulk increased. Halver saw a void shield flare again, and again, until finally the first one failed. The strike cruiser had multiple shields, of course, but the initial overload merely dumped an even greater strain on the rest of their systems. It would be a matter of seconds before the rest gave out, and then it would simply be a brutal battle of attrition between the *Unseen*'s ordnance and the *Dawnblade*'s hull armour.

The light of explosions glinted off distant fragments, and Halver thought for a moment that the prow of the strike cruiser had been blown apart, but then he realised what was actually occurring.

'Boarding pod launch detected,' another servitor reported. There were ten of them, Halver saw; each one flaring out around the narrow corridor of destruction with which the *Unseen* was punishing the *Dawnblade*. The choice being presented to Va'kai was clear.

'Activate defensive turrets,' Va'kai ordered, 'so long as that does not interfere with the power required for main weapons.'

'There could be fifty Primaris Marines within those pods!' Xettus barked.

'And we will deal with them if they get here,' Va'kai replied tightly. 'Right now, I am focused on keeping us in one piece!'

The strike cruiser's other void shields failed, a kaleidoscopic collapse that left the vessel naked and unprotected. Guns the size of assault craft raged silently into the void, lances stabbed beams of searing energy outwards, and other, more esoteric weapons fired as well, if Halver was any judge. Not even the Imperium's finest shipbuilding could hope to stand for long against such a barrage.

The *Dawnblade* died, and it died messily. It was torn apart, disintegrated from bow to stern as the *Unseen*'s firepower chewed it up. Va'kai kept his weapons firing until they failed, until the remnants of their enemy was filling the viewports as a fireball of wreckage.

Krozier Va'kai opened the channel on the internal broadcast system, and spoke as calmly as though he were issuing a routine instruction to a maintenance servitor.

'Brace for impact.'

The *Dawnblade* struck.

The space hulk's superstructure rang with the force of the collision. Qope Halver had to grab on to a cogitator bank to prevent himself from being thrown across the bridge: Xettus' thralls were not so resilient, and slammed into the far wall and each other with distressed hisses and crackles from their vox-units as their limbs snapped. Halver froze, waiting for the first telltale creaks and groans as the *Unseen* began to rip apart.

They never came.

'Moderate impact damage,' Va'kai reported, scanning his feeds. 'Hull punctures in a few places, nothing severe. We turned a battering ram into a wreckage storm – it lacked the concentrated mass to impale us.'

'The pods?' Xettus demanded. Va'kai waved a hand at his read-outs.

'I am working from something like a dozen patched-together systems, here. Ascertaining where a boarding pod has attached itself to a vessel is hard enough at the best of times, and this is most certainly not that. I will detail teams to do sweeps, but any loyalists who get aboard are going to be vastly outnumbered. We may have to reduce the number of legionnaires we land from the *Unseen*, in order to maintain an appropriate security presence.'

'What about the rest of their fleet?' Halver asked.

'The rearguard have engaged them, and the vanguard are doubling back,' Va'kai reported. 'They will bloody our noses before they are done, but they pose no serious threat now. They knew they could not defeat us in void combat, so they threw everything into trying to decapitate us. It was a bold gamble, but it failed. Now we can land uncontested.'

'Hydra Dominatus, my brothers,' Xettus said, turning away from the hololith to stare out of the viewports at the orb of Qampar.

'Hydra Dominatus,' Halver echoed, fingering his boltgun once more. Whomever he was acknowledging as Harrowmaster, he would be glad to have his feet on a planet again, and an enemy in front of him whom he could kill.

DOWNREACH

Tulava had never properly explained to Solomon how she warp-walked, but in all the times she had done it with him they had never once rematerialised in mid-air; or, even worse, within solid matter. The sorceress' ability had a far shorter range than teleporters, but unlike those machines, which even with the technological genius of the Adeptus Mechanicus or the New Mechanicum were something of a jump into the unknown based around hope and best guesses, Tulava appeared to know where she was going before she re-emerged from the warp.

Sometimes that involved appearing in front of a crowd of enemies, but even when plucked without warning from his restraints in a Kharybdis drop pod, Solomon was ready for battle at a moment's notice.

They were on a defensive rampart atop a wall, amidst wailing sirens and gunfire. Solomon snatched his bolter up from where it was mag-clamped to his thigh, and began firing before any of the black-clad soldiers running to their posts had registered that there was now a Space Marine in their path. He killed three before any of them managed to raise a weapon, and two more before they pulled a trigger. The last one got a shot off, a hotshot blast which glanced off Solomon's pauldron and left a burn mark across one of the hydra's heads. Solomon's return shot struck the trooper in the neck, blowing off their head and half of their torso.

'You–' he began angrily, turning to address Tulava, but was cut off by the taste of burned sugar on his tongue, and the sorceress' scream of effort as she sent a psychic blast of force rippling through the air. It struck the barrel of a skyward-pointing battle cannon on a turret fifty yards away, and knocked it sideways: the defence gun still fired its shell, but the shot roared wide rather than striking its intended target at what would have effectively been point-blank range.

Instead of being blown apart, the Kharybdis landed with a rockcrete-shattering *thud* in the central courtyard. Its storm launchers activated, blasting out a wave of destruction that reduced the contents of the courtyard to smithereens.

'You're welcome,' Tulava mumbled, staggering, clearly weakened by two huge efforts in quick succession.

'Get behind me,' Solomon instructed, stepping around her. His subvocalised instruction sent the scales on his armour rippling to their reflective setting as more hotshot lasgun-armed troops began to emerge from the turret's postern. The protection it gave was no longer complete, thanks to his and Tulava's run-ins with Mechanicus guard servitors in the depths of the Anthras node, but it was sufficient to keep him insulated from the two blasts intended for Tulava, which instead struck him harmlessly while he selected a new type of ammunition from his magazine, looted from the forge world's armouries. 'Time to see if the tech-priests knew what they were doing.'

He raised his relic bolter, and fired a single shot. The metal storm frag-round detonated just in front of the tightly packed group of defenders, cut through their body armour like it was paper, and shredded them into meat.

'Impressive,' Tulava wheezed, peering around his elbow.

The doors of the Kharybdis crashed to the ground, and the vox-net erupted with roars as the First Strike poured out, looking for living enemies on which to vent their bloodlust. Solomon's first instinct was to vault over the internal parapet, drop to the courtyard, and join them; or more accurately, attempt to direct them. However, the battle cannon was still operational, and was declining its barrel to open fire at their only way off this moon.

Solomon sprang forward, reaching the blood-slicked bodies he had just killed within a few strides, and hurdled them to crash into the postern door and knock it from its hinges. The chamber beyond was a guardroom that also housed the controls for the battle cannon. There were two humans by the targeting cogitator bank, each one aiming an autopistol at him.

Their reflexes were too slow, as humans usually were.

He reached out with his bionic arm, extending the fingers without thinking, and seized one of the cannon operators, then threw him into the other with bone-breaking force before either of them had properly processed what or where he was. He pulled a frag grenade from his belt, primed it, then wedged it between two cogitator banks and withdrew to the doorway.

'You do not want to go in there,' he told Tulava as he remerged. The sorceress had not yet finished picking her way through the corpses of the fragged defenders, and she flinched involuntarily as the grenade detonated, destroying the battle cannon's controls.

'"Get behind me", you said,' Tulava grumbled. 'Staying behind you is a lot easier when you don't go racing off!'

'You can warpwalk, can you not?' Solomon said lightly, taking a moment to get a more tactical perspective of their surroundings. There was no universal layout for Administratum complexes across the galaxy, but there were just enough defensive enhancements to this facility for its clandestine nature to be obvious to a trained observer such as himself; even without the presence of the battle cannon, which judging by the top of the turret, had previously been shielded from prying eyes by a decorative dome that retracted when a threat appeared.

Solomon let himself feel a twinge of excitement. So much of the last two hundred years had involved keeping his emotions under tight control, lest he overreach himself in his eagerness. Time and time again, he had fought down disappointment and accepted lesser successes, when the Serpent's Teeth were denied their original goal by chance, or the unknowing interference of unrelated parties, or even, on occasion, a surprising level of competence from the Imperium. However, his information had been correct in terms of the nature of this place. If the rest of it was accurate, he was on the verge of a personal triumph greater than any he had achieved before.

He reined himself in again. He might yet be frustrated in his primary purpose, but eliminating one of the Inquisition's ghost sites would still be a victory. For all of the enhanced defences, there was no possibility that anything here would have the capability to resist a dozen Space Marines. Anything the enemy wanted to protect was worth destroying. By such small successes was the greater battle won.

'I can't warpwalk at the moment,' Tulava was protesting. She looked even paler than usual.

'Then we shall have to travel in a more conventional fashion,' Solomon told her. He reached her side within a second.

'Wait, what–'

He picked Tulava up under one arm, and stepped off the walkway. It was approximately a thirty-foot drop to what was left of the internal courtyard after the Kharybdis and its storm launchers had finished with it, and the servos of his armour absorbed the impact without trouble.

Not that you would have believed it if you listened to Tulava.

'Argh! My *ribs!*'

'Your ribs are undamaged,' Solomon said calmly, setting her on her feet. 'I would have heard or felt it if they had fractured or broken.'

'*You* would have felt it?'

'You complain like a child,' Solomon said, then opened a vox-channel. 'First Strike, report.'

Nothing answered him apart from howls and roars, and the sounds of bolt pistols and chainswords. Solomon ground his teeth, and tried again.

'Lord Amran? Brother Dinal?'

Still nothing. It appeared that even the Apothecary was lost to the joy of battle. It was frustrating, but not useless: even if the First Strike were not heading for their goal, all of the complex's defences would surely gravitate towards them, leaving Solomon and Tulava comparatively unmolested.

'That was revenge for me snatching you out of the pod, wasn't it?' Tulava groaned, straightening up with a wince.

'I am Alpha Legion,' Solomon said, triangulating the location of his bloodthirsty battle-brothers through the noise of their progress. They had gone into the northern wing, which was at least where his source had indicated the vault to be. 'We are above such petty concepts as revenge.'

'Solomon, I don't know how best to concisely recount the events of the last ten thousand years, but–'

'This way,' Solomon cut her off. He moved only at a slow jog instead of a run, but that was still enough to leave the sorceress struggling breathlessly after him.

It was unclear exactly how many of the complex's inhabitants knew of its true nature. The troops guarding it did not need to know what secrets they were protecting, merely that they were to kill any unauthorised intruders. The Administratum adepts whose bodies Solomon was now encountering alongside their black-armoured protectors were unlikely to have any greater insight. Perhaps they wondered why they warranted such staunch defences; more likely they gave thanks to their false god that they were so lucky, and gave it no further thought. It was even possible that no one here actually worked for the Administratum at all, but simply believed they did; that everything was part of an Inquisition cover operation, with only a handful of ranking individuals who knew who the complex's true masters were.

The level of defences might have sufficed against most attackers, but not the First Strike. They had hit just as hard as Solomon would have expected, and left a trail of destruction in their wake as they ploughed deeper and deeper into the building. Deeper was the operative word, in fact: starting from ground level, their path began to descend.

'It seems they remembered your briefing on where you thought the vault was, at least,' Tulava commented as they reached another stairwell spattered with blood.

'That seems unlikely, given they will not even respond to my hails,' Solomon remarked. All the same, his fellow legionnaires were moving unerringly in what he believed was the correct direction.

'Then perhaps the defenders are just pulling back to try to guard it,' Tulava said, setting off down the stairs with her force staff levelled.

'It feels too easy,' Solomon said, pushing past her to take the lead, despite her squawk of protest. 'They could draw us away from their most valuable artefacts by retreating along a different route.'

'You're overcomplicating it,' Tulava said, slightly huffily. 'These aren't Space Marines who know about Khornate berzerkers – they're humans who have been told to guard a certain door, or whatever, faced with terrifying killing machines. They'll be lucky if they stay alive long enough to get a shot off when they actually see what's coming for them, let alone have the composure to understand that the enemy's blood-drunk, and that they should abandon their posts as a tactical move.'

Solomon grimaced, but the sorceress' words made sense. 'I knew I kept you around for a reason.'

'For my insight into the Imperium's humanity?' Tulava scoffed. 'They would consider me damned thrice-over for the choices I've made, and I wield powers beyond the comprehension of all but their greatest hypocrites.'

'You are closer to them than I,' Solomon said absently. 'I remember so little of my life before the Legion that I truly might never have been anyone else.'

They had reached the bottom of the stairs, and a choice of three routes: a corridor to the right, its mirror to the left, or one directly ahead, down which the First Strike had left yet more bodies. Solomon's audio sensors picked up rasping, ragged breathing from near his feet. It seemed the First Strike had neglected to kill one of their victims as they tore through the defenders. It was a testament to their speed that Solomon and Tulava, advancing without any resistance, had not yet caught them.

Solomon reached down and hoisted the half-dead trooper off the floor, prompting a groan of agony. The man was wearing a sophisticated mesh jacket, reinforced with plasteel plates, but it had done nothing to stop a chainblade with a Space Marine's force behind it. His left arm was truncated at the elbow, and there was a deep, wet gash beneath his ribs on that side.

'Which way is the vault?' Solomon demanded. The man focused on his face, then bared his teeth.

'Go... to hell.'

'Give him to me,' Tulava purred, dropping into the voice she reserved solely for theatrically intimidating difficult Imperials whose tongues might be loosened by the threat of sorcery, and its damning influence.

'We do not have time,' Solomon said. He twisted the trooper around to face down the left corridor. 'Is it this way?' He got nothing except halting, agonised breaths in response, so he turned the man through ninety degrees, looking directly away from the stairs. 'This way?'

The reaction was minimal, and would have been imperceptible to most observers. Solomon was watching closely, however, and he caught the faint tells: a flicker of the eyes, and a tightening of the lips. Easy to mistake in a man caught in the grips of his death-pain, but still clear as day to Solomon. 'You can't trick a trickster' was an adage well known throughout the Imperium's criminal classes, and humans could give themselves away in a lie without ever saying a word.

Solomon snapped the man's neck with a flick of his wrist, and dropped him. 'This way.'

The First Strike were still heading in the correct direction.

They caught up to Raelin Amran and his legionnaires at the doors to the vault itself. The desperate last stand of the remaining defenders was eradicated within seconds, as black-clad bodies were cut down by swinging chainblades and point-blank bolt pistol blasts. Solomon saw Alboc's massive form close in on the last remaining trio while his battle-brothers were already decapitating corpses, harvesting skulls for a compulsion they did not yet fully understand. The big Alpha Legionnaire raised his chainsword, nearly scraping the ceiling above him as he did so.

Solomon caught sight of the middle trooper, whose chest appeared somewhat bulkier than those of her colleagues on either side of her, and recognised the shape of the belts of grenades strapped there, just before she detonated them.

Fire and force swept out in what seemed like slow motion. Alboc was immediately engulfed by the blast, which flashed towards Solomon–

–and broke in front of him like waves hitting a headland.

It was over in a second. The trooper's pyrrhic act had hastened the death of her and her colleagues by a few moments, but it had claimed one Alpha Legion life. Alboc lay on his back, thrown away by the force. The front of his helmet and gorget and half of his breastplate were missing, as was most of his face and a fair amount of his chest. Three of his companions had also been thrown from their feet by the blast, although with less obvious injuries to show for it, and the impact of it appeared to have finally jogged the rest from their frenzy somewhat.

Solomon turned to look at Tulava, who let her psychic shield drop along with the hand with which she had gestured it into being.

'Thank you for your concern,' Solomon said, 'but I doubt I would have been greatly affected at this distance.'

'Oh, I'm sure,' Tulava muttered, leaning wearily on her staff. 'I'd have been dead, though.'

'Have you considered being less fragile?' Solomon asked.

'Yes, you're right,' Tulava said sourly. 'I'll go to the Diabolicus and ask him to make me into one of his Dishonour Guard.'

'You have heard the screams of their making, just as I have,' Solomon said. 'You do not want that.'

'Lead me into another explosion like that, and my opinion might change.'

'Lord Akurra,' Raelin Amran rasped, having shaken some semblance of sense back into himself.

'Lord Amran,' Solomon said, not letting his distaste at the other Space Marine's excesses creep into his voice, instead replacing it with polite enquiry. 'Are you seeing to your fallen?'

Amran's helm turned towards where Alboc lay. Solomon got the distinct impression that the lord of the First Strike had to concentrate to distinguish his own battle-brother's corpse from those that surrounded him. Those already dead were little more than background to the worshippers of Khorne, unless their skulls were in the process of being freed from their original moorings.

'Bloodsinger,' Amran said, his voice thick even through the vox-grille of his helmet. 'Gene-seed.'

Dinal stepped forward, activating his narthecium. The damage to Alboc's battleplate meant that no drilling or cutting was necessary: the reductor plunged into his flesh twice, and the fleshy lumps of the progenoid glands were retrieved. Solomon was unsure whether they were intact enough to be of use, after the explosion that had killed their bearer, but that was not his concern.

'Where now?' Amran asked. He appeared to be struggling to form words. Solomon could hear the rasping breathing of several of Amran's followers. They were on the verge of losing control again, and the only living targets for their rage were himself and Tulava.

'Through there,' he said, pointing to the thick pair of blast doors in front of which the last troopers had died. They were slightly buckled from the force of the grenade explosion, but remained standing. That was not the case for long, after the First

Strike had placed a pair of melta bombs on them. Walking the razor's edge of bloodlust though they might be, they were still Space Marines, and they still knew the quickest way to get to potential victims.

The melta bombs activated, releasing a concentrated blast of super-heat, and the doors largely melted out of existence. The First Strike poured through the gap, knocking the still-molten remnants aside in their eagerness to further wet their blades with the blood of whoever might be within, and without a backward glance at the body of the warrior who had been their battle-brother for decades, possibly centuries.

Solomon followed more cautiously, with Tulava trailing behind him. He was not anticipating living defenders within the vault itself – assuming his intelligence had been correct, and they were indeed in the correct place – but he was not prepared to rule the possibility out. There might be more esoteric defences in any case: battle-servitors, perhaps, of the sort they had encountered in the tunnels on Anthras, or some other Inquisitorial toy. This was an Ordo Malleus facility, after all, and the radicals amongst them were prepared to use virtually anything to further their own purposes; even sorcery and daemonhosts, in extreme circumstances.

The vault was not huge – not the cavernous chamber of endless unmarked crates that Solomon's mind's eye had conjured when he had first learned of it – but it was still a sizeable space in which a careful pilot could have parked a Thunderhawk, given an appropriate entry point. Great racks marched across it, many of which were burdened with boxes. Some containers were no larger than a child's hand, while others could have comfortably accommodated a Space Marine in full armour. Other shelves were bare, awaiting new arrivals, or having at some point been cleared of what they had once held. In one place, the racks gave way to something free-standing which was at least twenty feet high, and completely shrouded under a huge, heavy cloth cover which was weighted down at the edges, and covered with strange symbols. Solomon got the impression that it might be a statue of some sort underneath there, but he could not be sure; nor was he completely certain, despite the patient read-outs from his helmet's sensors insisting that no such thing was taking place, that it was not moving very slightly.

'What now?' Tulava asked, looking around. 'Is there some form of index, or…?'

Solomon reached out and removed his helmet. He wanted to breathe in the air of this place for some reason, as though he could find his quarry by smell. He registered only dust and the faint metallic scent of the racks, overlaid by the stink of blood and the whiff of fyceline from the weapons of the First Strike.

He narrowed his eyes. Some of the dust on the shelves had been disturbed recently.

Very recently.

'There may be a cogitator bank,' he said, looking around. 'Or perhaps whoever accesses this facility brings the inventory with them, to avoid it being stored on-site.'

'You can't expect us to go through every box here…' Tulava began, but broke off when Solomon whirled around to face her.

'I *will* go through every box here,' he said. 'Every box, every crate, every compartment. I will break everything apart and search in the crevices, if I have to!' He clenched and opened the fist of his bionic arm. He was so close! 'If what I seek is not here, then so be it, but I will not be thwarted by a lack of thoroughness!'

Tulava's face had screwed up into an expression of concern, which was now shifting into controlled alarm. 'And are you expecting *them* to go through every box here?'

'Akurra!'

The word came from behind Solomon. It was growled out from between teeth, and dripping with saliva. It was almost unrecognisable, but Solomon knew who had spoken even as he turned back.

Raelin Amran and the First Strike had spread out through the chamber, but were now clustered together again, and advancing towards Solomon and Tulava.

'No blood here,' their leader snarled. 'No skulls. No prey!'

'Ready?' Tulava asked from behind him. The skin on the back of Solomon's neck detected a faint chill as she drew in her will, ready for him to throw himself flat and her to unleash a blast of psychic force, just as they had done so many times before.

'Wait,' he said instead. He knew his own capabilities, and Tulava's, but his armour was already damaged, and she was tired. Eleven Alpha Legionnaires would have been a tall order at the best of times, let alone under such circumstances, and especially when the opponents in question were on the verge of completely losing control to the Blood God. You could manipulate the worshippers of Khorne more easily that most, you could bait them and distract them and outwit them, but combat was where they made up for all those shortcomings. If you were actually fighting the followers of the Skull Throne, you had already lost half of the battle.

He would not lose this opportunity, not now. The First Strike were slipping, but they were still Alpha Legion, and they were not fully lost yet. Reason could still prevail. He opened his mouth to try diplomacy.

'*Solomon.*'

That word was not uttered by anyone within the room. The faint crackle, the multi-directional nature of it, the echoes: it was coming from hidden vox-units.

Solomon knew that voice.

'I am so glad you decided to–'

A less intelligent warrior would have stayed to listen. They would have stood, rooted to the spot by shock, as they were taunted. Not Solomon Akurra. If your enemy felt secure enough to speak to you, you were standing in the wrong place. He snatched Tulava up again, and immediately ran for the doors.

'Wait, what are…? Detonate! Now!'

The First Strike lurched into pursuit as soon as Solomon moved, their hair-trigger senses activated by the sight of a living being fleeing. The fact that Solomon was not running from them was immaterial; nor was their movement born from any sense of self-preservation, whether or not they had heard the order to detonate. He was running, and so they gave chase.

But they had started farther from the doors, and they were not fast enough.

Solomon was through and into the passage beyond before the explosions began to rip up from beneath the floor of the vault, and out from the walls. He cut right immediately, and was rewarded for his choice by not getting caught in the eruption of flame and dust that billowed out of the doorway on his heels. As soon as it subsided, he veered back into the original corridor, making for the stairs to the upper levels. He could already hear the creaking of strained masonry, and the patter of dust falling from the vault's ceiling growing into a tide.

'The roof's coming down!' Tulava yelled, from across his shoulder.

'I am aware of this!' Solomon replied. He reached where the injured trooper had unwittingly given him directions, and took the stairs five at a time, ignoring the grunts from Tulava as she was jolted around.

'I can… probably… get us out… of here!' the sorceress gasped, in time with his footfalls.

'Save your strength,' Solomon instructed her, eyeing the cracks running along the ceiling.

'Thank you... for your... concern.'

'This is not concern,' Solomon said. 'I will need your powers soon. Do not waste them now.'

A hotshot las-bolt blazed past him as he stepped out of the stairwell. The daemon in his bionic arm had aimed and fired his boltgun almost before he had registered the threat, and the three black-armoured complex troopers fell in sprays of blood and splintered bone. Solomon did not stop moving, but sprinted onwards towards the central courtyard.

'Can you... put me... down yet?' Tulava demanded.

'You could not keep up,' Solomon replied. 'Patience, we are nearly there.'

He set the sorceress down when they reached the doorway through which they had left the courtyard in the first place. Mere minutes had passed since the Alpha Legion's arrival, and the dust and powdered rockcrete from the impact of the Kharybdis' landing and the devastation wrought by its storm launchers still hung heavily in the air. He stole a look, then ducked back into cover.

'Eight hostiles,' he reported.

'Should be easy for you,' Tulava replied. The sorceress was still clutching her ribs, and a thin trail of blood leaked down from one temple where a scrap of stone or some similar small projectile had caught her.

'Two have a heavy bolter set up, and another two have a lascannon,' Solomon said. His armour would not protect him against such firepower, not in the condition it was in. 'The rest have hotshots. They are covering the Kharybdis, using it as bait.'

'I can warpwalk us inside it, but we'll be sitting targets until you can get the doors up,' Tulava said. She flinched as the floor beneath them shook. 'But I don't fancy our chances if we stay here.'

'Agreed.' Solomon removed two grenades from his belt. 'Be ready to move when I tell you, and make as little noise as possible.'

He primed the triggers, and hurled the blind grenades in different directions out of the doorway.

They detonated almost instantly, spewing out thick clouds of dense, black smoke, and emitting fizzing, hissing noises as they did so. The smoke was not just a visual obstruction; it also contained infrared bafflers, and broad-spectrum electromagnetic radiation and chaff. Even Solomon's helmet sensors were unable to penetrate the cover thrown up by blind grenades, so the targeting systems of the troopers would be completely foiled.

There was no question that an enemy was at work, of course, but when the smoke engulfed them the troopers' vox-equipment would be rendered non-functional as the signals were bounced and scrambled by the electronic agents within. Unable to see any potential targets, and unable to check in with each other, each one would have to make their own decision on what to do.

'Now,' Solomon said.

Power armour, composed as it was of thick plates with an external power source, was not a naturally stealthy form of protection. The Alpha Legion were adaptable, however, and Solomon's ceramite-shod feet barely made any more noise on the courtyard's surface than did Tulava's old Militarum-issue combat boots as they hurried to where Solomon knew the Kharybdis was. So thick was the cover belched out by the blind grenades that he could not even see it until they were within a few feet, at which point it loomed up out of the murk like some many-limbed terror from a nightmare.

'Get inside, and get down,' Solomon whispered. Tulava

nodded, and slipped past one of the mighty stanchions that stood between the lowered doors.

She made no noise that Solomon could detect in doing so – certainly none that would have been audible to the troopers still mired in the blind grenades' obscuring fog. One of them, though, chose that moment to open fire.

It was an unsighted las-blast which did not come within ten feet of Solomon, or the pod, but it was enough to spark the rest into action. Other hotshots responded, beams criss-crossing through the murk in a loose web of high-powered energy, which were dwarfed in turn when the lascannon opened up.

Solomon had no wish to test the protective powers of his armour against such a weapon, especially given that it was damaged. He lunged for the Kharybdis' control panels, and activated it.

Or tried to.

The machine-spirit that powered the pod was ancient, and malignant, and stubborn. It did not recognise Solomon, and had no intention of complying with his wishes. However, it was not the only spirit present.

Solomon laid the palm of his bionic arm on the main cogitator bank, and bid it go to work. The daemon bound within awoke and lashed out, and through whatever passed for its senses, Solomon felt the snarl of the Kharybdis as it was attacked. Solomon's daemon knew nothing of door hydraulics and propulsion systems, of course, but it understood fear and intimidation, and it relished the opportunity to bare its teeth.

The Kharybdis subsided, cowed into obedience. This time when Solomon activated the controls to close the doors, they responded.

There was no mistaking that, even through the cover thrown out by the blind grenades. The troopers went from taking wild shots at whatever might be stalking them through the murk to targeting the pod, guided more by the sound of the doors and their memory of where it was than by what they could see. Solomon ducked instinctively as heavy bolter fire ricocheted off the drop pod's hull: the shards of shells could have gone anywhere, including inside, but it appeared that luck – or some other power – was with them.

'Can we take off yet?' Tulava yelled, from the ball she was hunkered into.

'In a moment,' Solomon said. Taking off too early would see the doors potentially ripped from their hinges by air resistance. Tulava spat a curse as a lascannon blast caught the pod, sending the electronics flickering, but they came back online within a moment, and the doors shut with a hiss of atmospheric sealing.

'Protect yourself,' Solomon instructed Tulava, and activated the engines.

A Kharybdis drop pod, unlike smaller and later variants, was not a one-way vessel. It was an assault ship in truth, albeit a specialised one, and it could take off under its own power rather than being collected after use. It had not, however, been designed for use by anyone other than warriors of the Legiones Astartes.

The kick of the thrusters buckled Solomon's knees, for he had not had time to secure himself using the flight restraints. Tulava, now encased in a protective sphere of psychic energy, groaned as the effort to prevent her physical body from being crushed took its toll on her mental self. The G-forces were punishing, but they were moving. They were leaving Downreach behind them.

And not a moment too soon.

The Kharybdis had external pict-feeds to give the warriors it carried a view of where they would be landing, and what would be waiting for them outside, although Solomon suspected that it had been many years since the First Strike had paid any attention to what they showed. What they showed him right now, though, was the north wing of the Inquisition site being swallowed by the earth, as the explosion that had detonated beneath it brought that entire side of the complex down on itself. Countless tons of steel and rockcrete collapsed, burying whatever remained of the blood-crazed legionnaires.

And with them, the Ordo Malleus' relics.

Solomon watched in silence as the picture pulled back. The Kharybdis soared into the sky, punching up through the atmosphere of Downreach, until the complex was nothing more than a dot in the midst of a mottled, green-and-brown landscape.

'I'm sorry, Solomon,' Tulava said, fighting her way up to her feet. Their acceleration had decreased now, as they approached the edge of the thermosphere, and the sorceress was able to relax her psychic shielding. She was still unsteady, even so, and Solomon was glad he had not called on her to warpwalk them out of trouble on the moon, lest the G-forces of their take-off had overwhelmed her abilities and crushed her very bones against the drop pod's deck.

'You have no reason to be sorry,' Solomon told her. 'It appears that our pet snake has fangs after all. Hart sought to kill me with the very information he provided us. Perhaps he thinks he is still his own man.'

'I am sorry, because there's now no way to get what you were after,' Tulava said. Then her brows lowered. 'You're surely not thinking of going back–'

'Calm yourself,' Solomon told her. 'I will not be returning to Downreach.'

She nodded sombrely.

'But that does not mean that my prize is out of my reach,' Solomon continued. 'The manifests were genuine, the artefact was present. Hart was overconfident to gloat before he triggered his trap, but he would not have left such an item there for me to claim should I have not been killed, and he does not have a puritanical enough mindset to destroy it.'

Tulava's eyes flashed. 'You think he has it with him?'

Solomon smiled. 'Yes. He will be on a ship – I do not believe he would risk remaining groundside when he expected us to assault, lest our attack be more wide-ranging than he antici-pated. His ship will almost certainly be in orbit around this moon, however, or the signal delay would have been too great for him to risk his speech, foolish though it was.'

'But how will you find him?' Tulava asked.

Solomon activated the Kharybdis' communicator. 'Diaboli-cus Secundus, come in.'

The hiss of static was replaced by the distinctive voice of Yallamagasa's subordinate body. *'Lord Akurra. Was your ven-ture successful?'*

'Not yet, Secundus,' Solomon replied, 'but I am getting closer. I am sending you the timestamp for when a tightbeam carrier wave would have been sent to my location, suitable for remotely detonating explosives. You would, of course, have been moni-toring all broadcasts in my vicinity.'

'Of course, Lord Akurra.'

Solomon smiled like a viper.

'Then find me the point of origin.'

HINDSIGHT

'Your overconfidence is a flaw,' Tythus Yorr rumbled, the words sliding into place like leaden slabs over a tomb. His presence in Hart's chamber on the *Star of Kings* was a red thundercloud, threatening lightning. 'You should have detonated as soon as they were in position.'

'We set enough explosives to bring half the complex down,' Hart said. 'They will all die there.'

His words did not sound convincing, even to himself, and the bitter taste of disappointment sat heavily on his tongue. The other warriors with Akurra would surely have been caught in the main blast, but the Ghost? Rumours of the Alpha Legion were hard to come by, and virtually worthless in any case, even amongst those who were their factors – or had been impersonating their factors, Hart reminded himself – but still, Solomon Akurra had a reputation for getting in and out of places he should not be able to.

It was the first time that Kayzen Hart had laid eyes on the

warrior he had helped raise to power. It had been a strange experience, even via the imperfect medium of a grainy pict-sentry signal sent to the small Lampyridae-class lighter he had commandeered back at the space port on Qampar, using his Inquisitorial seal and the looming presence of his lifeward. Akurra looked alarmingly... normal. He could have worn the armour of most Imperial Chapters without seeming out of place. Truly, corruption in the soul was not necessarily reflected on the face.

Hart looked up at the glowering features of Tythus Yorr, with its prominent cheek scar and the silver service stud on the brow. 'My friend, calm yourself. Perhaps I was rash – perhaps the warning allowed Akurra to escape. Nonetheless, we drew a dozen Traitor Astartes into a trap today, and slew them, which is a triumph in and of itself. Furthermore, a variety of heretical artefacts were destroyed along with them.'

Yorr's cheek twitched. 'What of the artefacts you retrieved before we planted the explosives?'

'They may yet be of use,' Hart said. 'The ones I left behind were far too tainted, and should have been disposed of long ago – they had been collected and stored there by fools. And Nessa calls *me* radical! Ha!' He snorted. 'The ones with us warrant further study, however.'

'And the... *item?*' Yorr asked, distaste dripping from his voice. Hart found it interesting – almost amusing, although he would never admit it to his lifeward – how a Space Marine could spend his life wading through the ichor and entrails of his enemies without complaint, but be so utterly disgusted by an inanimate object based solely on its history.

'It has mysteries that may benefit the Imperium, if they can be unravelled,' Hart said firmly. 'It was said to be a fearsome weapon. If its effects can be reproduced–'

'It is a foul thing,' Yorr cut him off. 'It should be destroyed.'

'You have told me how the Deathwatch have access to weapons that incorporate elements of xenos technology,' Hart pointed out. 'We do not know this weapon's origin. It may indeed be of xenos make. If so, how would we be doing any different to what the Ordo Xenos does? To what you have done?'

Yorr's lips tightened, and he looked away. 'It is not the same.'

Hart opened his mouth to attempt to reassure Yorr further, but was interrupted by a flashing light indicating that the captain wanted his attention. He had left strict instructions that he was not to be disturbed except in the most exceptional circumstances, and he was fairly sure that the twin threat of Inquisition and Space Marine would have ensured the captain's compliance to those orders, so it seemed likely that this warranted his attention.

'Yes?' he said, opening the comm channel to the bridge.

'*Milord inquisitor, sir,*' came the nervous voice of Captain Verhardt. '*We have been commanded to hold position, and prepare to be boarded.*'

'By whom?' Hart snapped.

'*Milord, another inquisitor, milord–*'

Hart cut the link and cursed. 'Nessa!'

'Unless your popularity has increased remarkably,' Yorr agreed. Hart shot him a glance, but the Space Marine's face gave nothing away. Throne, but the Consul had an odd sense of humour, at times.

He opened the channel again. 'Ignore that order, and evade whatever ship she is approaching on.'

'*Milord…!*'

'He may not obey you,' Yorr said quietly. 'He is caught between two inquisitors, both of equal rank.'

'I am here, and Nessa is not!' Hart spat. 'If he has any sense of self-preservation, he will obey me! Captain,' he said into the transmitter, 'I cannot feel the ship moving! Why are you not evading?'

Only silence answered him, even though the steady green light showed that the channel was still open.

'Captain?'

'How close does Inquisitor Karnis have to be in order to exert her control over someone?' Tythus Yorr asked.

Hart swore under his breath. 'To the bridge, and quickly!'

Yorr got there first, of course, despite the cramped conditions. The discharge of an autopistol echoed through the corridors, and Hart arrived to find Captain Verhardt being held immobile between the Crimson Consul's massive armoured gauntlets, with the sidearm in question on the floor. There were no other crew aboard the *Star of Kings* to cause problems, other than basic servitors: Captain Verhardt was his own master, but no one else's.

He was also smiling, and sweating. The second was a completely understandable reaction to being in the grip of a Space Marine, but the first was not.

'There you are, Kayzen,' he said, as Hart entered the bridge with Helorassa drawn. The deferential, head-ducking man who had piloted them from Qampar to Downreach, and then back into orbit, had gone. Hart knew who had taken his place.

'This is becoming an obsession, Nessa,' he said, scanning the bridge. Unfortunately, the read-outs of the myriad ancient instruments meant little to him. 'You drove me from Qampar, could you not be satisfied with that? Should you not be there, helping to coordinate the defence?'

'And leave you to make off with your pick of tainted relics?' Nessa said, through the mouth of Captain Verhardt. 'I would be doing the Imperium and the ordo a disservice. Luckily, it was not hard to find the details of the vessel on which you fled.'

'Check your read-outs, Nessa,' Hart advised. 'You will see that the facility is destroyed, and the artefacts with them. I lured the Alpha Legion in, then detonated explosives.'

There was a pause, while Verhardt's face went blank. Then it reanimated with a sneer.

'In which case you will surely not object to us coming aboard to check that nothing slipped into your pocket on your way out.'

'You tried to kill me!' Hart shouted into Verhardt's face. 'Again!'

'Because you are a deceitful worm, Kayzen Hart,' Verhardt said, his voice laced with someone else's venom. 'I cannot see into your mind, but I *know* that you are trying to deceive me even now. However, I am fair, and I am content to see for myself the proof of your treachery before I destroy you.'

Hart sighed, and stabbed Verhardt in the heart.

The lighter captain gasped in sudden pain, and his eyes went wide in shock. Hart thought he saw an echo of Nessa Karnis in them for a moment, and hoped that the psychic feedback of her possession had allowed her to feel, just for a moment, the sensation of his powerblade slicing into her internal organs.

Yorr released Verhardt as Hart withdrew his blade. The captain fell to the deck, and Yorr's brow furrowed. 'I cannot pilot this ship, Kayzen.'

'Leaving him alive would simply give Nessa another tool with which to attack us,' Hart said grimly. 'But if I broadcast a distress signal and order another ship to take us on board–'

The *Star of Kings* trembled.

'Boarding lock,' Yorr stated. 'They must have already been close.'

Hart took a deep breath. 'I suspected it would come to this. One way or another, either Nessa or I will die within the next hour.' He eyed Yorr. 'My friend, I will be honest with you – I suspect even Nessa Karnis would balk at killing the last Crimson Consul without provocation. If you stood aside and denounced me, she might well let you live.'

'I am of the Adeptus Astartes,' Tythus Yorr growled. 'I do not fear death, and the Inquisition has no greater authority over me than does my own word. Nor will Inquisitor Karnis control my mind again, now I am prepared for her. I swore to be your lifeward, and I shall honour that pledge.'

Hart smiled in relief. 'With you by my side, my friend, I may yet have a chance at striking another blow against the Alpha Legion, even if they take this system.'

They advanced in pairs, eight of them clad in armoured void suits and carrying powerful, compact shotguns. Hart saw that much from the quick look he threw around a hatchway, and only jerked his head back into cover just in time before a shot thudded into it. The intruders' footfalls increased in pace as they closed in on him.

He was a distraction, nothing more, despite his drawn power-blade and his Ripper autopistol. These were void thugs, the crew of whatever vessel Nessa had commandeered, not true soldiers. Had they been properly trained, they would have checked the side chamber they passed on their way towards him.

Although it probably would not have done them much good, given that it contained Tythus Yorr.

The Crimson Consul erupted from it like a striking serpent, bolt pistol in one hand and combat knife in the other. The bark of shotguns was drowned out by the roar of the Space Marine's sidearm, and while his armour was sufficient to turn aside the solid slugs of his opponents, theirs did not manage the same. Hart looked through the hatch again after two seconds, when the noise had stopped. Yorr stood in the corridor's confines like a warrior god, his red armour newly wetted with gore.

'Is that all you brought, Nessa?' Hart shouted.

New light sprang into being farther down the corridor. It was wild light, flickering and swirling, and it cast enlarged, distorted shadows on the walls. The pyrokine, Evelyn.

'You know that it is not,' Nessa Karnis' voice replied. Hart glanced down at the body of the closest dead voider. His torso was a ruin, courtesy of one of Yorr's bolt-shells, but the man's full-face helmet was intact. When faced with the prospect of witchfire, any additional protection held an appeal. Hart eased himself around the hatch edge, reaching out for the corpse...

Fire billowed down the corridor, filling it from floor to ceiling, and engulfed Tythus Yorr. Hart jerked back into cover as the flames licked towards him, and he heard Yorr's bolter roar. The Space Marine had to be firing unsighted, both normal vision and infrared baffled by the flames, but his power armour would protect him for now, and Evelyn could surely not keep such output up for long. Yorr would ride out this firestorm, and then squeeze their necks–

Another weapon opened fire. Hart just had time to register that it too sounded like a bolter before Yorr spat a curse, and Hart heard him scrambling back into cover with a clatter of ceramite.

The fire died away. Very cautiously, Hart took a look.

The pair of them came stalking forwards. Evelyn had her hands held at her waist, palms upwards, with tame flames flicking around her fingers. Nessa Karnis' hands were empty, but her shoulder-mounted weapon twitched back and forth as though of its own accord.

A psycannon.

They were primarily designed for use against psykers, daemons, and the possessed, and the negative psychic energy imbued within the bolts of their ammunition could wreak terrible harm on such foes. However, they were still bolt weapons in basic nature, and that made them deadly in their own right.

'Unlike you, Space Marine, I do not need to see in order to shoot!' Nessa called contemptuously. 'You may have guarded your minds, both of you, but the sparks of your consciousness are targets to me!'

Hart glanced over at the doorway in which Yorr had taken cover. The Crimson Consul was on his feet and pressed up against his hatchway, but a chunk of ceramite had been blasted from his breastplate. The flesh beneath was ragged, and Hart was sure he could see patches of blood-slicked bone where the giant's fused ribcage was exposed.

Hart swallowed, and tried to control his breathing. He had accepted his death, or thought he had, but in combat with the servants of the Ruinous Powers. The notion of it coming at the hands of a fellow inquisitor, and Nessa Karnis at that, was enough to cause the long-forgotten threads of panic to begin winding themselves around his heart again. Emperor damn it, he would not go out like this! He could not!

The *Star of Kings* rang with the vibration of another collision.

'What was that?' Hart heard Evelyn say, and his heart leaped with hope this time. This was not their doing! Had some Downreach fleet enforcers noticed two ships docking with each other in orbit without permission, and come to investigate? That might lead to enough official confusion to make Nessa back down; at least unless she wanted to try shooting her way through them all and still claim the moral high ground.

'It's the Alpha Legion,' Nessa said, her voice dripping with disgust, and just a hint of fear. 'Kayzen's allies have arrived.'

'They are not our allies!' Tythus Yorr roared. 'I have dedicated my life to eradicating them!'

'You're supposed to be good with minds, Nessa!' Hart shouted desperately. 'Can't you tell that I'm telling the truth? I really did try to kill Solomon Akurra! If he's here, he's out for blood, but if we work together, we can take him down!'

'If you think–'

'Warp take you, Nessa, listen to me!' Hart yelled. 'If we kill Akurra, we have done a great thing for the Imperium! Even if we turn on each other immediately afterwards, at least those of us who then die will know that our deaths were not in vain. If you continue to attack us then all of us will die, and Akurra will get what he came for!'

'You have it with you?' Nessa asked.

'It's on the ship, yes,' Hart confirmed. 'It's in the cargo bay.'

There was a moment of silence.

'So,' he said, doing his best to sound reasonable, despite wishing death on his former colleague and her flame-fingered associate. 'What will it be?'

LEGACY

The Kharybdis' melta-cutters cycled down, and the protective hatches slid back to reveal the circular hole in the hull of Inquisitor Hart's ship. Solomon dropped through without hesitation. Under other circumstances he might have led a team around the outside of the ship and breached an airlock with melta bombs while the Kharybdis' cutters did their work, but not here, and not now, and not just because he was alone apart from Tulava, who had no void suit. He was hunting prey who thought they knew him, and the nature of his Legion. They would expect distractions, and he would not give them. If your opponent expected everything to be a feint, they would react too late to the true attack.

'Clear,' he reported, sighting down the barrel of his relic bolter. He had struck at the bridge, on the basis that should they secure his prize and depart, it would be more difficult for his enemies to pursue him with a gaping hole open to the void above them.

He turned the dead body on the floor over with his boot. A

human, presumably the captain of this vessel, killed by a thrust to the heart. A powerblade, judging by the cauterisation of the flesh around the wound.

Tulava landed clumsily behind him. 'Warp's blood, why don't these things come with ladders?'

'Quiet,' Solomon said, kicking the amplification of his helmet's audio sensors up. He could hear nothing apart from the faint whine of the ventilation systems, and the barely perceptible buzz of the bridge's systems. 'I hear nothing. No weapons fire.'

'But someone's already dead,' Tulava noted. She readied her force staff. 'So either everyone else is dead as well, or they've kissed and made up.' She grunted. 'Would it ruin my sorcerous mystique if I expressed a wish that just this once, something could be easy?'

'No,' Solomon said. 'You ruined that long ago.' There were two exits from the bridge: a hatchway directly ahead, towards the cabins, and a stairwell on the port side which presumably ran down to the main cargo hold. He moved towards the stairwell. 'Come on.'

The stairs switched back on themselves, and led out onto a gantry that ran around the cargo hold, and crossed over it both fore and aft. Solomon stopped and scanned around as he reached the hatchway, but there was nothing to be seen except for the pile of crates of various sizes in the middle of the hold floor below him.

The *clink* of Tulava's staff on the metal mesh flooring announced her arrival at his side. 'That,' the sorceress said dryly, looking down at the crates, 'is bait.'

Solomon frowned. It almost certainly was, although the crates looked genuine enough: they were of a similar nature to the ones he had seen in the Ordo Malleus facility before the explosives were detonated. However, where were his would-be ambushers?

He doubted their enemies would seek to set off an explosion sufficient to kill him on their own ship, given the possibility of structural damage to it, so a recurrence of the same trap seemed unlikely.

'I do not suppose you can bring them up here?' he asked quietly.

Tulava snorted. 'Not unless you want them coming at us all at once, at high speed. I can hit things hard enough to make them move, not pick them up and put them down again.'

'And you cannot warpwalk them?'

'I'd need to be touching them first, and I couldn't move them all in any case.'

'Very well,' Solomon said. 'We will save that as an escape plan. Stay behind me.'

'Are you going to move at a sensible speed this time?' Tulava asked, taking a fresh grip on her force staff.

'That depends on exactly what manner of attack comes our way.' Solomon stepped out onto the gantry, still holding his boltgun to his shoulder. Something felt wrong about this situation, but he could not see exactly what it was. Hesitation was potentially as much of an enemy as overeagerness, here. Sometimes you simply had to spring the trap just to find out what and where it was, and adapt from there.

He had taken three steps when something flickered in his helmet's display. It was as though his armour's sensors were trying to tell him that *something* important was on the opposite gantry, but his brain was refusing the information...

Solomon was prepared to take a warning from any source. He fired.

The bolt-shell impacted and exploded in a flash of light as it was intercepted by a conversion field, and suddenly the opposite gantry was occupied by four figures; or rather, they had been there all along, but a psychic warding had been persuading outside observers that it was empty. Solomon registered three baseline humans, one with a shoulder-mounted weapon, and the silhouette of a power-armoured Space Marine in livery he recognised as belonging to the Crimson Consuls.

If the last Crimson Consul was here, that meant Kayzen Hart was still here, which meant Solomon's prize surely was as well...

'There's only two of them! Fire!' Hart yelled, but the Crimson Consul had beaten him to it. The Space Marine's bolter roared, and the shell hit Solomon in the chest.

His battleplate held, but the force of the impact knocked him backwards into a safety rail which had seen better days, and which had in any case never been built to hold the weight of a power-armoured Astartes warrior. It gave with a creaking snap, and Solomon plunged backwards to the deck some fifteen feet below.

Even now, his reflexes were up to the task. He managed to twist in the air and land more or less on his feet, then sprang forwards, firing as he went. The other Space Marine stepped in front of Hart, and took a shot meant for the inquisitor's head on his pauldron. Then Solomon was in what passed for cover behind the stack of crates, although his enemies could flank him at any moment by moving around the gantry to the sides.

'Solomon!'

Purple-edged fire flared up, and Tulava appeared next to him.

'You were correct,' Solomon acknowledged, trying to watch both sides at once. 'It was a trap.'

'I threw a shield up as soon as you were hit,' Tulava said. She sounded shaken. 'That damned telepath shattered it with one shot – she's got a warp-forsaken psycannon!'

'Can you fight?' Solomon asked. He would not ask Tulava to warpwalk them out of here – not now, not when he was so close to success. But perhaps to a new vantage point, to ambush the ambushers…

'Give me a couple of seconds,' Tulava grunted, then cowered and covered her head with her hands as roaring flames licked out around the crates sheltering them. 'Emperor's blood!'

'No, you fool!' Hart yelled, and the flames subsided before they had done more than singe the ends of Tulava's hair. 'Not the crates! We don't know what fire might do–'

'They've got a wilder,' Tulava said, uncovering. 'What the hell are the Inquisition doing with a wilder?'

'A wilder?' Solomon asked, thinking through their options. If the Inquisition had a telepath, then warpwalking might not work: the psycannon could lock on to them as soon as they emerged.

'A wilder!' Tulava repeated. 'A witch, a wyrd! Can't you feel the psychic bleed? She's powerful, but if she's sanctioned then I'm a Cadian.'

'Then how has she not been possessed?' Solomon said.

'They're more susceptible, but that doesn't mean it's inevitable,' Tulava said with a shrug.

An idea struck Solomon. 'Can you help it along?'

'You mean, try to get her possessed?' Tulava looked at him as though he'd lost his wits. 'Solomon, if she's survived this long then she's got some strength of will, and she's not got any affinity to one of the Ruinous Powers that I can tap into, like with the First Strike. Anything powerful enough to possess her is *not* something we want to be in a confined space with, and it certainly won't be taking orders from me! Isn't it about time you used the song?' she added, testily.

Solomon grunted. 'I would have to be closer.' With a psycannon and a Space Marine bolter trained on their position, let alone psychic fire, he would struggle to get a shot away without drawing more in return than he trusted his armour to handle. 'We need a distraction.'

Tulava cocked her head. 'Clean? Or dirty?'

Solomon grinned inside his helmet, and laid one hand on the crate behind her. 'Clean.'

Tulava smiled back. 'Ready?'

'Ready.'

Tulava swept to her feet, swinging her staff with a scream, and unleashed a blast of psychic force that swept up and launched the pile of crates towards the Inquisition. They were not accurate missiles, but there was a lot of them.

Solomon saw something the size of an ammunition crate strike the fire-witch in the torso and send her tumbling off the gantry in a flail of limbs. The Crimson Consul literally punched another out of the air, then once more stood in front of Kayzen Hart and took Solomon's bolter shot intended for the inquisitor.

The telepath's psycannon roared.

All but the crudest of bionics were wired into the owner's nervous system to provide pressure sensation, but pain was not generally included. However, most bionics did not have a minor daemon bound within them, and as the blessed bolt smashed through his artificial humerus, Solomon felt an echo of the entity's screams, and what passed for pain amongst its kind. His arm went completely limp. What had been a malleable, morphous extension of his body was now no more than a lifeless metal framework dangling from his left side. His bolter dropped from his grip.

Crates were still crashing back down to the deck as Tulava yelled again, and unleashed another psychic blast, which struck the telepath before she could take a second shot. The woman dropped off the gantry like she had been poleaxed.

The Space Marine launched himself into the air with a roar of rage, combat knife clutched in one hand, straight for Solomon.

Instinct made Solomon try to ward him off with an arm that no longer worked, and the split second it took his mind to catch up with his non-functioning body allowed the Crimson Consul to crash down on him and bear him to the floor. Sheer fury appeared to have made the Space Marine forget his side-arm; he reared back with his knife in a reversed grip.

'For my brothers!' he bellowed.

Solomon bucked under him a moment before the blow landed and the tip of the knife overshot and scored the metal deck instead, giving Solomon a chance to swat the other warrior off him with his good arm. The Crimson Consul was knocked sideways, but began to scramble up immediately. Solomon snatched his bolter off the floor, and fired.

The shell smashed into the Consul's left knee, shattering the armour and striking through to the joint beneath. The Space Marine sprawled as his leg gave out. A few yards away, Tulava dropped with a shout of pain as Kayzen Hart's autopistol shot caught her in the gut and broke her concentration before she could unleash another strike.

Solomon began to sing.

'*Ney-ah tuku soma-nah, chora siru kae...*'

The Crimson Consul froze in place, the knife quivering in his hand.

'What are you doing, Tythus?' Kayzen Hart yelled. 'Kill him!' The inquisitor dropped down from the gantry and opened fire with an autopistol, not waiting to see whether the Space Marine heeded him. His shots were accurate, but were deflected by Solomon's armour.

'*...ala maha buru-tae, ney-ah tuku-mae.*'

It was a childhood rhyme from a culture that had not existed for two centuries, ever since the Imperium had left the world on which it had flourished as nothing more than a radioactive ball of rock. The odds of it being sung in the galaxy today were so astronomically small that they were virtually non-existent.

Which had made it the perfect preset trigger phrase to break the decade-long hypno-conditioning in a warrior who had been born on that planet before its death.

The Crimson Consul grabbed at his helmet and practically tore it loose, then clutched at his own skull as sweat streamed down his face. It was a face that Solomon had sorely missed.

'Kyrin,' he said.

His childhood friend looked up at him with uncomprehending eyes, beneath that ridiculous lump of metal in his forehead: a genuine Imperial service stud, ripped from a corpse.

'Kyrin Gadraen,' Solomon repeated, softening his voice as much as he could, but keeping his bolter steady. 'Come back now.'

The Crimson Consul shuddered, and closed his eyes. When he opened them again, an Alpha Legionnaire was in his place.

'Solomon,' Kyrin said. He smiled. 'It has been too long.'

The psycannon shot took him in his armour's power pack, which exploded.

Solomon switched his aim and opened fire as Kyrin pitched forwards. The telepath's conversion field flared into existence, but Solomon emptied his magazine at her, and the ancient technology could only take so much punishment before it gave out. The first shot that got through nearly cut her torso in half; the second one took her head off.

'Nessa!' Kayzen Hart shouted. The inquisitor shot a glance at Solomon and Kyrin, then his eyes lit on the contents of one of the crates, which had splintered and smashed when it hit the floor after being used as a projectile by Tulava. He gave a strangled shout and leaped forwards, dropping his autopistol in his desperation to grab the metallic objects which lay there. Solomon ejected the spent magazine from his bolter and reached for another, hampered by only having one hand to work with.

Tulava got there quicker.

The sorceress struggled up to sitting position, gestured with her force staff, and unleashed one last psychic blow. It struck Hart and knocked him across the deck, a few lengths of arcanely worked metal clutched in his arms. Solomon raised his bolter, ready to finally rid himself of this nuisance, but fast though he was, thought was quicker. The pyrokine had risen now as well, and seen the corpse of her mistress.

She screamed in rage, and white-hot fire gouted from her hands to envelop Solomon. This was no mere fire: it possessed physical force as well, sufficient to batter him backwards to the deck. His abused armour flashed desperate warnings at him as the temperature spiked, and his vision sparked and darkened as his tactical read-outs shorted.

'Run!' Solomon heard Hart yell, as the flames subsided along with the pyrokine's scream. His helmet was still blinding him, so he reached up and tugged it loose, just in time to see Hart hauling the sweating witch after him through the hatchway at the rear of the cargo bay. He got to his feet to pursue them, but paused as he saw what was lying on the deck.

Hart had got away with some of his intended prize, but not all. Four shards of metal still glinted there, the edge of one wet with a line of blood from where the inquisitor had managed to lay a finger on it just before Tulava knocked him away.

'Solomon!'

The gasp had come from Tulava, whose hands were pressed to her stomach. Her carapace breastplate had not saved her on this occasion, and the blood leaking from her wound was already starting to seep into her clothes.

'I don't mean to interrupt, Lord Akurra,' Tulava said weakly, 'but I'm bleeding, and some of us don't have blood that clots immediately.'

'Can you not heal yourself?' Solomon asked. 'Or summon an entity to do it for you?'

'I'm exhausted,' Tulava replied weakly. 'I need to sleep, recover my strength, and I would rather wake up again.'

Solomon hesitated. His own blood was singing out to him to pursue Hart and finally kill him, not to mention ripping the rest of his prize from the inquisitor's grasp. But while Hart was little threat, the witch was clearly dangerous.

More importantly, Tulava Dyne was wounded. Solomon and the sorceress had saved each other's lives so often they had stopped keeping a tally. She needed medical attention suitable for a baseline human or she would die, and a powerful and loyal ally was priceless within the shifting thing that was the Alpha Legion.

Perhaps it was better to take what he had here. It was still, after all, a triumph.

And Kayzen Hart could not hide from him forever.

'Kyrin,' he said. 'Can you stand?'

Kyrin Gadraen was already starting to lever himself up. Without the aid of his armour's power system, he was slow and clumsy.

'Stand?' Kyrin said. 'Perhaps. Walk? Not since you destroyed my knee.'

'I apologise, brother,' Solomon said. 'I needed to prevent you from killing me long enough to break the hypno-conditioning, preferably without killing you in turn.'

Kyrin reached one knee – his good one – and nodded. 'I understand. There were many risks I consented to when I agreed to your suggestion, including killing and being killed by my own brothers.' He shook his head in wonder. 'The conditioning was masterful work. I still remember the rage I felt at the Legion for what it had done to me, and the grief over the deaths of comrades I never had.'

'But look,' Solomon said, picking the blades up off the floor and showing them to him. '*Look*. This is our legacy. Your work helped us achieve many successes, Kyrin, but this... I never expected this, when you first infiltrated the Inquisition, and yet it is the greatest success of them all.'

The ship rocked slightly. If Solomon's guess was accurate, Hart and the witch had decoupled the adjoining vessel, and would be making good their escape. However, Solomon still had a ship of his own to call.

'I will signal the Diabolicus Secundus to retrieve us,' Solomon said. 'He will be able to attend to all of our needs.' He paused. 'Thank you, Kyrin, for your sacrifice. I am in your debt, as is the Legion. And yours too, Tulava,' he added.

'I think you've got a lot of people to persuade of your right to lead before they're going to agree with that last part,' Tulava panted.

Solomon looked at the blades nestling between the fingers of his gauntlet.

'That,' he said, 'should no longer be a problem.'

LAST STAND

Qampar thought it was prepared for war.

It had not been prepared for the Alpha Legion.

Qope Halver fired his grapnel, and the magnetic head caught firm on the roof opposite. He anchored the near end firmly behind him, attached his harness loop, and slid across the gap between the two buildings as smooth as silk. His Headhunters followed him, a succession of shadows in black armour. Far to the south, Titan war-horns bellowed as the Legion's captured Warlord and its pair of flanking Reavers systematically destroyed what remained of the loyalists' war engines.

Xettus' strategy had proved effective, although it relied greatly on Akurra's previous successes. The defenders had been hesitant, and largely unwilling to commit to bold strikes lest they find themselves outmanoeuvred yet again. The Alpha Legion had responded by simply ignoring most of the strong defensive positions, leaving only a cursory presence to warn their main force of any sortie, and delay it. Once the communication relays were severed, Qampar's troops were left cowering behind their fortification walls, unaware of what was happening on a wider scale, and unwilling to stick their necks out to find out in case they lost their heads.

It was a moot point, in any case. Had the Alpha Legion wished it, they could have annihilated resistance across the entire planet within a month. That was testament to how many different warbands had come together: Halver did not know exact figures, but he suspected they might now be approaching the strength of an Imperial Chapter. The Serpent's Teeth had numbered over a hundred legionnaires just by themselves, and then when you factored in the countless human militias, and other assets like the Titans, it was a stronger force than any he had ever thought he would be a part of.

However, eradicating all of Qampar's defensive capabilities had never been the plan, and so it was that Lord Xettus was advancing on the gubernatorial palace after less than a week of fighting. Low and high orbit belonged to the Alpha Legion, the ground defences had been dismantled, and the Lord Discordant did not come with the speed of a striking serpent, but at the leisurely pace of a conqueror.

That did not mean he had become careless, of course, which was why Halver and his team were on the roof of one of the many Administratum buildings around the palace. Halver suspected the clerics within had fled somewhere, although he was hardly concerned if they had not.

'Watchdogs,' Dommik Renn muttered, as they took up position overlooking St Stevanus' Way, the mighty boulevard leading up to the palace doors. 'Is this what we are reduced to? Akurra would have sent us ahead to either slay the governor, or have him in chains before the rest of the Legion had set foot on the planet.'

'Mind your tongue,' Vorlan Xhan replied. 'Lord Xettus may be listening.'

'My vox is off,' Renn said.

'How can you be certain, where the Lord Discordant is concerned?' Xhan pointed out. 'Regardless, Akurra is not here.'

Halver did not comment. He had heard nothing from Akurra since they had parted ways and the Ghost had gone with the First Strike. Akurra might very well be dead by now, but if Qope Halver had been forced to place a wager, he would have backed the former Harrowmaster to still be alive somewhere.

Once more, he wondered how wise it had been to pull Akurra and his witch out from under the noses of the Rustbloods on Anthras instead of executing them and having done with, but what was done was done. Halver just had to hope that it would work out to the benefit of the Legion; or at least, of him and his squad.

'Here they come,' Renn said, sighting down his Stalker-pattern boltgun. 'By the primarchs,' he added, anger colouring his tone, 'is that Vorgul of Second Fang he has made carry his banner?'

Lord Xettus was on his Helstalker, flanked by three of his own legionaires on each side, and trailed by a lone warrior carrying a standard on which was emblazoned the Legion's sigil, encircled by rusty chains. Behind them came three hulking combat automata which might once have been robots of the Adeptus Mechanicus, but if so, had been altered and corrupted beyond recognition. At a respectful distance farther back came the head of a great snake of baseline humans: the militias, and the prisoners they had taken. Xettus wanted Governor Alzyn to see how he had failed to keep his people safe.

It did not escape Halver's notice, through the scope of his boltgun, that although Xettus' bodyguard and standard bearer all bore the marks of combat to one degree or another, the Lord

Discordant and his mount were pristine. Halver was unsure whether that came down to excellent repair, superlative skill in battle, or simply avoiding the majority of combat, but something about it rubbed him the wrong way. It was not as if they were Emperor's Children.

The procession was entering the final approach now, which was flanked by nine statues of the supposedly loyal primarchs: four on one side, and five on the other. The defenders had covered them over, perhaps intended as some sort of sop to their new masters, so nothing more than their outlines could be seen. Halver scanned past them, looking for threats, and amused himself for a couple of moments by trying to work out which was which. The one with his arm outstretched like an orator was probably Guilliman; the one hunched over almost sulkily and resting both hands on something in front of him, possibly the pommel of a sword, might well be Dorn; and something about the pose of one wielding a sword two-handed suggested artwork Halver had seen of the Lion on other Imperial-controlled worlds. He was trying to work out if he could see the shape of a hammer anywhere, to try to pinpoint either Vulkan or Ferrus Manus, when the doors of the palace began to open.

'At least this one has not disappeared into a rathole in his own walls,' Xhan commented, as Governor Alzyn, bedecked in his chains of office, emerged atop the huge marble steps which led down to St Stevanus' Way. He had his own honour guard, but the silver-armoured humans with him were a poor reflection of the warriors accompanying Xettus, despite their immaculate wargear.

'He looks like he is wishing he had,' Renn said. Halver focused on the governor. Sweat was streaming down his face, and he was licking his lips almost constantly. His eyes were flickering around, as well, rather than being focused on the approaching

Xettus atop his Helstalker, which must have certainly been a terrifying sight, and normally enough to hold the gaze of any mortal. Checking for possible escape routes, too late though it surely was?

Something that had been bothering him clicked in Halver's mind. None of the 'statues' had anything that looked like wings, which meant Sanguinius was not present, which meant...

He glanced up from his scope for a wider perspective, saw where the governor was actually looking, and cursed.

They weren't statues at all.

Xettus had just passed the first two of them when they moved. All nine threw off their coverings at the same time, and armour flashed in the sunlight. Silver Templars!

One of the giants hurled something bulky at the combat auto-mata, and they convulsed as a haywire field enveloped them. The honour guard of Rustbloods were already firing, but they were outnumbered and outgunned by the Primaris Marines, who had been standing stock-still in poses imitating the statues that had until recently occupied their plinths. Halver fired, and his aim was true, but at this range his bolt-shell just caromed off a Templar's armour plating to little effect.

'Banestrike!' Halver yelled at his squad, already swapping out his own magazine.

'We're too far away!' Renn replied.

'Then get closer!' Halver ordered, slotting his new magazine in. There was no time for niceties, and no suitable target for his mag-grapnel on the stone plaza. Qope Halver stepped off the edge of the building, and dropped.

Imperial architecture came to his aid. Seven storeys straight down would have sorely tested the capabilities of both his armour and his body, but there were sufficient overhangs, buttresses, and gargoyles to break his fall somewhat, although his descent was far from graceful. He hit the plaza hard enough for his armour to flash up red warnings about the stress on the knee and ankle joints, but he was down.

'Va'kai!' he voxed, opening a channel up to the *Unseen*. 'How many boarders did you find?'

There was a brief pause, and then Captain Va'kai's voice replied, hazy and scratched with static thanks to the distance. *'Less than a dozen, which the magos' Dishonour Guard took care of. We're assuming the rest are still hiding somewhere, but searching this thing fully is virtually impo–'*

'They're down here!' Halver yelled. 'Most of those pods must have been empty! The damned Templars made us think they spent their strength assaulting the *Unseen*, but most of them must have shuttled down to the surface beforehand to lay a trap!' How many Space Marines would that strike cruiser have held? Thirty? Fifty?

Great slabs of stone in front of him were heaved upwards, and more Silver Templars clawed their way out of the ground, like the restless dead of legend. The same thing was happening on the other side of the ambush, but Qope Halver could only deal with what was immediately in front of him. However, at least he had the right tools for the job.

Banestrike ammunition. It had been developed by the Legion prior to the Horus Heresy for the specific purpose of penetrating the armour of the Legiones Astartes. Legion legend held that Alpharius Omegon had created it long before even the first whispers of Horus' treachery began to surface, in case any of his brothers' sons needed to be culled. It was rare even amongst the Alpha Legion – it was expensive and difficult to make, and sacrificed range for its greater armour-penetrating power – but Halver made sure his Headhunters always carried it, just in case.

The Templars were not expecting enemies behind them. Halver

slowed for a moment to aim, and fired into the back of the helmet of the warrior closest to him. The shot struck true, and the Space Marine's head exploded.

A trio of burning plasma bolts had already struck Lord Xettus before the ambushers realised that they had been outflanked in turn. The rest – eleven of them, Halver's sensors informed him – turned towards him as the rest of his Headhunters caught up.

It was a short and brutal firefight between expert marksmen at point-blank range, using weapons that made a mockery of each other's armour. Banestrike rounds penetrated Tacticus breast-plates to detonate inside chests, or smashed through helmet faceplates with as much ease as they had struck through other armour for ten thousand years. Bolt rifles blew off limbs, and plasma incinerators melted ceramite and flesh alike.

The final shots were fired at the same time, just under three seconds after the exchange had begun. The last Silver Templar's bolt rifle spoke, and agony erupted in Qope Halver's gut as the round splintered the protection provided by his ancient Mark VI armour and blew out half of his insides. His shot took his enemy in the neck, and the improved protection of the Tacticus gorget did not save the Templar from his fate. He toppled back-wards, lifeless, at the same time as Halver dropped to his knees.

He looked up. The fake primarchs had overwhelmed Xettus' honour guard, and the Lord Discordant himself was wounded, as was his steed, but who was that?

It was the banner-bearer, Halver realised, as his armour shrieked warnings at him about blood loss and major tissue damage, both of which he was already well aware. The legion-naire had ripped the standard from his banner pole, and was using the haft to fight with.

A strange, otherworldly wail reached Halver's ears, even above the noise of battle and the roar of the militia as it began to join the fray on the far side. Had the banner pole been topped and tailed with blades when it had still been bearing the standard, or had they suddenly appeared?

One of the Primaris Marines fell backwards, clutching at a massive gash that had nearly taken his head off. No blood spurted forth from the wound, merely oily black smoke. The standard bearer moved on, the double-bladed haft spinning through his hands, until he buried one end in another Silver Templar's chest, as though he were...

As though he were wielding a spear.

GHOST LEGION

The Pale Spear sang in Solomon's hands.

The Diabolicus Secundus had done masterful work in reconstructing the weapon of the Alpha Legion's primarch at short notice. Kayzen Hart might have escaped with the pieces of the haft, but Solomon had the blades. This was the weapon of his primogenitor, a weapon even more mysterious than the being who had wielded it. No one in the Legion knew the Pale Spear's origin; whether the primarch had created it, or found it, or been gifted it from one of the Emperor's storehouses of ancient, forbidden technology. Solomon could not imagine how many of humanity's foes had fallen to its twin blades, nor how many loyalists, once the Heresy had begun.

That number was already increasing.

The Silver Templars fought, of course – as did Xettus, wounded though he was. One of the Primaris Marines had fallen to the Helstalker's autocannon as soon as they revealed themselves, and another was cut down by the Lord Discordant's chainglaive.

One more was brought down by Xettus' bodyguard of battered Rustblood legionnaires before they succumbed to the Silver Templars' greater size and strength, and the sheer refusal of Tacticus plate to yield to combat knives and point-blank bolt pistol blasts.

The Silver Templars had paid Solomon little attention in the first second or so: one legionnaire with a banner was little threat when they were solely focused on killing Xettus. That changed when Solomon attacked. Armour parted like paper before the spear's edge, and flesh gave no resistance at all. The weapon felt natural in Solomon's hands, as though he had been born to wield it. He opened the throat of one of his enemies as easily as tearing open a ration bar, and impaled another a heartbeat later.

The daemon in his arm, newly repaired and resanctified by the combined efforts of Tulava and the Diabolicus Secundus, and disguised within the left arm of his borrowed armour, screamed a silent warning and flicked one end of the spear up behind him. Solomon felt the judder of impact as a weapon aimed at the back of his head was knocked aside, and the shot took one of the Templar's companions in the helmet instead. Solomon spun and lashed out, taking the Imperial's gun hand off at the wrist with one slash of the Pale Spear, then followed up with a thrust that splintered his enemy's faceplate and dropped him instantly.

Suddenly, there were only two Silver Templars left, and both had realised that Solomon was a threat. Their flankers on one side had been eliminated by Qope Halver's Headhunters, and the others were being swamped by the arriving militia. If they were going to finish their task, it was down to the two of them.

'Stop him!' the lieutenant barked at his companion. He was the one who had been pretending to be Guilliman; he lunged for Xettus with his power sword, and took one of the Helstalker's legs off at the second joint, trying to confirm his kill. The other Silver Templar, who wore lightweight armour and a skull-visaged helm, came for Solomon.

This one was quicker than the others, perhaps because of his armour, or relative lack thereof. Solomon ducked aside a moment before his enemy pulled the trigger of his bolt pistol, and the shell roared harmlessly past his shoulder. The other warrior feinted a thrust with his knife, which was more like a short sword, and as Solomon swept the Pale Spear up to parry, the Silver Templar fired again, directly at Solomon's chest.

The daemon in Solomon's arm was already twisting the Pale Spear, and the dual blades deflected the bolt-shell harmlessly aside.

The Silver Templar's face was hidden by his skeletal faceplate, but Solomon could imagine the shock written across blunt, noble features as he registered a feat that should have been impossible. The Imperial's hesitation was momentary, but sufficient. Solomon ripped the Pale Spear upwards, opening his enemy's armour from crotch to throat in one strike.

The lieutenant drove his powerblade through the Helstalker's head, and the daemon engine collapsed with a shriek that was somehow both infernal and mechanical. Xettus, his left side half incinerated by plasma, was thrown from his seat atop his steed, and landed with a clatter of ceramite on stone. The Lord Discordant struggled to bring his chainglaive up, and the Silver Templar drew his power sword back with a triumphant shout.

'For the Emper-*aaargh!*'

Solomon withdrew the Pale Spear from the lieutenant's thigh. The Silver Templar lurched around to face him, oily smoke gouting in the place of blood from the unnatural wound in his flesh.

'You are dishonourable,' the Space Marine hissed.

'You are surprised?' Solomon mocked him. It was so like a warrior of the Imperium to whine about his enemy's lack of honour after his own ambush had failed.

'You have my attention,' the lieutenant said grimly. 'Defend yourself, then!'

He attacked.

Even with the wound in his thigh, the Silver Templar was dangerous. His power sword was a masterful piece of work which sizzled faintly as it flashed through the air, and he wielded it with no wasted motion. Solomon knew within a moment that the blade would penetrate the plate he had borrowed from Vorgul as easily as the Pale Spear would the lieutenant's Gravis armour. It would all come down to who could land the first telling blow: the Primaris Space Marine of the Silver Templars, or Solomon Akurra of the Alpha Legion.

Solomon batted two thrusts of the powerblade aside, mindful of his angles. The Diabolicus Secundus had done his best work with the new haft of the Pale Spear, but it was still a common alloy, tough and durable though it might be. Solomon would have trusted that the complete Pale Spear could resist an Imperial power sword, but he had no intention of letting the symbol of his authority be sheared in two, so he batted his enemy's strikes aside and waited, counting on the Silver Templar's anger and desperation to do his work for him. The lieutenant knew he was about to be overrun, but if he could just dispose of Solomon then he might still have time to slay Xettus...

The end, when it came, was swift and sudden. The Silver Templar lunged a little too far, and overextended onto his good leg. Solomon sidestepped the thrust and sliced the Pale Spear through the lieutenant's knee joint. The other warrior fell with a shout of pain, and Solomon kicked his powerblade out of his hand, then planted the Pale Spear through his helmet.

The lieutenant twitched once, and then the last Silver Templar on Qampar was dead.

Xettus had managed to regain his feet, with the stubbornness common to all Space Marines, no matter their allegiance or origin. The eye-lenses of his helm were fixed on Solomon.

'You are not Vorgul of the Serpent's Teeth,' he declared, his voice rough with barely suppressed pain.

'I am not,' Solomon confirmed. He reached up to remove his helmet, and let the Lord Discordant see his face.

'You are named the Ghost for good reason,' Xettus rasped. 'Why did you come to my rescue?'

Solomon sighed.

'Because it was very important that no one killed you except me.'

The Pale Spear left his hand like a javelin, and sprouted from Xettus' chest. The Lord Discordant let out a wordless noise of pain, then collapsed. Solomon strode to him and ripped the weapon out again, making a further mess of his chest in the process, then struck his head off. Whatever boons Xettus' technomagical arts had lent him were not sufficient to survive decapitation.

The militia were watching in shock, but none of them stepped forward to challenge his brutal ascension back to power. None would dare. As for the rest of the legionnaires...

'Captain Va'kai,' he voxed, speaking quietly as he turned and began to walk towards the system governor, who still waited, trembling in fear, at the doors of his palace. 'Do you read?'

'Is that you, Solomon? Xettus proclaimed you dead, but I had my doubts.'

'He is the one who is dead,' Solomon said. 'How firmly under our control is the *Unseen*?'

'It is secure. I kept several teams aboard as a safeguard against any

rogue boarders, but that also serves well enough against any Rust-bloods who decide they want to contest our possession of it.'

Solomon smiled. 'Would that we all had your wisdom, Krozier.'

'It is good to have you back, Harrowmaster.'

Governor Alzyn was rooted to the spot as Solomon ascended the steps towards him. He did not order his bodyguards to attack, although whether they would have obeyed him in any case was another matter. Solomon did not intend to repeat Xettus' overconfidence, however: he raised his relic bolter and fired, placing four headshots before any of the bodyguards could react. They were dead before Alzyn even realised what was occurring, making his panicked crouch and shielding of his head with his hands somewhat redundant.

'M-my lord,' Alzyn stammered as Solomon crested the last step. 'I did not... I knew of the ambush, but I had no–'

'Peace,' Solomon said, holding up one hand. 'Please, rise. There is no quarrel between us, governor.'

Alzyn blinked, clearly wrong-footed, but he knew better than to disobey, and straightened up the best he could manage while still cringing. 'There isn't?'

'Of course not,' Solomon said with a smile. 'After all, you have bravely thrown off the shackles of the Imperium's clutching hands, and now stand proudly independent.'

'We... We have?'

Alzyn was not normally a timid man, if Solomon was any judge, but it was not every day that a baseline human was faced with a genetically enhanced warrior whom he had been taught was a monstrosity. Let alone when that warrior looked so similar to the ones he had just been colluding with, and was smiling at him politely. Alzyn had presumably expected torture and screaming death, and was now so busy trying to wrap his head around the possibility that this was not inevitable, that he was struggling to process anything else. The deaths of his bodyguards would already be forgotten: if they were not expendable to him, they would not have been bodyguards.

'Of course,' Solomon said. 'After all, your forces destroyed several Imperial bulk transports prior to our arrival. You cannot have expected that to be seen as anything other than a gesture of defiance to your former masters.'

'But we were told they were your ships!' Alzyn protested. 'That was how you took Beharis Delta!'

Solomon shook his head in mock disappointment. 'Precisely why we would not use the same tactic again. No, they were nothing to do with us – merely Indomitus Crusade supply vessels, I believe.'

Alzyn swallowed visibly. 'But Lieutenant Malfax–'

'Is dead,' Solomon cut him off. 'Neither he nor any others of his demi-company can confirm your story. Indeed, they are most likely also the victims of your treachery, in the eyes of the Imperium. And although that is not true,' he continued, 'you should know better than most that the Imperium cares little for what is true, and much more for what is *convenient*.'

He saw realisation sink in. Governor Alzyn would have made his own decisions based upon that very same criteria, because that was how the governors of the Imperium operated. What need was there for nuance when you had power? Why bother to engage in politics when you could just execute inconvenient potential rivals? Why investigate the reason for reduced production levels when you could simply send in the enforcers to kill the overseers – or the workforce, depending on your preference – and replace them from the endless mass of humanity that made up your planet?

What need was there to determine exactly how a planet had

fallen, when you could just brand the entire ruling class as traitors, execute them, and start over? There would always be others so eager to get their hands on the power and authority that they would care little for the fate of those who came before them.

Alzyn's voice was hoarse. 'What are you proposing?'

'Governor, let me be clear,' Solomon said. 'There are elements of my force that are considerably less disposed towards diplomacy than I am. It would be so easy for me to give them their head, and let them sate their bloodlust upon you and your world. That would satisfy them, and so fulfil a purpose for me. Or you can cooperate with me, keep the remains of your defences intact, and so be better able to defend yourselves when the next raiders come calling. That might be the Imperium, or it might not – after all, the Charadon Sector is a dangerous place, these days.' He paused, and saw Alzyn's eyes grow wide at the thought of being left unprotected from the various denizens of the galaxy.

'When the Imperium does return to your door, that also fulfils a purpose for me,' Solomon continued. 'They will either spend time, energy, and resources attempting to bring you under their control once more, which benefits me, or they will decide that an intact, defiant system is too much trouble for them at present. Then you can be free of their tithes and levies, which denies that to the Imperium, and that also benefits me.' He smiled. 'Of course, between now and then, a governor who managed to remain alive might decide his best chance of survival lies with appeasing the forces currently on his world, then taking what he can of what remains, and fleeing before the Imperium catches up with him. It is a large galaxy, after all, and sufficient currency can buy a great deal of anonymity, if one is careful. If the Imperium expends resources trying to find you... well, that also benefits me.'

Governor Alzyn was a politician, not a soldier, and certainly not an idealist. The flames of defiance, which had not been much more than embers from the moment Solomon began to climb the stairs towards him, flickered and died. He closed his eyes in shame, and bowed his head.

'What will you need from us?'

Solomon smiled. 'I will have a list prepared. Fear not, it will be modest compared to what the Imperium has taken from you as a matter of course. And we are far more selective about our levies.'

Alzyn looked up, uncertain. 'Levies?'

'Yes, governor,' Solomon said. 'Other Legions will recruit from death worlds, feral worlds, feudal worlds, the depths of hive cities, and so on – all the better to find the sort of compunctionless killers they value so highly. My methods differ. Force of will is important, of course, but the true mark of the Alpha Legion is intellect.'

He placed one hand on Alzyn's shoulder, and watched the governor flinch.

'I will need a directory of your system's schola progenia, and the most promising students aged between ten and fourteen years, Terran standard.' He moved his thumb slightly: such was the size discrepancy between the two of them that this was enough to brush the side of Alzyn's neck, and the touch of ceramite on flesh brought another flinch.

Alzyn bit his lip, and closed his eyes once more. 'I-I understand.'

'Good man,' Solomon said warmly. 'My congratulations, governor. Your decision has spared many millions, perhaps billions, from death. Only for now, of course,' he added. 'But what more can we ask for, from this uncertain galaxy?'

He removed his hand from Alzyn's shoulder, and turned away. Word of the ambush had spread, and other members of the

Legion who had been mopping up isolated pockets of resistance elsewhere in the city were arriving. Some were the leaders of different warbands: Xettus had intended to take Alzyn's surrender himself, with no others around to steal his thunder, but the lords of the Alpha Legion had seen fit to keep themselves close by nonetheless. Solomon saw them take in the mess of bodies, and Xettus' decapitated corpse, then focus on him.

The symbolism of the moment was not lost on him. He descended the steps from the governor's palace to greet them, having garnered the cooperation of the system, and carrying the weapon of their primarch. None of them had laid eyes on the Pale Spear before, of course, but the Legion's legends were sufficient for each one of them to identify it for themselves.

It barely mattered that there was no guarantee of its authenticity. It was a large galaxy, after all, as Solomon had just explained to Alzyn. He was not prepared to rule out the existence of another weapon, similar to that borne by Alpharius Omegon, and which had somehow ended up in the clutches of the Ordo Malleus. The important thing was first of all, that it served him as a weapon; and secondly, and more importantly, that his fellow commanders would see it as the Pale Spear. So long as they believed it was, it scarcely mattered what it *actually* was.

'Lord Akurra,' Roek Ghulclaw intoned. 'It appears that rumours of your demise were untrue.'

Solomon inclined his head to the lord of the Guns of Freedom. 'I always strive to disappoint my enemies. Sadly, Lord Xettus proved to be one of them.'

'You have spoken with the governor?' asked Jarvul Glaine of the Shrouded Hand.

'I have,' Solomon confirmed. 'He is cowed, and will allow us to take what we wish unopposed. Then we can leave him here as a problem for the Imperium to deal with.'

There were two Alphariuses present, and both smiled. 'It is always pleasing to see our enemies struggle with themselves,' said one.

'You are truly a worthy successor, Lord Akurra,' added the other. Neither took their eyes from the Pale Spear. To the Faceless, Solomon realised, he was probably either about to become a new primarch in all but name, or a usurper who held a relic that they would view as belonging to them, and who should be subtly killed as soon as possible. Fanatics were always a problem, no matter how useful they were.

'My lords,' he said. 'We are on the threshold of a new age. The galaxy has changed, and is changing still – it behoves us all to change with it. The Psyphos Subsector has been shown how tenuous the Imperium's protection is. At worst, our enemies will waste time reconquering it to their satisfaction. At best, the worlds here will wake up to the lies of their masters, and resist. Either way, this need not end here. We are stronger than ever, should we remain united.'

Keros Asid of the Sons of Venom tilted his head to one side. 'You are proposing more than an alliance, then? You wish to see us unified?'

'I have had my fill of striking from the shadows, and then withdrawing through necessity,' said Jarvul Glaine, looking around at the others. 'I would like the option to meet the armies of the Imperium in the field more often, should it be to our advantage to do so.'

'Your combination of subterfuge and force is an appealing one, Lord Akurra,' the first Alpharius said. 'The Faceless pledge ourselves to you.'

Roek Ghulclaw made a noise of discontent within his helm. 'I am not one of the Serpent's Teeth, and nor shall I become one.'

'I will not ask that of you,' Solomon assured him. 'I have a different suggestion. We are all Alpha Legion, but we are not all there is of the Alpha Legion. Nonetheless, a unifying name for our respective warbands would seem useful.'

'You have a name in mind?' asked Vyrun Evale of the Penitent Sons.

'One from history,' Solomon said, with an acknowledging nod to the Faceless. If anyone should appreciate this, it was them. 'The records of the Serpent's Teeth tell us that in the era of the Great Crusade, before Alpharius Omegon and his Legion were known to the Imperium, they still operated in secret. Rumours were whispered of their actions, but none knew who was carrying them out. Those responsible were given a moniker.

'The Ghost Legion.'

EPILOGUE

Kayzen Hart stared down at the lengths of metal – metal? Probably metal – on the floor of the cabin. It was the haft of the Pale Spear, the weapon of the primarch Alpharius Omegon. The Imperium had lost so much history over its existence, much of it destroyed deliberately. It was so infuriating that close-minded fools had simply decided to shackle the Imperium's defenders by denying them knowledge of their foes! The history of the weapon was lost somewhere, so Hart had no way of knowing exactly when it had come into the Ordo Malleus' possession, or from where. Nonetheless, the scant accounts of it that Lord Druman had found had been sufficient to convince Hart that this was what he had stumbled across, when he had happened to check the inventory of the Downreach site in case it held anything of use to him.

The door opened to reveal Evelyn. The pyrokine said nothing, simply looking at him instead.

'Well?' Hart demanded testily.

'The captain is displeased by the deaths of the crew members your traitor friend killed,' Evelyn said, 'but fear of the Inquisition still holds sway over him. We're leaving the system, and heading for Metalica.'

Hart grunted.

'You're a heretic,' Evelyn said, closing the cabin door behind her. 'You had a Traitor Marine as your lifeward.'

'Without my knowledge!' Hart protested. 'I saw Tythus Yorr interact with many other Space Marines during his time with me, loyalist Space Marines! Not a one of them detected anything out of place about him.'

'So you're incompetent, at the least,' Evelyn scoffed. 'But in addition to that, you knowingly communicated with the Alpha Legion, and gave them information.'

'Information designed to lead them to ruin,' Hart snapped. 'It is hardly my fault if everyone, including you and your mistress, failed to see the plan through! Besides,' he added, rising to his feet off the bed, 'who are you to declare me heretic, *interrogator?*'

Flames jumped into existence around Evelyn's hands, and Hart froze. The authority of the Inquisition might be absolute, but authority was not fireproof.

Evelyn held his gaze for a moment, until she was sure he was going to make no aggressive move, then let the flames die away again. She nodded at the pieces of the Pale Spear. 'What are they?'

'Parts of a legendary weapon,' Hart said. 'Akurra must have seized the rest, but I know he will want these as well. He will no doubt find some use for what he has, but it cannot be complete. Is it the haft which gave it its power, I wonder, or the blades?' He shook his head. 'It matters not. A trap can still be baited using this – it must simply be subtler than before.'

'You seem to be forgetting the part where you're a heretic,' Evelyn pointed out dryly. She had a clipped, rough accent, not smoothed out by her time with Nessa. Hart would have placed her as coming from a hive city, if he had to guess. 'I've got Lady Karnis' full report, ready for dispatch to her allies.'

Hart looked up sharply. 'It has not been sent?'

'Not yet,' Evelyn replied, shaking her head. 'She wanted to get confirmation of your actions on Downreach first. Don't get me wrong, I'm telling you this because I know you've got no way of stopping me sending it, unless you want your fate to be a lot quicker and hotter than what the conclave might think up for you.'

Hart considered. Burning to death was not high on his list of ways he wanted his life and career to end, but nor did he get the impression that Evelyn was taunting him; at least not simply for her own pleasure.

'What might I need do,' he asked slowly, 'to convince you not to send that report?'

Evelyn smiled. 'Nessa did say you were perceptive, in the end.'

Hart let that one slide.

'You need to maintain your reputation,' Evelyn continued after a moment. 'I want to build mine. I was hunting the Alpha Legion's operatives before I even came into contact with the Ordo Malleus, although I didn't know the nature of my quarry at that point. You can keep playing hide-and-seek with the legion-naires, if you want – I need the freedom to go after their cat's paws on my own terms.'

Hart shook his head. 'I'm not taking you on as my interrogator.'

'I've had enough of being an interrogator, you dim-witted bastard!' Evelyn snarled. 'I want the badge!'

Hart blinked at her. 'You want… to be raised to full inquisitor?'

'It happens,' Evelyn said, as though Hart did not know that. 'My mistress was killed. You're an inquisitor. You can raise me up to finish her work.'

'It's irregular,' Hart stalled.

'If there's one thing I've learned, it's that the entire bloody Inquisition is irregular!' Evelyn said with a laugh. 'If you grant me full rank, I've got no incentive to turn you in – that would only endanger my own promotion. If you don't, I *do* turn you in, and try to use the leverage of that to get the same thing from Nessa's allies.' She shrugged. 'One way benefits both of us. The other way potentially sees us both lose out. Although admittedly,' she added, 'you more than me.'

Hart bit his lip. It was blackmail, was what it was, and how could he let someone of such dubious moral character ascend to such a rank?

On the other hand, his work was crucial. Thanks to the short -sightedness and failures of others, what had been intended as an elaborate trap for a rising Alpha Legion warlord had turned into merely an opportunity for Akurra to solidify his power. Hart had to make that right, and he could not do that if a conclave got involved, especially not now his lifeward was revealed to have been an Alpha Legion plant all along.

There were far worse things to threaten the galaxy than an inquisitor of dubious background, and Solomon Akurra was one of them. If the price for Hart finally taking him down was the promotion of his old adversary's interrogator, so be it.

'I agree,' he said. 'I will make the necessary statements and recommendations. You will get your own seal. I will have no control if a conclave then decides to examine my decision,' he warned, 'but if you work fast, you may be able to head them off with proof of your successes after being raised to your new rank.'

Evelyn smiled. 'And in return, my mistress' report will remain unsent.'

'Tythus Yorr died nobly, a final badge of honour for the Crimson Consuls,' Hart added. 'And I keep these,' he finished, looking down at the Pale Spear's broken haft.

'I've no interest in them,' Evelyn said. 'It's a deal.'

'I still do not know your full name,' Hart said. 'I will need it, for my official statement of your promotion.'

The pyrokine stuck her hand out. 'Evelyn Darke. Originally of Vorlese.'

Kayzen Hart took her hand in his own. It was surprisingly cool.

'Then congratulations, Inquisitor Darke of the Ordo Malleus.'

ABOUT THE AUTHOR

Mike Brooks is a science fiction and fantasy author who lives in Nottingham, UK. His work for Black Library includes the Horus Heresy Primarchs novel *Alpharius: Head of the Hydra*, the Warhammer 40,000 novels *Rites of Passage*, *Warboss* and *Brutal Kunnin*, the Necromunda novel *Road to Redemption* and the novellas *Wanted: Dead* and *Da Gobbo's Revenge*. When not writing, he plays guitar and sings in a punk band, and DJs wherever anyone will tolerate him.

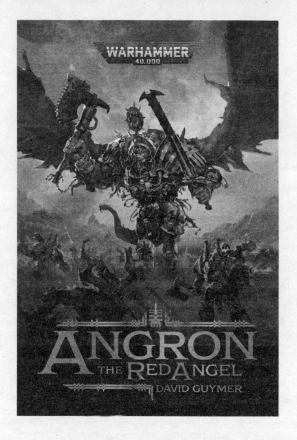

YOUR NEXT READ

ANGRON: THE RED ANGEL
by David Guymer

In the darkness of Imperium Nihilus, across half a million worlds cut off from the dim light of Holy Terra, a new beacon is born. The Red Angel has returned to an unready galaxy and everywhere, witting or no, his scattered sons heed the call to slaughter.

An Extract from
Angron: The Red Angel
by David Guymer

It was raining over Mount Anarch. Drops of liquid ethane
spotted the towering glassteel panes. In under one-fifth of
standard g, the rain was not falling so much as gliding, parad-
ing towards the desolate surface of Titan as though time had
already surrendered to its legions.

Graucis Telomane stared out through the cold grey eyes of
his own reflection. He could not remember the last time he
had looked so young, so naïve, but then it had been half a millennium since he last returned to Titan to set foot in this hall.

'No,' he whispered softly. 'Not here.'

'You are not ready, Telomane. Not for this. Grand Master Taremar is wrong to beg it of me and I refuse to permit it.'

In his memories, Justicar Aelos was a giant that he had never
quite been in reality. Experience had painted the warrior's hair
grey, as it had decorated his oath plate with records of valour.
In many ways, Graucis had outgrown his former mentor, but
he had never seen him again after this, and so he remained
the colossus of a newly initiated line brother's remembrance.

'I am ready,' he said.

'That you believe yourself to be so only proves how unready you are.'

'The Grand Master of the Third Brotherhood believes I am.'

A shake of that head, never greyer. 'There is a reason the Grey Knights do not temper their youngest brothers in battle. Do you know why?'

'No,' he said, frowning. 'Not here.'

It was raining over Mount Anarch. Drops of liquid ethane spotted the towering glassteel panes. Graucis Telomane stood at an empty table in the midst of an empty hall. The Saturnalium was deserted, silent but for the patter of the hydrocarbon rain and the slow mechanical grinding of the great orrery that made up the cathedral-like ceiling. Dark but for the stain left by several thousand candles. Illumination was not their purpose. Candles had been lit to bridge the two sides of the veil since humanity's first tentative dabblings with witchcraft. They were grey: the colour of wisdom, learning and defence against malefic forces.

The orrery continued to whir through its orbits.

Graucis looked up.

His fellow novitiates had called it the Deimos Clock. According to legend, it had been assembled and first set to motion by the forge moon's Fabricator General to commemorate its removal from Mars' orbit. Saturn rotated at its centre, a silver orb the size of a Rhino chassis held in a web of arcane suspension fields, its rings represented by concentric bands of crystal less than a nanometre thick. Titan itself was the size of a bolt-shell. Its orbit took it along a track of frictionless glass wire a hundred yards and more in radius, which it completed every three hundred and eighty-two hours. So flawlessly was the whole system rendered that, according to Justicar Aelos, a Grey Knight of sufficient acuity, patience and learning could deduce the exact time and Imperial Calendar year from the relative positions of Saturn and its eighty-two natural satellites alone.

And for eight and a half thousand years, it had been keeping perfect time.

It was 444.M41.

'No,' he said, becoming angry now. 'Not here.'

It was still raining. A crimson deluge splattered and sizzled against the consecrated silver and gold of his war plate. Before him it had been worn by Eygon of the Fourth Brotherhood, and by the legendary Paladin Phox before him. Graucis still had the suit, but this was the first time he would wear it in battle. The memory was bittersweet.

Justicar Aelos had been right, of course, but of the one hundred and nine Grey Knights who had teleported down to the floodplains of the Styx River that day, which of them had done so fully prepared to face the Cruor Praetoria and the Lord of the XII Legion?

Not the ninety-six who had gone and not returned.

Not the thirteen who did.

Graucis was the least of those on the field that day. Why he had survived while the likes of Dymus, Galeo and Taremar the Golden had been allowed to fall, he did not know, except perhaps as proof the laws of the tempus materium were grounded in unreason.

'No!' he yelled, into the twisted red-meat mask of hatred worn by the Emperor's son. 'Not here!'

Drops of liquid ethane spotted the towering glassteel panes. He was in the Saturnalium, in the Citadel of Titan, but seated now where before he had been standing. He kneaded the muscle of his thigh with the heel of his palm as though it ached, although of course it did not. Not here.

'Why do I keep on returning myself to this place?'

Nyramar, sitting across the table on the other side of a set regicide board, shrugged.

The other Grey Knight was one year Graucis' senior, but though they had been friends, it was a gulf he had always felt in more than just time. All that Graucis had accomplished in his years on Titan, Nyramar had achieved sooner. When he had passed through the final tiers of the Chamber of Trials to be inducted into the line brotherhoods of the Grey Knights, it had been Nyramar who welcomed him there in a warrior's armour. He looked none the worse here for his death. It would happen five weeks after this game had been played.

'These are your memories,' Nyramar said. 'What do you expect to find here that you do not already know? Or that you could fully trust?'

'To name a thing is to know it,' Graucis countered, reciting the words from the five hundred and eighteenth canticle of the *Liber Daemonica*. 'To know the daemon is to command its nature. I know the limitations of my own mind, brother, and the sanctity of my soul.'

Nyramar nodded, looking at the table between them as though planning his next move on the regicide board. 'Then look, brother. The answer you scry for is in front of you. You only have to see.'